BAT OUT OF HELL

BAT
OUT OF
HELL
AN ECO-THRILLER

ALAN GOLD

YUCCA

Yucca Publishing books may be purchased in bulk at special discounts for sales promotion, corporate gifts, fund-raising, or educational purposes. Special editions can also be created to specifications. For details, contact the Special Sales Department, Yucca Publishing, 307 West 36th Street, 11th Floor, New York, NY 10018 or yucca@skyhorsepublishing.com.

Yucca Publishing® is an imprint of Skyhorse Publishing, Inc.®, a Delaware corporation.

Visit our website at www.yuccapub.com.

10 9 8 7 6 5 4 3 2 1

Library of Congress Cataloging-in-Publication Data is available on file.

Cover design by Karis Drake, Subsiststudios

Print ISBN: 978-1-63158-062-8

Ebook ISBN: 978-1-63158-071-0

Printed in the United States of America

BAT OUT OF HELL

1

ABOVE THE CANOPY OF A JUNGLE IN INDONESIA

There are moments when words fail to define reality. Moments such as when the first Russian soldiers walked into the concentration camps of Nazi Poland and became witness to vast mounds of men, women, and children slaughtered by German industry; moments such as when astronaut John Glenn left the embrace of earth and stepped onto the surface of another world; moments when New Yorkers watched in silence as passenger jets flown by Islamist fanatics deliberately crashed into the twin towers of the World Trade Center, extinguishing three thousand human lives in an instant.

Moments when only thoughts, only the very deepest and most intimate of inexpressible emotions, could encompass the enormity of what the eyes were seeing and rationalize what the mind refused to believe.

Such a moment was now. As the helicopter hovered immobile over the village like a huge mosquito, it searched for a place to set down its passengers without crushing the myriad of dead bodies below. The seven passengers stared down in silence. This was their moment when words, any words of horror, incredulity, or uncertainty, were inadequate to express the fear flooding their minds. Amid all the noise of the helicopter, the passengers were lost in silence . . . introspection . . . searching for meaning in the incomprehensible. Words careened around their minds in an eccentric melange of incoherent thoughts. Yet as the helicopter balanced in the air and dust rings blew in concentric circles from the middle of the village, each passenger forced his or her professionalism to take control, and they became scientists again, able to focus on the immediacy of the task ahead.

Each of the passengers, excluding the pilot, was dressed in a hazmat spacesuit, with two separate and independent supplies of air from the tanks on their backs. Their visors were hermetically sealed against the possibility of external air somehow breaching the seals of the suits that separated the men and women from the outside world.

As soon as they were winched down onto the ground, the helicopter pilot was instructed to leave the area immediately, to return to the ship; then, exactly two hours later, when the scientists' air supply was three-quarters exhausted, a huge Sikorsky, suspending a large cage, would return for them.

Again, the helicopter would be suspended high above the jungle of Indonesia, they would be hauled sweating and naked into the Sikorsky and would climb into the cage with their samples of body parts, body fluids, and whatever biomass they felt might be pertinent to uncover the mystery. In the cage below the helicopter, they'd dress into paper uniforms and be deposited back on the aircraft carrier, the USS *John McCain*.

Once on board, they'd be no guard of honor. Instead, they'd take off their paper suits and deposit them into a xenon ultraviolet decontaminator. Stark naked, they would be sprayed with volumes of antiseptic and antimicrobial wash, then scrubbed head to toe by hazmat-suited sailors and jet-sprayed with hot water. Finally, they would be hot-air dried and dressed in forensic overalls. But that was for their return. The hard and hazardous part of the mission over, the men and women of the recovery team would assemble in the aircraft carrier's laboratory where the real work would begin . . . analyzing the biological samples to try to determine what new and fearsome pathogen had killed the 1,500 villagers of Minangkabau on the Indonesian island of Kasiruta.

The ladder descended until its top was a foot from the ground, a delicate act by the pilot as he used the controls to pirouette at the level of the treetops; the scientists slowly and awkwardly climbed down, reminiscent of the moon landing decades earlier. Once emptied of his passengers, the pilot immediately shifted the controls to vertical take off, not even giving them a traditional wave as he ascended like a bat out of hell to return to the safety of his warship anchored fifty miles off the Indonesian island's coast.

It took moments for the cacophony of the helicopter to disappear and return the jungle to silence. An odd silence. Most of the scientists had been into the jungle before, and each knew that its characteristic was a perpetual din, an orchestra of insects and animals screeching, howling, screaming, fighting, and mating. During neither night nor day was a jungle silent. Yet through their intercoms, giving their ears a semblance of the outside world, the scientists could hear that in their part of the vast jungle, there was an ungodly silence.

The team leader, Doctor Debra Hart, head of Virus Transmission Analysis at the US Centers for Disease Control and Prevention in Atlanta, realized that her scientists were in alien territory and had to be brought back to their professional present or panic would set in. Alone in an unfamiliar silent world, surrounded by bloated and contorted bodies, some partly eaten by wild animals, some turning a hideous blue-black in the decomposing heat of the jungle, their thoughts had no words to help them understand what had happened. Debra had to put words into action to help them back onto familiar territory.

"Doug, you begin to gather plant samples; Naomi, could you start taking the bloods; Rik, I'd like you to take biopsies of the skin lesions; Jim, could you take tissue samples; the rest of you know what you should be doing. I'll take an instrumental sweep of the area and collect air, water, and food samples. Jackie, could you help Ivan with the instrument box and begin to unload all the equipment and then you can do stomach samples. Okay, people, let's move. We've got two hours to get our stuff together before we have to get out of here."

Energized, retreating from panic into the certainty of their training and experience, the scientists set about their assigned tasks. They moved among the dead bodies as though they were negotiating a busy street in New York. No longer were these human beings—men, women, and children who had lived simple lives in an elemental jungle, innocent people whose connection with the outside world had been unwelcome and transitory. Now, right now in the immediacy of an urgent assignment under the aegis of the United Nations and the US government, requested by the government of Indonesia, alarmed by something it couldn't understand, these scientists were again in the familiar territory of their laboratories, thinking, analyzing, assessing . . . doing.

SIX MONTHS LATER

The audience was in no mood for surprises. The morning had been spent listening to the secretary of Health and Human Services defend her government's decision to allow local councils to be part of the decision-making process when potentially hazardous experiments involving viruses were undertaken by universities—decisions which had formerly been made by university presidents, boards of regents, and ethics committees. And the audience of leading researchers in the fields of bacteriology, virology, and pathogenic medicine were left angry and contemptuous when the secretary had left the stage with the Parthian shot, "Well, if you don't like what we're doing, vote us out next election."

Returning from a lunch of dried out chicken and soggy vegetables, they entered the afternoon session hoping that the next paper would be a meaty bit of science that they could get their teeth into. All in the room either knew Debra Hart or knew of her reputation as a fine scientist and exhilarating national spokesperson for her field of interest. Many of them were excited that such a brilliant and handsome woman would be addressing them for the next hour. Debra had been at the forefront of advancing the fight against the new and dangerous viruses that were gaining a foothold into the developed world, and they knew that because she was a cautious and committed scientist, her talk would be of particular interest to their fields of study. And they'd all read the cover story and seen the painting of her in a recent edition of *Time Magazine*, calling her the US's secret weapon in the war against viruses. For the two weeks that it took for the news media to become bored with the story, Debra had been constantly interviewed some time back as a result of the dreadful Ebola epidemic in West Africa that had killed thousands.

Introduced by the provost of Yale who was also dean of medicine at New Haven Hospital, Debra rose to applause and walked confidently to the lectern. But she felt anything but confident. What her audience didn't realize was that her speech could, probably would, spell the end of her career in public medicine. But it had to be said, and say it she would.

"What I'm going to say will not sit comfortably with many of you. Some may reject my thesis; some may openly criticize me to the media present today. But what I hope is that by my telling you what's kept me occupied for the past many months, I'll raise sufficient concern in your minds to encourage some of you in the field of virology to join me in my research.

"This will be the first time you've heard of my research because the authorities in Washington have refused me permission to publish what I'm about to tell you. I'm actually breaching a confidentiality and secrecy agreement, so this talk makes me liable to prosecution. But in the name of science, I've thought very carefully, and it's something that I've decided that I must do, regardless of the personal consequences to me.

"Which is the reason why I had to pretend that this session was about something relatively innocuous, in order to get out into the public space via the media present today, so that you could be told what's happening in the world of very nasty viruses."

The audience of scientists and doctors focused intently on her, a tall and intense young woman, gripping the lectern as though to stop it moving.

"I don't want to sound overly dramatic, but what I think I've discovered could mean that a catastrophic, new, and hideously virulent virus has found its way, as though by magic, across thousands of miles of oceans and land masses, to transmute and become an instant killer. I have no idea what transmission medium the virus used to travel huge distances . . . insects, birds, the wind . . . it's all conjecture at this stage. But the Ebola virus, colleagues, has left the villages of Africa and Ebola Mark 2, what you might call Ebola on steroids, has found its way into Indonesia. While African Ebola sometimes took a week to kill 60 percent of the people it infected, its evil twin Ebola in Indonesia kills 100 percent within hours. Be afraid, ladies and gentlemen; be very, very afraid."

She looked up from her paper at the audience in the room but found no satisfaction in the look of amazement on the thousand faces.

* * *

When the last slide of her PowerPoint presentation was replaced by the conference logo, and she had finished straightening her notes and prepared to step down from the podium, she realized that nobody in the entire audience was applauding. Scientists were far too sophisticated to act like normal people and to cheer and holler after a presentation. The most anybody—Einstein, Newton, Copernicus—should expect from an audience of top-level scientists was mild approbation, even an occasional smile and nod of encouragement from close colleagues. More often, those in the audience whose own research contradicted the speaker's lecture would shake their heads in dismay and loudly whisper that the speaker's research was flawed and incorrect.

In surprise, Debra looked up from shuffling her notes and saw that there wasn't a single movement in the audience. Faces were locked in shock, bodies in paralysis. For the past hour, she'd revealed slide after slide of her expedition to the Indonesian island of Kasiruta, shown them the bodies of the fifteen hundred dead men, women, and children, shown electron-microscopic slide after slide of the virus. shown them planograms of how the virus was thought to have invaded the victims' neural pathways that lead to the brain, and its rapid overwhelming instructions to close down the infected person's immune system until death came from the breakdown of capillary blood vessels in the brains of the victims, leading to what must have been unprecedented unbearable headaches, fainting, and death. Other slides had compared the Kasiruta Virus, as she'd dubbed it, to Ebola and other virulent pathogenic viruses.

But when she'd come to the method of transmission from animal to human and human to human, she'd drawn a blank. She'd told them that because of the rapidity of death and decomposition, there was insufficient evidence left on the bodies to determine how they'd caught the virus and how it had spread so quickly from person to person. As a final insult to the scientific method, the Indonesian government had ordered the entire village and surrounding area to be carpet bombed with Napalm, which had burnt over a thousand acres of the surrounding forest. At the end of Debra's talk, she'd informed her colleagues that, unfortunately, they'd have to await the next outbreak before they could get more evidence.

Gathering her notes, she stepped down from the platform. The emcee stepped up and, in a shaking voice, asked the audience to acknowledge her speech, which was met with halfhearted applause.

The Conference Coffee Shop

"That was a bold talk. Gutsy. I'm impressed."

She looked up from her notes into the eyes of a man she'd seen around the conference during the previous two days. He was a fatherly figure, not old enough to be grandfatherly, rugged from long exposure to the outdoors, but the sort who looked more comfortable in slip-ons than lace-ups. He sat, without bothering to ask the traditional "mind if I join you?"

Debra didn't want her coffee break to be disturbed, especially by some-one she'd not met and so presumably didn't work in her field—someone who would probably prove to be either a fawning fan or a puffed-up antagonist. Whenever she gave a talk, she was often overwhelmed by audience members who wanted to know more; an exhausting hour-long speech often turned into a half-hour longer fanfare with well-wishers wanting to praise or querulous opponents who wanted to air their knowledge. But she'd walked from the hall in the middle of the after-noon sessions and just wanted to be alone to reflect on what she'd said and especially on the audience's unusual reaction.

And most especially, she needed time to herself to think through the anticipated reaction in Washington tomorrow morning when the news-papers reported her speech. She'd breached her contract of confidential-ity, breached undertakings she'd given her boss, breached the trust that hundreds of people had in her, because she was absolutely determined that the public had a right to know, and especially that all scientific information had to be shared if it was to have any peer value.

He sat in a chair next to hers, put his cup of coffee down, and said, "Daniel Todd. Harvard. Associate professor of mammalian biology."

"What's a biologist doing at a virology conference?" she asked.

"Trying to get these guys to understand the dangers of bats," he said, somewhat more phlegmatically than the statement required.

Her interest spiked, she held out her hand, "Debra Hart," she told him.

He smiled and shook her hand. "I know. I was one of the guys who couldn't speak after your presentation. You really had the audience by their balls," he said. "Even the women. You could have heard a pin drop when you were presenting. I guess I was the only one who knew exactly what you were going to say next," he told her, sipping his coffee.

"Excuse me?"

"I've been waiting for this outbreak for a couple of years now. My only concern is that you've wasted six precious months before making the information public. Six months, Debra . . . I could have done a lot in those six months."

"I don't know what you mean," she said. "First off, I've had a lockdown notice imposed on me by Health preventing me from publishing anything for fear of causing a public panic. And secondly, this research is absolutely brand new. How could you possibly have known what I was going to say?"

"Because I'm not a virologist. I'm a mammalian biologist. I specialize in the order Chiroptera. Bats. I knew that you were researching something because some suit from the Department of Health in DC came to see me three months ago and asked whether I'd heard of you and knew anything about your research. I told him I didn't; I asked him what you had to do with bats, and he said 'nothing.' Then he asked all sorts of questions about colonies and spread and migration patterns and stuff like that. Never heard from him since. So I put two and two together, read that you were giving a speech, and here we are."

"Where are we?" she asked, having an uncomfortable feeling about where the conversation was heading.

"I think the vector for your killer bug is bats. I have no idea of the spreading mechanism because bats can't migrate directly from Africa to the Far East, so the pathogen could have spread in other ways that we need to understand. Or a natural virus in the bat's blood could have mutated into the Kasiruta virus that killed your village."

Now that she was no longer a distant figure behind the podium, he looked more closely at her. Divorced twice, he was attracted to women who looked like his former wives, and Debra was unnervingly like a more mature version of his first wife, Dione, who had been a blond-haired blue-eyed beauty making cow eyes at him from the front row of his graduate class when he taught at New York University all those years ago. Debra's hair wasn't blond; more a light shade of brown, but her eyes were what attracted him. He'd always been fascinated by women's eyes, and hers were clear, bright, and wise.

"Bats could be the vector," she said, "but I've had epidemiologists working on samples since we returned from Indonesia, and it could just as easily have been monkeys, spiders, ticks, mosquitoes, or anything. We certainly haven't ruled out bats, but it's less likely to be them than it is an insect infecting a larger animal. The infection could have entered the human body through sores, the air, food . . . we just don't have enough information," she said.

"I'm telling you, it's bats. I've been waiting for this for years, and all the stars are aligned. Today it's the jungles of Indonesia; tomorrow, and I mean tomorrow, it's going to be the jungles of New York and Washington."

She looked at him in astonishment.

ORLANDO, FLORIDA

Megan was a woman with four grandchildren by two of her three kids, a deacon in her local church, president of her local branch of the Democratic Party, and she'd once been asked to stand for city council. She looked around at the other women grouped on a busy street in the humid morning, the air still, the road heavy with traffic. There were twenty of them. They had gathered in silence outside Goldstein's Fur Shop.

Abe Goldstein had been watching them assemble on the other side of the road for the past twenty minutes before crossing over to block his entrance and window display. He feared that something was up. He'd gone outside his shop to inquire if he could help the ladies, but those that had arrived early had merely given him the cold shoulder, treating him like some pork butcher at a bar mitzvah. Now he knew from the experience of other fur traders in Miami, New York, and Washington what to expect.

On the one hand, the publicity was good—it brought attention to his shop, which could lead to sales—but on the other, bad publicity could damage his retirement plans. The fur trade had been *farshtunken* for years, and he was hoping to sell his shop to some schmuck who didn't know the future of furs was in real *tsuris*, go live in Miami with Zelda, and spend the kid's inheritance living like the people to whom he occasionally sold the odd ermine or sable. He couldn't remember the last time he'd sold a full-length coat, even to the wealthy Jewish retirees who spent the remains of their lives playing canasta and mah-jongg and looking to wed a replacement for Morrie or Saul or Ike who'd died at sixty-three of a heart attack when they lived in New York.

Abe eyed the women with trepidation. He'd already called the police, and although the captain owed him a favor for the discount he'd given him for the fur wrap he'd bought his girlfriend, the captain said that they'd be there the moment there was trouble.

Megan eyed Abe through the shop window. She'd seen him use the phone, presumably to call the police. She just hoped they didn't get here before the newspaper reporters and television people. She looked at her watch and wondered where Daphne and Chloe were. Everybody else was here. Women aged in their late teens, mothers in their twenties and forties, and grannies like her. Women assembled outside a shop that traded on the misery of harmless animals. Fur skinned in the cruelest of manners—animals trapped by the leg, some even chewing off their feet to escape the cruel teeth of the snares. The signs and banners were safely tucked away in Sally's SUV, waiting to be hauled out when the media turned up.

As so often the case, the media arrived in a convoy—two television station vans with satellite dishes eclipsing their roofs, three radio station vans emblazoned with their identification badges announcing garishly who they were, and then a couple of anonymous station wagons, presumably belonging to newspaper reporters and photographers. Megan smiled, knowing that her embargoed press release had worked beautifully. Right time, right place, and certainly the right headline on the press release: CHAT Women to bare their breasts for bears, foxes, and other endangered animals.

Megan marched over to the SUV and threw open the doors. She withdrew the signs and banners and handed them to the girls. Then she said loudly so that the media would hear, "Okay girls, bare it for the bears . . ."

At the signal, the women walked in front of the fur shop, put down the signs they were carrying, and in a fluid movement, stripped off their blouses, jumpers, and bras. Men and women passing stopped and looked in shock at the sudden expanse of naked flesh. Some of the men began to whistle and applaud; others, especially the women, frowned and tutted in disgust.

But Megan didn't care. Naked from the waist up, she bent down and picked up a sign that read SKIN THE TRADERS, NOT THE ANIMALS. Some of her other colleagues carried their signs and they formed a circle in front of the fur shop that they marched around, chanting their mantra, "CHAT to us . . . say no to fur."

The cameras flashed, the sound recordists set up their recorders, and the television cameras jostled with the crowd to get the best shots and angles.

All would have gone peacefully, had not Bob Gentle, Jill's husband, been carried away. Jill was one of the younger women marching in the circle, awaiting the arrival of the police and some manhandling of her naked torso, which she hoped would get onto the network news. But Bob, recently indoctrinated by Jill in the cruelty of the fur trade, found himself unable to control his emotions, and without fully realizing what he was doing, he picked up a car jack and hurled it through the window of Abe Goldstein's fur shop. A hush came over the crowd as the glass shattered, and large broken panes came crashing onto the pavement. The good nature of the demonstration evaporated at that instance. Abe came running out of the shop, shouting and gesticulating. The women stopped marching and looked in dismay at the broken window and the thousands of shards of glass on the floor.

Realizing how stupid he'd just been, Bob walked over to apologize to Abe; but as he stepped forward, out of the corner of his eye, he saw a blurred figure, wearing a parka with a hood pulled up to hide his face, suddenly appear from the back of the crowd. The figure, medium height and looking like some neighborhood punk, walked quickly to the broken window, crunching over the shards of glass on the pavement.

Having been robbed four times in ten years, Abe knew trouble when he saw it coming. Ignoring Bob, the person who'd thrown the tire iron, he stepped into the oncoming path of the young punk who was now close to the window.

"Hey kid," Abe shouted. "Get out from the window you goddam *goniff*. You don't go close. Hear! Don't touch dem furs. You get back."

The black-skinned pimply youth reached into the broken window, seized a mink stole from the closest dummy, and pulled it out of the shop.

Furious that the thief's dirty hands were touching something of such aesthetic beauty, Abe screamed, "you rotten little *mamzer*," and tried to wrest the stole away from him. The youth immediately pulled a knife from inside his parka and stabbed Abe through his heart, running away through the transfixed crowd before Abe's dying body had even hit the floor. The crowd parted like the waters of the Red Sea as the boy darted up the road, tucking the mink stole inside his coat as he ran.

Bob, Jill, Megan, and the others looked in horror at Abe as he lay in a tangled mess on the pavement, his white shirt oozing blood, which leaked over the shards of glass from his window as his life quickly ebbed away. A woman screamed. Megan screamed. Bob couldn't breathe and felt his knees buckling as he crumpled to the floor. The television cameras and reporters tried to capture what was happening, but it was all too quick.

And then the crowd heard the sound of police sirens, driving hurriedly toward the murder in order to stop bare-breasted women from making fools of themselves.

THE CONFERENCE COFFEE SHOP

Debra Hart shook her head. "It's just not scientific," she insisted. "It's conjectural, speculative. We're both scientists. We can't base conclusions on gut reaction. Only on experimentation, analysis, peer review, publication."

Daniel Todd agreed, stirring his third cup of coffee since Debra's session had ended. She was keen to go to the restroom and should have excused herself from the conversation half an hour ago, but Daniel had reached a point where she didn't want to miss a single word or nuance. At first, she'd thought that Daniel was a bit of a wiseass, out of his depth—probably very good in his area of speciality but had drawn wrong conclusions in a field about which he knew little. But for the past ten minutes, he'd convinced her that something was happening to the world's bat population that could impact her findings—indeed on the entire world of virus-caused diseases.

"Look, Debra, you're right that the transmitting agent could be mosquitoes or rats or fleas, just like in the days of the Black Plague. But we're living in an era that is unlike anything in recorded history. Mankind is changing the environment more quickly than even the most skeptical scientist once thought possible, and my guts tell me that bats are suffering more so than most. But your scientific mind is going to ask why? What's so special about bats? Well, these little buggers have lived apart from other mammals for fifty million years; they're the only flying mammal; so their metabolism, their blood, and other structures have had eons to develop in ways that are markedly different to land or sea mammals. Because they live in the tops of caves and trees, they haven't been subjected to the same evolutionary, environmental, or biological influences that other mammals have experienced. So in some ways, bats are unique. And part of that uniqueness is that they've built up immunity to diseases that kill other mammals.

"We might not have even noticed these changes for another million years, but since the start of the industrial era, we've made changes to our atmosphere, warming it up. Then to compound the problems for bats, we've taken away much of their traditional food sources by cutting down forests and fruit trees and planting biofuels for ethanol which goes into petrol.

"So because of global warming, bats have had to find food and shelter in new environments, like the middle of towns. We're seeing migratory patterns of animals that haven't happened in twenty-five thousand years, since the last ice age. The US bat population has halved in just a few short recent years, recent in geo-biological terms, at least. God knows what's happened to bat populations in other parts of the world where climate change is also having an effect.

"I agree that we have to continue serious scientific analysis, but listen to what I'm thinking. Firstly, bats are vectors for some hideous diseases that they carry but that don't affect them. Ebola, Hendra, Nipah, SARS, lyssavirus, rabies, Marburg, Mokola, maybe even AIDS . . . you name it and if there's a killer virus out there, then sure as apples, bats carry it. Their living conditions are hideous; they live in colonies, often in stinking caves where the floors are knee-deep in shit. They bite and scratch each other. They eat insects, often caught on the wing; they hang upside down . . ."

"If you think they're so awful, why devote your life to studying them?" asked Debra.

Daniel smiled as he shrugged. "When I was a kid, I couldn't understand how they could sleep upside down. I mean, didn't the blood rush to their heads and make them giddy? And how did they shit upside down anyway? So I began to study them in school, then in biology at college, then I did my PhD thesis on them, and I've been researching them ever since. Now, I reckon, I'm the right man in the right place at the right time. Pure luck."

"I still . . ."

"Look, over the past millions of years, bats have built up a resistance to the viruses they carry. And for all those millions of years, it hasn't made a lot of difference. They kept out of our way; we kept out of theirs. Only rarely do these viruses leave a bat's body and affect humans through our close contact with infected animals like horses and pigs and sheep.

"But have you ever wondered why there are sudden outbreaks of SARS or Ebola? Most people, especially scientists, don't even think of bats. Closest most people in the West have come to a bat is in a Dracula movie, or through Batman. Unless they have the odd bat in their belfry. But in the past couple of dozen years, bat populations throughout the world have been under huge pressure, in all continents."

He drank the last dregs of his cold coffee and nodded to the counter, asking Debra if she wanted another. She smiled and shook her head.

Then Debra asked, "I need to get this straight in my head. What you're saying is this: first of all, humankind is encroaching on the bats' grazing and feeding territory by pulling down their forests and turning their feeding areas into crop pastures. Once upon a time, they could fly over a forest and feed themselves on the fruits of the trees or eat insects above the forest canopy while they were on the wing. Now the forests are shrinking and crops like corn and wheat and rice and barley are taking over, and the bats can't find enough food for themselves. So while we're creating biofuels to feed our energy needs, the bats can't find enough to eat. Okay so far?"

Daniel nodded.

"But why does this make them so deadly, so suddenly. This can't surely be the first contact between a bat colony and human beings. Something has suddenly happened. Right?"

"Right," he said. "What's happened is that the worldwide bat population is suddenly under terrible stress. Not all of them, of course, but those where humanity has suddenly moved in and is living close by.

"You see, mankind is encroaching on traditional bat roosting areas, like forests and caves, by building houses and villages and cities where once there was peace and quiet. The bats are squeezed into tighter and tighter colonies, reducing the populations.

"And most serious, of course, is global warming, which is changing the face of the world. Forest fires, hurricanes, tsunamis, and fruit crops are changing their growing patterns; traditional areas no longer as welcome and habitable for bat colonies. They're like the canaries in a mine, and they can't adapt unless they move. Right now, their feeding areas are moving further and further away from traditional bat roosting areas," he said.

"They have to fly further and further to forage, which means that their body weight reduces through the use of the extra energy, and so they need more food just to stay still. And that's the cause of the problems we're going to be facing."

"Meaning?" asked Debra

"Meaning that bat populations from Africa to India, South America to Europe are under sudden and significant stress. And the rapidity of the changes to their environment hasn't enabled their metabolism to adapt on an evolutionary timescale. When human beings are under great stress, they get sick . . . migraines, elevated blood pressure, strokes, heart attacks. And when a bat population is under pressure, the viral load of the individual bat increases exponentially. The deadly viruses that bats once kept safely inside their bodies are now so massively increased that the viruses spill out when the bat sneezes, coughs, pees, shits, and farts. Sorry to be crude, but it's the quickest and most direct way of saying it. Nowadays, when they're flying over land with domesticated animals, and if the colony is under stress or starving, droplets from the bats fall to the ground, full of deadly viruses. Some of the droplets fall onto the feed of horses or pigs or cows. Even before it kills the agricultural animal, the virus can come out in its milk or through saliva or pee. There's a dozen ways it can get into human beings. Or it can simply be eaten, which is what probably happened in this village. I'll bet there was a feast of pig meat before those poor bastards died. I'll bet that's what killed them."

"And you think . . ." she began to say.

"I think that a bat colony near to your village was put under stress, probably by the Indonesians cutting down forests for their timber or changing the fruit trees to arable cropland . . . or something. I don't know because I wasn't told about it until today. But I'll bet you that the local bat colony was put under pressure and was forced to relocate. It probably starved and reduced in size over a couple of years. Remember that most bats only produce one live offspring a year, so the decrease in the population could have happened over a few short years. When the colony began to starve and had to move, it's a safe bet that the individual's viral load increased, the viruses mutated into your charming little bugs, a swarm of bats flew over the village, and droplets fell from their bodies onto foodstuffs or something near the pig pens or cattle. Once it was inside the host animal, it would have transmuted into something even more deadly, which would make the host sick, and if it was eaten by the villagers as their last meal, then it was good night and sweet dreams."

Debra remained silent for several moments. "This is pure speculation," she said.

He nodded. "Yep! But then so was almost every scientific discovery ever dreamed up until it was proven by analysis and experimentation. I've got a collection of recently gathered bat cadavers from Africa, and you should see what bugs we've found in their bloodstreams. And the viral count is terrifying. All because local villagers are encroaching on their roost sites. And have you been reading about the massive increase of bat colonies in the center of huge cities? They're taking up residence in the middle of our habitats because of all the food we leave out and throw away. There are now urban colonies of bats in parks and botanical gardens. Sure, everybody likes to walk through a glade and see a thousand bats hanging upside down from the highest branches of trees, but if their food sources dry up, if the farmers net their fruit trees or it's a dry season and there are fewer insects for the bats to eat, then they'll come looking for their feed at a house near you. And if their viral load is out of control because of stress . . . God help us."

"This is a doomsday scenario," said Debra.

Daniel shrugged and looked down at his empty coffee cup.

2

THE HUBERT H. HUMPHREY BUILDING
SW WASHINGTON, DC

The United States Department of Health and Human Services was housed in a squat and functional building on the corner of Independence Avenue and Third Street, just across the road from the Capitol Building, which housed the nation's lawmakers.

Debra had been to the building many times during her six years as head of Virus Transmission Analysis at the US Centers for Disease Control and Prevention in Atlanta. Although she was answerable to the CDC's chief operating officer, her real bosses, those to whom she was answerable for things way more important than budgets and targets, were housed in this building.

When the newspaper headlines earlier in the day had trumpeted "Killer Bug Spells New Threat to Worldwide Security," her boss had been called by his boss, whose boss wanted Debra to see her boss.

She stepped out of the taxi and drew a deep breath, knowing that this would be the last day of her employment with the United States government, and entered the north portal of the building. Signed in, badged, metal detected, and escorted to the carpeted and silent top floor, Debra was asked to wait in an anteroom before being summoned by Doctor Jonathan Bailey, deputy secretary of Health and Human Services. Only two people stood between Doctor Bailey and the president—his boss, DeAnne Harper, former lieutenant governor of Idaho, who was the secretary of Health and Human Services, and the White House chief of staff. Then it was the president.

In all her career of public service, Debra had never dealt with bureaucrats at this level, so her fall would be from a very great height—probably very public, and almost certainly very humiliating. But she'd anticipated some swift and nasty reaction from the bureaucratic hierarchy when she'd lied to her boss about the nature of her address to the conference she was attending. She just hoped that her boss, a really lovely and elderly gentleman scientist, wouldn't become a casualty of the firestorm that would be coming her way as a result of her very public indiscretion. As she went down in a screaming heap, she'd save her boss by admitting she'd lied to him. Hopefully, they'd believe her.

But she'd been infuriated by the gag notice that had been placed on her work, preventing her from exposing it to scientific scrutiny. So she'd determined that regardless of the cost to her career, the world had to know about this new and threatening bug. After her bisexual father had died from AIDS in San Francisco in the 1980s, a result of the conspiracy of silence for fear of causing panic that surrounded the HIV infection, Debra had determined never to keep scientific information from the community.

The bureaucratic minions walked softly along the corridors as she pretended to read a magazine in the outer sitting room. Her heart was thumping against her chest. She rehearsed the speech she would give to Jonathan Bailey before he thumped his desk and shouted for her to get out. She would try to tell him about scientific integrity, about the need for transparency in public health, and about the dangers of cloak-and-dagger attitudes applied to public medicine when the health, welfare, and lives of thousands of people might be at risk.

By the time the door to Doctor Bailey's office opened, her face was flushed and she was ready for the fight of her life. Yes, she'd go down, but it would be in a glorious heap of self-righteousness.

He was dressed in a charcoal-gray suit with a blisteringly white shirt and club tie. She didn't recognize what university the tie represented, but from the tall, lean, suntanned, and prosperous look of the man, she'd bet it was Ivy League.

He beamed a broad smile. "Debra? How good to meet you. I've read a lot about you, especially in this morning's papers."

Jonathan Bailey walked over, hand extended. His hair was turning silver gray; he wore the confidence of a seasoned politician, even though his early career had been in public medicine. He escorted her into his office, which was lush, exquisitely furnished if a bit too old-world for her, and they sat together on the leather lounge. She was mystified. If he was going to fire her, this was certainly not the traditional method.

"Coffee?" he asked, pouring her a cup from the tray that some invisible personal assistant had laid out on his coffee table prior to her entry.

They sipped their coffees; she was too confused to say anything.

"Let me come straight to the point, Debra. As head of the CDC's Virus Transmission Department, we've decided that you're the right person to be put in charge of leading a team to deal with the issue you raised at yesterday's conference. I have to admit we were a bit surprised that you gave your paper without consulting us first, but what's done is done, and now we have to ensure that this new virus and others of similar danger to our people, don't get into the United States. We're not going to be caught with our pants down again—like we were with the HIV virus—something about which you're all too familiar."

She looked at him in amazement, both for his offer of a fantastic job instead of firing her and for his understanding of her very personal demand for transparency in memory of her father.

"I want you to head up a task force to do two vital things; the first is to ensure national biohazard immunity to these new viruses, which are gaining ground in remote parts of the world, and the second is to determine ways of eliminating the source. And if that means eliminating entire animal populations, then so be it. Don't be surprised. It's not like the good ol' US of A going after terrorists in Iraq or Afghanistan. This is something we'll do with the approval and cooperation of the UN and other world agencies.

"Where we're notified of an outbreak of a virulent disease, we'll work with that nation's government to track its source and eliminate the vectors and carriers. This will be a cooperative effort of the USA, European countries, and many in Asia. But it'll be coordinated through the United Nations; so in effect, you'll work with the World Health Organization under the auspices of the UN. You'll build your team here, of course, but to all intent, you'll be answerable to the secretary-general.

"There'll be no bureaucrats who'll stand in the way of you and your team. This is separate from and outside of Homeland Security and FEMA. Naturally, your reports will go to them, but neither of them will have any oversight or budgetary control of your office. You'll be heading up a first-class scientific effort, well funded, well resourced. You'll have a very significant budget, the choice of any experts from any field in any university or private institution you want. You'll work from this building and report to me or my designated assistant. Well?"

She stared at him, still too stunned to speak. As though some external voice was talking, she heard herself saying, "I . . . I . . . er . . . ?"

Doctor Bailey continued, "This doesn't come out of nowhere, Debra. This is something we've been working on for months. When you and your team first came back from Indonesia and began reporting to my department on this new killer virus, it was the final piece of the jigsaw that I'd been putting together for more than two years. These outbreaks of deadly and incurable diseases . . . Ebola, SARS, the Hendra virus, and others . . . have been growing in frequency and getting closer and closer to home. Our home. Sixteen months ago, I called a top-level meeting of our staff, and they've been secretly talking to top academics about these eruptions. We've come to the conclusion that we can't be defensive but have to go on the offensive, and wherever and whenever they show up, we have to go in there with a hit squad of top scientists to search out, identify, and eliminate.

"Through the office of the secretary-general, we've got the agreement of most African and Asian governments who'll work with your team when an outbreak occurs on their territory. We'll pay half of all the costs involved and Europe will pay the other half. We are doing this as the lead agency because of our scientific prowess, which is why we have the total support of the UN, the World Health Organization, the World Bank, and other global agencies. We've been working hard these past many months to put this together," he said, resisting a smile.

"But why didn't I know about it?" asked Debra. She felt insulted that she'd been deliberately omitted from the team discussing the virus outbreaks. "I'm head of Virus Transmission at the CDC, for God's sake. This is precisely what I should have been involved in."

Doctor Bailey looked uncomfortable for a moment and said softly, "Yes, we thought long and hard about involving you, Debra, but our feeling was that this was less an issue about viruses and outbreaks, than it was about public health, public safety, and national security. Once you look at it through that lens, then the people you have to involve, people who deal in national security and international policy issues, tend to screw things down as tight as a drum. As a scientist, it was thought that you didn't need to be involved."

"But why wasn't this made public—at least to the scientific community?" she asked. "Why all this security? This is a major concern for the health and well-being of the community. Surely, like the outbreak of AIDS, you should have broadcast it far and wide and got every scientific mind in the field focused on the issue."

"That's precisely what the president was going to do at the World Health Conference in Rome next month. Unfortunately, Debra, you've kind of stolen his thunder. I was going to fly down to Atlanta and ask you, in rather less hurried terms, whether you'd consider heading up the new agency. But your speech yesterday . . . well, what can I say?"

Doctor Bailey looked at the woman who sat opposite him. She still had the spark of beauty glowing inside her, but she was one of those women who had put career before family, job before love. He wondered how many lovers she'd had while she was climbing the career ladder, and how many men were still in her life as she approached the wrong side of middle age. He wondered what was going through her mind right now.

STARBUCKS CAFÉ
CORNER OF THIRTY-FIFTH AND FIFTH, MANHATTAN

Tom Pollard, president of CHAT, Citizens for Humane Animal Treatment, was a man under siege. The appalling disaster of CHAT's anti-fur demonstration in Orlando, Florida, the previous day had resulted in him having to front for his organization on shows he'd sworn he'd never grace with his presence. Fox News, right-wing cable TV shows with dema-gogues screaming at him, right-wing newspapers with holier-than-thou reporters talking to him about his responsibility for the lives of human beings, not just animals. It had been hideous, but fortunately, there was the reality of a twenty-four-hour news cycle, and the cameras were now turned in the direction of some other poor hapless individual.

* * *

He'd just come from an emergency meeting of his board of governors who had carpeted him for not being there himself to prevent this trag-edy. They weren't interested in his rationale, nor that he'd been doing budgets all that day. He was the boss . . . it was his job to be everywhere. They hadn't fired him, but they'd put him on notice that if this sort of thing ever happened again, he'd be the scapegoat.

His chairperson, Donna McCabe, had been particularly scathing. She was new to the position, and Tom realized that his cozy relationship with her predecessor was not going to happen with Donna. She was a big time Washington law firm partner who flew down for the monthly board meet-ings. She had a mind like a steel trap and a frightening way of using a care-fully chosen phrase to spike his hubris whenever he tried to bignote himself and his achievements. He felt she could see right inside him, so he'd prom-ised her that not only would he put the Florida issue to bed, but he'd also ensure that no such demonstration ever happened again on his watch.

He'd been waiting in Starbucks for his contact to arrive for over fif-teen minutes. He didn't even know her surname. She was a middle-aged woman who worked for a government department in Washington. She'd given him fantastic information in the past about voting patterns of con-gressional representatives and senators, about their constituencies and families and likes and dislikes. All great stuff but little more than a good researcher could have produced in a week of hitting the books in the con-gressional library. But his contact's real value was in tipping him off about forthcoming bills pertaining to agricultural animals, domesticated and caged animals, pet shop regulations, import and export of animal skins and furs, and things like that. Thanks to her, a contact who'd come to him anonymously, he had become the darling of the animal rights movement. From a relatively obscure pen pusher to the nation's most effective activist and spokesperson on the inhumane treatment of animals, he'd taken his organization from an underfunded gaggle of hopeless amateur liberationists to the nation's best run, best funded, best publicized, and best-known advocate for the rights of animals in the country.

His contact didn't realize how important she was to him, and he maintained his relationship by dropping whatever he was doing when she rang him on the most private of his private mobile phones—one that he'd taken out in the name of a recently deceased person, the one that the FBI knew nothing about. When she was in New York and wanted to see him, he followed a charade, which was silly, but he did it to please her.

First, he'd leave his office and take a taxi downtown, then a subway uptown, then a cab to the Lower West Side, and then walk the ten blocks to Thirty-Fifth Street, looking behind him all the time to ensure that he wasn't followed. It was a ridiculous precaution because this Starbucks was so close to his office, but she'd insisted, and he just wanted to keep her happy. Confident that he wasn't followed, he'd entered the coffee shop, sat at a table with his back to the wall, and faced the door to ensure that he could scrutinize whoever walked in. And he'd been sitting like this for half an hour, which was fifteen minutes after she'd asked to meet him.

Suddenly the door opened and she walked into the shop. She was a faded Washington matriarch—big chested, dowdy, wearing clothes that had once been fashionable, carrying a handbag; nobody in New York carried a handbag.

She sat. He knew from past experience that she didn't like shows of emotion, and so he didn't attempt to give her a friendly peck on the cheek. Instead, he shook her hand and asked how she was.

"I'm in New York overnight. I have to be back in my office tomorrow morning for a meeting. I'm staying with my sister. She's expecting me for dinner, so I can't stay. And don't offer me any of the disgusting coffee they serve here. Let me just tell you what I have to tell you, and then I'll go."

Tom nodded. He knew better than to interrupt.

"This afternoon, there was a high-level meeting at the Department of Health and Human Services. It took place between the deputy secretary of state and a youngish woman who works at the Center for Disease Control in Atlanta, Georgia. You might have read the story written about her yesterday concerning some hideous new virus in Indonesia."

She looked at him closely, but it was obvious that he had no idea what she was talking about. "You really must keep up with the news if we're to work together, Mr. Pollard."

Stung, he said, "I had rather a busy day yesterday, you know. Perhaps you read of that death in Orlando at one of our CHAT demonstrations. A tragic occurrence."

She waved her hand as though the death of an old Jew was of no significance. "What I'm here to tell you, Mr. Pollard, is about the death of entire species. Species. We're no longer talking about the inhuman caging and death of cats and dogs in pet shops, or of the use of animal skins for the husbands of pampered women to purchase for them to wear and parade around in like tramps. This is the annihilation of entire species, animals that we were put on this earth by Almighty God to protect.

"What the deputy secretary has cooked up with this heartless Doctor Hart woman is a plan to eliminate all species of animals that are thought to be carriers of the viruses. Bats, birds, horses, pigs, donkeys, mice, rats. She's been empowered to eliminate whatever animal it is that might . . . might, mind you . . . be the carrier of these viruses. Can you imagine what that means, Mr. Pollard? This young woman has the right, under United States government decree, to decide which animal species may be causing some new virus to spread and then to eliminate it. It's genocide of entire species, Mr. Pollard. It's the greatest crime in the history of animal husbandry. In the Bible, God Almighty himself gave Noah responsibility for saving a male and a female of each kind of animal that existed before humankind fell from the grace of God's eyes. God gave Noah that right because he was a good man. Now the United States government is giving some girl the right to eliminate an entire species at her will. She'll be like a god herself, Mr. Pollard. Like a god. You have to do something about this, or there's never ever going to be a Second Coming. No redemption for humakind . . . confined to all eternity to . . ." Her words fell silent as she looked into the future.

Tom Pollard stared at her in disbelief. He had to get the details. One minute, his career was in the toilet; the next minute he would be an international savior of animals. So what did it matter that she was probably talking about ticks and fleas and mosquitoes and rats and mice? He would be the savior of species, and that would get him noticed internationally.

Landsdale Station
Fifty Miles Northeast of Toowoomba, Queensland

No matter how often he gazed at the enormity of the sky in the north, south, east, and west of his property, Doug Mauden was overwhelmed by the grandeur of design in the mind of the deity who had created it all. The vastness of the land stretched out in all directions around him, the red earth covered with bounteous crops. His vast cattle station and horse stud were the pride and joy of his life, as were the stands of gum trees under whose canopies kangaroos slept during the heat of the day and emus and wild dingos roamed freely. All was just as it was when his grandfather had acquired the station from a drunken landowner in a game of poker.

Doug's father had built upon the good fortune of his father and nurtured the station with careful custodianship, acquiring nearby farms during severe droughts for rock-bottom prices, until the family were the wealthiest and most significant landowners in the district. All was peaceful. Even his father's death had been peaceful. He'd died early one morning in the saddle while riding his favorite mare—the horse gently bringing her master home—feet still in the stirrups, hands gripping the reign, his face gently nuzzling the horse's neck.

Doug left the university in Brisbane to take over running the place and he hadn't regretted it for a single moment. He was a lay preacher at the local Baptist church, and when he eventually retired and handed over to one of his children, he'd finish his study for the ministry and as a venerable gentleman, hopefully would spend whatever time God allowed him to minister to a flock somewhere. Right now, the drought that was devastating farms and stations throughout the Eastern seaboard of Australia was his greatest concern. The land was parched; billabongs and other water holes had dried up long ago; crops had failed on nearby farms. But Doug and his family weren't too badly affected because twenty years ago, he'd run down the cattle interests to concentrate on breeding fine racers for Middle Eastern potentates, so now his income came mainly from horses, and he had the money and reserves to order in food, grain, and water to ride out the horrors of what God and nature, or more likely industrialized mankind and global warming, had caused the arid land.

He was content to run his stable of horses, make good money in most years from the horse sales, graze other people's horses, and when there was plentiful rain, grow crops to keep him in ready cash. Other than during the past four years of unremitting drought, it was a good life—hard work but honest and God-fearing work for those who were willing. Had his poor wife Susan not died two years earlier from cancer, life would have been completely perfect. Why on earth the Almighty should have taken such a good woman to His breast at the age of fifty-seven, Doug had no idea, but while his children wailed and said how cruel life was, he was content in the knowledge that he couldn't understand God's mind, and so he assured himself that, while the loss of his beloved Susan was truly raw and horrible, there was a higher purpose that he'd find out when he was removed from this earth to God's bosom.

Lying on his back on the parched earth that once was the bank of a fast-flowing stream of pure rainwater from the distant mountains, Doug looked up at the sky. It was a never-ending powder blue painted with an ethereal luminescence of a transparent cloud, and he could still see the distant moon, even though it was midday. He was at peace.

But his peace was disturbed by a distant scream. Frowning and sitting up, he turned toward what he thought was the direction and saw his eldest son riding like one of the Horsemen of the Apocalypse toward him.

As Ben drew closer, Doug could just make out some of his words. It sounded like trouble. A minute later, Ben reigned in his horse and explained why he'd come to take his father back to the homestead. It was trouble.

* * *

Veterinarian Peter Dobbs tucked his stethoscope back into the pocket of his white laboratory coat and stroked the horse's neck. The sick animal, breathing in shallow gasps, barely responded. Normally, horses needed to be calmed before he approached them. They were always spooked when they saw him wearing a face mask and rubber gloves in case the animal was infected with the bat-born Hendra virus. But this beautiful animal barely noticed Peter's approach as it continued to shiver and shake, its massive chest making liquid noises as it struggled to breathe.

Doctor Dobbs stood and walked over to where Doug, Ben, and other members of the Landsdale Horse Stud were waiting in anticipation of the bad news. They'd all been around horses long enough to know that whatever was ailing the stallion was bad—very bad.

"I'm afraid that it's very bad news, but I won't know for certain until I get the samples back from the laboratory. I've got to assume that it's a serious case of equine flu or Hendra virus, so I'm afraid I'm going to have to quarantine the stud. No movement in or out until I've reported back to the Ministry and I know what I'm dealing with. Equine influenza is seriously contagious, and your other horses could be affected. But if it's Hendra, then no human being must go near this beast without full protection. And that includes other smaller animals, like your dogs and cats. It's recently been shown that Hendra can be passed on to other species as well as horses and humans. Just be very cautious, for God's sake."

"Is he going to die?" asked Doug. "He's worth over two million."

"It's not looking good, I'm afraid. I've given him a massive dose of antibiotics, but if it's the virus, which it very well could be, then antibiotics are going to be of little use. I don't have any antiviral medicines with me, so I'll bring them round this afternoon. But I'm really serious, Doug, no movement of any of your staff in or out, no movement of any animals. Complete isolation. Everybody who's touched this horse must wash his or her hands with disinfectant. Same with shoes. We have to contain this thing, or it could spread and not only wipe out all the horses in your stud but close down the entire state."

Dobbs left the farm and drove at top speed back to his office in Toowoomba, where his responsibility was to report first to the local government veterinary official, then to the Ministry in Brisbane, and then return to the stud with antiviral medication. But he knew with certainty that it was too late to save the beautiful creature. Whatever it was that had affected the horse, it was vicious, potent, and dangerous. And if it was the Hendra virus, then it was more rapid and vicious than anything he'd yet experienced. The animal had only shown the first signs of sickness that morning. But just in case, he'd taken sensible personal precautions because other vets had died from underestimating the virus that could jump species from horse to humans. He'd book himself in for tests in a day or two, just to make sure.

Peter spent an hour in his office ensuring the biohazard material was properly handled by his staff before it was sent to the government laboratory, and then he made his phone calls. Before he called the chief veterinary officer for the United States Public Health Service, he had a cup of tea and took some acetaminophen for a headache that had suddenly come on. By the time he left his office with his antiviral injection and reached the outskirts of Toowoomba, he was in a cold sweat, and the headache had reached the point where he felt nauseous and unwell; his vision was blurred and made his driving difficult.

But he had to attend to the horse before he could allow himself the luxury of an early mark to end his day. Must've been a delayed reaction from the Cabernet Sauvignon he'd quaffed at last night's dinner party, though he couldn't remember drinking more than a couple of glasses. In fact, he could barely remember a thing. Try as he might, his short-term memory seemed to have collapsed. In a cold sweat, he tried to smile, promising himself that there'd be no more drinking midweek.

Later that afternoon, police were called to the scene of a crash in which Doctor Dobb's car had left the road and crashed at high speed into a telegraph pole, killing him instantly. At the same time as the vet, suddenly blind and screaming in agony from the crushing headache, had lost control of his car, silence descended on the Mauden homestead and the Landsdale stud. The silence of death. The only sound that broke the silence was the coughing and vomiting of three other horses that had shared the dead horse's paddock and eaten from the same pile of oats.

Until the alarm had been raised and forensic examiners got to work, the police had no idea of the reason the dead vet was speeding or why his face and hands were a hideous patchwork of blue-black blotches. When they arrived at the accident, they didn't know that the vet was on his way to attend to a beautiful black stallion that was already dead. It took an examination of his office appointments to determine where he had been going.

And it took only four hours for the local police to go to the farm to complete their investigation of the circumstances surrounding the death of the vet. There they discovered the owner, Doug Mauden, his son Ben, his other son Joshua, Joshua's girlfriend Rosemary, three stable hands, and two other people who had tried to calm a horse going crazy in a paddock, lying dead near the stable. By the following morning, Queensland's Chief Veterinary Office had ordered a hazmat team to be called in from Canberra. A one hundred square mile quarantine perimeter zone was quickly established around the famous horse stud. When forensic pathologists examined the cadavers, they wondered what pathogen might have caused the hideous blotches on the skin of the victims that made their faces look as though they'd been painted by some demonic artist.

As the sun descended into the west and dusk gently began to cast long shadows across the land, nobody collecting biological samples of plants, soil, and animal tissue from the stud or examining the dead bodies of the human beings, bothered to look up into the sky. Had they done so, they would have seen a swarm of distressed and famished bats, from a distant roost, flying over acres of sunflowers and other crops grown for human consumption and biofuels, desperately searching for a source of food they could eat—increasingly scarce because of the drought that was gripping Australia.

MUKUBOINA VILLAGE
ON THE BANKS OF THE ORINOCO RIVER, VENEZUELA

The woman Danthia, a native of the Warao tribe in Delta Amacuro State, looked up for a moment to watch a canoe, paddled by tribesmen she didn't know, drift lazily down the Orinoco toward the distant sea. But she only looked away from her child Nanrita for just that moment. She wanted to make her mother's eyes the very last thing that Nanrita saw before she drifted away into death.

The tribe's leader had told the mother that her eyes must be the last thing the child saw before she died, for then the girl would carry those eyes into the sky as her soul was released and she joined her ancestors in the uplands. With the knowledge and experiences of her mother's eyes, the little child would wander the home of the gods and understand everything with the mind of an adult.

Somewhere in the distant high mountains, which shielded the river from the setting sun, Danthia knew that the souls of her other children were being taken care of by her mother and father and ancestors, who enjoyed a life of luxury without pain and disease.

Danthia had no tears for her dying Nanrita. There were no more tears left in her body. She'd wailed when her first child, her youngest daughter, had died three months before. She'd cried when one of her sons had died shortly afterward. She'd cried far less—felt far less shocked—when her second and then her third son had died of the same illness. Now her Nanrita was about to die and join her three brothers and her sister in the uplands. She would be left then with no children, and that was good because she wouldn't feel any further grief.

Danthia was disturbed from her reflections by the appearance of Doctor Judith in her hut. Always a friendly sight, Doctor Judith's face was haggard, drawn. Danthia doubted that she'd slept very much these past couple of weeks since she'd returned from Caracas, trying to persuade the authorities to take some responsibility for what was happening to the children of the village. The villagers had gathered when they heard Doctor Judith's boat in the distance coming around one of the massive bends in the river. But as her boat was being tied to the jetty, one look at her face told the villagers that they were not going to be helped by the government people who lived in the city, that they were on their own, and that their children would continue to die. Soon there would be no children left in the village, and in a generation, the village would be no more. Nobody knew when, in the distant past, the ancestors had built the village on the banks of the Orinoco, but soon it would be no more.

"How is she?" asked Doctor Judith.

Danthia shook her head gently so as not to disturb the little girl.

Doctor Judith took her stethoscope out of her pocket and listened to the child's heartbeat. It was barely discernible. Soon, maybe within the hour, her heart would just give out as the virus, or whatever it was, overwhelmed the little girl's defenses and she succumbed, as forty-six children had succumbed in the past three weeks.

To hell with those stupid bastards in Caracas, Judith thought. Arrogant, self-righteous, pompous bureaucrats. Even the minister of health had dared to tell her that she was wrong. The man was an engineer, for God's sake. He knew nothing about medicine. When she'd tried to make him understand the results she got back from the University of Alabama, proving that the virus that was killing the kids was a new strain of rabies, he'd shaken his head and told her that it couldn't be rabies.

He'd had her escorted from his office when she thumped the test results down on his desk and ordered him to open his fucking eyes and read the fucking facts. Big mistake. Being an American, she was only tolerated in Venezuela solely because she was an academic—especially because her relationship with the country had been so long.

But to see the children of her people die in front of her, to feel so utterly useless, not to fully understand what was causing the destruction of the society, and especially to see it happening only to the children. Nobody believed her when she said that it was the vampire bats. The nearby oil-drilling rigs had uprooted and disturbed the roosts of tens of thousands of vampire bats that, two years ago, had relocated in the jungle along the banks of the Orinoco. The villagers loved to shoot them down from the trees with their bows and arrows. But since that time, the children had begun to fall sick, and it could only be the bats that were causing it. The bats flew down at night and sought out the warm body of a sleeping animal. Often they'd suck the blood of cows or horses. They'd land nearby on the ground and crawl surreptitiously over to the animal and make a small incision on the leg. They'd inject an anticoagulant and suck the blood until they were full—then fly away.

Rabies caused by bats was common in the rural parts of Venezuela; often bats flew in the middle of the night into a village and sucked the blood of sleeping children. Normally, it caused fever, terrible itching, especially in the feet, and could lead to paralysis if not treated. Sure, there were deaths in unvaccinated people, but in these cases, the disease took months to kill. But this latest outbreak was fatal within days— sometimes if the child was undernourished, in hours. She'd contacted her university, alerted them, and sent them samples. The results of the electron microscopy of the blood and brain tissue showed a new and virulent strain of rabies.

It had surprised the scientists. One of her colleagues had told her when he'd phoned to give her the results, "this is supercharged rabies. I've never seen anything like it before."

But nobody in Caracas believed her.

Teatro di Populi
Rome, Italy

Perhaps it was meant to be thus. Perhaps she'd been born to achieve this moment. Since she'd graduated top of her class from high school and became valedictorian, since she'd left Vassar with the university's and regents' medals for most outstanding scholar, and since her doctoral thesis had been picked up by Harvard University Press to be reworked into an academic textbook, Debra Hart had come to realize that what people said about her was true—that she was brilliant, quirky, and an intellectual who lived on the edge constantly seeking answers to questions others didn't think to ask.

She sat before a vast audience in the theater, which had been creatively rebuilt in the middle of the nineteenth century on Roman ruins, and tried to concentrate on what the president of the United States was saying. Did he know that she hadn't voted for him? Was there a way for him to find out? She really should pinch herself to stop smiling at such a ridiculous notion.

But the moment, the location, the event . . . were all threatening to overwhelm her. She was so far out of her comfort zone of laboratories and scientific conferences and meetings with other professionals that she seemed to be split into two people . . . one who was in Rome sitting near the US president as he addressed a global health conference, the other was a young and unconfident girl, distant from these surroundings, listening from elsewhere and wondering what Debra Hart was doing on a stage in Rome with all these important people.

Yes, she'd addressed many conferences before; no, she didn't suffer stage fright. Yes, she was scared as hell, and she wouldn't even be speaking today. She was there to support her president as he told the world of the US initiative that was supported by all of the ninety-seven governments that the United Nations and the United States had approached, whose lands were liable to sudden and devastating outbreaks of deadly viral diseases. And sitting beside her on the platform in front of an audience of staggeringly important world health professional bureaucrats and frontline doctors and scientists, was the director-general of the World Health Organization, the deputy secretary-general of the United Nations, a director of the World Bank that would manage the funds donated by the United States and Europe for the enterprise, and the prime minister of Italy. And she was placed fifth from the president of the United States, alongside the secretary of health. She! Debra Hart. Fifth in line. Yes, she thought . . . yes, I'll pinch myself and will wake up in Atlanta because this can't be happening to me.

As though sensing the thoughts running through Debra's mind, the president turned to her from the lectern and said, "And leading the

high-impact team will be a scientist with whom I know you're all familiar, one of the world's leading virologists who heads up the biological
crisis unit of the Center for Communicable Diseases in Atlanta, Georgia,
Doctor Debra Hart."

The audience applauded. She smiled but didn't know what to do.
Nathanial Jefferson Thomas, President of the United States, turned
toward her and nodded in appreciation, encouraging her to stand to
receive the acknowledgement of the audience.

"I know with absolute confidence that Doctor Hart will lead one of
the finest international teams of biohazard fighters in the world, available
to any country anywhere that suffers any outbreak of a deadly, yet previously unknown viral or bacteriological contagious disease at any time.
Our friends and allies, as well as those who don't see eye to eye with us,
all will be helped. The requests for frontline assistance will come to the
biohazard team through urgent applications for assistance to the World
Health Organization or the United Nations. They will pass on any
request directly to Doctor Hart's secretariat who will react immediately.

"As I've been saying, the sudden eruption of these dangerous, deadly
viruses could be a factor of man-made global warming, could be because
of increased urbanization, could be because of a sudden insect plume
caused by changed climatic conditions, or because much of our food
production areas have been converted to growing biofuels . . . could be
due to things that are happening in nature that we simply don't understand. But we have to fight them, in our own nations when they affect
our population, and especially at the source of the infection," said the
president, who took a moment for the import of his concept to sheet
home to the health professionals.

"Let me tell you what it is that we're going to be doing. As I've said,
ladies and gentlemen, during the past four or five years, we've had a series
of sudden and unprecedented eruptions of viruses not previously seen
before in human beings; some have for the first time, crossed the species
border, meaning that those diseases that affected other animals are now
mutating to affect human beings. We were first warned about this when
gay men began dying in the US, but we were unaware then of the ways

in which viruses could cross the species boundaries. It took us years to understand the nature of the HIV virus, and even now, we're only coming to grips with its treatment, not yet its cure. As to the source of the virus, we still don't really know.

"The HIV virus that causes AIDS could be, probably was, one such issue, and we all know how that has devastated so many of our brothers and sisters. SARS is another, as is the influenza A subtype virus H5N1, better known as avian or bird flu. There's the deadly Hendra virus that spreads from horses to humans, the Ebola virus that so recently killed thousands of people in West Africa, and a whole raft of other diseases that so far have only killed a relatively small number of people.

"Small, that is, until recently. We're now recognizing that primates were probably the vector of HIV, which spread to humans, but while we know they acted as a reservoir, we don't know what caused the primate HIV virus to infect them. And we know that pigs were the source of the virus that wiped out the entire populations of five villages on Indonesian islands and others in the jungles of Malaysia and Thailand during the past year, but what suddenly gave it to the pigs? Villagers in Indonesia and Malaysia and Thailand have been eating pork for millennia, yet suddenly something in pork is instantly fatal to human beings.

"What is of greatest concern to us is how the disease gets into the higher animals. Ticks, perhaps, mosquitoes possibly, fleas, birds, bats . . . who knows? That's what our brightest minds are currently working on . . . because if we can wipe out the source of infection for higher and often domesticated animals, then we can stop the spread of the disease to humans. Yes, scientists throughout the world are working on vaccines to prevent people from falling sick if they're unlucky enough to be infected by the virus, but as all of you scientists and health professionals here know only too well, viruses can mutate quickly, and any vaccine will be largely ineffective against some new strain that mutates when it enters a new host. So just like the Great Fire of London cleansed the congestion and conditions that had created fertile ground for the Black Plague, our team of biohazard scientists will be like a cleansing firestorm, identifying the source of infection, eliminating it, quarantining any infection, and preventing the spread into our cities, our homes. Unlike our tragic ancestors in England in 1666, we won't allow entire populations to fall foul of some new and monstrous disease. When we identify the source, whether it's mosquitoes, ticks, bats, birds, or whatever, we'll eliminate it before it has a chance to infect large numbers of human beings."

* * *

When the US presidential address to the World Health Organization Annual Conference was over, the VIPs were escorted to their cars and driven to the Quirinal Palace, where the Italian president was waiting to greet the visiting US party. Debra drove to the Italian president's residence in the limousine along with DeAnne Harper, the United States secretary of Health and Human Services; her husband; and Deputy Secretary Doctor Jonathan Bailey. The president of the United States, along with his wife, was riding in a heavily protected convoy with the Italian Prime Minister Doctor Angelo LoPresti.

Away from prying microphones, Doctor Bailey said, "Well what did we all make of the reception to the president's speech?"

Debra was inclined to give her opinion but had been warned both by her boss in Atlanta, and in a whispered conversation with Doctor Bailey just before she got into the limo, to allow the secretary the floor whenever possible. She was arrogant and a merciless self-promoter, but she had the ear of the president, and it wouldn't do to get on her wrong side. So Debra held back.

"I think it went over very well," said Secretary Harper. "Face it, after all of these hideous, sudden outbreaks in Indonesia, Malaysia, Thailand, the Sudan, Somalia, Benin, and Brazil, the Third World is running scared. And when China was the first to come on board, it was game, set, and match for the developing world. After the Ebola epidemic in West Africa, it was obvious to them that they could see half their populations destroyed, and when you don't have the resources to fight such disasters, you have to rely on a big brother. Sure, most people there today realized that we're doing this to protect ourselves, but they were also smart enough to realize that while we're protecting ourselves, we're also protecting them. No, I think it went very well. A good speech."

"You know, Madam Secretary, much of the content of the speech was provided by Debra," said Doctor Bailey.

DeAnne turned and acknowledged the younger woman. She smiled. "I'm really glad to have you on board, Doctor Hart. I just hope that you and your team can meet our expectations."

"We'll certainly try to, Madam Secretary. But you know how difficult it is, sometimes, to find the cause of a sudden viral infection," Debra said, not wanting to sound too defensive.

"What worries me most," said the secretary, "is if one of these horrible diseases gets into a city. In the countryside, even in the Third World, it can often be quarantined and contained; that's why Ebola didn't spread from Liberia and those other countries. And when a few doctors and nurses brought it back, we were able to contain it quickly. But we all know what happened when AIDS got into the wider community of San Francisco. It had devastated the gay population of the West Coast, New York, Chicago, and other major cities before we managed to get a handle on HIV. I stay awake at night terrified that one of these viruses will cross species and find its way into the heart of our homeland. God knows, Ebola and SARS are terrible enough, but they're usually in some African jungle or in China or somewhere far away from us. I read that paper you sent to me, written by that Harvard scientist; you remember, the one on bats and their viral load . . . is that a reality?" the secretary asked.

Debra nodded. "It's still speculative, but with bats now inhabiting inner cities, it's something that I think we should become very serious about researching."

* * *

Debra stationed herself against one of the walls of the reception hall while watching the president of the United States being introduced to Italian, European Union, and other high-ranking health ministers and their departmental officials. Quirinale Palace contained one of the most sumptuous rooms in which she'd ever been, at least under these circumstances.

Along with her widowed mother, she'd taken the occasional holidays to the beauty and culture spots of Europe; she'd been inside the Vatican, Windsor Castle, and all over Vienna's Schonbrunn Palace, but only ever as a tourist, hurried by guides, prevented by guards. For the first time in her life, she was within a historic building as an invited guest, with rights to touch the priceless objects, sit on the opulent furniture, and drink wine with the residents. And there were fewer more opulent or sumptuous palaces in Europe than the Quirinale.

Built in 1573 by Pope Gregory XIII as his summer residence, it had served popes, both as the site for their conclaves and as home and offices for the Papal States until 1870 when the hapless Pius IX lost them. Then it became a royal residence for the King of Italy and now housed the president of the Italian Republic.

The steps leading up to the palace from the Via del Quirinale had impressed her greatly, and as the car drove toward the palace, she could barely wait to be deposited at the foot of the stairs so that the tourists would look and gawk and give her the feeling of being like the Queen of England. Would she turn and wave . . . no, she'd let them guess who she was.

But her girlish fantasy evaporated as the driver, naturally, drove around the palace to a secure entrance. She felt stupid for even thinking that the president of the United States would get out of a limo on the pavement like some Hollywood hunk at a movie premier, walk up the stairs through a gaggle of sightseers, and shake hands with the president of the Italian Republic when he reached the top.

It was when she had alighted from her car, following the secretary of health into the palace, that she truly understood Gibbon's expression . . . the glory that was Greece, and the grandeur that was Rome. She'd never, ever been invited to be a guest somewhere as grand, as magnificent, as plush. Having spent her life in universities, laboratories, functional government buildings, and purposeful offices, being inside a venerable European palace and surrounded by the wealth of former ages and offered wine and canapés by liveried flunkies in powdered wigs was an experience she would find hard to define either to her future self or her family.

She had been escorted and announced as she entered the reception hall, where the president of the Italian Republic and his wife and the Italian prime minister and his wife greeted her at the door. The prime minister kissed the hand of the secretary of health but shook Debra's hand. And so she'd entered the inner sanctum where she and five hundred other guests were gathered. The vastness of the room gave her the feeling of being one of few, rather than part of a crowd, and she gravitated toward one of the walls where she stood nursing her glass and observing how people who felt completely at ease in such surroundings behaved.

One she observed was the president of the United States. She'd never met him until this afternoon, but had been at Health and medical receptions when he'd been a guest and found him, from afar, to be intelligent, personable, and comfortable within himself. Her opinion of him was that he was neither as arrogant as Bill Clinton nor as ignorant as George W. Bush but a brilliant orator in the style of Barack Obama. President Thomas was the first man with a doctorate in a scientific discipline to be elected to serve his people from the White House; already well into the beginning of his term, he was elected with a very comfortable majority over a born-to-rule Bostonian whose campaign never recovered from the photographs of him making a drunken fool of himself with a Fox News female reporter.

Debra was impressed by the facility with which her president sashayed from one conversation to another, immediately finding a thread in a conversation that involved the person meeting him, often for the first time. Attempting to read his lips from a distance, he seemed to be saying immediately after the introduction, "Yes, I know the city where you come from. I was there four years ago . . ." or "Good to meet you at last because I was just saying to my cabinet colleagues that we really should see more of you in the White House."

It was practiced small talk, a skill at which she was an utter incompetent. When she was at scientific conferences, she and her colleagues wouldn't indulge in small talk but would rather come straight to the point about this virus or that research.

She was brought back to the moment when she saw that a man was suddenly standing next to her, appearing out of nowhere like a faithful retainer. She turned and looked at an elegant European—suntanned, brown hair graying at the temples, in his mid-fifties but still obviously immensely healthy, probably athletic from regular ski holidays in the Swiss Alps.

"Doctor Hart, I am Professor Enrico Maria Giulini. I head up the virology unit of the University of Rome."

She held out her hand, and he clasped it to his lips and kissed it. She was touched and felt a ridiculous frisson of excitement.

"May I say, Doctor Hart, that there has never been a mission more important than that with which you have been entrusted. Without wishing to sound like some adolescent hysteric, the very future of vast numbers of the human race is at stake, and our authorities have failed to realize this until now. For years, I have been warning my government of the potential of widespread infections from these new strains of viruses, but I have been marginalized by low-level bureaucrats as a scaremonger. Now your president makes an announcement, your secretary of health joins him, the United Nations and other world bodies come on board, and my government rushes to catch up. Suddenly I get urgent phone calls to see the minister to explain what I've been trying to get him to understand for years. I'm criticized by my government that I didn't think of your initiative before you did and that thanks to my incompetence, Italy is playing second fiddle to the United States. Ridiculous."

She burst out laughing. "I'm sorry, but that's all really so stupid, isn't it? It sounds like just the sort of thing that happens in the United States."

"Very stupid. But at least we have some action now. If there's anything you need, anything which Italy or my university can assist you with, please don't hesitate to ask. Thanks to you, I'm now being listened to in high places. Who knows, I might even get some equipment I've been begging for these past ten years."

She was warming to this gentle man. Elegant, sophisticated, handsome even, he reminded her of her father . . . the father she knew and loved before he caught AIDS from one of his lovers.

* * *

Possibly, it was her laughter at the Italian professor's jokes that caused the president of the United States to turn and look at her. Possibly, it was the simple fact that the conversation time he'd allotted to the German minister of health had run out, and the president was getting bored with all the facts and figures being aimed at him as though they were V-2 rockets. Or possibly it was one of the myriad of hidden signals—a scratch of the left ear, a surreptitious turn of the right elbow—that caused the president's press secretary to approach him, excuse himself most sincerely, and guide the president away from the rigidly boring minister.

For some reason, the press secretary, whose face was almost as familiar as the president's from the daily press briefings he gave in the West Wing, escorted the president over close to where Debra was standing, talking animatedly to Professor Giulini. Without bothering to wait for their conversation to enter a natural break, mid-sentence, the press secretary said, "Excuse me Doctor Hart, Professor, the president would like to speak with you."

With well-oiled mechanical timing, the president glided into the group, held out his hand and said, "Doctor Hart, I've heard so much about you. It's good to meet with you at last. Professor, I wonder if you could spare Doctor Hart for just a short time."

The press secretary gently took the Italian by his arm and led him to the buffet table, chatting amiably all the way, as though the conversation they had just begun had been taking place for hours. Debra was amazed by the fluidity with which the short but intense maneuver had just been carried out. Nobody had been offended, nobody felt ignored, yet she was free for a conversation with the president. And she knew that as soon as what he needed to say or find out had been satisfied, he'd glide off to someone and somewhere else and she'd be left alone, wondering what just happened.

"So Doctor Hart, you're our new virus fighter," he began. "Quite a job."

She wanted to say that it was daunting but that she was well up to the task. However, her throat suddenly closed up and she was rendered speechless. She suddenly realized that she was standing inches away from Nathanial Jefferson Thomas, the most powerful man in the world, an intellectual and political giant, a mountaineer and scientist, a business leader and author of two well-received political and philosophical tracts, a man even the most jaundiced media compared to Teddy Roosevelt. And Debra turned her mind to making comparisons between the hapless President Bush, the rutting President Clinton or the emasculated President Obama; it seemed to her that the new man in the White House was being treated like a god by the media. Now she was standing next to him, touching his shoulder, and all she could gasp was a ridiculous, "Yes, sir, big job."

She tried to free her mind of its frozen state by concentrating on the fact that she wasn't standing next to her president, but some new boss. Yet it wasn't easy. By any accounts he was an extraordinary man. Not only was he a brilliant scientist before entering politics, he'd made a fortune as head of a multi-billion dollar clean water facility taking sludge from around the country and using microbes both to turn it into drinking water and generate enough electricity to power a dozen small towns. Nathanial Jefferson Thomas was a natural leader of men, one who had come into politics in the middle of his life, stood for congress, and was drafted into the vice presidency in his second term. When, in the middle of his presidency, the incumbent had been forced to step aside because he'd developed early-onset Alzheimer's, Nathaniel had taken over the presidency and had recently won the next election in his own right. He was a Renaissance man, but she hadn't voted for him because she was a lifelong Democrat and he was a Republican. Now that she could see close up how gorgeous he was, she regretted her political leanings. Like millions of other young women in America, she'd suddenly fallen for him like an adolescent teen. She knew she had to get a grip on herself, and bit the inside of her cheek.

"Have you got your team together yet?" he asked.

"Some," said Debra, recovering her composure and her voice. "I've got a top-line bat biologist from Harvard, some virologists and bacteriologists from Oxford, a wonderful geneticist from Tel Aviv, an epidemiologist from Paris, and I think I'm going to ask the Italian gentleman I was just speaking to if he'd join the rapid response team . . . from the work he was telling me about, he seems just what I need."

The president nodded in approval. "I'm not one to interfere because I'm a firm believer in the checks and balances of the separation of powers, but I wonder if I could impose upon you to see if there are any African or Asian or Arab scientists who you could incorporate. I realize, Debra, that the scientific skills you require in your team are far more important than the culture or nationality of the scientists you're choosing, but it would be very useful politically to my administration and its relationship with the WHO and the UN if some scientists on the team could come from these blocs. If the team is exclusively composed of Americans and Europeans . . . well, I'm sure you understand the sensitivities."

"Of course, sir," she said. "And as a scientist, I know you'll understand the importance of getting the best people for this job. But I'll see who's really good in these fields in non-Western universities and try to enlist them."

He smiled. She felt a charge of electricity surging through her body at his world-famous smile, which had been compared by the editor of *Paris Match* magazine to a thousand-megawatt generator, able to light up a town.

"You know, Debra, we really should have a reception at the White House when your team is complete. A dinner to honor the men and women who have come forward to accept the challenge. Have you been to the White House?"

She laughed. "When I was a kid, I did a tour. I even fantasized that I'd be the first female president."

He grinned. "I hope you'll wait until I'm out of office before you run." He put his hand on her shoulder, the touch of an older brother. She felt ridiculously fragile, as though a puff of Roman wind from the open curtains would blow her over. It was as though she was on her first date. God, but this man was sexy.

"Would you show me around the White House?" she asked, and suddenly felt herself flush and she knew she'd gone the color of beets. "Oh my God, I can't believe I just said that. I'm so sorry, Mr. President. It just slipped out. I don't know what came over me."

Nathanial Thomas laughed and squeezed her arm. "I'd be offended if you didn't let me show you around. I'll show you the Oval Office and the staterooms, and all the other places that are so famous. I take special people on special tours. And you're a very special person because we're all relying on you to keep us safe from harm."

Suddenly she felt the press secretary's presence beside his president. After a whispered conversation between the two, the president said, "You'll have to excuse me, Debra. I must speak with the prime minister. Now you just contact my personal secretary and arrange that tour when you get back. Make it sooner, rather than later."

And he was gone. She watched him walk away. Debra spent the next fifteen minutes totally alone, unable to speak, still in the company of the most powerful and sexiest man she'd ever known.

3

St. Stanislav's Primary School
Cricklewood, North London

It was a game the children had played a dozen times before, especially when the teachers were engaged in supervision duties on the other side of the playground. The kids, aged between five and nine, from parentage as diverse as China and Libya, Uganda and Northern Ireland, stood beneath the huge two-hundred-year-old oak tree, and threw stones into the canopy hoping to dislodge one of the dozens of bats that had taken up residence.

As they threw their stones and gravel upward, shouting with delight as each pellet left their hands, other younger kids who didn't have the muscular strength to throw that high, sang:

> What are you doing, Mr. Bat
> Hanging upside down?
> Stop your sleeping, Mr. Bat
> You'll lose your grip
> Your feet will slip
> And then you'll all fall down

The bell rang, the children screamed one last time, and scampered off to their classrooms, leaving the bats shivering in fear and trying to regain their sleeping posture.

The following morning, one of the smallest and youngest of the children who attended St. Stanislav's, Fergus O'Mara, kissed his mother, walked away from her toward his classroom, and, as he did most mornings, ran his hands along the top of a low wall that separated one playground from another. He didn't notice the tiny spots of shiny congealed liquid that had dried in the early morning sunshine. Nor did anything prevent him from digging into his school satchel and having a quick bite of the chocolate biscuit his mother had packed for his mid-morning milk break.

But as the teacher droned on during the day about playground rules and not throwing things into the oak tree, telling the boys that the tree had been their age even before the Victorian age, young Fergus began feeling a bit sick to the stomach.

Half an hour later, the teacher was surprised when Fergus vomited over his desk and the floor. The lad was helped to the principal's office and stayed there, feeling worse and worse, until his mother came hurriedly from her work at the local supermarket to take him home.

The following morning, Fergus, comatose and shivering, was rushed to Cricklewood General Hospital, where he was diagnosed as having all the symptoms of parvovirus B19. But Fergus's consulting physician told the pathologist who had just delivered the results to him, "This is like a parvovirus on steroids. I've never seen symptoms like this before. Normally you'd expect an *erythema infectiosum* rash on the cheek and a rash on his chest and limbs. Perhaps a low-grade fever. But this kid is as sick as a dog, and yet parvovirus is the only thing that fits all the symptoms. There's got to be something else in his system that is potentiating the parvovirus, but God only knows what it is."

The pathologist shook his head. "I've examined his fluids and tissues and I can't find anything except for parvo. If there is something else in there, something giving the parvovirus balls, it's not showing up in our test results."

The consulting physician nodded gloomily. "Then I'm keeping him under quarantine for a couple of days to see what develops."

Fergus died that night. Antipyretic and anticonvulsive injections didn't help him at all. He suffered a raging fever that even an ice bath couldn't bring down. When he died, screaming that his head hurt really badly, the attending medical staff was stunned by the look of his body. It seemed as though he'd just been in a ten-round heavyweight boxing match. The kid was black and blue, with huge blotches ranging in color from purple to jet. As his life slipped away, blood oozed from his nose, his mouth, and his eyes. His breath sounded as though he was under water. The physicians and nurses looked on in horror as his body seemed to disintegrate in front of them.

And the mystified medical staff was even more surprised when four more children from the same school were brought in during the following two days, suffering identical symptoms. It was then that the hospital called in the chief medical officer for London.

A quarantine area was set up around the school, and all students, administration, teachers, kitchen staff, and cleaners were ordered to be driven by ambulance to a biohazard reception center in Ealing, West London. Blood tests were done, and those found to be carrying the parvovirus were segregated and given massive doses of medicines. Twenty more people died during the following four days.

Dozens of police and ambulance vehicles raced to the school, their alarms cacophonous in the narrow, restricting streets; their flashing red and blue lights cutting the air like laser beams. It disturbed the small bat colony that had been forced to roost in the old oak tree for the past three years after their traditional roost site had been bulldozed for a new housing development. Now, terrified and in a panic, the bats had risen from their sleep and flew off following the bat colony's scouts where a new roosting site had been discovered far away. For the first time in a year, the oak tree was suddenly free of bats.

But nobody, neither teachers nor pupils nor ambulance nor police nor neighbors saw the entire diminished and frightened bat colony leave their oak tree home for the last time. Everybody was too busy trying to deal with the situation on the ground.

* * *

Britain's chief medical officer, Professor Lord Soames of Tewkesbury, read, and reread the national emergency safety alert broadcast report that wouldn't be published or put onto the airwaves without his signature.

The urgency of the situation in North London was paramount; every minute wasted would almost certainly lead to further catastrophic problems; but to be too hasty could lead to a national panic, the consequences of which would be horrific.

Yet to delay was unthinkable. Men, women, and children were dying of some hideous new infectious outbreak. Hazmat teams were crawling over the area. There was no traffic in or out of Cricklewood, Kilburn, Golders Green, Neasden, or West Hampstead. Residents, many of them elderly and in the throes of panic, had been ordered to remain indoors until the source of the infection had been identified. Food was being delivered door to door to residents in the quarantined areas by men in spacesuits, which simply added to the panic. And what increased the level of fear among the residents was the arrival of fleets of ambulances, driven by men wearing breathing apparatus and hazmat suits, carting people off to the hospital. Those neighbors watching out of windows thought that the patients were suffering from the disease, whereas all that was happening was that the elderly, infirm, or sick from other causes, were being taken to someplace safe and isolated for their normal treatments.

It was a disaster of unimaginable proportions. The prime minister had been on the phone every hour, and the media calls bombarding his office had been unprecedented—not just local media, but papers and broadcasters from all over the world. A hideous infectious outbreak in some Third World famine- and poverty-stricken area was one thing . . . but in central London?

This made Lord Soames stop and think before he acted, much to the fury of his staff. The infection seemed to be localized to a huge area of North London, but it hadn't yet spread to other districts of the capital, nor had it shown its horrible head in other towns or cities. So to put out a central infection alert to all doctors and hospitals that a virulent infectious organism, whose transmission procedure was as yet unknown, whose carrier was unknown, whose source was unknown but was 100 percent fatal to anybody infected could be counterproductive. Such an alert would instantly cause regional quarantine procedures to be put into effect with all the fear and trepidation that alone would create. And the disruption to the business and cultural life of the largest city in

Britain—for potentially no reason if the contagion was confined to this area in the North.

Lord Soames's thoughts were interrupted by a tall grave-looking young man at his office door who said, "Malcolm, we must have that report immediately if we're to initiate the alert before tonight. Have you decided whether or not to sign it?"

Years of public medicine tempered his answer. "No, not now. Nothing beyond North London. We'll review the situation in six hours."

The young man shook his head in amazement and left the room. Lord Soames called out, "Get me a hazmat suit. I want to go to Cricklewood and see for myself."

His assistant turned in surprise. "But the protocols say that you have to remain in this building because of the . . ."

"Alistair, I know the protocols as well as you. But you forget that I've been in Sierra Leone when there was an outbreak of Ebola and I worked with the frontline people who treated the victims. I know what to look for. Maybe the reason our people haven't been able to trace the source is that they're looking in the wrong direction. Now, get me the hazmat equipment and get my driver to bring the car round the front, will you."

"Certainly, Malcolm. Police escort?"

"Absolutely not . . ."

* * *

It took two days for the rapid response team headed by Debra Hart to arrive in London and assemble in one of the conference rooms of the Department of Health. They came from the United States, Israel, Italy, France, China, Australia, Mexico, and Russia. Other members of her team—those who didn't deal with frontline issues, but were world-class laboratory scientists—were put on alert to drop everything and anything they were doing, including family holidays, and await the arrival of samples for laboratory analysis.

Two days had passed since the UK's chief medical officer, against the specific instructions of the prime minister, had notified the World

Health Organization who, as the coordinating body, had then informed the United Nations and had authorized Doctor Hart to pull together her team to travel to England. Doctor Hart had immediately arranged for leading laboratories at Oxford and London universities to make ready all the analyses and other equipment she would require when she had samples to send them. She arranged with the Metropolitan police to have high-speed drivers available to transport the samples by the quickest possible methods—PolAir helicopters if necessary.

Lord Soames stood as Debra Hart and four of her colleagues entered his office. He'd just endured the most aggressive and unpleasant phone call from the prime minister who'd shouted at him for demeaning his country's reputation, making it seem as though they weren't able to look after Britain's own problems. Soames had shouted back that his responsibilities to the people of England were infinitely more pressing than meeting the prime minister's concerns about Britain's medical reputation, and had slammed down the phone. As a statutory officer answerable to Parliament, he couldn't be fired, but life from now on would be far from pleasant.

Soames walked around his desk and shook Debra's hand. "Doctor Hart, what a pleasure to meet with you."

She introduced him to the others on her team, and as they sat, she got straight down to business.

"Okay, Lord Soames, could you bring us up to date on what you've done to identify the source since we received your last report yesterday evening."

"It's still a mystery. We've had our top people examining virtually everything in and around the school, which was the source of the original outbreak—insect carcasses, food from the canteen, skin, hair and body tissues from everybody, animal dander, urine, feces, soil . . . you name it, we've tested for it. We just can't seem to find the vector or the reservoir," he said.

"And have there been any more outbreaks?"

"We've confined it to the staff and pupils at this school and a couple of hundred or so unfortunate men and women who live in the immediate surrounds. And there have been isolated cases in the more distant surrounding streets north of the school. We've also had a dozen or so cases in the area of North and North East London, quite a way from the school—but not many. We have no understanding of how the disease could have spread north and in such isolated areas. Unless one of the kids or parents or staff traveled to those houses, we'll probably never find out because tragically they've died so we can't ask them," he said, his voice strained and weary from a few snatched hours sleep here and there in the past week.

One of Debra's team, a tall, rangy man who'd been introduced as Professor Daniel Todd, a mammalian biologist from Harvard, interrupted and said, "Do you happen to have a topographical map of the spread of the infection?"

Soames nodded, and his assistant shuffled through a series of boards until he pulled one out and propped it up on the desk.

Professor Todd stood and walked over to have a closer inspection. The rest remained quiet as Daniel picked up a pencil from the desk and drew some lines joining up dot points between sites of infection breakout.

He turned and looked at Debra, then at Lord Soames who was studying the lines Daniel had just drawn.

"That's a flight path, Lord Soames. The reservoir of your infection flies. It's either birds or bats. I'll bet that if you follow the path northwest, you'll find a food source. Tell me, are there bats in or around the school?"

Soames looked at his assistant who shrugged his shoulders.

* * *

President Nathaniel Thomas was in the middle of writing a telling phrase into the speech he was due to deliver the following evening to the Daughters of the American Revolution. He wanted to deal with the way their nation had changed for the better as a result of immigration and tell those attending, who he feared would be far-right matriarchs, that change can be a force for good. But just as he'd defined an interesting philosophical argument that his speechwriter hadn't thought of, his phone buzzed.

"Excuse me, Mr. President, the British prime minister is on the phone for you. Will you take his call?"

Nathaniel frowned. He wasn't expecting a call from Alistair Blain. He'd last spoken to him a week earlier when he'd first heard of this terrible outbreak, but the man had been quite off-putting, even arrogant. When he was abusive or angry, his Scottish accent became much stronger, and Nathaniel found him hard to understand. He didn't think he could put up with another bout of Blain's high-handed British superiority this morning.

"Could you see if Prime Minister Blain will talk to Jenny Tan over at State?"

A moment later, his secretary buzzed through again. "I'm sorry, sir, he insists on talking to you. He said he wasn't interested in talking to flunkies."

Flunkies? Jenny was the most brilliant secretary of state since Henry Kissinger. "Okay, put him through."

He waited until the secretaries and personal assistants had finished checking that their various bosses were ready for the call, and the red light on his phone suddenly flashed.

"Mr. Prime Minister," he began. "Good to speak with you."

"Mr. President, how are you?"

When pleasantries were over, the prime minister of the United Kingdom came to the point. "Nat, I'm going to be very direct, as I'm sure you'll appreciate."

"Wouldn't have it any other way Alistair."

"I find it quite objectionable to have this team of yours in my country, taking over from my scientists, telling my people how to fight an infection."

So that was what it was all about. Great Britain puffing up her chest—"Rule, Britannia" for the twenty-first century. "Alistair, I'm sorry you think that way. You were a supporter of my move for an international effort to deal with epidemic outbreaks."

"Sure, when they were in Third World countries. Africa, Asia, South America. Where they didn't have the skills or the infrastructure to deal with what could become a pandemic. But this is England, my friend. England! We have the best scientists and medical laboratories in the world. We're the last country that needs some visiting firemen to put out a blaze in one of our cities. No, Mr. President, call off your dogs. Thank them for their efforts but have them go home and deal with outbreaks in nations that can't defend themselves. Not England!"

Nathaniel drew a deep breath and tried not to get angry. "Alistair, before the WHO team got there, your scientists hadn't a clue about the source or the cause of this outbreak. Within minutes of the World Health team arriving, they'd sourced it to birds or bats. That's one step closer to eliminating the problem. This could be a national emergency; surely you can't object to a bit of help, can you?"

Had it been a videophone, Nathaniel would have been able to see the British prime minister's nostrils flaring in anger. "We haven't needed US help since the Second World War, Mr. President, and even then you only came in at the last minute and took charge. Look, we're not a mendicant begging for assistance. We're one of the world's most advanced societies, and it's doing the morale of my people no good at all to know that our top brains are playing second fiddle to some international circus here for the glory. Order them home, Nathaniel, or I'll kick them out."

The phone slammed down. Nathaniel looked at it in shock for several long moments, not quite believing what had just happened. Slowly he replaced the receiver and thought for several seconds. Then he picked it up again.

"Shirley, get me Jenny Tan, will you."

* * *

She was tall and slender, and twenty years earlier she could have been a catwalk model lifting Armani to higher and higher levels. Her Asiatic eyes, blond hair, and porcelain skin defined her Japanese and Swedish heritage. Born in New York, she had been a precociously brilliant student and in her mid-thirties had become dean of political science at Yale. Advisor to the United Nations secretary-general, board member of the

World Bank, and numerous other high profile positions had brought her to the attention of Nathaniel Thomas when he stepped down from his bioengineering business and began his run for congress. They'd stayed in close touch ever since, and when he began his run for the vice presidency on the joint ticket, he'd encouraged his running mate to make Jenny the ticket's adviser on international political issues. Her brilliance, contacts, and global perspective had enabled both of them to triumph over their opponents in the television debates and town hall meetings. When he became the occupier of the Oval Office on the sudden incapacitating illness of the president, Nathaniel had asked for, and received, the resignation of the secretary of state and had put Jenny in charge. Her extraordinary skill as a negotiator, seducer, and power-packed intellectual had won over numerous intransigent world leaders. It was Jenny's brilliance that had cobbled together nearly one hundred countries to accept a rapid response team to make change in a nation where there was a sudden outbreak of a virulent disease capable of causing a pandemic.

And now the first to sign the agreement, Britain, faced with the reality of an international team in its territory, was suddenly saying that it didn't need or want help.

"Of course he retains sovereignty, Mr. President. He's the prime minister."

"But he's a signatory to the UN Charter on Pandemic Diseases. He was the second after us to agree to be bound by the terms of the charter. He signed on the goddamn dotted line. Surely we've got the right to insist that our people stay there."

"Firstly, it's not a pandemic. Not yet. It's been confined to an area of London. It hasn't crossed a national border. Secondly, the charter states that the UN can only ask if it can place its rapid response team within the boundaries of a signatory nation that is suffering an outbreak, but it has always given the government of that country the right to determine how long they'll stay and under what conditions. It's the same terminology as is used in UN charters governing peace keeping forces . . . they're invited in and they can be expelled at the will of the government. It all comes down to sovereignty, I'm afraid, Mr. President," she told him.

He breathed deeply. "So that snotty English bastard can kick us out and we might suddenly have a global outbreak of an incurable disease on our hands . . . just because he sings God Save the Queen in his bathtub."

She nodded.

"Okay, get over there by tonight and talk to him. See if you can convince him that our people have to stay. Remind him that this disease might be under containment at the moment, but it's 100 percent fatal. If it breaks out somehow, it could be as devastating at the Black Plague."

Jenny nodded. "I'll get over there immediately." She stood to leave his Oval Office.

"Jen, just be careful, won't you. Don't do anything stupid like going on a site visit to this infected school just for a photo opportunity."

She looked back and flashed her universally famous smile. "You're the politician, Mr. President. Not me."

* * *

Protocol demanded it, but the foreign secretary was infuriated at being dragged from his bed to greet Air Force Two at Heathrow in the middle of the night. The British government had been informed hours earlier that the US secretary of state was making an unofficial visit to speak with the prime minister about the WHO's rapid response team's tenure in Great Britain, but nobody at Number 10 had thought to inform the foreign secretary. Suddenly the prime minister's personal assistant had remembered protocol, and although he wouldn't be in the discussions that Secretary Tan would be having with the PM, the foreign secretary had to greet her on the tarmac, kiss her on the cheek as she descended the plane, and ride with her to the US Embassy where she'd catch up on a quick nap before breakfast at Downing Street.

As she descended the steps from the huge Boeing 747, she smiled at Paddy Cronin and knew from his hunched up body that right now he'd much rather be in bed. Beside him stood the tall and elegant figure of the United States ambassador to the United Kingdom.

"Paddy," she said as she stepped over to kiss him. "I'm so sorry to have dragged you out. You know I hate all this protocol business."

"Jen, my darling," said Cronin, "without all this protocol business, there would be no Great Britain."

She smiled and shook hands with her ambassador, who hung back as they walked to the convoy of cars to enable the two leaders to speak in private.

When he was sure that nobody could overhear, Cronin said, "Now, what the hell are you doing in the UK? Why are you seeing our esteemed leader? The bugger's told me nothing whatsoever, just that you're here representing Nathaniel and talking privately. What's it all about?"

"Can't tell you, my sweet; your 'lord and master' Alistair Blain and my 'God who walks on water' Nathaniel Thomas have had a lover's tiff, and I'm here to ensure that they continue to screw each other, in the nicest possible way, of course."

They got into his Rolls Royce. "What was the quarrel about? Oh, come on . . . you know I'll keep *schtum*."

"Darling, of all the foreign ministers of all the countries in the world, you're the least able person I know to keep *schtum*. However, a man of your insight should be able to hazard a guess."

She remained silent.

"I assume," he said, "that it has something to do with our sovereignty over dealing with this horrible disease that's suddenly erupted. The PM's been ranting and raving about it since yesterday."

She smiled, patted him on the knee, and said softly, "Isn't London beautiful at this time of year."

Paddy Cronin sighed. "Oh shit. I was afraid of that."

* * *

Five hours later, Secretary of State Tan was sitting in the dining room of 10 Downing Street with the prime minister of the United Kingdom, eating a breakfast of grapefruit, toast and English marmalade, muffins, and Earl Grey tea. In silver salvers on the credenza were bacon, sausages, cooked tomatoes, mushrooms, and something that he'd explained was bubble and squeak, a dish that sounded as disgusting as it looked. She'd passed on the cooked stuff, contenting herself with a continental breakfast.

When she'd first met him three years previously, she'd found his Scottish accent lilting and his speech lyrical. Now, in the pit of his barely restrained anger, she found him hard to understand, harsh, and ruthless.

"Jennifer, my dear, you're failing to understand. These scientists of yours are unnecessary. Our people can handle this crisis. We handle medical crises all the while."

"They're not my scientists; they're from the World Health Organization. And I'm well aware, Alistair, of the quality of British medicine . . ."

"No, you're not! Our researchers from the UK have won the Nobel Prize for medicine twenty-eight times in the past century. We're world leaders. We don't need some Israeli or Frenchman or Italian to tell us how to conduct this investigation."

"This is a global problem, Alistair," she insisted. "We've seen outbreaks erupt in the past couple of years in Niger and Venezuela and Indonesia and . . ."

"Precisely. The reason we signed the charter was to help these Third World countries whose populations could be eliminated by a pandemic. But not us. Not Britain. We can handle our own problems, thank you very much."

She felt like shouting at him but sipped her Earl Grey to calm down. "Alistair, can't you see the message you'll be sending to the Third World if Britain kicks the rapid response team out? Think about AIDS and Thabo Mbeki of South Africa. Remember what his minister of health did?"

Alistair Blain wiped his mouth with a napkin and said, "No, remind me."

Jenny Tan reached down into her briefcase and withdrew a letter. "This was sent to the president of South Africa in 2006 by the world's leading health professionals."

She handed him the letter. He took it and put on his reading glasses.

Mr Thabo Mvuyelwa Mbeki
President
Republic of South Africa

Dear President Mbeki

EXPRESSION OF CONCERN BY HIV SCIENTISTS

We are members of the global scientific community working on HIV/AIDS who wish to express our deep concern at the response of the South African government to the HIV epidemic.

HIV causes AIDS. Antiretrovirals are the only medications currently available that alleviate the consequences of HIV infection. The evidence supporting these statements is overwhelming and beyond dispute. We are therefore deeply concerned at how HIV science has been undermined by the South African Minister of Health, Dr Manto Tshabalala-Msimang.

Before and during the XVI International AIDS Conference, Dr Tshabalala-Msimang expressed pseudo-scientific views about the management of HIV infection. Furthermore, the South African government exhibition at the Conference featured garlic, lemons and African potatoes, with the implication that these dietary elements are alternative treatments for HIV infection. There is no scientific evidence to support such views. Good nutrition is important for all people, including people with HIV, but garlic, lemons and potatoes are not alternatives to effective medications to treat a specific viral infection and its consequences on the human immune system. Over 5 million people live with HIV in South Africa. According to the best estimates of South African actuaries, over 500,000 people without access to antiretrovirals have reached the stage of HIV-disease when they now require these medicines to save their lives.

He looked up from reading the letter without bothering to finish it and said, "But this is precisely my point. Your team has to deal with Third World, not First World nations. I don't expect my health minister to recommend potatoes for the treatment of whatever is happening in Cricklewood. If he did so, I'd fire him instantly. "

"And that's precisely *my* point, Alistair. If idiots like this South African health minister or counterparts in other Third World nations see Britain standing alone, refusing help, being all puffed up and isolationist and patriotic, then it'll be a clue for how they should act. The only way we're going to deal with this problem is by every country, yours and mine included, saying to the global community that these outbreaks are a worldwide problem, and the world has to come to every country's aid to deal with them."

The prime minister handed her back the letter. He sighed. "Look, Jennifer, don't think I'm unsympathetic to your argument. My problem is that there are rumblings in the media about this team. Not their professionalism or their expertise—simply the fact that the disease must be far worse than we're admitting if a country like Great Britain has to call for help with a problem that we're incapable of solving ourselves. The public panic has been huge because of this damn outbreak. Your team suddenly flying in like supermen to Gotham City has made the panic a lot worse. It's as though the British government is out of ideas, out of control."

"How bad has the panic been?" she asked.

"As bad as it gets. Britons are stoic in the face of adversity. During the war, we all pulled together during the Blitz. When the Islamic terrorists killed fifty people on the trains and buses, the first thing we Britons did was to show them we weren't going to be intimidated, and we immediately got back on the trains and buses as though nothing had happened. Life went on as normally as possible. But this! Microbes falling out of the sky infecting anybody and everybody. A mortal enemy that's too tiny to be seen by a microscope. An indiscriminate killer of men, women, and children that could hide in soil or leaves or food or birds or bats and one touch and you're dead. The whole of London's in a panic. Outside of the quarantine areas and restrictions on travel, people are leaving the city in the hundreds of thousands. The streets in Central London are empty. The suburbs are ghost towns. The Midlands and north of England are overcrowded with people begging for hotel accommodation or staying in overcrowded conditions with relatives.

"We've done everything in our power to calm people down, to tell them that the infection is isolated, but nobody's listening. People are hoarding food, medicines, liquids. It's an end-of-the-world scenario being played out in England's green and pleasant land," he said, stirring his tea for the umpteenth time. "We have to convince our people that we're handling the situation calmly and efficiently, or we'll be in terrible trouble. And we have to show Britons that we're doing it on our own. That's why your team being here has been such a disaster for my government."

She nodded, and for the first time understood the enormity of the prime minister's problem. It wasn't just his countrymen and women who were in a panic; it was also him. From the way he was sounding, he was one decision away from imposing martial law, from ordering armed police on every street corner, from creating concentration camps and badges for aliens. He was making his country seem as though it was Nazi Germany before the war. She had to convince him that his country was simply suffering from an unidentified virus. Once the reservoir had been established, it would be eliminated, and the problem would be solved.

"How's about we take the pressure off your shoulders by getting the secretary-general of the United Nations to have a press conference in which he says that, with your consent, he invoked the conditions of the charter and Britain is leading the way by inviting in an international team, working with some of the best British scientists around. That it was you who said this is a problem that the world has to work together to solve, and as a result, you've strongly suggested that the team comes into Great Britain to assist your scientists and medical practitioners. And that you've done this to assure Third World countries that international cooperation is the only way we're all going to beat this new and undiscovered menace and that this is how all nations, even the world's most developed, have to behave in the face of a future epidemic."

The prime minister of the United Kingdom smiled for the first time since she'd entered Number 10. "Could you get him to do it?"

"Absolutely. And you'll hold a press conference, televised at precisely the same time. You could even be joined by satellite—he in New York, you in London—so that it seems as though you and the secretary-general are singing from the same hymn sheet. Surely, that'll take the pressure off your government. And it'll explain to the people of Great Britain why the rapid response team is here. At least that level of panic might be ameliorated."

He stood from the table and helped himself to more food from the credenza. "That could work. You're a smart lady, Jenny Tan. Very smart."

4

OFFICES OF MIDNIGHT RECORDS
LOWER MANHATTAN

His face was one of the best known in the world. People living in rural China, in South American shantytowns, and on the steppes in Mongolia were as familiar with his craggy jawline, his hairstyle, and his aviator glasses, as were black metal aficionados in the heart of Chicago, Paris, and Moscow. Everybody knew his voice, which ranged from growling threats in lyrics such as "If you do it, I'm gonna getcha getcha getcha," to the universally imitated "when a man loves a woman, his heart's a shared vessel," a line that earned him an additional fortune in royalties since it had been taken up by greeting card companies.

As a singer and a songwriter, his sales had eclipsed the Beatles and the Rolling Stones put together. He was America's favorite recording artist. According to a cover of *Time Magazine* last year, he was the "Voice of America."

Jay Silvester, mega-philanthropist—intimate of Hollywood super-stars, network talk-show hosts, prime ministers, and presidents—sat and listened in amazement as Tom Pollard, president of CHAT, Citizens for Humane Animal Treatment, told him what the British government was about to announce.

"You're shitting me. You're fucking shitting me," he said.

Pollard shook his head.

"Birds?"

"And bats."

"You're shitting me. Tell me this is a joke."

"My source in our government has found out, and remember she's got the ear of the health secretary, that all flying animals—birds, and bats in London and immediately surrounding districts—will be caught, culled, murdered, exterminated. Poisoned. Gassed. These morons from this rapid response group . . . freakin' lunatics. . . have decided without a single scrap of evidence that the cause of this outbreak in North London is a virus found in the body of birds and/or bats. They're not sure, and so they're going to exterminate every animal that flies. Birds and bats. Of course, all our research shows it could just as easily be mosquitoes or other flying insects, but no, they've fixed their minds on birds, and that means good night and good-bye. And it's just to placate Londoners. The other thing our research scientists have told us is that if the virus is localized to a relatively small area of London, that it can't possibly be birds or bats, but has to be fleas or rats something in the food.

"But no," Pollard insisted, "instead of looking at the obvious, they're mounting a PR campaign, going for the most visible target and showing Londoners that they're doing something. It's disgusting."

Jay Silvester sipped his mineral water and looked at Pollard over the lip of the glass. When the appointment had been made, he'd agreed to give the dude half an hour for the pitch, which Jay assumed would be for money. Jay was the world's highest grossing performer, higher even than pretty-boy actors of Hollywood, myrmidons of Tinseltown, those puffed up nonentities who couldn't remember more than a couple of lines of dialogue per scene and had to have a director tell them how to look and walk and eat and talk. Yes, he was friends with the superstars, actors whose faces beamed down from massive roadside billboards, but deep down, he had no respect for any of them. And Jay knew what each and every one of them made . . . tens of millions per movie just for their names on the covers of magazines and most of the motherfuckers couldn't even act to save their lives. Put 'em on a stage, and . . . *kerpowee* . . . they'd be struck dumb in fear of the audience.

But Jay had to go out live in front of his fans every night for months while he and the band were on tour, and he had to perform every note to perfection each time he sang. Nobody told him how to do his job. And because of his vast wealth—he didn't even know how much, but his managers assured him that it was a couple of billion—he was always a prey to parasites and con artists, so he had every appointment vetted by his staff, every phone call recorded, every letter opened and read by his secretaries so that he'd never, ever, be accused of plagiarism or rip-offs or anything.

It had taken Pollard a week to set up this appointment, a week of begging, pressure, and persistence. The dude had been researched, analyzed, scrutinized, and sanitized because nobody got to see Jay Silvester on business without Jay and his people knowing everything about the dude. But this dude had come up kosher, so Jay, being a huge cash supporter of CHAT and having donated 10 percent of the proceeds of one of his albums to them, had agreed to see him.

At first, the dude had seemed nervous, shuffling his feet. Jay hated people who were nervous. He always joked, as somebody diffidently approached him, that he wasn't the fucking president of the United States or the pope for god's sake. But his personal assistant was always reminding him that when he was meeting a fan or some low-life reporter for the first time, Jay might be full of confidence, but the fan or the reporter was in the presence of somebody world-famous and might be nervous. Still, he didn't expect the president of CHAT, who he'd met once or twice at receptions, to be nervous when he was alone in a room, just the two of them—man to man.

And the dude had brought him news that the Brits were planning to kill all the birds in the skies of London just because they were panicking over some fucked-up virus that had only killed 452 people. Shit, that was how many died on the roads in a day, and nobody was talking about killing all the cars.

"So what do you want me to do, Tom? You want money for a campaign or what?"

Pollard shook his head. "No, no money. I want you to go on national television and condemn what the British are planning to do. If we . . . you . . . can put pressure on the government of Britain, the people might rally and stop this hideous slaughter of innocent animals."

"Okay. No sweat. I'll have my people set it up. First off, though, I'll need proof that the Brits are actually going to kill the birds, though. I can't get the media in here to beat the drum and then make a fool of myself."

"I can't give you proof, Jay. Only to tell you that my source, who's highly placed at Health, has found out the plans and has told us. She's been 100 percent correct about everything she's told us in the past, and these plans are well underway. She's seen them. That's why she came and told us."

"Can I speak to her?" asked Jay.

"Sure. I told her you wouldn't act without proof. So she agreed to reveal her identity once and once only. And only to you. Here's her phone number at Health. She's waiting for your call. She suggests that instead of you phoning her on her direct number, you phone the switchboard and ask for her. That'll prove to you that she really works there."

Jay nodded, put on his headphones, and Skyped the numbers on the piece of paper Tom gave him. Within moments, the phone was answered.

"Department of Health and Human Services," said the receptionist in Washington, "how may I direct your call?"

"Could I please speak to Miss Christine Knowles."

"Certainly, putting you through to Miss Knowles's office."

He looked at Tom, who was sitting there, much more confident of himself.

"Miss Knowles's office," said the assistant.

"Hi, could you please tell me Miss Knowles's position in the Department of Health?" he asked.

"Sure, Miss Knowles is Deputy Under Secretary of Health and Human Services."

"Might I speak with Miss Knowles?" asked Jay, suddenly impressed.

"Who may I say is calling?" asked the assistant.

Jay looked at the piece of paper Tom had given to him.

"Tell her Mr. Underwood is calling her. Jonathan Underwood."

"Certainly, Mr. Underwood. Hold the line a moment, will you please."

A couple of seconds later, a husky female voice answered and said, "Good afternoon, Mr. Silvester. I was hoping that you'd call."

PRIME MINISTER'S RESIDENCE
DOWNING STREET, WHITEHALL, LONDON

The secretary-general of the United Nations cut an elegant figure on the screen. Tall, muscular, and blond-haired, the chisel-faced severity of SvenPeter-Knut Berentsen glaring through the large television monitor at the assembly of the world's media in the pressroom of Number 10, belied a wickedly funny personality kept firmly hidden except in private, a refreshing development since the austerity days of the humorless Ban Ki-moon. Standing beside the plasma screen and the face of the secretary-general was the homely and profoundly brilliant prime minister of the United Kingdom—Scots-born but knowing that for his audience, he had to modulate his Highland accent, especially when it came to question time.

"Let me begin by saying," Secretary Berentsen said, "that I am extremely grateful to the prime minister and the citizens of Great Britain for allowing the rapid response team to work with and learn from the local scientists and medical professionals in the search for the cure of this dreadful virus. Great Britain, as we all know, is blessed with some of the world's most acclaimed men and women operating in these fields of science and medicine, but as the prime minister was the first to realize when I asked him to allow the rapid response team into his country to assist, this is a global problem and requires all the nations of the world to work together.

"Over the past three or four years, a total of nearly half a million people throughout the world have been struck down with new and virulent viruses, the source or sources of which are still a mystery. Without global cooperation, finding a reason and a cure will be longer, and more difficult and will lead to many more unnecessary deaths. As the prime minister has so generously shown, international cooperation is our passport to ultimate success."

The reporters were furiously scribbling down the secretary-general's words. They continued to take down notes when the prime minister took up the theme of cooperation and stated that if a leading nation like Great Britain, which itself was at the very cutting edge of brilliant scientific and medical research, could work side by side with the rapid response team, then every nation in the world should be willing to do the same.

When the set speeches were over, the first questions were addressed to the prime minister. They were simple questions, planted by the press office and asked by tame reporters in the audience, to which he gave simple answers.

Then Maggie Tynan, one of the House of Commons reporters who worked for the political desk of the BBC, stood to ask, "Do either you, Prime Minister, or you Secretary-General, have any comment on the statement made by rock star and environmentalist Jay Silvester from New York in the past hour, condemning the British government's decision to exterminate every bird and bat in the United Kingdom?"

Surprised reporters turned to stare at her. The prime minister looked at Maggie in utter shock. "Excuse me?"

It took the secretary-general a couple of seconds before the question had traveled across the Atlantic to the United States, but he looked as shocked as the prime minister did.

She repeated the question.

"This pop star is saying we're going to do what?" asked the prime minister.

"Kill all the birds and bats in the UK. Apparently one of the conclusions of the rapid response team is that this virus has been spread by flying animals, and a recommendation coming to you today is for a mass extermination of all birds and bats. Jay Silvester and Citizens for Humane Animal Treatment have held a press conference at the Waldorf Astoria saying that mass extermination of British birds is the next phase in fighting this virus," said Maggie. "They're condemning any such move by the British government and saying . . . I quote . . . 'Britons must not allow their government to exterminate millions and millions of innocent birds. If it does so, the voice of Natural England will be silenced.'"

She continued to glance at the notes handed to her at the beginning of the PM's press conference and said, "Silvester says that other reservoirs for this viral outbreak have been eliminated, and birds and bats are the most likely candidates for the spread. However, he goes on to say that the virus could have many causes and that the execution of all British birds is species genocide and immoral."

Recovering slightly, Alistair Blain said, "I haven't seen the video or any reports of this press conference, but I seem to recall that Mr. Silvester is a pop singer and doesn't have the knowledge or qualifications of British scientists or the rapid response team working to find the source of this outbreak. How on earth Mr. Silvester came by this information, which hasn't been seen by me, if it exists, is a matter I'll investigate. And as I understand from US newspaper reports, this organization, this Citizens for Humane Animal Treatment, was responsible for the death of a man recently in Florida. However high profile Mr. Silvester is, I hardly think he's in a position to pontificate about this virus, what's spreading it, or how we're dealing with the outbreak."

Not willing to let the spotlight fall on any other reporter, Maggie quickly continued, "Would you deny, then, Prime Minister, that if the source is found to be birds, you will order their mass extermination?"

"I'll neither confirm nor deny anything. I won't comment further until I've seen the latest report from our scientists. As of this moment, I am informed that we have no definitive understanding of how this virus has infected so many people. And I'm certainly not going to speculate as to what the carrier might be. But be assured that whatever it is, we will deal with it efficiently and thoroughly, whether it's birds or rats or fleas or whatever," he told her. "Our primary responsibility is the safety and security of the people of Great Britain, not protecting birds or bats."

His press secretary shuddered when his boss had said these words. He could see tomorrow's headlines now, and he was terrified of the response.

There was uproar in London and in New York, with questions flung haphazardly at both world leaders. Their respective press officers decided that it was time to extricate them from the fray, and with thanks and excuses mumbled into microphones, the two men smiled, waved at the reporters, and exited stage left.

When he was in the corridor walking back to his private office, his press secretary asked softly, "How could you have said that about not protecting birds. Do you realize the effect that'll have on the lunar left? On the animal lobby? On rural voters?"

But Alistair Blain hissed at his press secretary, "And how the hell could you have let me walk into that? Why didn't you warn me this fucking pop star had said we were going to kill all the birds in England?"

"Boss, I didn't know. I swear. I didn't even know this Jay Silvester person was going to be holding a press conference. I'll find out all the details, and we'll put out a press statement . . ."

"Too fucking late. The damage is already done," the prime minister snapped, walking rapidly ahead of the hapless staff member.

The prime minister only had to wait fifteen minutes before the first headlines started to appear on BBC News and the other broadcast channels.

The unctuous announcer said, "Reports are circulating that a plan is being drawn up to exterminate all British birds if they're found guilty of being the carrier of the London virus which has so far claimed the lives of nearly five hundred Britons. In an effort to halt the spread, Prime Minister Alistair Blain would neither confirm nor deny that such a plan existed, but international superstar Jay Silvester says that his organization has reports that point to species of British birds as being the culprits. Our reporter, Maggie Tynan, has just been at a press conference at Downing Street."

The screen changed to show one of the most famous front doors in the world, with two police officers standing like statues on either side. The camera panned sideways to show Maggie, microphone in hand. Her head was pointed theatrically toward Number 10. Slowly, deliberately, she turned to face the camera and said, "While the entire nation is in the grip of panic about the London virus, could it be that tomorrow, Britons will no longer hear a dawn chorus of robins and finches and jays? Well, that could happen if Prime Minister Blain agrees with a top secret report from British scientists studying the cause of the virus outbreak crippling the capital, claiming that it's our feathered residents that are responsible. Just hours ago in New York, rock legend

Jay Silvester, an environmentalist and animal rights activist, stunned reporters by revealing what he claims is the content of a recommendation about to be made by the rapid response team assisting local doctors in attempting to uncover the source of the virus outbreak. That recommendation is the capture and extinction of all flying animals above the level of insects. Birds and bats. These animals, according to the report, could be the reservoirs of the deadly disease. If the recent concerns about the bird flu from Asia haven't been worrying enough, to add to the grave concerns, recent research has identified birds as the cause of the pandemic of influenza in 1918 that killed anywhere from twenty to one hundred million people worldwide. When I asked Prime Minister Blain whether he'd follow the recommendations of the team to cull all birds, this was his response . . ."

The screen cut to a flustered prime minister before the podium, listening intently to the question Maggie had asked, not half an hour earlier.

Thirty feet away from where Maggie was standing and presenting her live report, deep within the bowels of Number 10 and silenced from the outside world by two layers of bombproof glass, the PM's flustered press secretary froze as he heard the scream, "Get me that fucking report. Now!"

Conference Room No. 4
The Waldorf-Astoria, Manhattan

Had it been a quiz for who had the most famous face, followers and fans would have been torn in two. DeLile Carpenter, the great-granddaughter of a tobacco farm slave, was the most famous and richest media personality in America—possibly the world. Jay Silvester was as rich and famous as a rock star actor in Hollywood movies, promoter of environmental and animal liberation causes, and friend and confidant of Third World presidents and prime ministers fighting the colonial hegemony of the United States and its European allies.

Despite the clamor to snare him for Fox, CNN, ABC, and print and radio media, Silvester's press people had granted an exclusive interview only to DeLile on NBC; she had attended the press conference and now was sitting three rooms away from the ballroom where the other media had been gathered. She sat opposite Jay in an armchair. He chose to sit in a dining room Carver chair to give his body greater definition, and hence more gravitas during the interview. He didn't like his body looking awkward on couches when he was being interviewed by late-night TV talk show hosts; it made him feel awkward, and if there was one thing he prided himself on, it was that for a man approaching his mid-forties, he was in remarkably good shape.

DeLile shooed away the technician who was fiddling around with the lapel microphone and adjusted it herself. The boom mike would be positioned over Jay. Lights were adjusted and smoke alarms were turned off in case their heat activated them during the interview, and two cameras were dollied in and out to get precisely the right angle for DeLile's left-side profile. Last minute makeup was applied to both, now that the lights were making the room hot, and the floor manager was reminding DeLile of the cues he would use and the questions she would ask. It would be a live cut to the studio, interrupting the prerecorded current affairs show *24/7* with breaking news.

Listening intently on his headphones to *24/7*'s director back in the studio, the segment director said loudly, "Okay everybody, we go live in sixty seconds. Clear everybody except the talent from the set, please. Jay, DeLile, do you want water?"

Both shook their heads and cleared their throats. They'd rehearsed the first couple of questions and rubbed their teeth with their tongues to get that momentary shine when the viewers first saw them.

"Thirty seconds people. And counting," The makeup artist quickly dabbed a sudden shiny spot on DeLile's forehead and rapidly disappeared.

"Ten, nine, eight, seven, six . . ." The director stopped speaking and held up his hand using his fingers to count them into DeLile's introduction.

"The killing of all birds flying over Great Britain. Is it possible? Could it happen in the United States? Could the bald eagle be hunted down as a killer not of wildlife but of human beings? And could the British government *really* be planning to exterminate all the cute little feathered friends in a species holocaust on the other side of the Atlantic? Yes, if you believe rock megastar, environmentalist, and animal activist Jay Silvester. Jay, we've just seen a clip of your press conference just a few moments ago when you stunned the entire world by your announcement. Can this be true? What information do you have that tells you England is planning a mass culling of all of its bird population?"

He gave her his best and most endearing smile and said softly, "I don't say things which aren't backed up with fact, DeLile. Look at every statement I've made these last dozen or more years, about global warming, poverty, overcrowding, the rising cost of food, mass starvation, and you'll see that it's all come true.

"In the case of the Brits killing their birdlife because of these isolated and possibly unconnected deaths in London, all I can tell you is that I've had an advanced copy of the report that the rapid response team is going to be giving to the British prime minister and to the World Health Organization in the next few hours. I have to say that the report is utterly shocking. Remember that this doesn't come out of nowhere. During the scare with bird flu not so long ago, South Korean officials murdered all the poultry in Seoul to stop the spread of any new outbreaks. They killed fifteen thousand chickens, ducks, pheasants, and turkeys. There wasn't much of an outcry because these tragic animals were caged or farmed and were going to be killed and eaten anyway.

"But what Britain is planning to do is entirely different, and I don't think that the British people, most of whom are animal lovers, are going to stand for it. They're planning to lay poison traps to murder the birds where they roost. By the tens of millions. The voice of Britain will be extinguished; birds will die in excruciating agony. It's monstrous, and I just hope that our president takes a stand against this barbarity and persuades the prime minister not to agree. There are other ways to stop the spread of this virus, and there's no proof that birds are responsible for spreading it."

DeLile asked, "But how can you be so sure that birds aren't responsible for the outbreak? After all, hundreds of innocent Britons have been killed by this virus and to date, nobody's come up with a source."

"Listen up, DeLile, if you know anything about history, you'll realize that when people are in a panic, they always look for someone or something to blame. Women with warts were burned as witches in the middle ages . . . do you know why? Because the populace, the Church, and the authorities didn't know the cause, they blamed people who were feared . . . old women who looked off. They called them witches. Nobody knew until the last century that rats and fleas spread the Black Death, the terrible bubonic plague in centuries past that wiped out a third of the population of Europe. So who did they blame? Who did they slaughter? Foreigners living in their midst.

"And it's not just diseases which make people go crazy like the British government is doing today. Whole communities of innocent Jews were burned to death and hunted down because some Christian kid was killed. Without any proof, they accused the Jews of killing Christian kids and drinking their blood.

"I could go on and on. The wrong people have been blamed and killed because of our irrational fears. And now the British government is going to kill every bird in the United Kingdom because they're so terrified of this sudden outbreak. Well, maybe, just maybe birds are responsible. But every bird? Caged birds in pet shops? Pet budgies bringing joy to some little old woman in Birmingham? Pigeons in central London? And why suddenly now? Why suddenly have birds become responsible for all these deaths?

"Look, DeLile, I'm no scientist. I'm just an ordinary rock singer, trying to do his best for today's kids and future generations. That's why I honestly believe that we should all think deeply about these issues. It seems to me that a top-ranking group like this rapid response team should be looking at all possible sources, like fleas or spiders or mosquitoes or rats, as the likely reservoirs for this virus. Maybe like the Black Death, this virus was transported into England by a stowaway rat on a cargo plane or in the hold of a ship that had just come from Africa or Asia. But to kill all the birds of England . . ." He shook his head sadly and looked down at the floor, fighting back tears.

DeLile reached over and touched his knee. And thirty-seven million Americans felt his pain.

Department of Health
White Hall, London

"Who?" asked Debra Hart.

"The secretary of state," said the breathless receptionist. "The American lady," she whispered in her British accent.

"Who?" she repeated in astonishment.

The receptionist told her again.

"The American secretary of . . .?"

Debra heard an angry "oh for God's sake, give me the phone." Suddenly one of the world's most familiar voices came on line.

"Doctor Hart. This is Secretary of State Jenny Tan. I'm in reception and would like to see you immediately."

"Yes. Of course. Sure. I'll be right there."

A moment later, Debra's astonished colleagues saw her run from the conference room without an explanation. She descended the stairs three at a time, ran down a corridor, burst past two armed security guards who hollered after her, and ran across the public areas into reception.

"Secretary Tan, what an unexpected surprise. I had no idea you were in London," Debra said, out of breath and desperate to compose herself.

"Neither did anybody else, Doctor Hart. Can we go somewhere private?"

Debra led the secretary of state and four members of her entourage back in the direction from which she'd just come. They walked in silence. The demeanor of the secretary was an indication that any conversation would be low on civilities and high on purpose. And having been locked in meetings all day at the Health Department, Debra had no idea what was wrong.

One of the senior people from the Health Department paced ahead so that the guards on security detail would allow the secretary through without any further embarrassment. Her sudden and unannounced appearance had strained the normally staid British civil servants into apoplexy. Known for impetuousness—she had once turned up uninvited to the Russian president's dacha with a bottle of vodka and spent the entire night drinking until he'd agreed to join with the US in a peacekeeping force in some African trouble spot—the decision to seek out the leader of the rapid response team had been hers and hers alone. It had been made without consultation with her president or the British prime minister, just after she'd just turned off the cable news channel and the interview between DeLile Carpenter and Jay Silvester.

They walked in strained silence toward the suite of offices set aside within the Health Department for the rapid response team. As they entered the conference room, the ten men and women looked up from their deliberations and were shocked to see the US secretary of state standing there. And from the look on her face, she wasn't a happy woman.

Everybody stood as the secretary entered the room. She sat in Debra's chair at the head of the table.

"Madam Secretary, I don't understand why you're here. Why you didn't let us know you were coming," said Debra, knowing that serious trouble was brewing.

"Is it your intention, Doctor Hart, to recommend the culling of all birdlife in Great Britain?"

Debra looked at her in shock. "How did you . . ."

"Yes it is," interrupted Daniel Todd.

"No it's not," insisted Debra. "We simply haven't come to that decision yet. Anyway, how did you find out about it? We haven't released our interim findings yet. We've sent a draft to the secretary of health in Washington because of the political nature of what we're about to do, but that was top secret. Did he tell you?"

"No, I found out from NBC," she said, the restrained fury in her voice making her position apparent. "DeLile Carpenter and Jay Silvester have just had a charming little fireside chat on NBC in front of tens of millions of Americans, telling them precisely what your report is recommending. It's out there, Doctor Hart. In the public arena. So right now, some Joe *Schmuck* on the streets of Hoboken knows more about your decisions than the president of the United States of America."

Stunned, Debra said, "It can't be."

"It is."

"But how?"

"That's what I'm here to find out. I can't tell you what an unmitigated disaster this is. I've come over here to have a private conversation with the British prime minister to try to convince him not to kick you out of his country, that we should all cooperate and show the Third World how we work together. And just when he's approved the idea, suddenly we're into media hysteria about species genocide. About killing all the birds in England. The prime minister has called an emergency meeting of his cabinet at Number Ten and God only knows what decisions will be made. It could be the end of your work here. He could demand that your team leaves. Now what the hell kind of security are you running in this place?"

"I can assure you, Madam Secretary, that our security is watertight. Every scientist sitting at this table has been thoroughly vetted by the FBI, Europol, and MI6. We've taken our security protocols from the Center for Disease Control in Atlanta, which was based on CIA modus operandi. All our notes, discussion papers, CDs, PowerPoints, and discs are numbered and logged and released strictly on a need-to-know basis from a secure server by way of a code known only to me and my counterpart in the UK. The distribution list is to the men and women assembled here, as well as the British minister of health, the secretary of health in the States, and the director-general of the World Health Organization and the secretary-general of the United Nations, and . . . and that's it. Every memo is encrypted and when it's received, decryption can only be done through a formula known exclusively between the recipient and the sender. If a leak has occurred, Doctor Tan, it's occurred somewhere further up the pipeline and not from this room."

"That remains to be seen. These gentlemen are security experts from the US Embassy in Grosvenor Square. They'll be examining every aspect of your security systems from top to bottom. When they've finished, they'll report to me because I'll be mounting an investigation to determine where this leak came from, and when I've . . ."

Debra steeled herself and said, "No, you won't."

Everybody in the room looked at her in amazement, not least Jenny Tan.

"Excuse me?"

"I said you won't be investigating the security of the rapid response team. You won't be placing your spooks in here, and there will be no report coming to or from you."

"Doctor Hart, are you aware of who you're talking to?"

"I'm well aware, Madam Secretary. But are you aware that our mandate to operate doesn't come from the United States government, or from the British, but from the secretary-general of the United Nations, the General Assembly, and the World Health Organization? This team is mine to lead, not yours to investigate. We will naturally cooperate fully and closely with these gentlemen because we must find and plug the security leak, but if they wish to work with us, then they'll work under my direction and report to me and my counterpart from the UK, Professor Lord Soames. We will report jointly to the secretary-general, and he may, if he chooses, report to you and the president."

Debra had never spoken to anybody as important in this way before. She wondered where her strength had come from. And she wondered how soon her neck would be on the chopping block—after all, she was only a couple of miles from the Tower of London.

The ethereal silence filled every nook and cranny of the walnut veneered room. The creaking leather chairs were silent as not one single person moved a muscle, other than Jenny Tan's middle finger drumming on the tabletop. For interminable moments, nobody breathed.

The US secretary of state nodded. "You're quite right. It was my error of judgment, for which I apologize, especially if I caused you or your team any embarrassment. My purpose in being here is to avoid any future leaks and subsequent panic, which is, I'm sure, your aim as well. Would you be willing to have these gentlemen assist you in the security issue?"

Debra nodded, barely able to speak. "Of course."

"Good. You're a ballsy lady. Now, can you please fill me in on this bird culling issue. We've got a real problem, and I need to be able to handle it."

Again, Daniel Todd spoke out. Despite being witness to a potential volcanic eruption between the two women, he saw that the emotions in the room were settling and found his voice. "Actually, Madam Secretary, it's probably not birds at all. It's more likely to be bats."

"Bats?"

Daniel nodded. "It's possible that it's birds, but the nature of the virus we've taken from the first victims is a pathogen which is often associated with the blood of bats. We've found parvovirus and other coronaviruses which are known to infect many animals like chickens and pigs and are passed on to humans. SARS is a typical trans-species viral infection, and there are many similarities between what's infecting these British people and the SARS virus which infected Asians. My view as a biologist is that it's bats which are the reservoir of these pathogens."

"And have bats been found?" asked Jenny Tan.

Daniel shook his head. "No, but we've found bat guano in an oak tree and on the ground inside the school where the infection was first reported. A school where the first victim was a pupil."

"And are there bats in this oak tree?" she asked.

Debra interrupted. "That's the interesting thing," she said. "We know from interviewing the uninfected children that there was a small colony of a hundred or so roosting in the tree until the first infection. Something scared them away, presumably to find a new roost site. We have no idea where they are now. We reported this to the secretary of health in Washington, and the minister in London, who are monitoring our work on behalf of the secretary-general and the WHO."

"So where the hell did this pop singer get the idea that we're going to kill all the birds?" she asked.

"In our report, we included birds as a possible reservoir, but we only ever said that birds *could* be the source; we never ruled them out, but likewise we never said that they were, nor that we'd be advising the British government to cull all birds. Our report was largely about the bat population. Obviously, the person who leaked the report isn't a scientist, because they've misunderstood what we said."

"Misunderstood? If what you're telling me is in the report, then I don't think anybody misunderstood what was being said. This is a case of media manipulation, deliberate lying for headlines. We have to fight fire with fire, so I need to put out a statement denying that we're calling for the extinction of all birds in the UK," said Jenny Tan. "Is that okay with you guys?"

"Yes," said Debra.

"No," said Daniel at the same time.

Jenny Tan looked at both scientists. "Let's not get precious here, guys. We're in crisis mode."

"Can I just say two words to you, Secretary Tan," said Daniel. "Palm oil."

"'Scuse me?" said the secretary of state.

"Palm oil. Innocent and innocuous enough. Used in thousands of foodstuffs around the world. It's ubiquitous. But where does it come from? Malaysia and Indonesia. The governments of those two countries, in concert with growers, are currently bulldozing and destroying areas of forests and jungles the equivalent size of six hundred football fields every hour . . . every hour . . . habitat for all sorts of endangered animals, in order to plant palm oil to satisfy the food industry. Bats in these two countries are having their traditional habitats and food sources destroyed by mankind to supply the insatiable demands of the human food industry. Coincidentally, it's also sending the Sumatran tiger and the orangutan to the point of extinction. But some of the earlier outbreaks of these sorts of terrible plagues have been in Malaysia and Indonesia. Villages, which I'll bet my bottom dollar, are on the flight paths of bat colonies which are desperately searching for food, fruit, or flying insects. The sources of fruit are being bulldozed, and the insect populations are either being sprayed or are relocating because their traditional jungle habitat is under constant destruction. Without food sources, the viral load in the bats' blood is massively increasing, and I'm certain that the viruses are mutating and causing the problem. But I've got to prove it. I have colleagues right now in these countries and dozens of others around the world catching bats in these types of areas to investigate their blood. We should know the answer soon.

"If I'm right, then these stressed-out bats are the source of the infections and people below their flight paths are dying of terrible and previously unknown diseases. It's probably bats, but it could just as likely be birds or fleas or flies or mosquitoes or something which uses the air to find a food source. So to say that we're not going to cull flying animals is premature. We just don't know at this early juncture," said Daniel.

He looked at Debra for support, but she just shrugged.

Jenny looked at them both. "Okay, guys, let's get this sorted. Now."

5

Tom Pollard, president of Citizens for Humane Animal Treatment, was still basking in the glory of Jay Silvester's overwhelming success. Pollard had been called everything from a self-gratifying jerk-off merchant by a right-wing blog artist to a PR genius by the *Wall Street Journal*. Today, he was certain in the knowledge that his PR coup would cement his reputation as the leader of the animal rights movement throughout the world.

Two more years with CHAT and he had no doubt that he'd get a call from some giant corporation offering him a VP's job as head of communication on a salary of a couple of million.

He sipped his coffee and for the tenth time that morning, reread the headline in the *New York Post*: Rock Star Slays Brit Plan to Crop Birds. Another headline: Wing It—Silvester to UK. The funniest was: Silvester the Puddy Tat to save Tweetie-pies.

All the media had reported the interview between Jay and DeLile on their front pages. All had flown into a rabid frenzy of condemnation of the rapid response team and the British government for even contemplating the mass extinction without definitive proof. They had all come to the same conclusion . . . a massive and hysterical overreaction based on inadequate information. A demand to cease any planned culling of birds until positive and irrefutable proof was available. None had any problems with actually culling the birds, if they were found to be the source of the viral outbreak; they cited the killing of poultry and some wild migratory birds in Asia to stop the spread of bird flu, which had been done scientifically, humanely, and with full knowledge of the circumstances.

Only Tom Pollard, his Washington source, and a handful of others knew the actual content of the rapid response team's report that said that bats were the probable source of the outbreak but that birds couldn't be ruled out until further tests had been conducted. But why let facts stand in the way of a great piece of PR?

He couldn't help smiling as he contemplated the next board meeting. He might even ask for an apology for the way in which they'd rebuked him for the death of the old man in Florida. Maybe now they'd realize just how overwhelmingly important his PR skills were to the organization. And maybe now his new chair, Donna McCabe, might warm to him and not treat him like something off the pavement she'd just trodden in wearing her $2,000 Jimmy Choo's.

His thoughts were interrupted by the phone. He glanced at the wall clock. He had a conference call with the UK branch in fifteen minutes, but it was too early. He picked up the phone.

"Tom, it's Maya Almarta for you," said his secretary.

"You're kidding."

"No! Really! She's on the phone."

He stabbed the flashing line and immediately recognized the voice of the most beautiful actress in all of Hollywood.

"Tom? I got your number from Jay Silvester. He tells me you're the go-to guy who's doing something about this terrible thing with the birds in England."

"Good to speak with you, Maya. And may I say that in all of New York, I'm your biggest fan. And yes, it's a terrible thing which the Brits are doing, and I'm working my guts out to try to save these precious birds."

"What can I do to help?" she asked.

"Where do I start? You've got one of the best-known faces in the world. If you could reach out to your media contacts in LA and speak out against this atrocity. I'll fax you the sheet of talking points so you have all the latest research at your fingertips."

"Oh, I think I can do better than that, Tom. A media interview lasts a couple of minutes. But we want to stop this insane slaughter, don't we? So why don't we do two things which will not just get great media coverage but will make the world sit up and take notice?"

In his mind's eye, he could see the smile on her face. Intrigued, he asked, "Okay . . . what?"

She paused. It was an actor's pause. Pure effect. Tom loved it. "What does America do to a dictatorship, say one in the Mideast like Iran, which is doing nutty things?"

He remained silent.

"It creates a boycott," she said.

Tom Pollard immediately knew where she was going with this and realized that he would have to hand over his PR genius's crown to Maya.

"I'm going to get every actor and actress that I know in Hollywood and throughout the world to stop buying British products. But that's not all. Not by a long shot. I'm going to get my fellow thespians to refuse to act in any British movies, television plays, or on the stage until the British government agrees not to kill all its birds."

He continued to remain silent. He was overwhelmed. Suddenly, this was one of the most manipulable and exciting stories of his life.

"Tom?"

"I love you," he said softly.

She laughed. Hers was one of the most famous laughs on the screen. People paid money to hear her laugh. "Do you think it's a good idea? You don't think I'll get laughed at, do you?"

"Oh no, Maya. This will be huge. I promise that the headlines will be massive. And international. When can we meet up? We need to work on this together," he said.

They arranged a time for him to fly out to LA. When he'd said his good-byes, he buzzed through to his personal assistant.

"Cancel my conference call with the UK. Book me on the next flight to LAX."

"Tom? Are you going to meet Maya?"

"Yep."

"You know she's a lesbian, don't you?"

He didn't.

It took less than twenty-four hours for Maya to organize to have twenty of Hollywood's most luminescent men and women actors sit on a podium in the Roosevelt Hotel at 7000 Hollywood Boulevard before dozens of television cameras and over five hundred reporters seated in rows that stretched to the back of the hall. Reporters had come from every newspaper, radio, and television station in California when news of the event was announced. International reporters and camera crews had flown in. The room was packed with hot lights, cables snaking across the floor, microphones like the heads of gorgons on the table that was covered with flowers, and curious hotel staff who hung agog around the walls. The hotel's staff was used to celebrities but not this number all gathered together in their conference hall.

The twenty actors were world-famous and nobody could remember when so many had come together for a press conference. Seated in the middle of the table was the glorious face and shining blond hair of Maya Almarta, surrounded by Jay Silvester and Tom Pollard. Hung from the curtains at the back of the assembly of actors was a huge banner reading

WANT TO STOP CRUELTY TO ANIMALS?
CHAT TO US AT
CAMPAIGN FOR HUMANE ANIMAL TREATMENT

When Maya moved slightly forward toward the microphone, the buzz in the room came to an instant halt. Tom looked at her and was overwhelmed by a desire to reach out and touch her. She was so utterly, impossibly, flawlessly beautiful. Her skin was translucent, her hair rich and full and perfumed, her eyes vibrant with youth and passion. She was taller than he had imagined, but when they'd met at her house in the Hollywood Hills just yesterday, she made him feel so at ease, so comfortable in her presence. He was lost then, and he was still lost now, despite the frantic preparations.

She gave a delicate smile and said, "Good afternoon, ladies and gentlemen. I, and my fellow actors you see here today are horrified by the plan of the British government to kill its entire birdlife population. Accordingly, we have decided . . ."

THE OVAL OFFICE

Nathanial Jefferson Thomas was sitting at his desk, going over aspects of a bill that he was considering vetoing, when his chief of staff, Felix Unterman, knocked on the interconnecting door and walked in unannounced.

"You'd better see this," he said, pacing over to the television monitor in the wall cabinet. He switched it on, and suddenly the gray plasma screen was filled with the stunningly beautiful face of Maya Almarta. President Thomas looked up from his papers and frowned.

They listened to her live press conference for several long moments, and then he heard the line that turned his blood cold.

From three thousand miles away, Maya said, "And so we, the actors of Hollywood, will from now on refuse to act in British movies with British directors or with British crews. We will refuse to purchase British-made goods of all forms. We won't travel to Britain on work or on pleasure. We will continue our boycott of all things British until the government of Britain comes to its senses and reverses this immoral plan to kill all the birds in Britain."

The moment she had finished speaking, there was a cacophony of questions shouted at her. Unterman turned off the television.

"But I thought Jenny Tan's statement had calmed things down. It couldn't have been more plain. There's no plan to kill any birds. Not now and probably not at all. What the hell are these people in Hollywood thinking?" the president asked.

"I have no idea, Mr. President. But truth isn't playing a very large role in this thing. Right now, we have a disaster in the making on our hands. I can't overstate how dangerous this is. These Hollywood stars have got a pulling power of unlimited strength," said Felix Unterman.

The president looked at his chief of staff and shook his head. "Oh, come on, Felix, just because a bunch of stars refuse to buy British, you're saying that they'll bring down the British economy? The government?

Get real! These are celluloid heroes. Make believe people. Kids might be influenced but not adults. This is just a publicity stunt. Cheap headlines. We overreact, and we'll give it legs. We ignore it, and it'll be yesterday's news."

"Mr. President, you have no idea what we've just witnessed. This is a boycott that could spread around the world. Okay, it's not going to bring Britain to its knees, but it'll be a disaster for Prime Minister Blain's government. And imagine what reaction it'll have on Third World governments when they get a viral outbreak. Nobody's going to call in the rapid response team in case Hollywood gets its collective knickers in a twist."

Unterman walked over and sat in front of the presidential desk.

"What do you advise?" asked the president.

"You call a press conference immediately to refute what Maya Almarta has just said. Don't ridicule her . . . tell the world that she's got guts and courage and that sort of pandering bullshit but that she's misguided because she hasn't got the facts. Then get Jenny Tan over here from England. Get the head of the rapid response team over here immediately. With them, we'll get a second bite at this cherry. We'll hold another joint press conference and give the very latest and most up-to-date facts on how we're dealing with this virus outbreak. I'll contact the secretary-general and encourage him to say how misguided these Hollywood types are."

"And that'll do it?" asked the president.

"No, but it'll hold it until hopefully we find the source. Mr. President, this Maya person has just lit a powder keg. We have to stop it exploding in our faces."

* * *

In a coordinated exercise between CHAT in the States and the UK, within hours of Maya Almarta's globally publicized appearance on television, huge posters began to appear on highways and in city centers in both countries. The Hollywood megastar's billboard-sized face took up half the space beside a more distant drawing of the countryside in which dozens of sharpshooters in army fatigues were taking potshots at multicolored birds flying away to save their lives. The caption read: SHOOT DOWN THIS EVIL LAW . . . NOT OUR BIRDS.

And the phones, faxes, and emails began to arrive at the offices of congressional representatives and senators and members of the British Parliament. An avalanche of correspondence. So much that the Department of Health's email server was overwhelmed and crashed, pumping out tens of thousands of phatic apologies. Frustrated bird lovers were forced to contain their rage.

Alistair Blain, Prime Minister of the United Kingdom, looked at his entire cabinet, gathered at Number 10 to address a series of circumstances that had erupted over a matter of days and looked set to damage severely the standing of his government, despite it being one of the most popular since polling began. More than anybody in the room, the politically savvy Blain knew how quickly public approbation could turn to loathing on an emotive issue.

For an hour, debate had flowed freely. Nobody was accusing anybody. Nobody was forced into a demeaning apology. Rather, as a body mandated to govern the nation, the cabinet had come together to seek out a way of handling the immediate crisis, to deal with a mounting national frenzy against a bird cull that wasn't going to happen anyway.

Minister of Defence Doug Francis said softly, "A denial won't do it, Prime Minister. Not with this tsunami of anger thanks to this Maya woman. You just won't be believed. Anyway, Jenny Tan has already spoken out and denied that there are any definitive plans to cull the birds, and she wasn't believed. I'm afraid that you have to assail this CHAT group. Not softly, gently. You have to go for their jugular. Secretary Tan tried to be politic and it patently didn't work. You've got to go for their balls."

"If I attack this Maya Almarta woman, I'll have every movie lover going for my balls."

"Not her," insisted Doug Francis. "CHAT. Go for CHAT. Say that this Maya person is misguided. She's a wonderful role model for young people, but she's been fed inaccurate information and there's no plan whatsoever for culling birds."

"But I can't say that, Doug," insisted the prime minister. "The fucking report from this rapid response team is public, and it doesn't specifically deny that all our birds will have to be slaughtered. It specifies bats as the most likely source, but it also specifically says that birds could be a reservoir."

"I know, but you can come out and say that you'll never, ever allow the culling of birds."

"And what if birds are found to be the source? I'll be forced to admit that I lied and I'll have to order their butchering, and it'll be the end of our government," he said.

"If birds are the cause, that'll happen anyway, whether or not you go on television in an hour's time and say that our birds are safe. If we do have to order a cull, history will call this government 'the bird murderers.' And that's regardless of what this filthy virus epidemic is doing. Our bird-watcher friends, our bird lovers, don't seem to care if a thousand of their fellow citizens drop dead of some deadly disease, but harm one feather of the little flying fuckers, and you're worse than Hitler," said Francis.

The minister of health said, "Let's just pray to God that it's not birds but bats. That's the likelihood, anyway. Bats are far more liable than birds to be the reservoir. And fortunately, very few Englishmen go weak at the knees over bats. Most people hate them or are terrified of the dis-gusting little bastards."

"What's the latest?" asked the prime minister.

"We've got thousands of people in woods and forests and fields and copses looking for this fucking colony that came from the school. We've gone into every barn and church steeple and other places where bats roost. But once we've found the colony and can do autopsies on the corpses, we'll identify the virus in their blood and then panic over. Let's see this Maya bitch shed crocodile tears and cuddle some fucking vam-pire bat and beg people to boycott us. She'll be laughed off the planet."

* * *

Debra Hart had never been in the first-class cabin of a passenger aircraft; the most luxury in which she'd ever traveled was in business class. And she'd certainly never flown aboard any aircraft even remotely resembling Air Force Two, the vice president's Boeing C-32, a modified 757.

The steward had just served her the best piña colada she'd ever tasted in preparation for her meal of lobster thermidor, kipfler potato salad, and a vintage chardonnay. She watched as Jenny Tan, sitting two tables away with three advisors, talked in hushed terms about a report that had just been delivered by the communications officer on the flight deck.

Yep, she thought—this is a life I could easily get used to. Except that in four hours, she would land at Andrews Air Force Base just southeast of Washington, DC. From there, Marine Two, a White Hawk helicopter, would take them directly to the lawns of the White House where they would be escorted into the Oval Office for a face-to-face meeting with the president.

Debra didn't normally drink, except for the occasional glass of red to accompany a friend over dinner, but her nerves were on the edge from the rapidity of events during the past twelve hours. The secretary of state had been quite insistent once she'd heard about the amazing press conference by this Hollywood publicity-seeking rabble-rousing actress that had caused a call from the president. He insisted that they both come over to the White House and make a joint press conference on the lawns of the Rose Garden, explaining why the recent broadcasts and news media beat-ups about the mass culling of Britain's birds was so very wrong.

Debra had insisted on staying with her team and not entering into the political dynamic. She'd told Jenny Tan that as a scientist commissioned by the United Nations, it was inappropriate for her to speak at a press conference with the president of the United States; but Secretary Tan had been equally insistent that science had to take a backseat to the imperatives of calming the British people down, and that could only be done by some very persuasive PR. She'd called Professor Lord Soames who had spoken to the minister of health who had phoned the prime minister, and word had come down the line that she should make a quick trip to the States to hose things down. Just to check, Debra had phoned the WHO and the office of the secretary-general of the United

Nations, and they had been equally supportive of the necessity of her making the trip.

So here she was, treated like some high-powered diplomat on board Air Force Two, luxuriating in the glory of high power, even if it was only illusionary and very, very temporary. She mischievously thought about picking up the phone next to her seat, pressing the numbers to speak to the pilot, and direct him to land in Martinique so she could spend a couple of weeks on the beach. But she was pretty sure that a number of first-timers on Air Force Two had done precisely that, and she didn't want to hear groans coming from the flight deck.

Maybe she could phone her mother and stepfather in Maryland, tell them where she was and that within half a day, they'd see their daughter standing next to the president of the United States, making a major statement of public policy. They would be so proud and would invite all the neighbors in to watch their daughter on television, standing shoulder to shoulder with the world's most powerful man . . . and it was then that she suddenly became hot and sweaty . . . and icy cold all at the same moment.

After the president's phone call, Secretary Tan had hustled her to leave the Department of Health and drive to the US Embassy in Grosvenor Square where a helicopter was waiting to take them to Air Force Two parked in a secure area of London's Heathrow Airport. It had all been so last minute, so rushed, that she hadn't had time to get a change of clothes from the rooms set aside for her in a Ministry apartment in Kensington. And she suddenly realized that she was wearing a knit top and jeans, ideal for clothes beneath a lab coat, but hardly appropriate for a press conference with the president of the United States.

She stood and walked over to the secretary of state's table. All four people looked up in surprise.

"I'm sorry to interrupt you, Madam Secretary, but I've just realized that I left in such a hurry that I don't have any suitable clothes for a press conference. Would it be possible to stop off at a dress shop in DC before we go into the White House?"

Jenny Tan smiled. "Debra, there's a full wardrobe of men's and women's clothes in every conceivable size and shape and color kept in the basement of the White House. The staff there will give you something gorgeous to wear, and if it doesn't fit perfectly, there are seamstresses who'll do an instant alteration. No cost. Stop worrying; you're not the first person who's suddenly needed to get dressed into something special. These days, the White House operates twenty-four-seven and nobody in the building comes to work dressed for every unexpected occasion."

Debra smiled in relief, thanked the secretary, and returned to her seat, wondering how she could get a job in the White House without spending $500 million to become president.

* * *

They were the most famous corridors, the most famous walls. She'd seen accurate representations on the television program *The West Wing*, as well as thousands of shots from TV news footage. She felt a sense of familiarity when she walked along the carpeted passages, through doors, down stairs, and past paintings of George Washington, Thomas Jefferson, and John Adams. But despite her familiarity, when she walked into the Oval Office with its regency colors and heraldic carpets, she was overcome by the alchemical power of the place, a power that transformed base thoughts into lustrous ideals. This was the Oval Office, where John Kennedy had conceived of mankind leaving the boundaries of this earth and where Bill Clinton had tried to bring peace to the fractious world. And sitting behind the famous desk, made from the wood of the HMS *Resolute*, a present from Queen Victoria to President Rutherford Hayes in 1880, sat Nathanial Jefferson Thomas, president of the United States of America.

Dressed in a beautiful Armani duck-shell-blue suit with black high-heel pumps and a silk red scarf tied like a choker around her neck, her hair and makeup freshly done in the White House beauty salon, Debra was led into the office by the president's butler. Once deposited in the center of the room, the butler silently disappeared, leaving just Debra, Jenny Tan, and two of her advisors standing.

The president came around his desk, kissed Jenny on the cheek, and shook Debra's hand. "Good to see you again, Debra. I hoped to be able to show you around the White House in more pleasant circumstances as I promised you in Rome. Still, you're here, and we've got a situation on our hands."

They sat down on the comfortable lounges facing each other, the presidential seal standing out from the rest of the carpet. She glanced down at it. She'd seen images of it a thousand times from photos that showed the young son of President Kennedy hiding underneath the desk, to dramatic long shots of President Nixon talking to the Apollo 11 astronauts. But she was one of a tiny minority of people who had ever been invited into this office and who had been privileged to see the carpet and its seal close up.

President Thomas noticed that it had captured her attention. "He's hardly known today except to historians of the presidency, but Rutherford Hayes, the nineteenth president of the United States was responsible for the creation of that seal which we use on the carpet. He was also responsible for acquiring the presidential desk. His election was fiercely disputed because he won by only a single electoral vote, and so he was the only president in our history to be elected by the decision of a congressional commission. Unless, of course, you count that prostitution of our democracy when President George W. Bush beat Al Gore because of the close call with the Florida vote being decided by the Supreme Court."

She listened in admiration of his knowledge. Both of them had doctorates in science from prestigious American universities, yet she had stayed in research all of her life, and he had used his doctorate to build a spectacular business career followed by an unprecedented rise in politics. She bit the inside of her lip to stop herself from becoming too much like a girl.

"Okay, Jenny, fill me in," he said.

Jenny Tan explained what she'd been doing with Debra Hart and her rapid response team during the past three days. It was obvious that the source of the problem was bats. Bats, she insisted. Not birds or fleas or rats or anything else.

"Can you prove it beyond all measure of doubt?"

She shook her head and nodded to Debra to tell her to take up the explanation.

Debra cleared her throat and said "No, sir, we can't give an unequivocal scientific determination because, as of yet, we don't have the proof. There's the percentage risk that some species of bird might be carrying this particular viral load, like migrating birds carried the avian flu, but the British scientists we've been working with have killed and examined dozens of birds from different common species and the only viruses they're carrying are the normal ones that don't cross boundaries into humans. They're completely harmless to us and most other mammalian animals.

"You see, Mr. President, the virus that is killing the British is confined to a narrow vector. A flight path that fans out from a single point into a narrow cone and weaves through the air over the outer suburbs of London, but the narrow cone remains intact, which means that a group of creatures is keeping in contact with each other in flight. While some species of birds, especially migrating birds, fly like that, it's much more likely to be bats. And that's what we said in our confidential report, where we said it was probably bats, but we covered ourselves by saying it could be birds until we've excluded them. We didn't think the report would leak so we may have been a bit too loose in our statements.

"To prove it was bats, we've followed the flight path by identifying the incidents of infection, and it falls within the dimensions of a cone. We know where it started . . . at the school in Cricklewood in North London because that's where the first infection was detected. And we monitored the spread of the infection northeast. Unfortunately, the bats were disturbed by all of our activity on the ground and they've roosted somewhere else. We don't yet know where. And we don't know where they swarm to in order to feed. But we've monitored the infection en route so we know in which direction they're flying," she told him.

"But why can't we track them by satellite navigation?" asked the president. "We've got the world's most sophisticated equipment in geostationary orbit around the globe. We can photograph a fly on a horse's ass in Siberia. Surely, we can identify a swarm of bats at night with ground or over-the-horizon radar or satellites. Can't we?" The president demanded.

"We've tried everything, boss," said Jenny Tan. "The British Royal Air Force has observation aircraft flying at night over the flight path; we've used the radar equipment at Royal Air Force Brize Norton in Carterton near Oxford but nothing positive. We've had loads of false positives but nothing concrete so far. Because it's so close to London, we have thousands of birds and bats and planes and helicopters and fixed-wing aircraft flying over or near the area. Sure, we've seen what we think might be a swarm of a hundred or so bats, but it could be birds or even a strange weather phenomenon. We're never sufficiently confident to be certain, and by the time we've directed a helicopter to the coordinates, they're long gone . . . and they don't appear again the following night. It's very frustrating, Mr. President. It's almost as though they know we're trying to find them, and they're getting clever at keeping out of our way."

"Okay," said the president, "so if and when you find them, what will the British do?"

"Clear the area of human beings within a five-mile radius and fumigate the roost with an anesthetic gas which will put them to sleep. Some will drop to the ground; some will cling there. They'll all be collected in biohazard vans, taken to an ultra-high security lab, and we'll examine the blood and other tissues. The area in which they've roosted will be cleaned up by hazmat security teams to ensure that any viruses that are in the soil or on the ground will be removed.

"If any trace of the virus is found, the bats still alive will be quarantined and used for experimentation. We'll try different things to see if we can find an agent that can fight the virus," Debra told him.

The president looked at his watch. "Okay, time to go out and face the press. Secretary Tan has told you about the protocols for a conference of this nature. Jenny will stand on my left, you just behind us both on my right. I'll speak first, explaining that there is no immediate intention to kill the birds and that it's almost certain that the reservoir of this outbreak is bats; then I'll introduce you and explain why you're at the White House; after that, I'll then call on Jenny to give a perspective of what we're doing about this sudden outbreak of these viruses throughout the world and the problems that we'll encounter if we don't adopt proper measures to fight them. She'll talk about restricting travel, migration, isolation . . . and that's why we're contemplating such draconian measures. But she'll also stress that the chance of the vectors being birds is incredibly small.

"I'll call for questions. If one of the reporters asks specifically scientific questions, I'll turn and nod to you, Debra. You then step forward, I'll step back and to the right of the microphone, and you step forward front and center and answer the question succinctly. Just answer the specifics of the question . . . don't add or volunteer additional information that you think that they should be told. If you do, you'll only open yourself up to cross-questioning and dilute the impact of what I have to say. This is a press conference in which we tell the world that we're not going to wipe out birds. It's not a lecture on the science of these viruses. Remember that, Debra . . . we have to convince the world that we're not bird killers. Nothing more. Okay?"

Debra nodded and smiled. She looked confident as they stood to walk from the Oval Office into the Rose Garden, where hundreds of people had gathered and were seated awaiting the president. But in her knotted stomach, she felt anything but confident.

6

Exhausted from travel exacerbated by the time difference between California and New York and having caught very little sleep on the red-eye, Tom Pollard, president of Citizens for Humane Animal Treatment, turned off the live broadcast from the White House, swiveled around to look at his assistants, and asked, "Well?"

"That fucks us up. Totally. We're screwed. The president has just derailed the train. We can't expect Hollywood to pretend to know more about the science of these viruses than the White House, can we?" said his PR assistant, Jackie Medway. "Now that the president has said that no birds will be culled, it's the end of our campaign. Who's going to go out on a limb for bats?"

Pollard turned to another assistant, who nodded in agreement with Jackie. Others in the room signified their agreement with her.

"Which is why I'm president of CHAT, and you're not," he said. "This is just the break we've been hoping for. A flat denial by the White House. And presumably, the British prime minister will say the same thing from 10 Downing Street or from the House of Commons. With a bit of luck, the secretary-general of the United Nations will do exactly the same thing. Straight out, 100 percent denials. Perfect. Couldn't be better for us."

His team looked at him in wonder, frowning at his denial of the obvious.

"Okay, give," said Jackie. "What's going on in that Machiavellian mind of yours?"

"Why is everybody rushing to deny something? What are they hiding? What secret reports are there that they're too scared to show the public? Why don't they make everything available on the web? And then we'll believe them. And when they do put everything on the World Wide Web, we'll demand to know what they've kept hidden from us, locked in their secret buildings and offices. Is there something going on that is just too frightening, too dangerous for us to know? Is the entire world population in danger? Will this be a repeat of the Black Death that killed a third of the population of Europe? Why aren't they telling us what's really going on? The media has been muzzled, but I demand a face-to-face meeting with the president of the United States so I can put these very questions directly to the man in whose hands is the fate of all humanity, these questions about the survival of the human race. I must speak to him and him alone . . . and when he refuses to meet with me, I'll demand to know what he's hiding."

Tom Pollard sat back in his chair with a smirk on his face. "Pure media manipulation. It'll keep things going until the next outbreak and the next animal they're going to victimize."

"You can't. This is too serious to run a scare campaign like that, Tom," Jackie insisted. "You'll just drive people into a frenzy. It's too irresponsible. And our organization is about protecting animals from people, not about finding the truth behind human diseases. Our mandate is animal welfare. You're letting this Hollywood stuff go to your head."

"Bullshit. We're trying to stop the mass killing of birds in England and probably other places as well. A campaign like this will drive people right into our hands; we'll have a huge increase in membership and the donations will keep us afloat for a thousand years."

He could feel the unease in the room. People were shuffling uncomfortably in their seats.

"Okay, what don't you like?" he asked.

His staff looked sheepishly at each other; nobody was overly willing to speak first in case they incurred the wrath of their boss. But Jackie had made her feelings plain, and so she was less inhibited than the others were. "Look, Tom, the Hollywood thing was manna from heaven. And you exploited it brilliantly. But now there's been a blanket denial by the president himself; we're in a corner. We've done our job; it's time for us to back off. To contradict the president and the weight of scientific evidence he's got, we'll effectively have to call him a liar and that'll put us offside with a hundred million Americans. This could backfire on us really badly."

Tom sighed. He was surrounded by drones. What had Jay Silvester called them . . . myrmidons? His office was full of myrmidons, robotic individuals who couldn't think outside the square, who lived their lives within parentheses just doing what they were told to do by their boss. But when this was over and things began to calm down, he'd have to fire the lot of them, get in new staff, women with balls who shared his vision, who could contribute and add to his ideas, not have people try to shoot him down just because they didn't share in the brilliance of his vision. When he joined CHAT, it had been a Mickey Mouse organization begging for donations. Now it was international, front page, and feared by world leaders. When he first came on board, it had been a boy's club; he'd gotten rid of most of the men and replaced them with women who did what they were told.

"Guys, we have two separate and distinct jobs in this organization. They are to protect all animals from the cruelty of human beings and to grow CHAT into a global institution that will prevent the abuse of animals. Nothing that the president said undermined our approach through our Hollywood friends. He's just told the world that if birds are found to be the source, the British government, or indeed our own, will eradicate bird populations. Look at what the Asian governments ordered when the bird flu epidemic happened. Tens of thousands of birds murdered and all for what? A couple of human deaths in rural areas, probably caused by malnutrition, overcrowding, or drinking contaminated water or something. What we're looking at here is a massive overreaction by authorities that will lead to a mass extinction . . ."

Jackie interrupted, "Tom, the report said that it was almost certainly bats and almost certainly not birds. We can't keep going on about birds being in danger of species extinction when everybody now believes that the culprit has been proven to be bats."

"What if I could get a couple of top-line scientists to say that these viruses could be spread by birds? High-profile scientists. Nobody could say specifically that birds don't spread these diseases because nobody's yet proven that bats do. And that puts us on the front pages again, demanding more proof before anything is done to harm the bird population. Right?"

"And which reputable scientist is going to put his nuts on the line to make a statement like that?" asked Jackie.

Again, Tom smiled his legendary smirk. "Leave it to me. Okay, everybody out. I have calls to make."

Studio 4
BBC White City, London

With only four hours sleep since the early-morning phone call from Tom Pollard, author, environmentalist, and commentator Gerard Sobel desperately needed the cup of coffee that the assistant floor manager handed him. It was BBC coffee, weak, tepid, and colored sludge brown, the antithesis of the Nespresso machine coffee he'd recently given himself as a gift, but it was an approximation of what he needed, for which he was grateful.

He checked his notes before walking toward the brilliantly illuminated set where a settee was waiting for him and where he would be sitting alongside the two presenters who would question him about his radical interpretation of the president's and the prime minister's recent statements. He knew both of the presenters, having been on *Good Morning Britain* several times in the past few months. This time, though, it would be different. This time, his appearance wouldn't be known only to homemakers, shift workers, and the unemployed. This time, he'd make national, possibly international headlines.

Mandy Sawyer, the leggy, toothy presenter who was talking to the show's director, saw him tiptoe over the snake-like tangle of cables on the floor, weave his way through the three cameras, and extend his hand toward her.

"Gerard, good to see you. Okay, you sit there. We're doing a filmed segment about the oldest continuously used toothbrush in England, and then we'll cut to you in about ninety seconds."

He sat on the couch, arranged his clothes, and ensured that he looked morning fresh. The time passed in a flash, and he only just had a chance to clear his throat when he heard Mandy, sitting beside her co-presenter Daniel Cohen, comment upon the previous segment. "What an amazing story . . . how often do you change your toothbrush, Dan?"

"At least once a month," her co-presenter replied with a laugh. "How she could have kept that thing for twenty years is beyond me."

Mandy laughed. "Me too. But on to more serious topics." She turned and looked directly at camera two, her face suddenly taking on the image of gravitas, and she spoke personally to each of the three million viewers. "I'm sure you all saw Prime Minister Alistair Blain when he said that birds are definitely not the cause of this terrible virus outbreak in North London. He was echoing a statement made by the US president, Nathaniel Thomas who said that all evidence showed it was bats, not birds, that are the reservoir. But that hasn't satisfied our next guest. He's England's most popular environmental writer and scientist, Doctor Gerard Sobel, who joins us in the studio this morning."

She turned toward him, and a long shot was picked up by camera three. "You disagree with what's been said, Gerard?"

"I neither agree nor do I disagree, Mandy. I've listened carefully to both statements, our own prime minister's and the president's, and frankly, they were long on rhetoric and very short on science. They were like a couple of spin doctors putting a slant on a story to keep the natives happy. But this outbreak is far too serious for spin. This is an outbreak that threatens the life of every man, woman, and child in England, and for our political leaders to dismiss a possible carrier just because the government will cop a bruising in the polls if it talks about the culling of all birds is just wildly irresponsible. I'm a naturalist, an animal lover, dedicated to protecting all species from the damage human beings have caused to the environment, but even though the killing of all birds is too awful to contemplate, if it has to be done to save our lives, then so be it."

Daniel Cohen interrupted, "But do you have any evidence that birds could be the carriers? The president and the PM were quite specific in their denials."

"That's the point. I have no evidence that it is birds. But far more important, I have no evidence that it's not. And until somebody, some reputable scientist, proves with 100 percent certainty that it's bats or fleas or something and not the bird population, I shall keep on thinking that it quite likely could be birds."

Mandy started to speak, but Gerard spoke over her, "And if you examine their statements, they talk in vague and general terms—non-scientific terms—about likelihoods and probabilities. Dear God, we have hundreds and hundreds of people dying in agony from some terrible contagion. How utterly irresponsible to try to assure us that it's not one particular species of animal, when those very animals . . . birds . . . are known to have been responsible for deaths of human beings from the virus they were carrying in their blood. It was avian influenza, and it crossed species and killed human beings. We'll never know how many Asians died of avian flu, simply because their health records and reporting methods are so poorly kept. And those authoritarian governments in that part of the world tend to hush up these sorts of outbreaks. Did a thousand people die? Ten thousand? We'll never know. But I'll tell you one thing . . . if I lived in the countryside of England, I wouldn't be very happy if I saw a tree full of rooks or crows. I'd want to know what was in their blood. And I'd tend to live my life indoors until our scientists have found the cause and cure for this deadly virus."

The interview continued for several more minutes until the cross to the news. When the studio went dark, Gerard shook hands with both presenters and was praised for his "great television" by the director as he walked back to have his makeup removed.

As the taxi drove him back to his home in Wimbledon, he pondered the headlines. Gerard's warning was carried by the BBC news and picked up by local radio stations. Only the BBC carried a recording of his voice. The others repeated what he'd said, and one had followed up with a statement from some Department of Health bureaucrat who parroted the line that the prime minister had taken the previous night.

And then his phone began to go berserk. Newspapers wanting to interview him, international media wanting him in a central London studio for a feed back to their countries, Department of Health functionaries asking whether he'd consider popping in for a cup of tea and a chat to discuss his latest statement, and they'd show him the scientific proof negating what he'd said on television.

After ten phone calls, the taxi driver commented, "You're busy today, Guv."

He didn't have a chance to answer because the phone immediately rang again.

"How'd it go?" asked Tom Pollard.

"You could say that I've put the cat amongst the pigeons. When your bloke comes out on American television and says what I've said, all hell will break loose."

"He already has. He just stopped short of accusing the US president of crimes against humanity. The news media has gone wild. Ballistic. The White House is plugging holes like it was a sinking ship."

"That's the way it's going to be here too if I know my media."

"Thanks, Gerard . . . I owe you one."

"Oh," said Gerard Sobel, "you owe me all right. Big time. Talk tomorrow when we've seen the headlines. And I'm already working on follow-up media ideas. We should be able to keep this going for some time. Oh, and Tom, I'd keep low if I were you. Let us experts handle this for a couple of days; then, when there's a mass popular movement toward species extinction, that's when you come in and save our little feathered friends."

"Agreed," said Tom. He pulled it off again. He put down the phone and allowed himself a couple of moments to ponder the past twenty-four hours. A wildly successful press conference in Hollywood with one of the most beautiful women on earth telling him that she'd do anything to help his cause, frantic denials by the leaders of the United Kingdom, the United States, and UN, and finally the icing on the cake—two well-known media environmentalists putting CHAT right back into the middle of the debate. He couldn't help smiling. Was there nothing he couldn't do to create headlines . . . the lifeblood of his organization?

DEPARTMENT OF HEALTH
WHITEHALL, LONDON

The television program ended with a hiss as the screen in the conference room turned to black. The eight men and six women looked at each other. Debra had conferred second-in-command status on Daniel Todd. As a professor of biology at Harvard, he was equally as qualified as the rest who sat around the table, except that his English was far better than the Italians, Africans, Asians, or scientists from the Middle East who were part of the rapid response team. The three scientists from England's Oxford and Cambridge universities had been warned by the minister not to make public announcements, so Daniel was the last spokesperson standing when Debra was away.

The team had just listened to Doctor Gerard Sobel pontificating on some morning show about how birds might be the vectors for this viral outbreak. He'd single-handedly managed to undo the strong statements of the prime minister and the president, who had assured the public that birds were in no danger.

"Your opinions?" asked Daniel.

Janet Wheelwright, an Oxford don was the first to speak. "The man's an arse. He's a failed scientist, a failed policy maker, and he's found his fifteen minutes of success as a public commentator. He's the darling of the media because he's willing to say wildly unlikely things on television without any science behind his pontifications. My view . . . just ignore him. He'll be forgotten by tomorrow."

Others around the table nodded, and Daniel was about to say something when his mobile phone rang.

"Daniel," said Debra, her voice echoing across the Atlantic. "What was the reaction in England to the broadcast?"

"Debra, it's only just been broadcast. I've just switched it off."

"Didn't you pick it up on CNN?"

"It was on some morning show on a commercial channel over here."

There was silence on the line.

"What broadcast are you talking about?" asked Daniel.

"An American scientist from Tulsa State University has slammed the president for minimizing the danger from birds. He's said that until there's 100 percent proof that it's bats, birds can't be dismissed as a reservoir for this virus."

"Oh shit!" said Daniel.

"What?"

"That's exactly what some Mickey Mouse environmentalist named Gerard Sobel said on British television just now. We've just this minute turned off the TV. It was a live broadcast. It sounds like a joint effort across the pond. The United States and England joining forces to whip up a frenzy."

"What organization was your guy representing? Our guy in the States was representing himself alone. Or claimed to be."

"Same here. But who knows."

"Okay, we've got to hose this thing down or it'll get out of hand again. Can you get on to the British media, hold a press conference, and say that it's not birds?"

"Debra . . ."

"For god's sake, Daniel. In your guts, you know it's bats. Just this time, go public and put people's minds at ease. If you don't, the panic will be catastrophic. Nobody will come outdoors for fear of a bird flying overhead."

"Is that what your guy over there said?"

"Yes, or words very close . . . why?"

"That's why our guy here said. You don't think . . .?"

"Hold the press conference this morning. I'm meeting with the president later on this evening, our time. Just put this thing into a bottle, will you. We'll work out who's behind it when it's died down."

She disconnected the phone. Daniel turned to his colleagues at the conference table and explained what he had been asked to do.

"But how can you say it's definitely not birds, Daniel, when we haven't positively determined the vector?" asked Professor Wheelwright.

He didn't reply.

* * *

It wasn't his first time in front of the media, but he never felt comfortable. Unlike the president of the United States, who could make carefully constructed statements and refuse to answer questions shouted at him over the noise of Marine One on the lawns of the White House, Daniel knew he would be peppered with questions. It was a delicate balancing act between his professional integrity and scientific reputation . . . and his team leader's clear instructions to bottle up the bird issue.

He decided not to make a statement, but instead began his comments in the Ministry's media room in front of one hundred or so journalists, cameramen, and sound recordists.

"You will no doubt have heard your prime minister's comments that birds are not to blame for this outbreak of viral deaths. And no doubt, you'll have heard Doctor Sobel on television earlier this morning, saying that we have no evidence that birds are not responsible. Doctor Sobel, somewhat mischievously, opened up doubts in people's minds once again.

"As a professor of mammalian biology at Harvard University and as a member of the rapid response team, I'm here to tell you that bats are by far the most likely reservoir for this recent outbreak and other outbreaks in other parts of the world. Despite the outbreak of avian flu a decade back, which killed a small number of people, there is almost no doubt in our minds that birds are not responsible for these eruptions. I repeat, ladies and gentlemen, birds are almost certainly not responsible.

"The worldwide bat population is under stress from global warming, the depletion of their food source due to the massive transfer of agricultural and fruit-growing land to the growth of bio-energy crops, and loss of their habitat due to human encroachment. Where these and other changes in the environment bats live in have occurred, the viral load of these mammals has increased; in some cases, the viruses have mutated to become deadly and cross species into farm animals and human beings. So yes, it's spilling out into the human population. But let me put the population of England at ease by saying that it's not birds . . . it's bats."

A reporter shouted out a question. "Professor, you say that bats are the far more likely cause of this modern day plague. And just yesterday, the prime minister also said that birds were definitely not the cause. Are you also saying that birds are innocent of causing this outbreak in North London, that they're not the cause?"

He squirmed in his seat. The Ministry PR man had briefed him on answering this question. "Look, it's almost certain that birds are not . . ."

"Almost?"

"Well, you can't rule them out completely . . . we're scientists and we have to . . . well, not until we have positive proof that bats are the reservoir and until we find the particular bat colony that has caused this latest outbreak, then we can't absolutely rule out birds, but . . . "

"So birds could still be the culprit?"

"Yes, of course they could. But they're probably not. What do you mean by culprit? We won't know until . . ."

The rest of his sentence was drowned out by reporters shouting questions at him. The Ministry PR man, seated on the back row, groaned and put his hands over his face.

Debra Hart groaned at the same time, three thousand miles away. Seated in the James S. Brady Press Briefing Room of the White House where daily briefings were given to the world's White House correspondents—empty now because the media wouldn't return to the building until the next scheduled briefing at 5:00 p.m. that night, Debra watched a monitor tuned to the BBC as her second-in-command made a hash of the media conference. She turned to the president's deputy press secretary, Kia Markovitch, a fifteen-year veteran of three administrations and asked, "What now? This thing just won't go away."

Crossing her long legs in the confine of chairs, Kia used the remote to turn off the plasma screen. "It won't go away because people are shit-scared of anything that could cause them fatal harm. We've tried to stop the panic over birds. And if the strategy had worked, it would have been marvellous, because bats are just far less known and common, so blaming them would have been great, especially as a lot of people have a repulsion toward bats. But if there's the slightest possibility that birds could be the cause, then panic is still the go."

"We just have to find the colony of bats that has caused this outbreak and prove it to the world," said Debra.

"First, we have to try to get to see the president as soon as possible and tell him what's happened. I'm afraid that you might have to fire your second-in-command, in public, for causing panic. That might calm things down a bit," said Kia.

"Fire Daniel? No way. He's one of the best members of the team."

Kia stood and said, "You may have no choice. If the president says he has to go, and that'll be my strongest recommendation, then go he must."

The two women walked out of the pressroom and down the corridors toward the wing where the Oval Office was situated.

"Kia, a couple of days ago, I had a run-in with Secretary Jenny Tan about my authority. Much as I respect the president, and recognizing that it was he who suggested me for this position, I'm afraid that I'm not answerable to him but to the secretary-general of the United Nations. It's my decision as to who I fire, not yours, not Secretary Tan's, and not the president's."

Kia stopped, walked, and turned to face Debra. She gave her that famous look that she gave from the podium of the pressroom whenever a reporter asked an inappropriate question, a withering look but one steeped in bemusement, as though asking silently, *Can you really be that stupid?*

"Debra, do you really want to stand tall against the full might of the president of the United States of America? 'Cause if you do, girl, ain't no way I'm going to stand between the two of you."

* * *

It took them half an hour of sitting in the anteroom of the president's office before they were told by his personal assistant that they could enter the Oval Office and see him for just fifteen minutes before his next appointment. They stood in front of the inner door waiting for it to open. When it did, the senate minority leader walked out, the president's arm around his shoulder. The two men shook hands, reminded each other of a squash match that had been rescheduled a dozen times, and President Nathaniel Thomas greeted the two women warmly.

Seated on the couches, Kia brought the president up to date on the situation during the past three hours.

"Who are these environmentalists?" he asked.

Kia and Debra filled him in.

The president thought for a couple of seconds before saying, "They're just taking advantage of the situation. They're just beating it up for personal publicity. I could have told you something like this would have happened. I don't think it's anything to concern ourselves about. Problem would be if we reacted to the reaction . . . if I went to the media and denied what these two commentators are saying. Then the public would get into a rare old panic. If we ignore them, they'll have an afternoon in the sunshine, and by tomorrow morning, something else will have distracted the public's attention."

Debra looked down at the carpet, realizing the naivety of her decision to send Daniel to be on television.

Kia said softly, "I'm afraid that it might be too late to do nothing, Mr. President."

She explained what had happened in the United Kingdom. The president nodded as he listened. He looked at Debra and was concerned that she was obviously horribly uncomfortable.

Kia continued, "And so, having made that gaffe, I think the only thing to do would be to instruct Debra to remove Professor Daniel Todd from the team. Make him a sacrificial lamb. I think that's what you should be doing, Mr. President."

Debra held her breath for a moment and only began to breathe when she heard the president say, "Firstly, Kia, I can't fire anybody. I can't tell Debra what to do; only the secretary-general of the United Nations can do that. Secondly, it would be an unwise move. Daniel Todd didn't tell any lies. I can't recommend firing somebody for telling the truth. Neither I nor the British prime minister ever said in our media conferences that birds were definitely not the cause of this outbreak. We were very careful about how we addressed this issue. We said that birds almost certainly weren't the reservoir, but we said that the reservoir would probably turn out to be bats, and we were working hard to prove it. And from what you've told me, that's exactly what Doctor Todd said. Look, this thing will blow over soon. Debra and her team will find the cause. We'll destroy a couple of colonies of bats; nobody will be too concerned. Situation over."

Debra looked up at the president and realized that he was expecting her to say something. "Absolutely. Once we find the bats, it'll take us just hours to prove that the virus is in their blood."

Kia shrugged and accepted her boss's decision. He could see she was uncomfortable being contradicted in front of Debra and said softly to the two women, "Ladies, do you know the story about the white swan?"

Both women shook their heads. He continued, "Well, in all of Europe from time immemorial, people knew swans were white. That's how they were defined. It was an absolute, immutable rule of science that swans were white birds. It was in all the nature books. And then in 1697, a Dutch explorer saw a black swan in Western Australia, and that's why we've had to develop the Law of Falsifiability, which states that a hypothesis can only be scientific if it is refutable. Otherwise, it's just unscientific. So the immutable rule about white swans had to be rewritten."

He looked at Kia and said, "Sorry, Kia, but I'm not prepared to ruin the reputation of a man like Daniel Todd because he won't give me an immutable rule that later turns out to be false. He's a scientist and he's told the truth, and it's our job, not his, to make the American people come to terms with it."

The president stood, as did the two women. "Kia, I wonder if you could allow me some time alone with Doctor Hart."

Surprised, Kia nodded and left the room. It took Debra a moment to realize that she was alone with the most powerful man in the world in the world's most famous office. He was a man who was tall, brilliant, muscular, good-looking, and devastatingly charismatic; he'd been called a once-in-a-century politician, a man who was held in both awe and affection by the American people. When he first came to power, he was called a second Teddy Roosevelt, but now, even after years in the vicinity of the Oval Office, he was known as a Renaissance man, another Kennedy, a moral Clinton; he was a charmer with a serious bite; in debates on television, he used his looks and charisma to seduce his audiences and his brilliance and encyclopedic knowledge to overwhelm his opponents.

He was a Republican because he believed in the freedom of the marketplace to find its own level, but his social policies were akin to Democrats. He had the support of fully 68 percent of the American people, a phenomenal approval rating for a man who'd been this long in the White House. When he'd first taken over the presidency following the incapacity in office of the recently elected president, he'd served the remainder of the four-year term, and, unlike the one-term President Johnson who'd taken over after the assassination of President Kennedy, Thomas had offered himself up for election in his own right and had won overwhelmingly. The Democrats had struggled to find a third-rate politician to run against him because they didn't want to waste a top class candidate against a certain winner, knowing that the American people would give the hugely popular President Thomas a second term.

"Come over to the window, will you please Debra."

He led her to the windows at the rear of his desk that looked out at the green magnificence of the White House gardens. There was no sensation of heat or cold from the bullet- and blast-proof, double-thickness windows, which hermetically sealed the president into his office and away from the outside world. There was no smell of blossoms, no wind to gently cool her flushing face, no feeling of being as one with nature. It was as though she was a visitor to a museum, and nature was one of the exhibits. She stood close to him and could feel his warmth. She realized, for the second time in his presence, that she wasn't breathing.

"Beautiful, isn't it," he said.

She nodded. Her voice failed her.

"You know Debra, I never sought this office when I was the vice president. I know that every VP secretly harbors a desire to step out from the president's shadow and take on the top job, but that never, ever, was my intention. If my president hadn't shown increasing signs of memory loss through Alzheimer's within months of being elected, I would have been happy just being a VP. Giving a bit of advice here and there, sitting, and banging my gavel in the senate, opening and closing pony and trap shows, attending weddings and funerals of world leaders. Despite what might be written about me, I don't have politics flowing in my veins. What I do have is the desire to do some good for the American people, to leave a legacy, and to ensure that the nation is better off financially, culturally, and socially, than when I came into office."

"Uh huh?" she said. She was mute. What could she say? Was this the opening gambit for him to seduce her? Did he look on her like a Monica Lewinsky?

Uh huh? Did she really just say "uh huh"? What a stupid thing to say. She was mortified, a second time, by the inanity of her response. She was expecting him to put his arm around her. To pull her close to him. To kiss her on her forehead, then on her lips. To lead her onto the couch and make gentle, then passionate love to her. She felt a surge of electric intensity flow to every part of her body.

But why was she thinking like this? It was so far away from her true character. She was behaving like a hormonal teen. It was silly, unworthy. And worse, much worse, it was an insult to a president who had never made even the slightest suggestion of a move toward her sexually, not even the subtlest and most guarded innuendo or the most tangential of seductive comments. Maybe it was wishful thinking on her part. Yes, he was married to a beautiful woman; yes, he had three kids and was a devoted family man; but 60 percent of married men have affairs during their marriage, and it had been so long since she'd had a relationship . . . sex . . . the joy of feeling herself lost in the embrace of a man . . . that if her commander in chief demanded it of her, for the sake of her country, she'd have to consider allowing herself to be seduced by him.

She waited breathlessly for his next move.

"Debra, I wanted to say to you in private that I have a very real fear that this outbreak in the United Kingdom could be a precursor to what might happen in other major population areas. US cities . . . New York, Washington, Chicago. We've recently seen tuberculosis reemerge in our population of homeless. We recently had thousands, tens of thousands of our best and brightest citizens dying of HIV/AIDS. With untrammeled international air travel, with our borders being so porous, how far away can these new diseases be from entering our homeland?

"I can't have that happen on my watch. I simply won't allow another AIDS kind of epidemic to strike down the very best and brightest of our innocent men, women, and children. If it's money you need, staff, assistance, all you've got to do is ask. You know that I can't say this to you officially, which is why I asked to speak to you in total privacy, but as you know, my background is in science, so I'm probably more able to understand the ramifications of what's happening than other politicians. I know the kind of dangers that face humanity if these viruses spread. We've seen it with the Black Death, with the influenza epidemic after the First World War, and recently with outbreaks of AIDS and the Ebola virus.

"The world was incredibly slow to move on climate change and global warming because politicians were, frankly, unsure, unaware, and probably too scared to admit to the truth. I don't want this to happen with this latest series of viral outbreaks.

"I wanted to talk to you privately and not to be repeated, that I, as president of the United States, am very well aware of the dangers we face, and of the stresses and strains you're under. I've already instructed the Center for Disease Control in Atlanta, your boss, in fact, to begin a top secret research facility based on what you're doing. It's a backup to help you with the science and forensics to track down and destroy these viruses.

"Because of the political necessity of ensuring the cooperation of some intransigent Third World dictators, we put you and your team under the control of the United Nations, but Debra, if you want anything . . .

anything at all . . . money, help, transport . . . anything . . . you've got an open line to me. I'll facilitate anything you need to ensure the safety of people throughout the world. My secretary will give you my direct number. Only a few people have it. It rings on my personal assistant's desk. Tell her precisely what you want, and if it's truly imperative, she'll be instructed by me to put you straight through, even if you interrupt a meeting. That's how seriously I view what you're doing. You'll report to the secretary-general, Debra, but it's me, the United States government, who is in largest measure funding you, so talk to me as a friend and mentor first if you need help and advice. Now, is there anything you want?"

She shook her head. If she told him what she really, truly wanted, why her body had suddenly started to ache and throb and what it was currently demanding, she'd probably be kicked out of his office. Debra wanted to pinch herself for utterly inappropriate thoughts, wrong in time, place, and person. But she'd been under so much strain and pressure during these past traumatic couple of weeks and had neither opportunity nor place to find an outlet for relief that her body had taken off on its own, regardless of propriety and occasion.

She wondered whether the death penalty could be invoked for her sexual harassment of the president of the United States.

7

UPSTATE NEW JERSEY

Only a farmer would have known that the number of bats flying over his acreage this year was noticeably smaller than in previous years. And only a farmer who'd been working his land day and night for decades would have realized that the actual numbers of bats swarming from a cave in the New Jersey Highlands just north of Pompton Lakes had shrunk by three-quarters. The dramatic decline from the 1980s to the present day coincided with the apple and pear and stone fruit trees having been plowed into the ground to be replaced by the rich harvest of canola and sunflowers and other oil-bearing plants for which the food companies paid good money—plants that the fruit bats couldn't eat. For years, in declining numbers, they searched the area for alternative feeding grounds, but the paucity of supply had made the colony wither to a fraction of its original size. Where once there had been a huge family of thousands of bats, today, there were barely a couple hundred.

But it wasn't just the difficulty of finding new food sources that were causing increasing problems for the large brown bats. What made the bat colony really stressed was the construction of a new tourist center in the heights overlooking Pompton Lakes in the Ramapo Mountain State Forest, adjacent to where the bats slept in caves during the day. The noise of excavators, bulldozers, dynamiting of rock overhangs; seventy construction workers on site from early morning to mid-afternoon and using the mouth of the bats' cave for shelter during meal breaks to escape the heat of midday; shining flashlights into the bats' eyes and inviting friends and visitors to peer at the bats hanging upside down and trying to sleep—all had a deleterious effect on the remaining number of bats in the colony.

Fighting and squabbling, tearing of flesh, and death of bats had become a common occurrence in the months since the construction began. Young were no longer born to overtly stressed females, and in the unseasonably hot summer, now that the weather pattern of North America had changed since global warming took hold of the climate, food sources became more and more scarce.

None of this would have been known to Katrina-Joy Elder, a thirty-something school teacher at the Benjamin Franklin Nursery and Primary School, in Newton, upstate New Jersey, who had taken her class to the Wantage County Petting Zoo as she had done every year for the past five years. The toddlers loved it, and it gave Katrina-Joy an opportunity to have a day out of the classroom in the warm summer sun while her little ones were looked after by the petting zoo's education officer. In preparation for the children's visit, the animals had been well fed to make them docile. For some, a new bale of hay was cut open and distributed, which the little animals ate greedily. And the piglets had been given specially enriched food pellets in their trough, a trough that lay in the open paddock, which itself lay beneath the flight path of the stressed bats from a cave overlooking Pompton Lakes in the Ramapo Mountain State Forest.

Twenty-five little children, boys and girls aged four and five, were screaming with joy at the face painting, laughing at the bouncing wallabies, hugging the animals close to their bodies, thrilling to the pony rides, and adoring the chance to bottle feed the newborn. And the newborn were in abundance. There were baby bison, ponies, kangaroos, emus, goats, sheep, pigs, ducks, fluffy chickens, and lots more. The children kissed the baby animals, fed them, cuddled them, and named them with their own special names, regardless of the names chosen by the zoo's staff.

Their day continued with a picnic where, after washing their hands with soap and water, the children sat on rugs and ate sandwiches, fruit, and drinks from their lunch boxes. The day ended when the exhausted children were lined up, counted, checked off the register, and piled back on to their school bus to be deposited an hour and a half later into their school's parking lot, watched in envy by younger children who would have to wait a year or more before it was their turn. Parents were there

ALAN GOLD

to collect them, and they returned to their homes to an excited family who demanded to know what they'd done during the day and to enthuse over the souvenirs that the zoo had given to the children as a memento of their visit.

It was when the education officer was clearing up after the kids' visit that she noticed one of the piglets was lying on the ground, breathing in a shallow manner, with mucus oozing out of its nose. She immediately rang for the zoo's vet, who came and carried the piglet to the infirmary. Blood tests were taken, bottled, sealed, and sent to a veterinary laboratory in Hackensack, New Jersey. But the piglet died before the bottles had been delivered. Concerned, the vet ordered that its body be sealed in biohazard material and sent for postmortem investigation to New York University.

While the twenty-five youngsters were bathing and laughing as their mothers and fathers tried to get the face paint off their noses and ears and out of their hair, the body of the piglet was being rushed south to the laboratory that had been warned by the zoo's veterinary officer. When it arrived at the university, the piglet's corpse was immediately quarantined and samples of mucus, tongue, muscle, blood, nerve, gut, lung, liver, and other tissues were taken and rushed for analysis. The danger everybody was concerned about was swine flu, which had last reared its head in Fort Dix in 1976. President Ford had ordered the inoculation of the entire US population, and it was estimated that five hundred people had caught Guillain-Barre syndrome from vaccinations and twenty-five people had died as a result before the mass inoculations had been stopped.

Swine flu was the very last thing that the United States needed right now, especially with the panic throughout the world caused by these virus explosions. The professor in charge of the animal health laboratory of the university decided that even before he'd received the results of the tissue analysis, he ought to phone the nation's chief veterinary officer and alert him to the possibility.

While the phone calls were being made, the first of the twenty-five children from Newton, New Jersey, who would die in agony during that night, awoke from her sleep, clutched her head, and began wailing from the awful pain caused by her severe headache. Small for her age with a low body weight, the little girl, Jessie, had a history of asthma and skin rashes, for which her doctor had prescribed very low continuous doses of pediatric antibiotics. They had repressed her immune system, which caused the new strain of virus she had inhaled from the piglet she'd been cuddling hours earlier to ravage Jessie's tiny body.

When they heard her screaming in agony, Jessie's parents rushed into her room, fearing that she'd had too much sun, and gave the child a dose of infant's analgesic, holding her close, assuring her that she'd feel better in a few minutes, mopping her brow, singing her songs. The little girl lapsed into a coma and the relieved parents, thinking that she'd merely gone back to sleep, removed the blankets, covered Jessie with a single sheet, kissed her tenderly, and turned off her light. Jessie died three hours later of massive organ failure without recovering consciousness while her parents slept next door soundly.

WASHINGTON, DC

About to descend the air bridge which would enable her to board the Boeing 757 to London, Debra Hart was stunned when two burly Secret Service men pushed through the crowd of passengers surrounding her, without any apology, and asked for her identification. Astounded travelers looked at Debra with suspicion as she demanded to know what this was all about.

"Ma'am, please show me your passport," said one of the officers.

She fished in her bag while the ground staff tried to encourage the other passengers to board the aircraft, but they were both fascinated and concerned by this sudden security interchange. Was she a terrorist, a criminal . . . what? They waited breathlessly.

"What the hell do you want?" asked Debra, frightened and embarrassed as she struggled to find her documents in the depths of her hand luggage.

"Ma'am, please identify yourself. You're wanted back urgently."

She fished in the bottom of her hand luggage for her passport, eventually finding it. When the Secret Service men were satisfied that this was, indeed, Debra Hart, they escorted her from the gate lounge, leaving her fellow passengers in a state of confusion and panic. A few refused to board the flight, saying that they wouldn't travel across the Atlantic with her luggage on board.

"Sir," said the ground controller, "that lady had no luggage."

"Then I'm definitely not getting on board. That's just how terrorists kill innocent passengers."

His panic spread through the rest of the passengers. The flight to London was eventually canceled.

In the car on the way to the White House, Debra stopped asking her sentinels why she'd been dragged from the airport back to the center of Washington when she realized that they simply didn't know.

At the White House, she was greeted by the president's personal assistant, who escorted her into the Red Room. She'd given up asking why she'd been forced to return and sat for ten minutes in a state of confusion, concern, and anger.

Suddenly, the door opened, and the president of the United States, followed by DeAnne Harper, the secretary of health and her deputy secretary, Doctor Jonathan Bailey walked solemnly into the room. They sat on the opposite side of the table to where she sat and looked as though the end of the world was nigh.

"Debra, I'm afraid I have some very worrying news. Overnight, twenty-five children have died in upstate New Jersey. They'd all been to some kid's zoo near to where they live. A pig is thought to have been the source of the infection. And the hellish thing is that early analysis shows it to be the H5N1 virus," said the president. "It's arrived, Debra. The nightmare is here, in our towns; it's killing our people."

"H5N1?" she said. "But that can't be. It's bird flu. An influenza virus only found in Asia, China and Vietnam."

"And a variant caused seven hundred and fifty thousand human beings to be infected in Hong Kong in the late sixties," said Doctor Bailey. "Debra, you'd be the first to know that these viruses can combine by exchanging homologous genome subunits by genetic reassortment and pass mutated variants onto people. Only a relatively small number of people died from the Hong Kong flu and from other influenza attacks in recent years. But from very early reports we're getting from the virology people at New York University, where the tests are being conducted, they think that the H5N1 strain has mutated and is much more dangerous, far more virulent.

"We think that what's happened is that the pig who died harbored influenza and that it mutated into some deadly variant that has killed these poor kids. And it might not just be the very young and the old who are in danger of fatal consequences. We're just now getting reports that some of the parents of the dead kids have shown symptoms and are in the hospital. We're quarantining the entire town . . . no entry or exit. We'll clamp down on the area. If this breaks out, all hell will descend," said Doctor Bailey.

"But where did this come from?" asked Debra, feeling horrified and shell-shocked.

"That's what we want you to find out," said the president. "That's why we can't allow you to return to the United Kingdom. Now that this problem is on our doorstep, we need you here. You'll have access to every resource imaginable. I'll invoke emergency powers to co-opt every virologist, scientist, medical practitioner that you need for your assistance. But we have to find the source of this damnable thing before it kills more children."

She remained silent, staring at the three people opposite her. Never in all her career had she imagined a moment like this, when three of the most important people in the United States looked at her for answers to a problem of such breathtaking magnitude. She never had much faith in herself and was always surprised at the way people respected her for her achievements. But to have the president and the secretary of health and . . . one thing she knew. The next thing she said must set their minds at ease.

So she did everything in her power to make her voice sound stable, solid, and professional. If only they knew that she was quivering on the inside. "I don't understand something. Doctor Bailey, perhaps you could tell me. I assume that the parents of this piglet, the one that died, were tested for diseases before they were admitted to the zoo?"

Bailey nodded. "I guess so."

"That's standard procedure these days," she said to the president and the secretary of state. "Which means that the piglet must have been born relatively disease-free, or at worst acting as a reservoir for viruses that pigs normally carry in their bodies and that generally don't do much harm. So the virus must have got into the pig since birth. In other words, it could have been a virus that the piglet ingested and that acted as a co-host or initiator or accelerant of a normal virus in the pig's body and created the deadly mutation that crossed species into the poor children. Because it was a new strain of virus, the pig didn't have any resistance to it, and so it caused the animal's death. On that assumption, the disease must have been airborne or carried through a vector like this bat-born virus in North London. Are there any reports of bats in the vicinity? Doctor Bailey?"

He shrugged. "I don't know. We've only just been made aware of the situation. We haven't even begun to think about what could have been the vector. Look, it's only just happened; we have a lot of work still to do."

"Okay then, that's my first port of call. Madam Secretary, Mr. President, I'll need you to get the coast guard and air force to examine their flight logs for the previous forty-eight hours in order to see if they've been monitoring swarms of bats or birds in the immediate vicinity. I know it's dangerous to jump to conclusions, but if this is a variant of H5N1, then it has suddenly mutated from a common bat or bird virus in the body of the piglet, and that's why our people are dying."

"What do you need?" asked the president.

She told him. The secretary of health made notes, as did Doctor Bailey. It dawned on her that she had suddenly taken control of the meeting. She was giving instructions to the president of the United States of America and his senior cabinet secretary. If it weren't so serious, she'd have smiled.

* * *

By the time the morning news shows began to cover the tragic events in upstate New Jersey, the doomsayers were already on the airwaves, thumping their tubs. Tom Pollard, president of CHAT, Citizens for Humane Animal Treatment, was savvy enough to keep a low profile and tell his staff not to talk to the media under any circumstances. The death of people in the United Kingdom was one thing, but twenty-five kids in New Jersey and God knows how many moms and dads and uncles and aunts would follow was too close to home to make political capital.

But that wasn't the case for the Reverend Jeremiah Jesus Higgins, pastor to a congregation of fundamentalist Christians called the "Brothers and Sisters of Eternal Salvation in the New Jerusalem," headquartered in Lower Manhattan. He demanded and was given time on Radio Station KVVX, broadcasting through syndication to seven hundred radio stations throughout the East Coast of the United States.

Speaking to the host of the show, Marty Ziller, the Reverend Higgins said, "I knew this was going to happen. I have been predicting this occurrence for ten, fifteen years. I tell you, Marty, that it was revealed to me by the good Lord himself. He came to me in a revelation and told me that salvation was at hand. But that at the beginning of this awakening of humanity to the Second Coming, we would have to suffer the death of the innocents to bring mankind to his senses. Twenty-five beautiful little children, God's children, have been taken from us, and all because the American people have strayed from the word of God, from the very Bible itself. The only way to stop this plague in its tracks, Marty, is for every single American man, woman, and child, to fall on their knees and beg forgiveness from the Lord Almighty Himself. Beg, I say to you. Because this plague can be cured immediately and overnight by the flick of the good Lord's finger. But He won't do it, no He won't unless Americans repent and beg forgiveness and go to church and prostrate themselves in the sight of the Lord, and . . ."

The Reverend Jeremiah Higgins continued in this vein for the next five minutes, continuing to blame the tragedy on the moral laxity of the American people until the show's host interrupted him. "Reverend. I have to stop you. I've just been told by my producer that the president of the United States himself has phoned in to speak with you."

"Excuse me?"

To the utter astonishment of every one of the twenty million syndicated listeners to the radio station throughout the United States, a familiar voice came on the line.

"Reverend Higgins. This is President Thomas. I don't usually do this, phone in to radio stations, but I decided to in your case, because my communications staff alerted me to what you've just been telling the American people to do, and so I've spent the past few minutes listening myself to your comments about the tragedy unfolding in New Jersey."

Trying to recover from the shock, Reverend Higgins said, "Well, Mr. President, I hope that you'll join me in telling the American people how we can go about curing this . . ."

"Mr. Higgins. On behalf of the American people, let me tell you some home truths. You're an ass. A buffoon. You're a know-nothing bag of hot air. How dare you come on public radio blaming the American people and pontificate about matters of which you know absolutely nothing! You're a disgrace, sir. You dare tell the American people that this problem can be cured by asking the Almighty for forgiveness. You moron. This is a virus, a lump of inanimate chemicals that only comes to life in the body of a living thing. A virus, Mr. Higgins, that is caused by some agency that we're desperately trying to understand. This is a global problem that affects Christians and Jews and Muslims and those who believe in many gods and no gods at all. This is a medical problem, you idiot, and scaring people into believing that there's a divine agency causing it can only do great harm to those of us who truly have the welfare of the world's population in our hands. Now, Mr. Higgins, get off the radio, stop scaring our citizens, and beg forgiveness from the great American people for your self-serving hypocrisy."

The president slammed down the phone. Reverend Higgins was, for the first time in his life, speechless. The producer of Radio KVVX's *The Marty Ziller Hour*, frozen into immobility because of what had just happened, didn't have a clue how to react, cut to a commercial break, and in doing so, missed the immediate follow-through that would have given him the biggest scoop of his career.

But even though the president's intemperate intervention, compared by commentators to the type of caustic observations that an often frustrated Harry S. Truman made in public, was the second lead item on all news programs—an item that producers broadcast to follow their lead item dealing with the outbreak of the viral disease in New Jersey, that didn't end the professional Bible-thumpers from using the children's deaths as an excuse to promote their causes.

Except now they had a president who didn't pander to the religious right in middle America and who, to the voluminous cheers of East and West Coast America, had told a fundamentalist preacher to go jump. The liberal media loved it. After electing president after president who had shown themselves to be neutered by the God-fearing angel-believers in the middle of the nation, Americans at long last had a twenty-first century president who wasn't afraid to call religious hypocrisy by its true name. It became a cause célèbre and threatened to dominate the more hysterical media outlets with instant listener and viewer polls springing up to determine whether or not the president had been right to speak that way to a man of the cloth. Possibly because he was reacting to the terrible deaths of these children, a huge majority of the population thought that the president was spot-on and applauded him.

But Higgins, and the other religious leaders using the tragedy to increase their profiles and donations to their churches, were only a sideshow to the problems that President Thomas and the American people were facing. In the town of Newton in northern New Jersey, an impregnable quarantine cordon had been placed around the town, as it had been placed around the Wantage County Petting Zoo and an area of 100 square miles in the vicinity. Terrified residents begged for information from the police and men in white hazmat suits. Information officers, sent by the president to brief residents, media, and officials, told everybody everything they knew. The president's instructions were to hold nothing back, provided it was based on fact and not speculation or rumor.

Debra Hart flew to the affected area in Marine One. Her first port of call was to the zoo, where she spoke at length with officials. She had discussions with the county medical officer and then, when she realized that the veterinarians had things well in hand, asked to speak to wildlife offi-cers from the nearby Ramapo Mountain National Park. Too far to drive in the haste of her trip, the pilot of Marine One said he'd happily fly her there. It took him only ten minutes to arrange a new flight plan with the local air traffic control, and they took off for the twenty-minute journey. The White House telephoned ahead to expect a visitor, but when the astonished rangers left their cabin at the approach of the famous helicop-ter, they simply didn't know what to expect.

In amazement, they watched the marine colonel land the helicopter on a flat area of the empty parking lot one hundred feet from the visitor's center, and as the doors opened, the first out was the copilot who osten-tatiously and facetiously saluted as he would the president as Debra stepped down onto the ground. She walked toward the four rangers, who didn't know who she was and weren't sure whether or not to salute as well.

"Hi," she said and introduced herself, explaining quickly what she was doing there.

Ranger Will Saville invited her and the crew of the helicopter inside the empty visitor's center for a cup of coffee, apologizing as they walked through the door for their lack of preparation, but they'd only just been phoned by the White House.

"Mr. Saville," Debra said, "I'm here because I think that a rural area might be the source of this horrible outbreak of disease that claimed the lives of so many little kids in Newton, west of here. There are quite a few national parks in New Jersey, and we're looking at each one."

Will Saville shook his head. "Doctor Hart, we've got the cleanest drinking water in the area. There're no diseases in the park. We keep a special eye on what's going on because we have so many visitors from New York."

"Do you have bats in the park?" she asked.

"Sure do. They're in a cave up on the heights, close to where the new visitor's center is being built. You get a great view of New York City from up there. This visitor center is too small for the number of tour-ists we get every month, especially in summer, and so this here visitor's center is being converted into the ranger's hut because it's close to the entry from Interstate 287 so we can keep our eye on who's coming into our park."

She nodded. "Will it take us long to get up to the cave?"

Will shook his head. "No, it's ten minutes to the park. If you want to see the bats, I'll take you up in the SUV, but you gotta remember that it's a bit noisy up there because of all the construction and all . . ."

As they drove further up into the park's heights, Will asked, "What's your interest in bats?"

"Just interested. We think there's a possibility that they might be the source of the infection that killed the children."

"But the cave is just a maternity center for them. The entire colony uses the cave in winter when they go into torpor, but the rest of the year when it's warm, they use the park's trees to roost. Only the pregnant mothers use the cave when they're breeding at this time of year. Their body temperatures raise the temperature inside the cave so that it's a nice, cozy environment for when their young are born," Will told her.

"How many bats are in your colony?"

"Years ago, when I first came here, there were thousands of bats. But the numbers have crashed. We had some people from New York Uni-. versity up here, some years back, doing a count and they figured that there were less than two hundred. Today, I think there are even fewer," he said.

Fifteen minutes later, Debra was standing at the entryway to the bats' cave. It stank of guano and was fetid, rank, and squalid. An environment ideally suited to bats, if everything she'd learned from Daniel Todd was correct. She also noticed that there were old food wrappers from the construction workers laying about on the floor, thrown down casually, thoughtlessly.

"How many people are working up here?" she asked.

Will shook his head. "Dunno. Maybe sixty; maybe eighty. Depends on what they're doing. If they're dynamiting rock, it'll be a lot more because they have to have safety inspectors and all sorts of experts. If they're bulldozing or jackhammering, they'll be fewer because it's largely mechanical. If they're building and constructing . . . I don't know, ma'am. Upward of one hundred."

"And do the men eat in here?"

Will laughed. "Not inside the cave. It stinks. And the floor is crawling with beetles which live off the bats' shit. So the men only take shelter from the sun in the shade of the cave mouth. I've taken coffee with them when I've been up here. They're rough diamonds, but they're okay. Why? You really think that . . ."

"I'm not thinking anything, just want to try to get a grip on the environment around here. I want my people to collect some bat droppings and a live bat if possible. I'm going to radio through to Marine One."

She went outside into the open air, away from the entry of the cave and picked up the two-way that the captain had given her. She asked him if he could patch her through to the White House. When she got through to the personal assistant with the number given to her by the president, she instructed the young woman to contact the veterinary department of New York University and get the scientists to collect the samples she needed. And she gave strict orders that anybody who entered the cave was to wear full hazmat protection including air-breathing equipment. Also, a mobile shower and disinfection van was to accompany them for when they left the cave.

When she disconnected, she turned and smiled at Will Saville. But before she could ask him to drive her back, the ground under her feet shook as though there was a minor earthquake taking place. She turned and saw that a giant excavator was using a pneumatic power tooth to punch deep holes into the stone to weaken and fracture the granite and then a separate bucket would carve out vast scars of earth and rock at the construction site.

"Can I borrow your flashlight?" she asked.

She knew the risks to her, but decided to walk just inside the entryway to the cave . . . holding her breath as she entered. But she could tell instantly that the stench was overpowering. Urine and ammonia and the putrid reek of decomposition. She had to breathe again, and so she soldiered on, shining the flashlight into the black depths of the cave. As she walked deeper and deeper, she became aware that the shadows cast by the flashlight's beam were making her frightened. Silly, because she was within running distance of the cave mouth . . . yet there could be black or grizzly bears in here, or other animals like mountain lions who might like to take a bite out of her. Especially as she could feel the vibrations of the giant earth-moving equipment outside, which must be causing a disturbance to animals that used the cave as a daytime sanctuary.

She was about to walk out when she shone the flashlight beam up into the ceiling of the cave. A shudder of horror rocked her body as she looked at what the brilliant light had illuminated and saw, high on the roof of the cave—quivering—dozens of bats. They were hanging on nooks and crannies, in little pits in the rock wall, or from spurs in the roof of the cave. And as the ground beneath her feet vibrated, so too did the cave walls. And the bats. The groundbreaking, jarring, massive machinery outside was affecting the peace and tranquility inside the cave. Daniel Todd had shown her videos he'd taken of bat colonies asleep in caves. Those bats were docile, still, only the occasional one moving and altering its position, but these bats were behaving very differently. They were shaking, as though they were frightened.

Debra walked quickly out of the cave and into the brilliant summer sunlight. She had been terrified of breathing the same air as the bats, touching the same surfaces, being in the same place. She would have to get the analytical results as quickly as possible if she were to quell this outbreak. But in her heart, she already knew the result. Although she certainly wasn't an expert on bats, she knew a sick colony when she saw one. And this was a depressed, depleted, and stressed-out colony. God only knew what the viral load was within these creatures' blood. It must be a cocktail of every malevolent disease that could cause mayhem in the human population.

And if what she instinctively knew was proven correct, they would have to be exterminated. Immediately.

8

Tom Pollard, president of CHAT, reacted in anger when his phone rang. He was in the middle of reading the *New York Times'* story about the discovery of bats in some cave in upstate New Jersey being the most likely source of the infection that had taken the lives of twenty-five kids, and, at last count, seven adults in a small town. As he read, he tried to figure out an angle he could use, but for once, caution took control of his promotional instincts, and he knew in his heart that he shouldn't try to capitalize on the tragedy by coming out in public and trying to defend the bats. The public hated bats. There would be zero public concern about their fate, and having been responsible for the deaths of young children, the chance of Americans wanting them to be spared the executioner's wrath was non-existent.

And the stakes were too high for Tom and CHAT to become involved in the debate. Only a day or two ago, Tom was listening while the president of the United States crucified some asshole fundamentalist minister for making capital over the deaths of these poor kids, and Tom certainly wasn't going to get a tongue lashing from President Thomas.

He picked up the phone and hissed, "What?"

"Sorry to disturb you, Tom, but there's a man on the phone who insists on talking to you."

"Who?"

"He refuses to give his name. He just says that you'll want to speak with him."

Without waiting for permission, his PA put the call through.

"Who is this?" asked Tom.

"I don't want to give my name because I can assure you that the Feds are listening in right now. I just want to know whether you and CHAT are going to do anything to save these bats. They're about to be slaughtered by the United States government . . . they may already have been slaughtered . . . but it was Americans who make them carriers of these deadly viruses, and instead of making restitution, we're going to kill the victims of our transgressions. Are you going to do something to protect them? Yes or no. And don't think that it'll just be these bats in New Jersey that are slaughtered. Every bat and probably every bird in America is threatened."

"Who are you?" asked Tom.

"Think Pollard. Think about who could be asking such a question, when the whole of America is baying for the innocent blood of these creatures. Think about who really is concerned about the earth, its creatures, its ecology. Not a bunch of shitheads like you and your CHAT-erers who strip naked in front of pet stores to make television pictures. Not an organization that gets airhead Hollywood movie stars to cry crocodile tears about cuddly, fluffy animals. I'm a man who thinks that all life is sacred, from the humblest insect to gorillas and polar bears; animals that mankind is pushing to extinction because of his insatiable greed and desire. I'm a man who speaks out and points the finger at who's really responsible for the mess the earth and all its creatures are in. So do you know who I am yet? And are you and CHAT going to do anything to save these bats?"

Light dawned when he began to put two and two together. Pollard knew who was on the phone. He was the very last person to whom he wanted to speak.

"Professor Stuart Chalmers, I assume."

"Are you and CHAT going to do anything to stop the slaughter of these bats?" he insisted.

"I don't want to talk to you, Chalmers. Don't phone here again."

"Moron."

Tom Pollard put the phone down. His mind reeled, going over the conversation, trying to pinpoint any threats. The last thing he needed was to be associated with the fanatics of the Whole Earth League. And there was no doubt that the police or the Feds were monitoring his phone calls as well as those of Chalmers and his fellow fanatics in WEL.

If Tom contacted the FBI about the phone call, it would score him some brownie points and might get them off his back. Or should he leave it alone? The Feds would have recorded this phone call, so if he didn't report Chalmers' contact, he could be seen to be acting in complicity, and it would be a black mark against him. There was only one decision, and he'd already made it.

He picked up the phone, opened his address book, and dialed the number of the FBI district officer who had recently warned him that CHAT's activities were close to breaching federal regulations, especially if he'd ordered the crime across state lines to break a window of the fur shop in Florida. This phone call from Stuart Chalmers and its implied consequences would be reported by him to the Feds. At least, when the shit hit the fan, he wouldn't be caught in the updraft.

* * *

A thousand miles away, Professor Stuart Chalmers, department chair of the Philosophy Department of the University of Wisconsin School of the Mind, replaced the receiver and smiled. The FBI was monitoring his phone calls and would certainly have monitored CHAT's phone and now would be buzzing with what Chalmers was planning to do. They assumed that he would be planning an assault by his Whole Earth League. Something big—something showy—something to do with the bats! He smiled. How wrong they would be.

Chalmers loved the cat and mouse game he played with the Feds. Twelve major terrorist assaults this year alone against electric utilities, animal transport and haulage firms, government offices, and God knows who else—and even though he'd been questioned each time, they'd never had the evidence to charge him.

Nor would they this time, when Chalmers and his handful of lieutenants in the fight to save the earth and its flora and fauna from the ravages of humankind, committed the greatest homegrown antigovernment assault in history. Okay, not as big as 9/11 but this one would be against Americans . . . by Americans. More spectacular than the Oklahoma bombing, he would strike at the very rotten heart of a corrupt system of government that slaughtered animals that had been prostituted by humankind's intervention, nature's creatures changed by humans to become unwilling and unwitting killers of little children. Not that he truly cared about little children . . . or big children . . . or people or, if truth were told, even some animals. Some of them, like snakes and rats and spiders and yes, bats, made his skin crawl. It was his philosophical mind that wanted to protect them from humanity, not his emotional mind. His ineffable joy came from knowing that he could make the United States' law enforcement authorities look silly and stupid, knowing that they knew he'd committed these crimes, but being unable to prove it.

And soon, he'd rise up above the law enforcement buffoons and attack the US government itself. And he'd even warn the authorities before he did it, just to give them a heads up. Not a big warning, of course, but rather a hint that something might be awry so that when the inevitable senate or congressional investigation took place, somebody would uncover a telephone warning to some district office of the FBI that had been ignored, that hadn't been acted upon, and the Bureau would have some explaining to do by shocked politicians in their splendid isolation in Washington, pontificating and thumping desks.

He'd warned them a day or two before every assault his group had committed, but his warnings had never been heeded in the past. He smiled to himself as he mused on the past two decades of being the most carefully guarded secret in the FBI's annals—the man they'd most like to exterminate . . . the man they were unable to prosecute.

The US system had brought this on itself, and bats and kids were the innocent victims. And while the Feds were monitoring his movements in New York, assuming that he'd gone there to do some dastardly act of terrorism, all he'd really be doing was giving a lecture; and at the very moment that he was teaching in front of an audience of hundreds, one of his WEL group would be preparing to commit a huge act of aggression against the government. While he was being monitored by the Bureau, while he was asleep in his motel in Manhattan, the act would be committed. And in the aftermath, when the dust was beginning to settle, no matter how the cops and the Feds tried to pin it on him, he'd come out of it as clean as the driven snow. Nor would they, or could they, connect any associate with him. All his meetings were held covertly in different locations, and he was known to be a total loner in his private life. It was a delicious irony.

Soon the American people would feel the wrath of the Whole Earth League and be forced to change its ways. Mickey Mouse organizations like PETA and CHAT were brilliant for distracting public attention from the real eco-warriors, men like him and the dozens of handpicked troopers from around the world who'd joined him in the most secret and underground resistance movement the world had ever known, dedicated to reversing the ravages that humanity had wreaked on a globe that was theirs to share, not dominate. Dear heavens, how he hated humanity . . . how he hated all living things . . . how he hated.

WEL had become one of the most covert and tightly run organizations by adopting the modus operandi of Al-Qaeda and some other Arab terrorist organizations; only a tiny number of those at the very apex of the organization knew its structure. These were the handful of people who ran the organization but who recruited those locally to do their dirty work.

The minions below were organized into cells, and those cell leaders only knew the name of one man or woman at the top of the next cell up. Chalmers had organized it along Al-Qaeda lines so that the only numbers that could be busted by the police were miniscule, and even if they were tortured, they simply didn't know who else was involved. Which was the reason for their success in the early days; so if one cell was busted, it was virtually impossible for the police or the Feds to work their way up the chain of command to Chalmers and his colleagues who ran WEL. Perfect decentralization. Perfect cover for him—an honest and nonviolent, though profoundly controversial, philosophy professor.

Yeah! Right!

He was front-page news in the *New York Times*, and everybody in the United States knew of his radical ideas—his demand for an end to all human destruction of the environment and the earth's remaining fauna and flora—but equally well, everybody thought he was an amiable nutcase, somebody so off the planet as to be laughable. Even the senate of his university had demanded his dismissal, and had it not been for the president who'd insisted on academic freedom, he'd have been on the streets.

Only the Feds, police forces in twelve states, and a handful of hardcore reporters thought that they had an inside understanding of what the true Professor Stuart Chalmers was really up to. But thinking and proving were two completely different things. That was precisely why he played the cat and mouse game with them. Because whenever Stuart made fun of the authorities, he knew that it was too dangerous to drop his guard, to get sloppy. The moment he started to believe himself invincible, he'd make a mistake and be thrown into prison for the rest of his life.

CHAT and the other animal protection groups were the focus of public disquiet, of conscience-prickers, but in the end, their nude demonstrations, moronic protests by starlets with banners, and the occasional prison sentence for throwing paint on a fur coat or breaking windows in a pet store, were nothing more meaningful than hot air. They were to eco-terrorism what Andy Warhol's fifteen minutes of fame was to intellectual genius. The real job of rescuing Mother Earth from the evildoings of human beings had to be left to men and women who'd put their lives on the line and think nothing of taking the lives of perpetrators. Just as a soldier in a war was entitled to take the life of an enemy combatant to protect himself and his colleagues, so WEL had decided that as the soldiers defending the natural world, they were entitled to take lives in order to protect what was incapable of defending itself from the brute force of humanity. The men and women who were the soldiers of WEL killed without compunction those men and women who destroyed without compunction. They were dedicated last-ditch warriors trying to prevent the destruction of the earth by the most destructive animal who'd ever evolved . . . man!

Professor Stuart Chalmers was a perennial suspect by the Feds of being the kingpin of the Whole Earth League, but that was only because he regularly lectured to large numbers of adoring kids about the evils of humanity and what it was doing to the ecosystems. Yet despite the court orders, the searching of his rooms at the university and his home, despite having him followed and bugged twenty-four hours a day, there was never ever anything that even remotely connected him to WEL.

Like Al-Qaeda, he'd learned never to communicate WEL business by phone or in writing. Instead, he personally gave his orders and instructions to those in his inner circle, who traveled to their lieutenants in America and other parts of the world and spoke only to the person in charge. Conversations were always in parks or open spaces to avoid listening devices. Hands were held to mouths so that lip reading experts couldn't interpret what was being said.

The members of the inner circle then went to see other lieutenants until the second tier structure that was involved in the action had been informed. These lieutenants would then communicate directly, and in precisely the same manner, with cell leaders who had to carry out the assaults. There was virtually no possibility of tracing the instructions to Chalmers.

And today was the day to activate his most audacious assault against the hubris of humanity. Today, he would set in motion an assault against authority that would make America reel back and take notice of the destruction it was wreaking against Mother Earth.

When his new project came to fruition . . . he leaned back in his chair and smiled to himself. All hell would break loose. Literally. He just couldn't wait.

THE WHITE HOUSE
WASHINGTON, DC

No matter how confident he tried to portray himself, Daniel Todd was overwhelmed by his first time in the White House. Few ordinary people had ever been at the center of the US executive government, yet when Daniel sat in the Roosevelt Room with Debra, waiting for the arrival of the president of the United States, he came close to being struck dumb. Used to addressing audiences of hundreds, he said a short prayer to himself to ensure he was able to speak clearly, crisply, and without error to the audience he was about to address, an audience of a handful of the most influential people in the world.

Sensing his unease, Debra said, "You really mustn't worry about talking to the president, Daniel. He's a scientist, a keen listener, and very interested in what you've got to say."

Before he could respond, the door suddenly opened and a tall, thin middle-aged woman walked in. She smiled at Debra and nodded to Daniel. "The president will see you now, Debra," she said crisply.

They rose and followed her down further corridors—sound muffled by the royal blue carpet—and as they approached, the door to the world's most famous office was opened by the president's PA.

President Thomas was sitting at his desk, writing. He looked up as Debra and Daniel entered his room. Debra introduced Daniel, and the president escorted them to the sofas.

"What's your assessment, Professor Todd?"

Clearing his throat, Daniel said with halting confidence, "One can't be definite without the electron microscopy of the virus that should be here within a day or two, but I'd say you could be pretty confident that the bats that Debra found are the source of the infection that killed the children."

"I can't wait a day or two. If those bats swarm tonight and more people die . . . well, the prospect is too awful to contemplate. If you're pretty sure, I'm giving the order to destroy the colony," said President Thomas.

"Sir," said Daniel, "there could be other causes. There could be . . ."

"Sorry, Daniel, but I'm taking no risks. I held up the destruction of these bats for sixteen hours because Debra begged me to wait for you to arrive here from London. I have no intention of waiting another moment. The American people will accept the death of a colony of bats; they'll never accept the death of a human being when our best minds were pretty confident that they knew the source."

The president stood and stabbed a number on his telephone. "Go!" he said.

The order was given to the general in command of the Situation Room in the basement of the White House. He instantly picked up another phone and spoke to the colonel in charge of the fumigation squad from the Chemical and Biological Defense Division at the Pentagon, who had positioned themselves outside of the cave in the Pompton Lakes in the Ramapo Mountain State Forest.

The colonel simply nodded to the Sergeant in charge of the squad who told his men to uniform up. They donned their full-face breathing masks over their white hazmat uniforms and walked toward the mouth of the cave that had been sealed with a heavy rubber curtain. Walking through the curtain's airlock they pulled the tubing through the aperture and deep into the cave. The lights in the cave had been muted so as not to unduly disturb the bats, but several of them were flying around in an obvious panic that their radar couldn't find the cave's mouth. Laying the tubing on the floor of the cave, the Sergeant pressed the light on his intercom to instruct the men waiting outside to begin the fumigation process. Within seconds, the end of the tube emitted an eerie yellow gas that floated to the ceiling. The chemical, a close relative of mustard gas, quickly filled the part of the cave in which the fumigation troop was standing. They shone flashlights into the roof of the cave and saw the bats twitching. Some left their perches and flew around in obvious distress. Others, still asleep, breathed in the deadly gas and quickly dropped to the floor of the cave, convulsing for a few moments in great suffering. Others died where they hung, their claws clinging in death throes.

It took only minutes for all the bats in the cave to die. When there were none flying, those dead but still clinging to the roof were removed by long poles. The men picked up the tube, still pumping out its deadly gas, and moved further in. It took them two hours before they were totally confident that each and every living thing inside the cave had been destroyed. They emerged from the cave, climbed into a large trough, and were immediately pressure-sprayed from above and the sides with hot water to wash away the residue of the gas; then they were sprayed with bleach, antibacterial and antifungal chemicals, and disinfectants; and finally, a hot air blower was brought in to dry their hazmat uniforms.

When the procedure was completed, rubber-gloved assistants in breathing masks helped them off with their uniforms, which were immediately stuffed into a mobile incinerator and burned. The fumigation team was followed into the cave by a disinfectant team that sprayed the entire inside walls and ceiling of the cave with three specific types of antibacterial, antifungal, and antiviral disinfectants. That took a further three hours. Finally, a hazmat team was sent into the cave with mechanized digging equipment to scrape the floor of the cave back to solid rock. Aside from samples of the bats' bodies for forensic investigation, the entire floor of the cave—guano, insect and bat bodies, and chemicals—were scooped up and loaded into special drums that would be taken in a military convoy to be burnt to a cinder in a 1,500 degree furnace. Then the ash would be collected and dumped in a unused 1,000 meter deep mine shaft in geologically stable Utah which, along with numerous other deadly cocktails collected over the years, was guarded every minute of every day by an army detachment.

Debra and Daniel were having dinner in the Lafayette Restaurant on Sixteenth Street NW when she received a text message on her cell phone. She looked at it and nodded to Daniel. It was a simple coded message, "MA", meaning mission accomplished. It was a parody on the obscenity of the former President George W. Bush saying that the United States mission in Iraq was accomplished with the overthrow of the hideous ruling family of Saddam and his psychopathic children, a prelude to years of anguish and cost in American lives and money.

"They're no more," she said.

Daniel nodded. His face didn't betray any satisfaction. He didn't like the thought of being the destroyer of animals he'd come to know and love. He never thought that he'd be the cause of a colony of bats being destroyed when they were the innocent victims of humanity's push for room to grow and feed itself. If anything, it was the law of the jungle, of a species that was destroying what stood in its way because suddenly the species threatened them. It was the sort of thing that nature had done through evolution since plants and animals first colonized the earth. One species developed and wiped out another . . . Homo sapiens wiped out

Homo Neanderthal; Aboriginal man had wiped out much of the mega-fauna. It was a progression—the cruelty of Darwinian survival of the fittest. And inexorable logic demanded, as the president had so forcefully put it, that the American people get upset about the death of a few bats rather than hysterical about another child's death from this virus.

"What if it wasn't the bats, though?" Daniel asked Debra. "What if it was birds or some insect? Jesus, Debra, what could we be dealing with here? Is this the beginning of another pandemic or plague? Are we dealing with species' extinction? Our extinction?"

"Remember when you first approached me all those months ago at that virology conference at Yale? Remember, you said that the source of the virus I was investigating, what had wiped out the villagers in Indonesia, was almost certainly by bats. I remember so clearly what you said to me. It was along the lines of, 'Today it's the jungles of Indonesia; tomorrow, the jungles of New York and Washington.' I've thought you were talking crap then, but I totally believe you now. My problem, what I really don't understand, is what's happening . . . why it's happening. This outbreak in the UK, in New York State? Okay, I understand the outbreaks in South America and Asia, but England? The United States? What the hell is happening to the world?"

Daniel smiled and reached over the table to hold her hand. She felt a shock of surprise as he'd never shown her the least bit of physical interest. He'd only ever once touched her and that was to shake her hand when they'd first met. She didn't react to him.

As though he didn't notice her reaction, he said, "You remember some of what I told you in that coffee shop at Yale, but you haven't remembered what else I said. I clearly remember the conversation because you were the first medical person who'd taken me seriously. I said that the worldwide bat population has plunged in the past dozen or more years. The populations are under huge pressure . . . everywhere. We're encroaching on their habitats, they're developing disastrous fungi that are killing them, we're fucking up their food sources, and let's never forget global warming. It's only just begun with the shrinking of the ice caps and our weather patterns beginning to turn nasty, but in five, ten, twenty years, the problems that are going to be caused by global warming will become the biggest problems humanity has ever faced. There are some species that can't adapt quickly enough. We all know about frogs disappearing and the colony collapse of bees. But bats are the real canaries in the coal mine. They're the early warning system that the earth is in revolt. Because they harbor all these viruses and their viral load goes through the roof when they're stressed, it's going to spill out and human diseases will proliferate like there's no tomorrow.

"All in all, Debra it's a real bad world out there for bats right now and tomorrow, it's going to be a whole lot worse. And with their stress and the massive increase in their viral load, the viruses in their blood will mutate. Today, individuals are dying; tomorrow, whole communities will be at risk."

"Surely bats aren't the only cause . . ."

"Of course not, but as a vector, they're a hidden menace and they're not taken seriously. Everybody knows about rats and fleas and the Black Death. It's one of the reasons why we're all so terrified of rats but not so much of mice that are seen as safe and cuddly. What's not understood by the public is that bats can harbor these viruses that jump species into human beings."

"Okay, but why Washington? Why London?" she asked. "I can understand a tropical village with its heat and unsanitary conditions, but the world's largest metropolises . . . and bats? Bats are country dwellers, not city folk. Sure, we have some flying foxes in our city parks and some bat varieties are in the barns on the outskirts, but bats in cities are incredibly uncommon, aren't they? It doesn't make sense."

"Really? Cities are sources of food. Bats need ready access to food. We're seeing more and more feral animals come into cities for their food . . . foxes, squirrels, possums, moose, bears, and deer are just recent arrivals. Rats and mice and dogs and birds have lived in inner cities for millennia, side by side with human beings who have taken control of the production and supply of food. Think about when you dig up the garden . . . suddenly half a dozen birds appear in the trees, looking down and watching you. The moment you go indoors to make a cup of tea, they fly down into the furrows you've made and pull up the earthworms that you've disturbed. Clever.

"So it makes sense for an intelligent flying mammal to come to the city for its food supply and its shelter when its food might be drying up in the countryside and its shelter under threat from developers."

Debra drank some more wine and asked, "Okay, so if this is going to be an epidemic or even a global pandemic, what can we do about it? No matter what the animal protectionists say, we're the dominant species on this planet, and we have to make it safe for humanity. Nobody's going to go back to pre-industrial revolution times and live within the rhythms of the earth. So are we going to have to kill all the bats? Is that becoming a real possibility?"

"We may have to," said Daniel. "But only in the inner cities and the surrounding suburbs where there are colonies. Most of the rural bats are probably okay."

She shook her head. "What about these villages in Indonesia and Malaysia and South America? They've been wiped out by these deadly mutating bat viruses."

"Sure, but we're pretty sure we know the reasons for that. And unless you eliminate every bat in the world or reverse the damage that humanity is doing to the ecology, it's something that we're just going to have to live with. Face it, jungle and rural villages have been impoverished—disease- and sickness-prone—since time immemorial. The vast majority of the world's populations are living in filthy conditions with no access to pre-ventative medicine, all on a dollar a day. It's the haves and the have-nots. We who live in the cities have wealth, community, access to medicines, control of pests and vermin, shelter, and cleanliness. And we can domi-nate the landscape and the environment like no other animal in creation. And if something gets in our way, we can eradicate it. We eradicated smallpox and most waterborne diseases. It's just a question of eradicating species higher up the evolutionary scale. It shouldn't be too much of a problem for scientists like us to eradicate our neighborhood bats."

"So what method do we use? Are we going to have bat patrols walk-ing city streets on the lookout for something flying other than moths or birds? Inner city radar won't work because of the buildings. Satellite navigation devices spying on our own towns and cities . . . drones flying down the canyons between skyscrapers? What?"

Daniel shrugged. "Scientists are good at analyzing and protecting and counting and stuff, but I don't think that too many of us are destroyers. I think we're going to have to leave that to vermin controllers . . . my God," he whispered, "did I just call bats 'vermin'?"

MADISON, WISCONSIN

He only ever ate at the Green Madison Restaurant when the situation required immediate action. A young first-year student had kindly carried a note to Jim Towney in the Agri-Science block of the university way across the campus from the Philosophy School, alerting him to be at this new restaurant at 12:30 p.m. sharp and to sit at a table facing the door.

At fifteen minutes to the half hour, Stuart Chalmers left his office and his building via a service entrance, quickly crossed the busy main street, and stood surreptitiously for five minutes in the alley to see if he was being followed. Satisfied that he wasn't, he walked by circuitous routes down Campus Drive toward University Avenue and then turned left toward the lakeside.

The Green Madison Restaurant was just a few blocks away. Stuart, assured that he wasn't being followed, hurried to the eatery and stood and waited for a full five minutes, hidden by a post but looking carefully through the windows. He wasn't looking at the table where his colleague Jim Towney sat; instead, he was looking at other tables to see if anybody was sitting there and trying to look inconspicuous.

Satisfied that they weren't going to be observed by the Feds, the police, or any other enforcement agency, he entered the restaurant ten minutes late and sat alone at an empty table overlooking the lake. He ordered vegetarian lasagna, a sarsaparilla, and unbuttered toast. Taking out that day's edition of the local newspaper and holding it high so that his mouth was obscured, he said softly, "Thanks for coming so quickly."

Jim Towney, sitting with his back toward Stuart's at the adjoining table, said, "What's so urgent?"

"We need to take immediate action to prevent further slaughter of these bats. Soon it'll be birds and anything else that carries a virus. It has to stop."

"Sure, but what do you want to do?"

"We have to off the secretary of health. Let everybody know that this is a man-made problem, and slaughtering animals is just delaying the inevitable. We have to put out a message that if you slaughter animals, we'll order the slaughter of the person responsible. Do it at your own risk."

Jim Townie was quiet for a moment. "Did you just say what I thought you said?"

"You heard," Stuart whispered.

"You want to assassinate the secretary of health. Kill DeAnne Harper?"

Stuart didn't answer.

"Why her? Why not the secretary of agriculture?"

"Because she's the one most closely associated with the destruction of the bat colony in New Jersey. Offing the secretary of agriculture is something we'll do later, once we've told the world that governments have got to get their populations to live in harmony in the natural world."

"Jesus, Stuart. Do you realize what assassinating a cabinet secretary will do? It'll have every Fed, every police force, every US marshal, every government agency after our balls."

"Right. As if we didn't have every one of them after them right now."

"But a cabinet secretary? That's almost as high profile as offing the president."

Stuart laughed softly. "I thought about giving it to him, but he's one step removed from the person responsible for ordering this slaughter of innocent animals. First her, then the secretary of agriculture. Harper is behind this rabid assault on bats, and the world has to understand the seriousness of her actions. It'll be a warning to other governments . . . stop this shit happening or shit will happen to you."

"And when the roof comes down on our heads . . .? Nobody's going to help us or fund us if we assassinate a cabinet secretary," Jim whispered.

"Nobody's going to blame us. Just like we weren't blamed when that old Jewish guy who sold furs got what was coming to him in Florida. CHAT was blamed because they have a publicity-hound spin-doctor asshole in charge. Nobody connected the Florida thing to us. Good, eh!"

Again, Jim remained silent. "So you set that up? That Florida killing. You set it up?"

His silence was eloquent testimony. The less Jim knew, the better. That was the way to ensure security. Stuart was only including him in this latest plan because it was important that he be seen in public in another city when the bomb went off.

The black kid who'd done the Florida killing would be happy to off anybody else for a grand. Even a cabinet secretary. He was a brilliant student but wildly irrational and probably insane. Stuart had nurtured him by giving him passes in his academic work that he didn't deserve, but there were moments when Noah, the black kid, had some breathtaking insights. Still, the pressure had been on Stuart to kick the kid out of school, and now he worked for Stuart on a freelance basis . . . and Stuart gave him free tuition from time to time.

One of the things Noah liked to do was to kill, so long as he didn't have a relationship with the person he was killing or know why he was doing the killing. He was a thug and an assassin with a sky-high IQ, one who needed money to live and needed the occasional intellectual nourishment. But it was the money that was needed most, and Stuart's money, sourced from wealthy and eccentric donors to WEL, was as welcome as anybody's was.

"Did we really have to kill that old Jew?" asked Jim.

"I didn't kill him because he was Jewish, but Jews control what's left of the fur trade, so I had to make it look like a street crime and not a deliberate murder. That's why I coordinated it with CHAT's demonstration."

"Why link it with CHAT? What's the advantage?"

"Who's under police scrutiny? Who got it right up their arrogant, useless ass when the media was on a witch hunt for somebody responsible for the old guy's death? Who's the focus of public attention? CHAT, that's who! When we off DeAnne Harper and her family, we'll leave a tiny bit of evidence which won't be easy to find. And when some forensic hotshot finds it, it'll be traced back to CHAT. It won't stick, but it'll be a nice red herring. Enough of those and it'll point to a probability that CHAT has been somehow involved.

"Me and you? We'll be covered by alibis. I'll be giving a lecture on the immorality of species extinction at New York University, you'll be lecturing in control of insect pests, or something, and everybody else associated with WEL will be publicly engaged in an official activity, far away from Washington. The Feds will have no way of connecting the . . ."

"Her family? Did you say we were going to off her family?"

Irritated, Stuart hissed, "Jim, this is war. If we don't protect the earth and its creatures, nobody else will. This is a case of survival. If we have to rid the world of a destroyer of the ecology and her family, so be it. Get used to it, buddy, or get out."

A silence again descended on the two tables as Stuart was brought his meal. It was mushy, unappetizing. Nobody except a specialist knew how to prepare vegetarian food. Ordinary chefs who thought they'd make a profit out of vegetarians simply took the quickest and most obvious route to its preparation; few realized that cooking vegetarian was totally different than cooking meat and fish.

"So when are we going to do this thing?" asked Jim.

"Much sooner than they'd realize," Stuart told him. "I've arranged a lecture at NYU for next Monday. I've checked your schedule and you're giving a talk here. So are most of the others. On the assumption that she doesn't suddenly change her schedule and that she remains in Washington, that's when it will be."

"And how do you know that she'll be there?"

Stuart smiled to himself. "Trust me. I have very good information."

"You've got somebody on the inside?" whispered Jim.

Again, Stuart remained silent and finished his meal stuffed with rice. He was no longer thinking about continuing the conversation with Jim Towney; he was wondering how to phrase the warning he was going to give to the FBI . . . a story about CHAT's plans to assassinate a high government official. Maybe he'd even say cabinet secretary, just to scare them; and provided his anonymous call from the disposable cell phone he'd buy later that day was made only an hour or two before Noah blew up the house in Washington, the Feds wouldn't have time to react. Yes. That was the way to go. All he had to do now was to work on the text of what he was going to tell them.

9

Little Jessie Marquis turned right out of the school gates and, under strict instructions from her mom, walked home along the pavement and well away from the roadside toward her home on Wilmont Drive in Hendersonville, a township in the eastern part of North Carolina.

She looked around to see who else from her class was walking in her direction. Most were met by their moms or older sisters, even a grandma or grandpa, but Jessie's mom and dad were working and so she had to walk home alone from school. Not that she minded because unless it was raining, she loved the ten-minute walk and used her imagination to peer through the hedgerows and try to see what lay behind in the hidden garden.

She was deep in her imagination, flying around a garden holding hands with a beautiful fairy, when suddenly she felt something real fly into her head. For the first instance she was unsure of whether she imagined it or whether it really happened, but when she felt something twisting and turning in her hair and scratching her scalp, she reached up to her head, felt something warm and furry, and screamed.

The little eight-year-old's hysterical screams of distress attracted a small group of parents who were holding hands with their children as they, too, walked home. Mothers ran over to Jessie to see why she was panicking. There were no strangers about, no cars or motorcycles, because this was a quiet part of town, and people helped other people when there were problems. And suddenly, for no visible reason, a little girl was standing on the pavement, frantically flicking her hair and screaming as if she'd been stung by a bee.

"What is it, honey?" asked a mother, looking anxiously around. The child didn't answer but frantically pulled at her hair trying to dislodge something. The mother looked closely at Jessie's head, and then she too screamed as a small Indiana bat dropped out of the girl's hair and onto the ground.

Horrified, mothers hid their children from the bat as it lay on the ground, squirming, struggling to flap its wings and eventually hiding its body in the flaps of its arms until it lay silent and barely moving other than an odd twitching.

Jessie stamped her feet in horror as she looked at the bat and wouldn't stop her screaming. The mother put her arm around the little girl but try as she might, the mother couldn't comfort her, and Jessie continued to look in terror at the bat twitching on the pavement. Other mothers, equally horrified, gripped their children and pulled them away so they couldn't see the bat in its death throes.

Marlene Devoss bent down and held her arms tighter and tighter around Jessie to comfort her and asked, "Darlin', how'd you get the bat in your hair?"

Crying and still distressed, Jessie sobbed, "I don't know. It just got there. I was just walking and then I felt it. It was so horrible."

"Okay, darlin'. First thing I'm going to do is to call your mommy. Then I'm going to take you to my house just down the street and drive you to the hospital, just so's the doctors there can make sure you're fine and all right."

"Hospital?" asked one of the other women. "It's only a bat."

Marlene turned and whispered, "Ain't you been reading the papers? These damn things got all sorts of diseases. You get you kids home," she said to the group, "and stay indoors. If there's one, there'll be plenty others."

As if prophetically, three other bats suddenly dropped from the sky not a hundred yards from where the group was standing. "I'm gonna call the cops," said a mother. "This ain't funny."

By the time the Hendersonville patrol car arrived, there were dead bats all over the road, pavement, in gardens, on roofs. There must have been hundreds. The patrolman who'd taken the call and who initially thought it was a hoax, called back to his base for instructions. His sergeant called Police Central in Raleigh, the capital of North Carolina, and they immediately contacted the Department of the Interior. Within minutes, the call had been routed to the Department of Health near the White House, where Debra Hart had her offices and staff.

It took just five hours from Jessie's initial hysterical outburst for the area to be cordoned off and for hazmat teams to arrive. Exercising emergency protocols, the blood of the dead bats was extracted, sent to a nearby laboratory, and examined, but no unusual diseases or viruses were found to be present. Debra read the report and demanded further tests to be done immediately. An entire forensic battery of blood, tissue, and organ tests were done, but except for rabies that was common in many bat species, no other viruses could be identified.

The director of the pathology lab who had conducted the tests was quite pointed when he said to Debra, "Doctor Hart, you can look and look, but you're not going to find anything which killed these bats. I could do a full postmortem that would give me the cause of death, but I assure you that they weren't killed by anything alien in their blood or body tissues. This could have been an external agent, a poison, or a neurological disturbance of some sort. What I can assure you is that their blood and other tissues are normal for bats."

Next morning, Debra and Daniel Todd flew to Raleigh, North Carolina, and then by helicopter via Charlotte to land in a field close to where the previous day little Jessie had encountered the bat. Residents looked out of their windows at the commotion but remained indoors, as though under curfew. Debra and Daniel were met by the chief of police for the area, who escorted them to the nearby police precinct.

Over a cup of coffee with his senior officers, Daniel asked, "Where is the closest bat population?"

A local sergeant answered, "Since the poor little girl had her encounter yesterday afternoon, we've been speaking to rangers and guides and folk like that. Most likely, the bats came from the Asheville area in Henderson County, a place called, appropriately enough, Bat Cave. It's fifteen hundred feet above sea level, and from what we've learned, that's where the Indiana bats go to hibernate over winter. We're told that there's a population of some twenty thousand of them in the cave. We haven't been up there to investigate because your instructions were to stay well away."

Debra nodded. "Right. We have no idea why the bats died or left the cave during the day, but because of all the other problems we're having with bats, it's best if you guys leave it up to us. No sense in you risking your lives without the special equipment you'll need to go in there. Okay, can you get somebody to drive us to the Bat Cave?"

The sergeant shook his head. "Best off to go there by helicopter. The terrain isn't all that good, and it'll take hours for you to drive."

* * *

Daniel and Debra donned their full-face masks, breathing apparatus, and gloves as they walked into the cave. They hadn't gone more than three or four hundred feet when Daniel turned to Debra and said, "This is all wrong."

Their flashlights revealed no bats in the roof or walls of the cave, but as they walked further and further away from the narrow entrance, they shone their flashlights on the floor and revealed tens of thousands of dead bats, piled high in a huge area.

"Goddamn it," said Daniel. "They've been poisoned. Some bastards must have filled the cave with poison gas." He whipped off his mask and smelled the air. "Chlorine. These bastards have made a chlorine bomb and set it off down here in the cave. The bats wouldn't have stood a chance."

"A chlorine bomb? Dear God, do you think the locals would know how to make chlorine?" she asked.

"You don't have to be a chemical genius. Just hydrochloric acid and manganese dioxide. The acid you can get from anywhere and the manganese dioxide is used in dry cell batteries, or somebody around here will sell the stuff. Put the two together with a bit of knowledge of chemistry, and you'll get enough chlorine gas to fill this chamber and kill every god-damn bat. It's criminal. Thousands of innocent bats, killed just because people were scared."

"But I don't understand," said Debra, also taking off her mask. "Chlorine is heavier than air. How could they have killed the bats on the ceiling?"

Daniel shrugged. "The initial reaction of the acid with the dry chemical would have sent out plumes of the gas. It would have filled the chamber before settling back down to the ground . . ."

"But how could bats have escaped out of the cave?" she asked. "How could they have flown to Hendersonville all those miles away?"

Daniel shrugged his head. "They might have just been irritated by the initial gas and managed to escape. But if they'd just breathed it or if some of the gas had got on the skin of their wings, the irritation and damage it would have done certainly would have been enough to have caused what happened back there yesterday."

They turned to leave the cave, having seen all that they needed. They walked toward the outside in silence. Once there, they took off their protective masks and faced the three local police who'd joined them but remained outside while the scientists did their work. Daniel explained what they'd seen within.

One of the officers, young and inexperienced, said, "Shame about the bats, but if they're the cause of all these deaths of folk, maybe whoever did this was saving us a lot of problems."

"If people are going to become vigilantes and take on the war against bats without any scientific rationale, then I think our problems are just beginning," said Daniel.

"I don't follow," said the police officer.

"Today it's bats . . . tomorrow birds . . . then some other species. The problem isn't the animals; the problem is humanity's inability to live as part of nature. We're stealing their habitats, we're changing the environment of the planet . . . this is a result of what we're doing and not what they're doing. If we keep on driving species to extinction like this, there'll be nobody left on earth but us. Our success depends on biodiversity. Get rid of the diversity and you'll get rid of us," Daniel said. He turned to

Debra, who nodded in agreement. What was obvious to them as scientists wasn't so obvious to lay people.

The police officer remained silent, but just looking at his face, Daniel and Debra realized that he and his colleagues weren't convinced. It was a Darwinian case of survival of the species, and dominant humanity had just shown how they were going to survive, regardless of the costs.

The group packed up in silence and entered the helicopter in preparation for their return to civilization.

WASHINGTON AND NEW YORK UNIVERSITY

The news of the slaughter of the North Carolina bats was on the front page of every newspaper in the United States. The line taken by most editorial writers was that the killings were wrong in principle, wrong environmentally, and wrong ethically . . . but completely understandable. The lead writer for the *San Francisco Chronicle* captured the mood of Americans by asking:

> Deplorable as the slayings were, who among us—mother or father— wouldn't have done precisely the same after witnessing the heartbreaking grief of the parents of the children in Newton, NJ, whose precious lives were cut short because of viruses caused by bats. While we must retain a sense of our humanity, surely it's this very humanity itself that caused the good people of North Carolina to want to protect their families by killing these flying death machines.

In the Great Hall of New York University, Professor Stuart Chalmers was talking animatedly in an early evening lecture to nearly three hundred students, faculty, and media, holding up the *New York Times* and reading aloud the opinion of the newspaper.

"Understandable?" he said, sarcasm oozing from his voice. "Understandable? Why should we understand the killing of animals completely innocent of any crime against humanity? Laboratory tests have proven that these bats were healthy, safe, and posed no risks whatsoever to people. This was vigilantism of the very worst kind. This was . . ."

"Bullshit," shouted somebody deep in the audience. "People before animals. Always was, always will be, asshole."

Many in the audience laughed. Some applauded.

"With that attitude, friend, the world's six and a half billion bipedal apes are in real trouble . . ."

People in the audience who'd come to the public lecture to agree with Stuart burst out laughing and many applauded. But Stuart wasn't having any of it.

"Before the rest of you guys feel too much pride in your efforts to save the planet, who here only eats free-range eggs?"

Half the audience put up their hands.

"Okay, you think you're doing something for the animals, but have you seen the condition of free-range chickens? Before you start criticizing guys like him who promote people before animals, why not look at how we're treating the very animals we're using for our food and clothing. There's nothing free-range about free-range chickens. You think I'm talking bullshit, friend? The poultry companies want you to think that their products are free range or free roaming because their chickens spend their lives in the sunshine, warm country air, and scratching up worms in a huge field full of grass and wheat. That's bullshit, friend. Research in the United Kingdom shows that less than 15 percent of chickens are able to get out into the farmyard. They've been bred to be almost incapable of walking. They're just huge egg-producing, meat-making, genetically engineered freaks, created like Frankenstein, to feed our emotional and physical needs . . ."

"Maybe so, but what am I going to eat with my bacon if not eggs?" shouted the same man, turning to the audience and encouraging them to join in his ridicule of the lecturer.

This time, nobody in the audience laughed.

* * *

While Stuart was lecturing in New York City, a meeting was being held in the Oval Office of the White House. Present were the president, at his desk, and sitting opposite him were the secretaries of agriculture and health and Debra Hart. Deputy secretaries and spokespeople sat against the walls on the periphery of the room, listening and taking notes. Daniel Todd, assisting Debra, sat alongside people furiously writing down whatever was said, wondering whether or not he too should be taking their thoughts down.

"Okay," said President Thomas, "as I see it from listening to you all, we've got three things to do immediately. The first is to reassure everybody that not every bat is deadly, and it's up to the government to examine the blood of every bat colony to see which, if any, need to be destroyed. The second is to mobilize every animal laboratory in the nation to capture and test the colonies near to them, inform us of the results, and in the case where bats harbor dangerous viruses, to destroy their colony. And the third is a public information campaign on television about the possible, if remote, dangers of bats and how to avoid them at all costs until we know that they're safe. Is that right?"

"Yes," said the secretaries of health and agriculture. Debra remained silent.

A low voice from the rear of the Oval Office muttered, "No, that's just so wrong."

In surprise, people turned to identify who'd just spoken. It was Daniel.

"Sorry, folks, but that's wrong. Dead wrong. You put out warnings like that on television, Mr. President, and you're going to have every jumped-up wannabe scientist publicity hound screaming doom and destruction from the rooftops."

He stood and walked toward the semicircle of chairs in front of the president's desk.

"Daniel, please . . ." said Debra softly.

"It's okay, Debra," the president said gently, "I'd like to hear from Professor Todd."

"Sir, you're going to make an announcement which says that bats are generally safe, but we've all got to be careful because some bats that are under stress are building up viruses which mutate and can cause real harm to people . . . so until we've got the situation under control, don't go near bats. Is that right?"

"Generally, I guess," said President Thomas.

"Okay. Now if I was listening to that announcement and I'm a scientist on the make, wanting publicity, I'd think that it was manna from heaven. First thing I'd do, wanting to get my name in the paper or my fifteen minutes of fame on television, would be to phone the media and say, 'scuse me, but bats fly and eat insects on the wing; they fly to distant fields and eat fruit. While they're silently flying unseen over your houses, their body fluids full of deadly viruses are expelled and in the morning, the bacon or eggs you eat could kill you. And don't go running around your back garden without shoes and socks, because if you have the smallest cut in your foot, you'll pick up the virus on the grass and it's good night Charlie. Not only that, but . . ."

"Okay, Professor. I think we have the drift of your argument. You're saying that a television education campaign could hurt us more than help us," President Thomas said. "So what do you recommend?"

"Newspaper adverts, sir," he said. "But buy the ads in specific papers where there's a bat colony or a flight path. Most bats have regular roosts and regular flight paths. As an example, sir, in Austin, Texas, there are a million and a half bats that fly every evening out from under the Congress Avenue Bridge over Ladybird Lake and fly in an almost straight line to their feeding grounds. So why would we trouble people who weren't underneath their flight path? We should publish newspaper ads that give full details of the problems we're facing, what we're doing about it, and most especially the standard flight path that the bats take over the area in which the newspaper is circulating. Get the paper to print maps that show clearly which cities or towns or villages are directly under the flight path of the bats as the colony leaves its roost and searches for food. If we can identify the towns that lie underneath, we can give a focused warning to the folk that live there. Then we wouldn't have to alarm the whole country. These days, sir, there aren't all that many bats around. We've done a pretty good job of eradicating many of them. That's why we're in this trouble."

The president looked at the secretary of agriculture, who shrugged. "I can see no problem with that idea, Mr. President. My people will do some work on it, and we'll report back in twenty-four hours," he said.

"They don't have to do any work," insisted Daniel. "They'll find out that I'm right. I know bats. I've worked on them half my life."

The secretary of health, DeAnne Harper, said, "If Professor Todd is correct, then I think his strategy is the right one for us to take. Why scare the pants off everybody when we only need to terrify a small proportion of the population that could be in immediate danger."

"Okay, that's what we'll do." He turned to the man on his right and said, "Mr. Secretary, will you and your agriculture department work with Professor Todd and ensure that what he's just said is correct . . ."

Daniel started to react but was cut short by the president. "Doctor Todd. We all respect your expertise, but this is a huge crisis for America; people are terrified of going outdoors. You know what's just happened in North Carolina. So before we follow your advice, which I'm sure we will, I need to test your hypothesis."

Daniel nodded, much to Debra's relief. Everybody stood and started to leave the room, but as they filed out, the president said softly, "Debra, could you please give me a moment of your time?"

She waited until the Oval Office was empty. Nathaniel Thomas led her over to the couches, where they sat. A butler appeared from nowhere and offered them coffee or other drinks, which they both declined.

When they were alone, President Thomas said, "When we first met, I promised you a private tour of the White House. Since then, I guess we've both been a bit busy, what with my normal presidential duties and you flying off to London to take care of things there and then having to hightail it back here. But I haven't forgotten about my promise, and I'm happy to show you around any time you want."

She felt herself blushing like a teenager and hated her body for reacting without the approval of her mind. "That's very generous of you, sir, but I know how busy you are, and . . . ."

"And you're up to your eyes in it too. There's a number of ways of looking at it. A couple of hours out of our schedules aren't going to kill either of us. And it'll have the advantage of making us both happy. What do you say?"

"How can I refuse an offer from my president?"

"Dear God, you make me sound like a mafioso. When do you want to do it? Tomorrow afternoon would be good. My wife is out of town, giving a speech in Chicago. About two?" he said, standing and escorting her to the door.

She was too stunned to speak. His wife was out of town? He didn't . . . he couldn't . . . would he?

* * *

Noah Simball, known to all his friends as No Slimeball, sat in the back of a black delivery truck that had its windows coated with a transparent film. He could see out, but nobody could see in. He'd been warned by Stuart that the Feds and protection services regularly scanned the area adjacent to the White House looking for parked cars, trucks, and vans that might be observing the comings and goings at the most powerful building in the world. He had also been warned about the electronic monitoring, the listening devices, scanners, movement detectors, and a dozen other things that showed the White House security people what was happening inside and in a broad sweep outside the building.

He was parked in Alexander Hamilton Place looking carefully at a guarded exit that fronted a tunnel. It wasn't a well-known tunnel because its entry was well concealed, but it was the unofficial way for cars to enter and exit the White House. As cars emerged from the underground parking lots buried deep within the building's grounds, they turned left onto East Executive Avenue, skirted the White House, and then went into Washington, DC's frantic traffic.

Knowing which car to spot, Noah waited patiently, as patiently as he'd waited for that old dude in Florida to come out of his shop and confront the crowd. Noah had a large stone in his pocket to toss through the store window to draw the owner out so he could stab him when he tried to prevent Noah from stealing the furs. But before he'd had a chance, some man had thrown a car jack and done half of Noah's work for him.

But this job was going to be a lot more difficult than offing some old guy. This was a job to off some high government official, and the level of security would be much greater.

Suddenly, a large black limo emerged from the tunnel. He could barely make it out because of the concealed entrance, but as it sped up the ramp from the underground parking tunnel into the grounds of the White House, he focused his binoculars on the car and its license plate. He sighed. It was the wrong car. Wrong plates. But another big black limo emerged fifteen minutes later, and this one had the right plates. He quickly hurried from the back of the van through the curtains and sat in the driver's seat, turning on the engine and gunning the pedals to be ready the moment the limo and two other cars had overtaken him. *Always stay two cars behind the target*, Stuart had told him. And that's just what he'd do. As a student of Stuart at the University of the Wisconsin School of the Mind and as a foot soldier of the Whole Earth League, he always did what he was told.

He followed the car northwest from the precincts of the White House toward Georgetown. At a brownstone just off Potomac Street, the limo slowed and stopped, depositing the secretary of health at a freestanding building with a neat front garden, a path that led to steps that ascended to a mahogany door in a three-story house. As if by magic, the door to the house opened as the secretary of health reached the top step, and the brilliantly lit interior gave Noah the feeling that the person he was about to kill lived in more comfort and wealth than he would ever know in his life.

Noah drove past the building as the limo pulled away, turned left on Prospect Street, and then left again on Thirty-Fourth Street. A final left turn brought him back out front of the secretary's home again. He drove past, parked his van a hundred feet away, and waited ten minutes. Then he started his engine and drove away—this time twenty blocks. He carefully checked his mirror every few minutes, and when he was certain that he wasn't followed, he turned a sharp right and parked 100 feet inside the road. No car followed him, so he started up again and returned by a circuitous route to the secretary of health's home. Again, he parked ten houses north of her house and waited. And waited. Tired, he pushed aside the curtain and went to the back of his van where he hunkered down and quickly fell asleep on a mattress.

The alarm on his mobile phone woke him at 2:15 a.m. Yawning, he had a quick drink of Coke and climbed back into the driver's seat of his van. He scanned the roadway and the parked cars. There was no traffic at all. He knew that the Secret Service made twice-nightly drive-bys past all the cabinet secretaries houses and that they'd have taken his van's license number. He'd bought these plates from an old man working in a used car lot in Alabama. It was a van the owner had for sale for two years and which would soon be turned into scrap. So when the Secret Service checked out the number, it wouldn't be flagged as stolen.

Looking back through the mirror, in the distance he could see that there were no lights other than one over the porch in the secretary of health's home. Good! Everybody would be asleep. And nobody would know what hit them.

It took Noah ten minutes to take the C-4 explosive out of its carefully hidden spot under the carpeted floor inside the van. The C-4 was wrapped in thick plastic, which was covered in coffee grounds to fool sniffer dogs in case he was stopped and searched; the coffee ground-covered tube was then encased in an airtight cylinder, which had been washed and scrubbed a dozen times to rid the outside of any possible trace of the explosive.

Washing the large package of explosives with a bottle of water, he plugged copper terminals into opposite ends and attached them to a transmitter, which was synchronized to emit signals at the precise megahertz range. This would activate and explode the blasting cap that in turn would cause the electrical impulse to create the explosion necessary to turn the C-4 from a harmless mound of gloop into a bomb that would destroy the foundations of the house and make the entire structure collapse into itself. He set the timer for two hours' time, meaning it would go off at about 4:30 a.m. while everybody was still asleep.

He pulled the balaclava over his head and left the van, walking in the shadows cast by the trees until he was opposite the secretary's house.

Standing in darkness, Noah put on night-vision goggles and looked carefully at the house and its grounds. There was no movement, nobody looking—nobody at all. Quietly, he crossed the road and walked to the large locked gate. He'd already found a part of the fence adjoining the next-door building that he could climb. Checking that there was no traffic on the road, within seconds he was over the fence and standing in the front garden of the secretary's home. He ran on the grass beside the path in case it had movement activation alarms. The path meandered around the house, and Noah quickly found what he was looking for. It was a coal grate, where coal had been dumped before houses got boilers and central heating. Noah lifted the coal grate and wormed his way inside the underneath spaces of the house. The coal storage room had been bricked over years earlier, but there was sufficient room for him to place the explosives so that they were close to the foundation of the house.

In the eerie green light of the night vision goggles, he checked the clock on the timer. It was perfect. All he had to do now was to connect the cathode lead to the battery terminal, and then the moment the timer hit zero, the battery would pass a jolt of electricity that would cause a high-pitched burst of energy, akin to the sound of a scream and designed to activate the detonator. Once the detonator exploded at the cathode end of the C-4 package, the thirty pounds of high plastic explosive would instantly decompose and the gases would escape at twenty-six thousand feet per second—causing the biggest explosion the area would ever see. It would be like an intercontinental ballistic missile being dropped on top of the house . . . only this would be from underneath. The gases would blow out the entire substructure of the house, and everything above would collapse within and it'd be *adiós* to anybody living upstairs. Noah couldn't stop smiling.

He was back in his van within six minutes. Stuart had told him not to hang around but to drive away. His hand rested tentatively on the ignition key. He knew he should turn it, gun the engine, and drive far away. He knew the consequences of being caught. But no matter what the rational part of his mind said to him, the emotional part told him to stay put and look at the end result of his beautiful night's work. Another pillar of the Washington establishment, another animal killer, was about to get her just rewards.

The minutes ticked past; time went incredibly slowly. Dozens of cars drove past him, even though it was the middle of the night. He checked his watch a dozen times. And eventually, after two of the longest hours of his life, his watch told him that within the next minute, there would be an almighty explosion.

He could barely breathe with the excitement. He felt an erection stirring in his groin. Thirty-twenty-ten-five seconds to go. He opened the window of his van and looked backward to the secretary woman's house. As his watch showed the precise time, he held his breath and waited. And waited. After ten seconds past the due time, Noah breathed out, suddenly worried that something had screwed up. Had he set the timer properly? Had he . . .

And as he was thinking, a brilliant flash of light illuminated the entire street, followed seconds later by the loudest explosion he'd ever heard, which tore apart the silence of the night. Even knowing what would happen, Noah was stunned by the sound. A blast of hot wind rushed past the van, catching him by surprise. And then he saw a thing growing in the distance. A brilliant white and yellow monster ballooning outward and upward, enveloping the trees with leaves and branches that instantly burst alight—the pavement, the roadway, the cars that stood silently nearby were suddenly picked up and hurled across the roadway. Everything in the immediate vicinity that was flammable was set ablaze as the fireball enveloped everything. Objects from inside the house began flying through the air—gates and bricks and tree branches and furniture and all the innards of the building, flying haphazardly in the light of the monster that roared and expanded in brilliance and heat and sound and fury.

Noah's jaw dropped in stunned silence. Windows of houses all around him cracked and smashed in the reverberation. It was a holocaust, a nightmare of the apocalypse, a war zone. Suddenly terrified, Noah tried to start the van's engine, but his hands were shaking so badly, he dropped the key. He scrambled for it, found it, and only just remembered to do what he'd been told by Stuart. He quickly opened the passenger side door and dropped a crumpled up piece of paper into the gutter. It was a business card. A card belonging to Lorrie Benson. The same Lorrie Benson who'd worked as a PA for Tom Pollard of CHAT until the previous year, when she'd resigned to live in Washington with her lesbian lover and their three cats.

* * *

Noah was shaking for an hour after he left the area. He'd never seen anything so exciting in all his life. He'd obviously used too much explosive, but what the fuck . . . it all added to the publicity value.

And the police were also in a state of shock when, ten minutes after the explosion, they arrived en masse to see what had become of a Georgetown house where there'd been dozens of reports of a massive explosion. The patrol car officers stood in front of the vast gap where once a large and very expensive brownstone had stood and wondered what in the name of God they were expected to do. Fires were raging inside the house; the garden where settees, chairs, and desks lay askew in flames; fires were ablaze in adjoining houses and terrified residents were trying to use sprinkler hoses to douse the infernos, and dozens of residents up and down the street were looking at the broken windows of their houses in horror and amazement. Some men and women in pyjamas were sitting by the roadside, nursing sores and cuts; some were wandering shell-shocked in the aftermath of the explosion.

Motivated by training and a need to take control of the situation, the officers got cordon tape from their cars and built a perimeter. Notebooks out, they began to ask residents what in God's name had happened. But nobody was game to go anywhere near the house, both because of the intensity of the fires and because it was nothing more than a shell with walls that were still standing and in imminent danger of collapse.

More distant residents, who were not directly affected by the blast, came outdoors when they saw the blue and red flashing lights from the patrol cars but started to return home when they heard the sirens of

ambulances and fire engines approaching. The police continued to interview residents, trying to gain an initial picture of the incident. Almost
every neighbor who had been asleep told them that it was undoubtedly
a gas leak; one elderly man who'd recently watched a Hollywood movie
where a similar incident had occurred, told the policeman that the gas had
accumulated in the basement, and then when the time clock had sparked
the pilot light from the boiler, it ignited the pool of gas and "whoomp."

The area was cleared so that the police forensic team could work alongside the fire department. The ambulances departed with just a couple of
residents who had been cut by broken glass and one elderly lady in a state
of shock who kept talking about terrorists and 9/11.

When the fire was extinguished, an investigation team began to sift
through the rubble in the early light of the dawn. It took just minutes
to discover the bodies of five people—a middle-aged man and woman
burnt beyond recognition and three children, one teen and two younger
ones, also burnt so badly that it couldn't be determined whether they
were boys or girls. And it didn't take long for the chief fire officer to say
to the police captain who'd taken charge, "This wasn't a gas explosion.
This was a bomb. The patterns radiate from underneath the foundations
of the house. It blasted the fuck out of everything. If it weren't for the
strength of the walls in the brownstone, it would have taken out a couple
of the adjoining houses as well; as it was, the solid walls concentrated the
blast upward. The poor bastards asleep upstairs would have been blown
to kingdom come. Their bodies would have hit the underside of the roof
space and they'd have come down on an inferno."

"Would they have known what was happening? Do you think they
suffered?" asked the captain.

The fire chief shook his head sadly. "Man, that was some mother of a
bomb. Whoever made it had no idea of the quantity to use in a confined
area; I'd say he used three or four times what was necessary. The poor
bastards asleep would have died before they could even have opened their
eyes. If that's a way to go, I'll choose it for myself."

Their conversation was interrupted by a patrol officer who approached
his captain and said, "Sir, I think you'd better hear this."

The captain followed him to his patrol car. The patrol officer's partner was in a conversation over the radio with a woman.

"That's not information I can give out, sir," she said. "That address is governed by security provisions and is locked down. I can't reveal the name or details of the occupant. I'm sorry."

The captain picked up the microphone. "Excuse me, ma'am, I don't know who you are."

"I'm the supervisor of Northeast Washington Atlantic Bell. Who are you?"

"I'm Captain Perry Arnaudo of the Twenty-Third Precinct. Ma'am, we've just had a massive explosion in this house. We suspect it was a bomb. That means terrorists. I don't want to have to call Homeland Security to monster you. All I want to know is who was in the house so I can inform next of kin."

She was silent for a long moment. "Okay, I'll give you the name, but that's it. The house belongs to Mr. Alan and Ms. DeAnne Harper. Captain, that's more than my job's worth. Now please, contact Homeland Security, but I can't give you any more information. Good night, sir."

Captain Arnaudo handed back the microphone to the driver. "Jesus Christ."

He walked away from the patrol car and stabbed his office number into his mobile phone. His assistant answered immediately.

"Hey Captain, what's happening down there? It's coming through on the news, and it's . . ."

"Don, shut up. Text me through the phone numbers for the White House and Homeland Security."

"Sir?"

"The woman whose house has just been destroyed was DeAnne Harper. In case you don't know it, Ms. Harper is . . . was . . . the secretary of health. This is a serious fucking terrorist attack. I'm clearing the area right now because where there's one bomb, there's often a second one that explodes sometime later to take out police and emergency workers and sightseers. Get on to the FBI and the security details for top government officials. Tell them what's happened to Secretary Harper and say that every cabinet and senior government person is on a potential hit list. Tell them that until we find out about this bombing, everybody on the protection lists has to have maximum protection immediately. That means now!"

10

Debra Hart was in the shower in the apartment on Third Street SW, loaned to her by the White House, when her mobile phone rang. She decided to ignore it and continued to allow the needles of hot water to prepare her for the day ahead. A day of meetings with officials from the Departments of Agriculture and Health to prepare the president's plans for how she would deal with the latest problems caused by the bats.

Toweling herself, her mobile rang again, and this time she answered it immediately.

"Ma'am, a car is outside your building to bring you to the White House. The president has asked that you'd come here as soon as possible," said the president's personal assistant.

"But I have to be in my office for an eight a.m. meeting with . . ."

"Doctor Hart, all meetings have been canceled. The government is in security lockdown. Please come to the White House immediately." The PA hung up, leaving Debra frowning. *Lockdown? What the hell for?*

It took her a mere ten minutes from the phone call to dressing, rushing downstairs to the black limousine, and being taken through Washington traffic to the White House's tunnel entrance just off Pennsylvania Avenue. Taking the elevator to the lobby, she was escorted by a Secret Service officer to the president's Oval Office. She was silent on the way through, knowing better these days than to ask questions of the security details. But what worried her were the glum faces of everybody she met. Normally they'd greet her with a smile or a kind word. Today, the building was funereal and seemed to be encased in silence.

"Debra, thanks for coming so early," said President Thomas.

She nodded. The office was full of people, groups of threes and fours standing and sipping coffee and speaking in undertones as though waiting for her to arrive. She sat on one of the sofas.

"I didn't want to begin the briefing before you got here," he said. "Ted . . .?"

Ted Marmoullian, Deputy Director of the Secret Service and on assignment as head of White House security, stood and began to address the large number of people. He was a middle-aged man with graying hair, but his body was that of an athlete. It was his eyes that spoke eloquently of his inner and outer strengths—cold, unforgiving eyes, without a single crease of mirth. He was the sort of man you needed to befriend because he'd make a dreadful enemy.

"Some of you would already know that in the early hours of this morning, the home of Secretary of Health DeAnne Harper was bombed. She, her husband, and their three children were killed instantly."

There was a gasp in the room from those given the information for the first time. People stared at Ted in amazement. Debra was horrified and put her hand to her mouth.

"The bomb was C-4, a plastic explosive. The entire house was destroyed. There're just walls left. All cabinet officers and senior government people have gone onto level six security. This was a terrorist assassination, and we can be confident that it wasn't the only one that's being planned. We've picked up nothing in our monitoring that this event was going to occur. There was an anonymous call made to an FBI Washington district office, which we're following through, but there was nothing whatsoever that would have identified Secretary Harper as the victim of terrorism. We have no idea at this moment who the perpetrator is or what organization he belongs to. Nobody has claimed responsibility, but that can take up to twenty-four hours to occur.

"There's one forensic clue, however. Some distance away from the scene of the incident, we found a business card, crumpled in the roadside gutter. It belonged to a woman called Lorrie Benson. She's currently being questioned by the FBI, but she was in bed when officers went to her apartment and seemed to be taken completely by surprise. There're no explosive residues on her body or her clothes, and she has an alibi for where she was the previous night. She was in a disco, and her alibi checks out until one this morning. After that, however, she has no alibi verification, but her partner and she swear on a stack of Bibles that they were in bed asleep when the bombing took place," he told them. "To be honest, Lorrie is in such a state of confusion and distress that either she's a brilliant actor or finding her business card near to the scene of the explosion was a complete red herring, either accidental or deliberate."

The president intervened. "Tell them why you picked her up, Ted."

"Her business card said that she was the personal assistant to Tom Pollard, the CEO of the animal liberation group, CHAT. But she hasn't worked for him for over a year. She left his office in Manhattan to come live in Washington with her partner. She swears that she's had nothing to do with CHAT in the past twelve months. We're checking her phone and banking records right now, but from the reports of the initial interrogation, I very much doubt that Lorrie is the person responsible. It's possible that her card was placed there deliberately to throw us off the track of the real offenders, but we're certainly not ruling out CHAT at this stage."

Shaking her head in consternation, Debra asked, "I don't understand . . . why would CHAT or any animal liberation group want to murder the secretary of health? It doesn't make sense."

"We have no information at this stage, ma'am. We'll keep you informed."

"Thanks, Ted," said the president. "I'm devastated by the callous murder of the secretary of health. She was a good friend, a terrific colleague, and the nation will miss her expertise terribly. But we have to try to fathom why she was the target of an assassin. Ted's right, of course, that this CHAT business card could be a coincidence or something designed to throw us off track, but it's too much of a concurrence to find animal liberationists somehow associated with this terrible deed, remembering that DeAnne was leading the fight against these bat viruses. When I was told what had happened in the early hours of this morning, my very first thought was that it was one of the lunatic fringe animal welfare groups. Why else, for God's sake, would anybody want to kill somebody in charge of America's health services?"

Recovered somewhat from the shock, Debra put her hand up for permission to speak. "Mr. President, as part of my work in fighting these infection outbreaks, we've kept a careful watch on the Internet traffic and weblogs of these animal protection fanatics. There are three that could have been responsible. They've all been sending out wild messages about retribution for the destruction of the bat population. We've told the FBI and they're investigating them. Animals Alive is based in Phoenix, Arizona; another is Care for All Life, based in Boise, Idaho, and the third is All Creatures Great and Small, based in Long Island, New York. We never took much notice of them, because . . ."

"What about WEL?" interrupted Ted Marmoullian.

"WEL? I don't know them," Debra replied.

"Not all that many people have heard of them," he continued. "WEL is short for Whole Earth League. They're an ultra-radical fringe group, set up like Al-Qaeda in cells throughout America and a number of other countries. They don't use the Internet or telephones to communicate. We know they've been responsible for some murders and for firebombing animal testing facilities, especially cosmetic houses and experimental laboratories, but they're as cunning as snakes and we've never been able to bring them to court. It's run by Professor Stuart Chalmers who heads some philosophy school associated with Wisconsin University. Frankly, Doctor Hart, it doesn't surprise me that you haven't heard of them. They don't use modern communication methods . . . they rely on personal messengers to pass on instructions from a small, tight central cabal. They're almost impossible to infiltrate."

"And you think that this WEL organization could have been responsible?" asked the president.

"Sir, our initial research puts this Chalmers guy giving a lecture in New York University yesterday evening, and he spent the night in the Holiday Inn adjoining the university. He was still there this morning, but our guys have picked him up and are interrogating him. They'll get nothing out of him, though. Unless he got a Learjet to fly him to DC, it would have been near impossible for him to have left his lecture hall at ten thirty last night, flown to Washington, committed the crime, and then to have flown back to be in bed when our guys knocked on his hotel door at seven this morning. And even if he was associated, he'll have covered his tracks like an Indian warrior. We've also picked up other associates of his, but I'm pretty certain that they'll all have cast-iron alibis."

"And your best guess?"

"Mr. President. I have no proof, but my guts tell me that if there isn't any evidence to prove that WEL committed this outrage, then they were probably responsible," Ted told him. "The clue that was left, the business card of this woman who worked for CHAT was . . . well, probably planted. It was probably contrived to throw us off the scent, but I'd be very surprised if CHAT were in any way responsible. This assassination is way out of their league. They're into spraying fur coats with paint, not murder. No, if anybody's responsible, it's either a completely unrelated terrorist atrocity, courtesy of some whacky paramilitary group who'll soon claim responsibility, or it was conducted by WEL. If it was WEL, it'll be a hell of a job getting evidence."

Others in the room began to make noises that they wanted to contribute, but the president held up his hand.

"So what can we do about them?" he asked.

"Unless we ignore the US Constitution or put the country on the highest level National Terrorist Emergency Alert, there's not much we can do to shake their tree, other than apply to a judge to hold them for further interrogation. But these guys aren't going to have left any evidence connecting them with the bomber who actually got his hands dirty and murdered Secretary Harper and her family. Whoever the bomber is, he'll be a couple of hundred miles out of DC by now; he'll have ditched the vehicle he used to commit the crime, probably selling it to some boondock car dealership way out of Washington, then he'd have paid cash for some old jalopy of a motor to drive away in, no questions asked, booked into a dive motel, showered to get rid of any explosives residue, gave all of his clothes to a local charity, and will be driving west, north, or south to disappear into the underground network of some city a thousand miles away. I very much doubt whether we're dealing with Islamic terrorists here, Mr. President. These maniacs are homemade. They look like us, talk like us, and think like us, and they know how to hide among their own so that we can't tell them in a crowd. Worst of all is that they use no modern communication devices so we can't monitor them or record their phone calls, emails, or text messages. They don't use Skype or any other Internet connection devices that the NSA at Fort Meade can monitor. It's going to be a nightmare, proving that they did this."

Ted Marmoullian surveyed the silent room. "And even more of a nightmare finding out what they're going to do next. Which is why everybody in this room is a target of these lunatics and has been placed under maximum security and protection. Don't even think about complaining, ladies and gentlemen. When it comes to White House security, even the president does what I say."

* * *

The meeting over, the group departed quickly and in silence from the Oval Office. Debra walked out after the majority had departed, hoping to speak alone with the president and to get his reassurance that soon everything would be all right, but he immediately went into an obviously private meeting with his chief of staff. From the few words she overheard, they were talking about how to break the news of the assassination of a cabinet secretary to the American people now that they were having their breakfasts and early news programs were beginning to report both the incident and who had been involved.

Debra walked through the door with a number of other people and was surprised to find that her path was blocked by a younger middle-aged man with brown hair graying at the edges. Like Ted, he was lean and athletic, but from his suit, shirt, and tie—and the bulge in his breast pocket that defined his gun and holster—Debra immediately knew that this man was a Secret Service protection agent.

"Doctor Hart?" he said, obviously recognizing her from the dossier he'd been given by his Department.

"Yes."

"I'm Agent Brett Anderson. I'm in charge of your security detail. Please follow me."

He turned and led her in a different direction from the way she'd entered the White House.

"I'm not a cabinet officer, and I'm sure that I don't need a security person?" she asked.

"I don't know why I've been assigned, ma'am. I'm just here to protect you. At all times, you'll walk behind me. You'll never enter a room without me entering first. In the street, we'll avoid crowds and only walk with the flow of pedestrian traffic, not against it. If we're walking, I'll walk a few paces in front. If I see somebody coming toward me who looks in any way suspicious, I'll slow down or stop, and you will keep walking up to me until you're close enough to touch me. That means my body will protect yours. If I say the word 'go,' you'll immediately walk quickly back in the direction from which we've come and I will deal with whoever it is that I've stopped in the street. You will not look back and check what's happening. You will continue walking until I catch up with you. If I haven't caught up, continue walking and enter the nearest shop or building with a large crowd. I'll find you. If I don't return, remain hidden and activate a number I'll put into your cell phone. Another security detail will be there within minutes.

"You will never arrange to travel anywhere, under any circumstances, without telling me in advance, enabling me to get my colleagues at the arrival point to check out the security."

She wondered if this included visits to the bathroom, but she remained silent because this was obviously very important to him.

He continued, "When you're in a room, you'll stand away from doors and windows. I'll enter first, and wherever practicable, I'll draw down the shades or curtains. You won't use private transportation, but only cars that have been garaged or parked under my supervision. You'll not open your own mail, answer the door, or identify your location when you're in conversation with people, even those you know well," he said.

He would have continued his litany, but she interrupted him, "Am I supposed to remember all that?"

"It'll become second nature until this emergency is over," he said.

"Look! This is ridiculous. Why am I being given security . . . I mean, I'm a scientist. I'm not a politician or a . . ."

"I don't know ma'am. I'm sorry, but we're not told of the political reasons for decisions having been taken. We're merely here to take the shot for you."

"Jesus!"

He immediately regretted what he'd said. "I'm sorry, ma'am, that's just an expression we use in the Service. I meant that I'm here to protect you against all threats."

"Okay, but who gave the order to give me protection?"

"It came from the top. You and cabinet secretaries and a number of key government officials."

"The top?"

"The Oval Office, via White House Security. You're being protected by order of the president."

"Can we go over those security instructions once again? And for God's sake, don't call me ma'am. I'm Debra. If you have a problem with that, then just call me Doctor Hart."

They left the White House via the secure garage built underground outside the West Wing and drove by a circuitous route to her office in the Department of Health. When they pulled up into the building's garage, Brett instructed her to stay low in the car until he'd examined the area. She watched him as he walked several car lengths in all directions. It was obvious that he knew precisely what he was looking for, and when he returned, he opened the door and escorted her to the elevator.

"What if there'd been somebody on the other side of the garage with a rifle?" she asked. "I was a sitting duck in the car."

"Bullet- and explosion-proof windows. They were more likely to injure me in the ricochet."

As they stepped out of the elevator into the building that by now was full of employees, she immediately sensed an air of unreality. It was a chill that hadn't been there when she'd left her office late the previous night.

The sense of emptiness was felt by everybody, as the awful news of DeAnne Harper's death became common knowledge. Women were sitting on chairs in hallways and on landings looking ashen-faced. Men and women walked around like ghosts; some had red eyes from crying. Most avoided her eyes.

Debra realized with a start that she hadn't reacted to DeAnne's death in the same way as people in the building. In theory, DeAnne was her direct link to the president, but she'd only met her on three or four occasions, and always on business. So when she was told of her death, the news had affected her in the way that the death of any nationally important person's assassination affected her—with shock and disbelief. But the people in the building were reacting to the loss of a friend, a colleague, a work-mate. Even though DeAnne wouldn't have known 95 percent of the people who worked in the building, the loss of such a senior government official . . . a mother, her husband, and three children . . . was heartbreaking.

They reached Debra's office, and as she was about to enter, Brett held up his hand to stop her and pushed open the door. Four people in there looked up and were surprised by the entry of a strange man. Daniel Todd stood and began to ask, "Who are . . ."

"Secret Service," said Brett pulling out his identification badge. "Who are you?"

"Daniel Todd. I'm Doctor Hart's assistant."

"Are all these people known to you?"

Daniel turned and scanned the group. Then he nodded to the agent. Satisfied that there was no immediate danger in the room, Brett opened the door and allowed Debra inside.

"Sorry guys," she said. "This is Agent Brett Henderson . . ."

"Anderson."

"Right. Brett is my security person. He'll just sit in here with a cup of coffee while we work. He shadows me until this nightmare is over and the bastard who killed the Harper family is caught."

"Debra, I'm so thankful you're here. The Internet traffic has been going haywire. Since we were told about DeAnne, we've been looking at the CHAT website and most other animal liberation sites, and their weblogs, and they're all going crazy. They're saying that DeAnne was assassinated. On the news, it said that it was thought to have been a gas leak." Daniel looked at Agent Anderson and frowned. "Why do you have security?"

"Daniel, I've just come from the White House. It was a bomb that killed DeAnne and her family. It was probably planted by an animal liberation group. I'd be surprised if the president didn't go on network television and address the nation. But I'm surprised that the websites are talking about it being an assassination. Nobody's said that so far. How did they know?"

Nobody answered.

"I don't understand? Why should she have been murdered? Why all the security? What's happening?"

Debra looked at her colleague and shrugged. "The thought seems to be that the animal liberationists are protesting about us killing the bats. They've been saying for some time, both in the UK and here, that humans caused the problems, and we shouldn't take it out on the bats. Crazy, but if you think about what PETA and the other defenders of voiceless animals have done in the past, in a nutty kind of way, it fits. There have been deaths and raids on laboratories and the murder of people associated with experiments on animals. And people in the fur trade. These people are fanatics. They're determined to save the earth and all its creatures, even if it means killing a few human beings on the way."

"Bats? They've killed a family of human beings to save diseased bats? It's crazy," said Daniel. "And why DeAnne? She's in charge of Health. I can understand them going after the secretary of agriculture or the president or somebody like that, but Health? It doesn't fit," he said.

"It fits in a perverted way if you think about it. DeAnne is . . . was . . . charged with protecting the United States against these viruses. The viruses are carried by bats. These wackos think that she gives the order for their extermination. Hence, they exterminate her and her family. It's insane, it's inhuman, but it's logical to their perverted minds."

Debra nodded and looked around the office at her colleagues. All were looking toward her for explanations, reassurance, and sympathy. But it suddenly dawned on her that there was more to their immobility than being in a state of shock. They were suddenly very frightened. As their boss, leader, and mentor, she had to do something or the office and all its work would come to a standstill.

"This has been a terrible shock to all of us. It's brought the reality, the dangers of terrorism close to the hearts and homes of everybody in this room. We're scientists, not security or military personnel. So if any of you, for any reason, wants to return to your universities or laboratories because of your concern for your personal safety, then not a word will be said against you. Of that, you have my promise. Please, friends, feel free to step forward and just say that you'd prefer to leave now, and I give you my word that nobody will think badly of you. We're all mothers, fathers, sons, and daughters in this room. We have to consider others, aside from finding a way of fighting this virus."

Silence descended on the room as not one person moved. When he saw Debra nod in appreciation, Agent Brett Anderson moved forward and said, "Ladies and gentlemen, Doctor Hart is in charge of the science of this organization. I'm responsible for security and to assure your safety. If any of you feel that you're being watched or that something unusual happens in your lives, immediately contact a number I'll write on your whiteboard and which you'll copy into your mobile phones. It's the emergency number for A3 level security. If you have genuine reason to be concerned at something . . . anything . . . ring that number and you'll have a dozen Secret Service men at your side within minutes."

"A3?" asked Daniel.

"A1 is a protection given to the president and senior members of the cabinet. That affords a team of Secret Service personnel at all times, day and night. Level A2 is for senior people associated with cabinet secretaries and gives twenty-four-seven personal security in shifts of three people for eight hours of each day, the sort of thing I'm here for on behalf of Debra. A3 is your security which means that a team is available in emergency within minutes of your call."

"And A4?"

"The number of the Washington Morgue," said Brett. He grinned, seeing the look of shock on everybody's face. Only then did everybody laugh. And get back to work.

11

The interrogation room was deliberately lit with a harsh and intense light so that the mirrored wall could conceal the banks of analysts who sat behind rows of computers, sound and video recorders on the other side. The interrogator's earpiece was alive with instructions from his controller behind the mirror, who was being fed with written instructions from a battery of experts.

Speech and body language specialists listened and looked at every nuance of the way he responded to questions and the manner in which he reacted physically as the interrogator was instructed to raise or lower the intensity of his questions.

Domestic terrorism authorities checked every answer he gave and prepared to instruct the interrogator to blow a hole in the subject's responses; but so far, he'd not made one single factual, timing, or geographical error.

After three hours of continuous investigations in an uptown New York office of the FBI, Professor Stuart Chalmers sat calm and poised while the two interrogators from Homeland Security continued to try to puncture his composure.

It was a simple question, though, which caused silent mayhem among the audience of watchers.

The interrogator asked innocuously, "So now WEL has killed the secretary of health, who's your next target, Stuart?"

Chalmers drew a deep breath, thought for a brief moment, and said softly, "The president of the United States."

"Excuse me," the slack-jawed interviewer replied.

Chalmers smiled, turned, and addressed the mirrored wall. "Just thought I'd throw you guys a bone so you wouldn't go to sleep. Surely you're bored by this inane line of questions, aren't you?"

Then he turned back to his interrogator and smiled.

"You think this is funny," the Homeland Security man said, suddenly becoming intensely angry with the academic's perpetually composed demeanour. He just wanted to reach across and break his nose.

"Oh Agent Carlson, surely you remember instruction number two in class 101 of the interrogator's handbook. 'Never lose your cool in front of the suspect. At all times remain calm and collected.' Y'know I've never really understood the use of the word 'collected' in that sense. I wonder what it means."

Again, he turned to the mirrored wall, "I wonder if one of you gentlemen could look that up for me and whisper into Agent Carlson's earpiece why it's used in that way in the sentence."

"Okay, we're wrapping it up. We know you were involved in this murder, Professor. We know you instructed some assassin to kill Secretary DeAnne Harper. And be assured that we'll trace it back to you, and then the full weight of the law will put you out of action for the rest of your perverted life."

"And as I've been saying for the past many hours, Agent Carlson, neither I nor WEL nor anybody that I know would contemplate taking a human life. Our mission is to protect and save all plant and animal life. Secretary Harper was, like you and me, a human animal. We're dedicated to care for her and her family as much as we're dedicated to protect bats and bees and flowers. You may not agree with what we think, but you have to believe me when I say that we've never knowingly or deliberately harmed a living thing. Now, if I could be released, I have a class to teach tonight, and I'd like to get back to my university."

Two hours later, Stuart Chalmers arrived at Kennedy Airport and checked in at his flight. He smiled at the two agents who had booked the same flight, acknowledging that despite their best precautions to remain anonymous, he had spotted them and knew they were tailing him.

He went over to one, who was reading a newspaper. "I often wonder why they waste time using people like you to tail guys like me when there's so much government surveillance equipment. The federal budget appropriation is over forty-two and a half billion dollars in this country for surveillance on American citizens suspected of involvement with terrorism. Imagine what Joe Stalin could have done with that sort of money. We have an hour before our flight. Do you and your partner want a coffee? At least we should get acquainted if you're going to be covertly trailing me all over America."

The agent looked up at him and hissed, "You might think this is a game, Chalmers. Okay, so you've blown my and my partner's cover, but a cabinet secretary and her husband and three children were murdered earlier today, and we know you did it. You talk about Stalin; how long do you think you'd have lasted in the Soviet Union in the days of Stalin, or in Iraq when Saddam was butchering his people or when ISIS was butchering anybody who didn't believe in Islam? It was the US of A, the land you detest, that put an end to those bastards. The only reason you haven't got a bullet in the back of your brain is that the America you despise is governed by the rule of law, and unfortunately, assholes like you know how to take advantage of it."

Chalmers smiled. "You're wrong, y'know. I don't hate America. I just hate Americans."

The agent watched Chalmers's back disappearing as he walked away toward the coffee shop. He wondered why US institutions like universities gave time and space to people like Chalmers or the vitriolic Muslim academics who were teaching hatred in their classes. Academic freedom? Civil liberties? Human rights? What about the rights of people like DeAnne Harper and her family to live in peace without being blown to pieces by some fanatic terrorist?

* * *

Secret Service Agent Brett Anderson knew it would have to come sooner rather than later. It always happened with people who had never experienced close body security before, people who were normally living their lives out of the public spotlight. Then, through circumstances they probably didn't fully understand, they were thrust into the glare of the media, arc lights, politicians, and others who lived their lives in sync with the biology of the 24/7 news cycle—a relentless parade of action and reaction, cause and effect, questions and answers.

Debra Hart told her group that she wouldn't be in the office that afternoon but was flying to Harvard University in Boston to see some electron microscopy that a team had recently done on some samples from Australia where two vets had died from the Hendra virus; apparently it was the first case ever reported where the virus had passed from bats or flying foxes into dogs and possibly cats, so she wanted to see its morphology to be in on the production of a possible vaccine.

As she nodded to Brett to follow her on her way out of the door, and as they walked down the corridor to the elevators, she asked him, "So, how did you enjoy your first experience of working inside a scientific group? Pretty dull, huh?"

"That's not what's concerning me, ma'am."

"Please don't call me 'ma'am.' It makes me sound seventy years old. Can't you cope with calling me Debra or Doctor Hart or something?"

"Debra, you've arranged a trip to Boston. You didn't tell me."

"Should I?"

"Yes."

She smiled, suddenly remembering that she'd broken one of the rules that Brett had given her. "You're right. I apologize."

He hated what was going to happen next, but it was straight from the song sheet. He steeled himself for the reaction.

"I'm canceling your trip to Harvard."

They'd arrived at the elevator where two other people were standing. She turned and looked at him in surprise. "Excuse me?"

"I'm cancel . . ."

"I heard what you said. Do you mean I'm not allowed to go?"

The others at the elevator turned in surprise and looked at Debra and Brett.

"Yes, I'm forbidding you to go."

"You're . . . are you telling me you're . . ." She was lost for words.

He turned away from her and faced the closed doors of the elevator, wondering what type of explosion he'd have to face.

"The hell you are," she hissed. "I'm the United Nations' chief scientific advisor right now on this issue, and if I want to go to Boston, I'll go to Boston."

"No, you won't," he said quietly.

"By what authority do you forbid me to do anything?" The two others at the elevator had turned back as the doors were hissing open but didn't want to miss a moment of the exchange.

"By the authority of the president of the United States. You will not be going to Boston or anywhere until my colleagues on the destination ground have thoroughly checked it out. You've given us no time and so . . ."

"I only made the decision ten minutes ago as a result of a phone call I made to the virology laboratory that's working with us. And anyway, how will you stop me? What'll you do, arrest me for boarding a plane?"

He forced himself not to smile, anticipating her reaction. "Yes."

She turned in shock and faced him. So did the other two in the elevator. "You'd arrest me?"

"Yes," Brett said simply. It was a scenario he'd played out a dozen times before with other important people who thought they could use their status to undermine his role in protecting their lives. He knew only too well how this scenario would play out.

"You'd arrest me? You'd actually arrest me for traveling to Boston?"

"No, I'd arrest you under National Security Enforcement legislation for failure to comply with a lawful request from a Secret Service agent."

Furious, she hissed, "You asshole. As soon as I'm out of this elevator, I'm going to phone the president of the United States, and then we'll see who's going where."

She was so predictable; it was almost like child's play. Even the most brilliant person, confronted with laws, restrictions, and empowerment they'd never previously experienced—out of their comfort zone—resorted to bluster and gales of outrage. An ordinary person would shout, "I know my rights," even when they didn't, but somebody like Debra, a close confidante of the president, would fall back on her connections to protect her. And he knew what would happen in a few moments.

"Debra," he said gently, "you can phone whomsoever you like, but you're not going to Boston and if you try to board a flight, I'll arrest you."

The elevator doors opened and the two other passengers walked out with huge grins on their faces, anxious for their watercooler moment when they could tell their colleagues what they'd overheard. Brett and Debra stepped into the building's foyer, he biting back a smile, she fuming with impotence. And if she continued to sing on the familiar song sheet, she'd soon start negotiating. Which is precisely what happened next.

"Why are you doing this, Brett? Playing the hairy-chested he-man? You know I have to travel. You know you can't stop me. So why?"

"Debra, at the White House, I said you have to tell me of your intention to travel to destinations. We have to protect you and ensure that when you land or arrive, you're in no danger. That means while you're still on the plane, I have to get my colleagues in Boston to be ready to meet you, escort you through the terminal and into a secure vehicle, while their colleagues are sanitizing the place you're traveling to so that they can ensure it's a safe environment. That's all I'm asking."

She remained silent as they walked to the second elevator that would take them down to the underground parking lot.

Softly, she said, "But you know I've only just arranged . . ."

"Which is why I'll allow you to go to Boston, on the condition that you take a later flight to give my guys time to do their jobs. Okay?"

She turned and looked at him in surprise. "You'll allow me?"

"Yes. Debra, you have to understand something. While you're under presidential orders for reasons of national security, I'm the one who makes decisions about where you go and what you do. You might not like it, but until this emergency is downgraded or called off, you are under a legal obligation to follow my orders. Now I don't ever want to get into the position, like just now, of pushing my weight around, but if I consider that something might endanger you, then I will take every step to ensure that you remain safe and well. I'm here to keep you alive, Debra, even if it means my own death. I'm not here to show you how hairy-chested I am. Please let me do my job so you can do yours and save lives."

They reached the armor-plated bulletproof car, and he asked her to stand well back while he examined the underside for bombs. She watched him on all fours, making himself dirty to ensure her safety. She realized that she'd gone too far and that he was, in reality, just protecting her against a very real threat.

And she wondered whether or not he did have a hairy chest.

* * *

The following morning, after all the safety checks had been made, Debra stood in front of the viewing panel of the electron microscope. She'd never before entered the Harvard University's School of Public Health and was amazed at the stunning array of ultra-modern equipment that the school used. Debra had landed at Boston's Logan Airport aboard a specially chartered flight just an hour before to be taken by a security convoy to Huntington Avenue where the school was located. Students along the way had turned in surprise as the convoy roared past, lights flashing. Traffic lights turned to green so the convoy wasn't halted, enabling her to get directly to her meeting with the chair of the Department of Virology.

And now she looked in surprise at the clump of chemicals in the aperture. "That's it?" she asked.

Professor Avi Mizrachi nodded and in his heavy Israeli accent said, "Dat's one of dem. Der are six others. We were concentrating on the morphology of the Hendra virus, but we also took blood and tissue samples from other bats in other locations where outbreak develop. Indonesia, Venezuela, London, Australia, and the others."

She stared at the color-enhanced image of the virus. Avi knew that Debra was as much of an expert on viruses as was he and that he didn't need to explain that in order to show the virus, he'd had to increase the contrast between it and the background. He'd used electron-dense stains to bring out its shape. His favorite, and the one that he'd used on all the virus samples he'd been sent, was a tungsten stain that scattered the electrons from his microscope's gun and the staining showed the detail of the virus to magical effect.

"So what's its structure?" she asked.

"Dey all different. Dat's astounding thing. The one from Australia, the Hendra virus, de von dat got passed to dogs, it's a mutational variant of the *Paramyxoviridae* family. Its morphology is different, though, in the protein casing. The entire virus is two hundred twenty nanometers long and one hundred twenty wide. Fairly average. But we're studying why so virulent. The other viruses are helical or are icosahedral. Seriously mixed bunch. To be honest, Debra, if you hadn't told me that they cause roughly same type symptoms, I say they attacked different organisms— maybe plants, maybe lower animals, maybe cause colds or sores. But such different viruses with such distinct shapes; to say they responsible for these hideous outbreaks . . . surprising."

"So finding a treatment, an antiviral drug common to all these infections, is going to be difficult," she said, walking from one screen to another to see what her enemy looked like.

Professor Mizrachi didn't answer. His silence was eloquent testimony to the uphill battle she was facing. "You have how many laboratories working on antivirals?" he asked.

"None. Well, just us, really."

"None? This cannot you do on your own," he said in tortured English. "This could be a pandemic. This worse could be than Spanish flu after First World War. Fifty million killed. Are you *meshuggah*?"

By now, a number of his colleagues had joined him and were listening to the conversation intently. They all knew of Debra, both personally having met at conferences or by her reputation in the Atlanta Center for Disease Control. And they knew her more recently by her television appearances standing beside some of the most powerful people on earth.

"Debra, you have to let researchers at Harvard work on antiviral drug . . . or drugs. And LA and Chicago and Paris and London . . . essential we find way of stopping this thing. Its virulence could wipe out a quarter or even a half world population. Think of Black Plague in the middle ages . . ."

His assault on her was halted by Brett Anderson suddenly appearing out of nowhere and handing her his telephone. "For you," he said.

She smiled and excused herself, taking the phone and answering it.

"Hi Debra. I have the president on the line for you. One moment please."

"Debra?"

"Yes, Mr. President." She didn't even notice the way Avi and the other Harvard scientists looked at her in amazement.

"Debra, I want you back in the White House as soon as possible."

"What's up?"

"Just get back here."

LATER THAT DAY, IN WASHINGTON

After the second appointment missed and ten phone calls to her mobile went unanswered, Kathy Moss, personal assistant to Christine Knowles, Deputy Secretary of Health and Human Services, phoned through to Human Resources to say that she was concerned about her boss's welfare. It was rare for Miss Knowles to miss a day's work, let alone not phone through with a reason.

Because of the security clampdown on government offices and personnel due to the murder the previous day of Secretary Harper, normal procedure—phoning several times before sending somebody around to her apartment—was replaced by a Secret Service officer going personally to her home. When there was no response, he broke down the door. The moment he entered, he phoned through to his boss.

"Code Red." He gave the address, withdrew his gun, and searched the apartment. When he was satisfied that he was alone with the corpse, he waited for reinforcements to arrive. His training told him not to touch a single thing but to wait for forensic scientists. Having ascertained that she was clearly dead and had been for probably many hours, he didn't even touch the note she was still gripping in her dead claw that once was her hand.

* * *

The president handed photocopies of the note around to his security people, those cabinet secretaries whom he'd invited, Debra, and his chief of staff. They all read it quickly, but the content was clear enough.

"The bitch," said the secretary of state. "So it was CHAT after all."

"Looks like it," said the president. "We've arrested their office staff for questioning, and we're turning over their computers and documents as we speak. But at least we know how the details leaked out about whether it was bats or other vectors that were causing this plague."

"Do you think there's anybody else at Health who was working with her?" asked the secretary.

The president shrugged. "We're questioning her direct reports and her administrative staff, but they seem genuinely stunned. Look, she was a cat- and bird-loving lonely woman with no husband or partner and almost no family, except a sister in New York, no social life and looking forward to a retirement of loneliness and ill health. From the reports, in her younger days, she was an up-and-comer, but for the past twenty years, she's been a time server with little enough to occupy her mind."

Nathanial Jefferson Thomas, president of the United States, looked around at the faces of his colleagues. But one of them was frowning.

"You have a problem Ted."

Ted Marmoullian, head of White House security, said, "Damn right I do. Sorry, Mr. President, but I think this letter is a crock. I know it's in her handwriting, but I think she's been the subject of a double-blind. She thinks that she was giving information to CHAT to help protect animals and that led her to the inevitable conclusion it was CHAT that killed Secretary Harper. That's why the old bitch whacked herself. But I'll bet you a bottle of fifty-year-old bourbon that they'll find nothing that will tie CHAT to the murders. I think this woman killed herself in grief because she felt responsible for a crime she thought she had helped perpetrate. But the real killers probably had no idea of Christine Knowles's existence. She was a bit player and CHAT's name was used by the people who organized the actual killing of Secretary Harper and her family. No, Mr. President, my money's still on WEL and that bastard Stuart Chalmers."

* * *

Unless it's a major assault against the country such as 9/11, the news cycle, even one obsessed with the murder of a cabinet secretary, tends to last little more than two or three days. Not that the news disappears; it just leaves page one to enter the graveyard of page fifteen and beyond.

But the moment the White House correspondents for the major television networks and newspapers of record began sniffing details of a lower-grade Health Department official who'd killed herself soon after the death of Secretary Harper and her family, the speculation ran white hot. Demands were made of the presidential media spokesperson, Aphra Howard, to front the correspondents so she could answer questions. After a hurried consultation with the president and a briefing from his chief of staff, she entered the media room and read a brief statement.

> DC police are currently investigating the death of Christine Knowles, Deputy Secretary of Health and Human Services, whose body was found in her apartment this morning when she failed to answer her phone and didn't turn up for work. We have no further details at this time and will release a full report as soon as the police and other authorities have had time to investigate her death.

She knew that the media throng would demand more. She was right. As she began to answer questions, the president watched her performance on closed circuit television from his Oval Office.

"Aphra, is it true that Ms. Knowles committed suicide?"

"I can't comment at this time."

"Is her death linked with the murder of Secretary DeAnne Harper and her family?"

"We're not ruling out anything at this stage until the police have concluded their investigation."

Smelling blood, two dozen reporters put up their hands, but the question went to Lyddy Outram, the seventy-nine-year-old veteran Mother of the House who worked for *Time Magazine* and who had outlasted five presidents. In her harsh and creaking voice, she asked, "There are rumors that Professor Stuart Chalmers was in police custody yesterday morning and was questioned about the possible involvement of his militant organization Whole Earth League in Secretary Harper's murder. Was Ms.

Knowles also questioned by police and is that the reason she committed suicide?"

Aphra Howard looked startled as the elderly reporter spiked her with a question she wasn't expecting. As was the president. But once the name of the WEL was out to the public, he knew that he had to contain this thing. He rose immediately from his chair and marched to the door to walk the short distance from the Oval Office to the media center in the White House.

"Don't, Mr. President," shouted his chief of staff who was monitoring the press conference. "Don't sir. Don't get involved. Aphra is quite capable of handling . . ."

President Nathanial Thomas paced along the corridors to the surprise of his staff and thrust open the door of the media room. As the entire White House media pack looked up in surprise, the front row stood, and immediately the whole room was on its feet. He mounted the podium and waved them to sit.

"Please excuse me, Aphra, for butting into your conference, but I was watching on my television and I wanted to answer these issues personally. It's important, ladies and gentlemen, that you hear this from the president of the United States."

He turned to the Lyddy Outram who'd just asked the question about WEL. "Lyddy, you've just mentioned Professor Stuart Chalmers and the Whole Earth League. We can neither confirm nor deny WEL's involvement in recent terrorist assaults against this country. Yes," he said as people in the room gasped and hurriedly scribbled down his explosive words, "I said terrorist. Of course we're waiting on forensic and investigatory evidence about Secretary Harper's murder and the killing of her entire family, but it's pretty obvious from the residue of the explosive C-4 found in the basement of her house that this was a planned, merciless, and evil killing of one of the most senior public servants who had devoted her life to the good of the United States. Not a gas explosion, nor an accident but a vicious terrorist murder of a fine American and her family.

"Which leads to the obvious conclusion that this crime was perpetrated by a person or persons who were not criminals, but criminal terrorists.

Perhaps an overseas terrorist, but much more likely, indeed almost certainly, a homegrown one; a latter-day Timothy McVeigh fighting for his or her perverted belief that animal life is more sacred than human life. At the moment, we don't have sufficient evidence against any one individual or group. We're concentrating massive efforts of all our branches of law enforcement against well-known radical animal liberationists. Yes, Lyddy, we're investigating WEL and CHAT and many other animal liberation groups. As president of the United States, I won't sit by and allow little children, men, and women in this country to die horrible deaths in order to protect an animal or insect species that is the vector for this new danger to our society.

"Some in America might have problems with us killing animals to protect ourselves. That's a topic that I'm sure will be discussed endlessly in ethics classes and university debating societies. But I'm charged by my oath of office to protect and defend this country. And by God, that's what I'm going to do, regardless of animal or plant liberationists, or any other extremist group who gets in my way."

He turned and walked from the podium, ignoring the shouts of the media to answer some questions. As he paced back to his office, his chief of staff, surrounded by his assistants, thought about the repair work he'd now have to do to mollify the entire environmental movement in the United States and overseas and wondered whether Dwight Eisenhower's chief of staff ever had to do more for his boss than arrange golf partners.

* * *

That evening, the early news segments on network and cable channels carried the type of headline that sent PR people and lobbyists into a flat spin. "In an extraordinary outburst, President Thomas launches an all-out assault on militant conservation and animal rights organizations as he vows to put people before animals."

The image on the screen of the newsreader was immediately replaced by the president behind the podium promising to protect and defend the country regardless of animal or plant liberationists. The clip was instantly followed by the anchor questioning the channel's White House reporter, positioned on the lawn outside the West Wing, asking him about today's unprecedented outburst. "Not within living memory, Angela, can any correspondent remember the president bursting into the White House briefing room, interrupting his press secretary, virtually expelling her from the stage, and launching into a full throttle assault like this. It was reminiscent of the fire and brimstone sermons of Pentecostal preachers thumping their pulpits. When he left the briefing room, his spokesperson, Aphra Howard, tried bravely to regain her composure, but you could tell that this was an extraordinary moment in presidential history, one which will be the talk of Washington town for years to come."

"So what does this all mean for animal species, Jim?"

"Well, Angela, that's the big question because if ever there was a declaration of war, this was it. The president was saying in no uncertain terms that if any animal species, be it bird, bat, farm animal, feral animal, or insect is found to be the cause of these hideous outbreaks and deaths in communities all around the world, then the president will order their extermination, regardless of outcries from animal liberationists. From his mood today, you can be absolutely certain that he won't tolerate any interference from animal rights movements, conservation NGOs, or animal welfare groups. I don't know how else to express it, Angela, but as of today, the United States is at war, at war with those animals that are making us sick. The weapon in this battle for survival is science, the enemy is . . . well, you tell me."

* * *

Debra Hart and the rapidly increasing number of assistants, colleagues, scientists, and doctors, who had joined her International Task Force working with increasing intensity in their laboratories and offices, weren't aware that there was a battle going on in the White House, a three-way standoff between the government, the media, and animal welfare organizations.

Because her role wasn't any longer that of a scientist but of administrator and team leader, she had been removed from both the laboratory and the spotlight beside the president of the United States. In her new and unaccustomed role as bureaucrat—the type of person she'd only recently felt little for but contempt—Debra's ear was almost permanently attached to a mobile phone, speaking in increasingly clipped sentences because of the volume of calls she was forced to take. Mostly, she spoke in her car, driven by her security man, Brett Anderson, as it transported her from meeting to conference, laboratory to government office, university to airport.

But her growing understanding of the politics of what she was involved in had recently become acute, and today, her radar told her that something big, very big, was happening on the political scene. She usually got a couple of phone calls from the media during the day, asking her for comments on what some politician or demagogue or religious extremist had said. Generally, she made a "no comment" or referred the caller back to the press office at the White House. But suddenly, starting in the middle of the morning, she was being called to make a guest appearance on high profile talk shows or to talk in-studio with some famous radio host.

When her phone had temporarily given her a few minutes of silence, she called the president's PA—a number she'd only dialed three times since he'd given her access to one of the world's most carefully guarded numbers.

"Hello Debra," said the PA.

"Hi, I was just wondering if something had happened that I'm not aware of. I'm getting all these calls from the media, and they won't tell me why they want me in the studio."

"Just refer them all to the press office, dear," said his PA. "The president made some . . . how shall I say this . . . confronting remarks in the middle of the morning about how he was going to put people before animals, and . . . well, not to put too fine a point on it, the shit's hit the fan. We're getting inundated with complaints from animal rights groups and Lord knows who else. Don't you get involved in it, Debra. You've got far too important a task to waste time with the sort of nonsense we have to deal with here."

She switched off the phone. It was the first time it had been properly turned off since she'd been given it by the White House. As they drove, Agent Brett Anderson glanced across at her.

"Problem?" he asked.

She laughed. "When hasn't there been a problem in the past couple of months?"

They drove toward George Washington University, where she had a meeting with some academics.

"I guess life is pretty tough for you right now," he said. "Do you miss your old lifestyle in Atlanta?"

"Some. But even though I was doing some cutting edge stuff down there, it was still pretty dull. All work and no play."

"You sound like me, Debra. Nobody in your life, aside from work."

She suddenly realized that even though they'd been side by side for days now, they'd never engaged in any personal conversations. She was too busy getting into and out of vehicles and buildings, reading papers and reports while he drove, making phone calls, and sending text messages. And now, to her embarrassment, she didn't even know whether or not he was married, had kids, a mother and father, or what his hobbies were.

"You're a workaholic?" she asked.

He smiled. "Not exactly, but there are ever-present dangers in this job, and I just never wanted to marry while I was a Secret Service agent. I don't want any kids of mine to grow without a father."

She was shocked. "Do many of your colleagues . . . I mean, have any of them died . . ."

He sighed. "More than a few over the years. We're the guys that jump between a gunman and our client. We take bullets destined for very important people. That's our job."

Until this moment, she'd viewed Brett as little more than her driver, a man employed to take her from place to place, but with a security blanket thrown in. Suddenly, she saw him as a man who would die to protect her.

"I'm sorry, Brett. I've underestimated your role. With all the fuss and bother over the past few days, I didn't stop to think . . ."

He smiled and reached over to touch her arm in friendship. "Don't worry about it. I should be invisible right up until that moment, which God forbid should ever happen, when suddenly you need me. And then I'll be there for you."

She sat back in her seat, his hand still on her arm. She liked the warmth, the personal touch. And she liked the fact that he'd said he'd be there for her. He was a rugged man, taller than her, far more muscular than most, but his strength was hidden by a natural softness, the gentleness of an intelligent man who ensured that his body was as highly tuned as his mind.

"What are your interests, Brett? I know nothing about you."

"Music. Mainly music. That's how I relax when I come home at night."

"And what type of music?"

"Opera; chamber music; mainly sixteenth to nineteenth century."

"Wow," she said. "I didn't expect that."

"Most people don't. I have a doctorate in ancient music. Before I went into the Secret Service, I was teaching the History of Music at Vassar."

She burst out laughing. "You're kidding! Vassar!"

He laughed as well. "Its reputation comes from the time when it was women only, but it's been coed for years. Unfortunately, I was forced to leave after just two terms because I ran afoul of a woman known as the Poughkeepsie Pitchfork. She was a militant feminist who wanted to return Vassar to its glory days of women only. She made up this story and spread scandalous rumors about how I'd had a relationship with a sophomore. It was completely untrue, and I was exonerated because the girl swore on a Bible that I'd never even touched her. But that didn't stop life becoming increasingly bitchy and unbearable with faculty and students, and no matter how I protested my innocence, there were remarks and looks and innuendo. So I saw work advertised for this department. I applied and here I am."

Softly, mischievously, Debra asked, "And honestly, between us, was there any truth to the rumors?"

"I could tell you, but then I'd have to kill you."

She looked at him in shock, but saw that he was grinning.

* * *

The first big gun to fire at the president was the CEO of People for Ethical Coexistence with Animals, Candice Shar, a former lecturer in the history of philosophy of science at Brandeis University who'd become increasingly horrified by the use of monkeys in medical experiments and had left her tenured post to head up what was now one of America's biggest lobby groups. She was appearing on *Meet the Media* in a head-to-head debate with the show's host, Mike O'Brien.

"Surely," O'Brien said, two minutes into the interview, "nobody could fault the president for putting human beings before animals."

She gave him her most devastating smile and remained totally composed, a trick she'd learned during her media training, "Of course not, Mike. If there's a vector that is killing people, then we have to rid ourselves of the vector. Indeed, science through the ages has always elevated humankind into the ranks of a separate species that must be defended at all costs—except when there was an exceptional departure from the imperative to care for humanity, of course, like the Nazis.

"But that's not what President Thomas is proposing. He's promising species extinction on the off chance that it's the species that is causing the problem. Sure, when it's viruses or bacteria like the Black Death, then we have to take measures to prevent a pandemic, and if that means killing sewer rats, so be it. Or when black cats were thought to be consorts of witches, the poor little things were slaughtered in the thousands by frightened townsfolk. But that's not what we're talking about here. President Thomas is talking about exterminating any species that might pose a threat to humanity. Might, not *is* . . . and that could include birds, mice, dogs, cats . . . you name it, and you'll find that huge numbers of virulent illnesses have been caused by some bacterium or virus or parasite crossing the species barrier into human beings. The proximity of people living cheek by jowl with animals sometimes causes these adventurous viruses or bacteria to cross the species barrier and infect horses or pigs or even human beings.

"If we handle the horses or eat the pork, very occasionally we could die. That's how there are occasional outbreaks of Ebola. And sometimes dogs or cats give their owners terrible medical problems when an animal parasite or fluke gets into the human body. But the president is talking about the extermination of heaven knows what numbers of animals, even entire species, just because of a miniscule number of problems.

"Look, Mike, the last thing I want to do is to cause a panic for pet lovers, but the last time somebody talked about exterminating a species because they were a germ dangerous to humanity, was Adolf Hitler. You know what happened to the Jews in the death camps of Europe, don't you? And I'd have to say that President Thomas is as much an agent of evil to cats and dogs and pet rabbits, as Adolf Hitler was to the Jews."

Astounded, Mike O'Brien said, "You're not serious, are you?"

"I've never been more serious. Who do you think caused these diseases in animals? Mankind, that's who! How? Simple! By the way we're extinguishing the habitat and because of global warming caused by our use of fossil fuels, we're making the viral load in their bodies explode because of the stresses we're putting them under. And so as the perpetrator of these problems, we're now proposing to exterminate the entire species to cure what we're responsible for. Is that ethical? I don't think so. And neither will the American people think so when they realize what the president of their country is planning to do to their pets."

* * *

Debra Hart hated early morning meetings, but when the president of the United States calls you personally and asks you to breakfast, it's incumbent to sound chipper and eager. She pulled on a dress, brushed her hair, still dampish from the shower, and ran downstairs from her fifth-level apartment. Normally, Brett would have just arrived to take over from the overnight shift, and the two of them would go for a five-mile morning jog as a prelude to her crushingly busy schedule, and then back to the apartment to shower and dress. He was the model of propriety and never intruded on her personal space in the apartment. And he even used to get her breakfast ready while she was in the bathroom. She really liked to hear a man busying in the kitchen while she was putting on her makeup and clothes. It was a sound she'd only heard once since she'd left her family home to attend the university—when she was living with a man, but it hadn't worked out and so most of her days indoors were spent in her own company.

Today though was different, for she knew that breakfast with the president meant there would be no exercise the whole day. Brett had been called by Ted Marmoullian and was told to meet Debra at the White House. As she left her building, she saw that the limo and two security vehicles were parked outside.

Ten minutes later, she was escorted into the Jefferson Room in the West Wing and sat at the table being scrutinized by a portrait showing the unyielding stare of one of the most brilliant men ever to live in this building. Lining the walls were buffet tables laid out with silver salvers covered by large silver domes. Her stomach ached smelling the divine food that lay beneath. Suddenly the door opened, and Nathaniel Thomas walked in unaccompanied. He was wearing slacks and a knit shirt and for the first time, Debra saw that he was lean and had a muscular body. He'd probably been for his early morning forty-lap swim and was now freshly showered. She stood as he entered.

Thomas walked over and gave her a peck on the cheek. It was warm and touching and friendly, a kiss between friends with no sexuality attached, but the moment surged through her body like an electric shock.

"Thanks for coming in Debra. Sorry to drag you from your bed."

He invited her to pick up a plate, and before she even reached the buffet, like a well-oiled Swiss cuckoo clock, two adjacent doors suddenly opened, and stewards appeared as if by magic from doorways and lifted the salver domes to reveal a smorgasbord of breakfast foods underneath. She chose poached eggs, four rashers of bacon, beans, French toast, and a slice of ham. The president chose just the eggs and whole grain toast.

"Debra, I've rather thrown the pigeons to the cat and there are a lot of feathers flying."

"Yes, Mr. President, the White House media center emailed me a video of your speech and also the reaction from the talk shows. I guess there's no point trying to hide our intent now, is there?"

"Was I wrong in saying what I did? I've had a lot of adverse reaction but a lot of support as well."

"I don't think it's for me to comment on whether what you said was right or wrong, sir."

He looked disappointed. "Debra, if there's one thing I've expected from you, and from my entire staff, it's to be honest in your opinions and to tell me what they truly think, especially if they disagree with me. I can't make a judgement unless I know all sides of an argument."

She smiled. It was so different from the George W. Bush or Richard Nixon White Houses when all they wanted to hear were opinions that agreed with theirs.

"What you said was right, sir, but the way you said it was wrong. You can't alienate conservationists and animal lovers if you want to bring a majority of the population behind you."

"Sometimes, you need something to cut through all the humbug and bullshit. We could have gone on for weeks not telling the American people what we know to be the truth until it had been established scientifically. And we could have evaded issues because we were scared that we'd frightening the citizens, or we could have sidestepped out of concern we might get one of the lobby groups off side. But I judged that this was one of those times when we just had to level with the public. People were scared, and they needed to know the whole truth, all at once, not dribbled out piecemeal in ten-second media grabs as I was entering my helicopter. Once the American people are informed of the full extent of the problem, they can cope with it. But if rumors start to fly around, they just don't know where they stand and that leads to panic."

She nodded. "You're right. But you've played straight into the hands of the animal rights lobby. They've now started a fear campaign that you're going to send storm troopers into people's homes at night and forcibly steal their puppies and kittens and baby bunny rabbits and kill them in the most heartless way. If you'd just said 'bats,' then you'd have a problem on your hands but not a disaster. This thing is turning into a category one PR nightmare. The animal liberationists are coming out in force now, and they're . . ."

He smiled. She looked at him quizzically.

"What?"

He continued to look at her and smile.

And then it dawned on her. "You did it on purpose, didn't you?"

The president remained silent.

"You deliberately forced the hand of the animal rights lobby, didn't you?"

As his tactic dawned on her, Debra smiled a beaming smile. "You provoked them to show their hand and to become extremist. Didn't you?"

He nodded. "What's happened now is that they're using Holocaust symbolism as I knew they would. They're calling me Hitler and going over the top. Before, they were using arguments of humanity and decency, so to shut them up, to spike their guns, I had to force them into a position where they'd take an extremist, hysterical position and put up the barricades to any scientific rationality.

"What's going to happen now is that the media will side with you and me because we're going to present ourselves as mild, reasoned, scientific, rational, responsible, and reasonable. You and me, we were the ones who were in danger of being painted as the extremists, as the murdering fascists who'd destroy all animal life in a Hitlerian orgy to protect the master race. But by spiking their guns, by forcing them out into the open, as soon as we explain to people what we're doing, we'll present the antithesis of their hysteria. We'll be saying that we're not going after people's pets. We're going after whatever is the vector for this mutating trans-species virus. We're going to say in all likelihood it's bats, that bats live in horribly unsanitary conditions, that we're going to euthanize only those colonies where the disease is found so that there's the least suffering or danger to the species."

"We?"

"We. You and me. We're going on television, on the talk shows. Directly into people's homes. I'm the president; you're the scientist I've entrusted with finding out what to do about this virus. We're the team. Is that okay with you? Because if it's not, I'm going to have to charge you for that breakfast you're eating."

12

For the first time since his adolescence, a time of self-doubt, introspection, and an explosive curiosity about sex, Stuart Chalmers was unsure of himself. As he walked, he felt as if the pavement was no longer solid but contained hidden traps and fissures through which he could fall at any moment.

Everything in his life for the past twenty-two years had been cogitated, planned, and programmed down to the minute. At the beginning of each year, he knew precisely what he'd be doing and where he'd be at the end of the year. From his graduate school studies to the nature of the thesis that had sparked the interest of a particular academic under whom he wanted to study at Oxford's Magdalen College where he'd been awarded a D.Phil in pre-Socratic philosophy, to his decision to accept a lectureship at a middle-ranking mid-Western university instead of Harvard, Princeton, or Yale so that he could build his WEL empire out of the sight and scrutiny of the FBI, all had been carefully thought through.

He'd constructed WEL so that nothing the organization did to shove aside humanity in his efforts to save the global biosphere could be tracked back to him. Long before Al-Qaeda became a household word, Stuart had constructed an organization that was so tightly controlled that it was impenetrable. It was impossible for security agencies to breach because nobody knew more about anything or anybody in WEL than who was at the same level. Even from the beginning of the era of the Internet and cell phones, Stuart had quickly realized that while they may be brilliant methods of communication, they would also allow governments to follow and listen in on the conversations and thoughts of its citizenry; so all communications from the very beginning of WEL were whispered, face-to-face and in parks and open spaces.

And from the early days, there'd been a surprising number of successes—closing down animal research laboratories, killing several high-profile medical researchers who experimented on nonhuman species, bombing the headquarters of food companies that factory farmed animals . . . the list of covert crimes his organization had committed was growing longer and longer. And the genius was that the blame almost always centered on other organizations like PECA, PETA, and CHAT. Best of all was the fact that the organization headed up by the vacuous airhead PECA boss Candice Shar, who ran People for Ethical Co-existence with Animals as though it were her personal fiefdom, and a number of other animal welfare NGOs were now under scrutiny for the recent murder of Secretary DeAnne Harper.

But just yesterday morning, the world seemed to have caved in on Stuart's head. The president of the United States himself had identified Stuart by name, at a White House press conference, as a person under suspicion. Since then he and WEL had been hounded by the media and just an hour ago, he'd been summoned to attend a meeting of the board of regents of the University of Wisconsin, where he was head of the Philosophy Department of The School of the Mind.

Okay, so most of the board were worthies from the local area and probably had little more than Bachelor's degrees; they almost certainly watched Fox for their news and information and thought that the Republicans were too socialist as a political party; but they had the power to close him down if they suspected that there was any fire behind President Thomas's smoke.

As he walked over to the administration block where the board of regents was meeting, he practiced what he'd say, assuming the nature of the questions he'd be asked.

The administrative secretary showed him in. The room made an unconvincing statement of a faux British university senate meeting room, replete with dark mahogany wood tables, dressers, walls lined with thousands of unread books, the obligatory oil paintings of previous regents, and patriotic flags unfurled in corners. At its center was a vast refectory table. Sitting around the table were twenty worthy men and women, dressed in somber clothes as though attending a funeral . . . his funeral. An empty chair had been placed at the end of the table, opposite where Professor Matthew Wadick, the president of the university, sat.

"Thank you for joining us, Professor Chalmers," he said. But there was neither courtesy nor warmth in his voice. "It must have come to your attention that the president of the United States yesterday identified you as a suspect in the dastardly murder of the Secretary of Health DeAnne Harper. I find it beyond belief that this university has been dragged into the very epicenter, the vortex, of such a treasonous terrorist act. This is one of America's finest universities, and for a senior member of our staff to be accused, by the president of the United States, no less, of a crime of the most amoral proportions is . . ."

"Perhaps," interrupted the professor of English, a man Stuart hardly knew, "we could ask Professor Chalmers what he knows, rather than make provocative statements that merely reiterate the content of today's newspapers. I was invited to a meeting of the board of regents, not to Torquemada's Inquisition. I would like to hear what Professor Chalmers has to say before we hang, draw, and quarter him."

Chalmers nodded to the professor of English. "For a man who has committed no crime, who has been falsely accused by the organs of governmental authority, who has been vilified by the media before I've even had a chance to state my side of the situation, I can honestly say that right now, I feel somewhat akin to Alfred Dreyfus."

He glanced around the table. Some of the men and women were frowning. From their quizzical expressions, it was obvious that they hadn't heard of Dreyfus. "He was the French army intelligence officer who was accused of treason in 1894. None of the evidence pointed toward him. He constantly protested his innocence and love of France. But because he was Jewish and France was a hotbed of anti-Semitism, he was found guilty and sent to Devil's Island.

"Like Dreyfus over a century ago, I've been accused of a hideous crime I didn't commit. In the place of anti-Semitism, we have a national epidemic of fear caused by microbes whose origin we don't know. That fear has mutated, like the virus we're trying to fight, into an irrational hatred of those of us who believe in a whole and integrated earth where every living organism, sentient or not, is precious. And this irrational hatred is being used by this government and this president to assail those of us who stand up for the rights of animals who can't defend themselves . . ."

"Professor Chalmers," interrupted the president of the university, "it is not appropriate for you to lecture us on ecology or environmentalism. We're here to listen to your response to the terrible accusations made against you by President Thomas just yesterday. And I must warn you that your very tenure, your role as teacher and researcher at this university, is hanging by a thread."

Chalmers fought back a smile. It was all so boringly predictable. He had practiced his response. "Might I remind you, President, and you ladies and gentlemen regents, that this very university was founded on the bedrock of truth—of teaching the young the principles of discovering that very truth by research, learning from it to become truly great citizens of this nation; that the underlying statute of this great university is to listen with an open mind, to learn from established facts, to dispense with falsities and misrepresentations and instead use the power of our minds to discover the very essence of certainty.

"Yet I am prejudged by you, President Wadick, as a guilty party who has to prove his innocence. All right, let me prove to you that I'm innocent of the crime perpetrated against this government when Secretary Harper and her family were murdered. I was teaching in New York at the time. Three hours after she and her family were killed two hundred miles away in Washington, DC, I was dragged out of my bed in Manhattan by federal agents and cross-examined about any association I might have had with this deed. My clothes were forensically examined and nothing whatsoever was discovered. And after intense questioning, I was released with an apology."

"Then why did the president name you as a suspect?" asked President Wadick.

"Because the organization which I have created, the Whole Earth League, has become the fall guy for the militant and insane animal liberation organizations which do commit terrorist acts. Organizations like the

Campaign for Humane Animal Treatment have, to my certain knowledge, killed people and bombed laboratories. And because they can cover their tracks so brilliantly because they're Machiavellian in their behavior, they've managed to tar and feather my Whole Earth League in the eyes of the authorities. I'm a one-man band. They're a multi-million dollar organization with vast resources, with PR departments and people who can advise them on explosives and bombing and such. Me? I'm just a professor teaching brilliant and beautiful young men and women how to think.

"These organizations do the crimes, and I become the monster. But ask yourselves one simple question: if I'm guilty as charged, why haven't I been arrested and imprisoned long before now? Not because I'm an arch criminal who can cover his tracks. Frankly, ladies and gentlemen, I'm just a philosopher, an innocent abroad. Yet I'm accused of running such a covert organization that not even the sophistication of the investigative authorities with all their electronic surveillance and cyber connectivity, can uncover what I'm doing. And no, ladies and gentlemen, I was not party to murder and mayhem, which I find ethically and morally abhorrent. No, the truth is that like Dreyfus, I'm a scapegoat. And if you fire me, then I become your scapegoat."

"Fine words, Professor, but you've still dragged the university into being front page news in the worst possible way, and . . ."

"And it's my responsibility to extricate you from this mess. Fire me and you'll go halfway to absolving yourself, but there'll still be questions about how much you knew and why you condoned a terrorist in your bosom for so many years. And if I resign and issue a statement of innocence, the smell will still attach to the university. But . . ."

Stuart Chalmers looked around the table. All eyes and ears were on him. Oh, it was all too easy, he thought. He was playing them as though they were eager parents sitting in the audience of a sixth-grade musical. "But if I call a press conference and publicly close down the Whole Earth League by denying any involvement with terrorism, if I say that this terrible disease which is ballooning out of control needs drastic and draconian measures to solve it, and animals and plants have to take second place in the scheme of things to the needs of humanity, then I'll come across as a voice of moderation and concern. And if I go further and speak on behalf of the university to assure the American public that we will throw the enormous weight of our scientific community behind all efforts to eradicate this terrible virus or bacillus, then we'll come across as the good guys."

He remained silent, waiting for the response.

* * *

"You're kidding."

Ted Marmoullian, head of White House security, shook his head and showed the president a copy of the press conference. Nathaniel Thomas read it in a few moments, skipping much but picking up on the main points.

"The unctuous, smarmy, rotten bastard. Okay, what does this mean?" he asked.

"It means he'll go even further underground. Now he's dumped WEL, he'll cut loose the few of the organizational cells we've been able to trace to him that we're currently monitoring, and we won't know what they're up to. It's been hell's own job in tracking his activities because he doesn't use the Internet, and we're pretty sure that when he uses the telephone, he buys a once only throwaway that is impossible to trace. But now he's made such a public demonstration of closing down his group, we're going to have to call in every favor the National Security Agency owes us even to find out where he buys his coffee in the morning."

"Dear God," shouted the president, "we've got the world's most sophisticated tracking and monitoring devices, we've got spy satellites and drones and vast arrays of everything, and we can't even find out what one philosophy professor is doing."

"Mr. President, if he presses a button connected to a wire in any part of the world, we can trace him instantly. But our entire monitoring and tracking system is built on the use of electronics and not human intelligence. If the guy doesn't communicate by any means invented since the eighteenth century, we're blind and dumb."

"Then for God's sake use human intelligence. The type that we used to use when Russia was the enemy and James Bond was the good guy."

"We're on it. But he has very few friends, never associates with other faculty, lives alone on a rented five-acre property, doesn't use gas or electricity but just burns wood, only rides his bicycle to school to teach and rides it back home again afterward. When he gives lectures, he travels coach at the back of the plane; if the ticket's purchased for him, it's somebody else's money but if he buys the ticket himself, he pays cash. He takes public transport to his hotel, talks to virtually nobody, and returns by public transport.

"He has one or two friends on faculty we know about, but we've hauled them in for questioning and they haven't given us a thing. He's Ted Kaczynski, the Unabomber, all over again."

Nathaniel Thomas thought for a moment, digesting the information. "So do you think that he's out of the picture now he's said he's closed down his organization?"

Marmoullian shook his head. "Never in a million years. He'll just activate resources we know nothing about. When he was questioned by the cops in Manhattan, he made a joke about you being the next target. They didn't take him seriously. I am."

* * *

It was a large park and a cold day. The wind, originating in the air above the massive inland sea that was Lake Michigan, was funneled down to Lake Monona, skimmed over the surface, and bit into their skin. But they were far enough from Wisconsin's state capital of Madison and its police and any Feds or NSA listening posts to ensure that what they had to say to each other couldn't be overheard.

Professor Jim Towney was a worried man and had demanded to meet with Stuart Chalmers sooner rather than later.

"First off," he said, still whispering behind his hand, despite the distance of the park bench from any lip-reader who could have been observing them, "you had no right to make the statements you did at the press conference without consulting me. And secondly, you . . ."

"Without consulting you?" said Chalmers. "And just who the hell do you think you are in this organization? You sit there in your academic gowns talking and plotting about saving the world, but you never stick your neck out. You never take risks. You're all talk, Jim. The most dangerous thing you've done in all your time as my second-in-command at WEL is to ride shotgun in the early days when I was planting explosives in cosmetics laboratories, or being my lookout when I was blowing up the offices of food companies using genetically engineered products. Don't get on your fucking high horse with me. I'm the one whose neck was on the chopping block when that idiot President Wadick hauled me in to the board of regents. I'm the one who was identified by the president of the United States as a terrorist. Me, Jim. Not you. So don't you ever fucking tell me what I should and shouldn't do, because you're nothing more than a myrmidon, a foot soldier, a subordinate who isn't paid to think but just to take orders, a yes-man who does what I say, when I say, and how I say."

"Go fuck yourself," Towney said as he stood to leave. But before he stormed off, he turned and said, "I was hauled in by the police yesterday. I was told that my association with you would be on my record. They said that unless I told them everything about you and your activities, my family, and my academic and personal life would be over. So don't fucking tell me that I'm just a subordinate. We run WEL together. Okay, so you're the big man out front. You're the guy who makes the speeches and who's written about in *Time Magazine*, but don't ever think that I don't take the heat for you. Because I do."

"Sit down, Jim. Stop making an asshole out of yourself. I'm sorry if what I said hurt you, but it's been a rough couple of days since . . . well, you know since when . . . and I'm feeling the strain. I shouldn't have said what I said. You've been a fantastic sounding board and a wise and valued deputy. But I had to do what I did yesterday. For all our sakes, if we're to have a future and stop mankind from destroying every plant and animal in his manic drive for supremacy. No organization is more important than the planet, Jim, and you and me, we have to save the planet from people.

"So I had to tell the world that WEL is no more. That we're supporting the president in his desire to save the human race. By doing that, the spotlight will fall on the other liberation and environmental groups. CHAT will be in trouble, not us."

He sat but was still upset by his friend's remarks. "So it's all over then. WEL is no more."

"Yep," said Stuart. He nodded and patted his friend's knee. "In the eyes of the media and the government, that's it. Good night and sweet dreams. But as far as you and I are concerned, we'll regroup after the virus or whatever it is has been cured. We'll get back together again and fight the good fight, but with so much media attention it's best that we just disband, cut the ties, and wait for the shit to stop hitting the fan. And I think it's best we don't meet again. If we do, the Feds will assume we're planning something."

Jim Towney nodded. "I'll leave first. You . . . you take care of yourself. We'll see each other again in better times."

They shook hands and Stuart watched Jim Towney walk briskly across the park to his car. When they'd first met all those years ago, everything had seemed easy. Humankind was destroying the ecosystem, exterminating species, employing its cruel and selfish mind to experiment on helpless animals, and creating monster species of pets and farm animals to supply itself with playthings or food for its own use. It was all so unnatural, and he, Jim, and a handful of others were the only ones who could see how evil and destructive the human race was. It, humanity, was the bacillus, the vast preying organism that was annihilating all the natural things in the world, and the human race had to be stopped.

All those years ago, it had seemed so easy when they'd been plotting and planning how to end the amorality of the human race in its manic destruction of the environment and plant and animal life. They'd been energized to do things. But over the years, it had been Stuart who had maintained the driving force and guiding light; Jim was little more than a hanger-on. He could have been so much more. He could have been one of the few, the very few, who'd had the foresight to try to save the biosphere. But he'd become prematurely old in mind and weak in resolve.

The animal kingdom knew what to do with those who were too old to contribute to the welfare of the pack or to fight for dominance in the tribe. The animal kingdom knew no mercy. And what was man if not a member of the animal kingdom?

A pity, in a way, that it had to happen to Jim Towney. But he was ineffective and a weight around Stuart's neck. He was running scared, and it wouldn't be long before the Feds returned and put pressure on him. Unrelenting pressure. And with absolute certainty, he'd cut himself a deal to save his neck at the expense of WEL and of Stuart. So he had to go. But which way? It had to look like suicide or an accident. And when it happened, Stuart had to be on the other side of the country—perhaps meeting with the FBI and becoming an informant against CHAT or one of the other groups. He smiled. What delicious irony—when the number two in WEL was taken out, the number one would be in a meeting with the Feds. Oh, it was a delicious and sweet mockery of the system.

But how to off Jim? And in a way that couldn't be traced back to Stuart? A car crash, maybe? Or a drug overdose at a faculty party? Or most likely, the unintended victim of a robbery—shot through the heart while the merciless killer was escaping after stealing an iPad or a pair of Nike shoes. He'd be the casual victim of mankind's insatiable lust for consumerism. And at his funeral, Stuart would deliver a heartfelt eulogy, a paean against the barbarism that was stalking the dark alleyways of humanity's unnatural urban existence.

He breathed deeply. He'd have to work it out before he bought a cheap telephone from some backstreet dealer and contacted the black kid who called himself No Slimeball. But was Noah Simball the right person? Was it too close to the killing of the old Jew in Miami, and the secretary of health in Washington? Probably, but Noah was as expendable as anybody else was, and Stuart's options were getting fewer by the day. So to protect himself and WEL, Noah would likely have to be killed afterward. Now that would be more difficult because, unlike Jim, Noah had street smarts. He would be no easy mark. And Stuart would have to do it himself.

He sighed again and stood to leave the park. Life was getting harder and harder, when all Stuart wanted to do was to put an end to mankind's destruction of all that was right and good in the world.

* * *

A thousand miles east of Wisconsin, in the Roosevelt Room opposite the Oval Office in the White House, Debra Hart was clearing her throat as she prepared to deliver what she knew would be a devastating report for the president and his most senior advisors. The sixteen chairs around the huge mahogany table were occupied by health and security officials, cabinet officers, the president and the vice president, and the president's chief scientific advisor. Seated around the walls were the deputies of the officials seated at the table, ready to take notes or to provide their boss with details, or facts. The thirty-four people in the room knew that they were in for a preliminary report from Debra's task force, but as with most preliminary reports, it almost certainly prefigured the final report that was probably weeks away.

Debra waited for the president to stop speaking before she announced what she knew would be utterly depressing. Nathaniel Thomas had been filling in his colleagues on the state of play with the terrorists who were threatening the fabric of the nation, who were determined to spare nobody's life in order to prevent the species extinction that was probably inevitable.

"So that, ladies and gentlemen, is about it. Professor Chalmers is our prime suspect, and I'm preparing to sign an order under the domestic terrorism provisions of the USA Patriot Act to arrest and incarcerate Chalmers while our law enforcement agencies sift through every square inch of his life since the day he was born. But now we'll hear from Doctor Debra Hart and the initial report of her task force into the identification and eradication of this deadly virus."

"Thank you, Mr. President. Unfortunately, though, it's not one virus, but many. And that makes it all the harder to control. In the past seven weeks, six laboratories in the United States and five overseas have been undertaking intense scientific analyses of the viruses extracted from the bodies of culled bats, birds, rats, mice, and insects, as well as the bodies of the victims of this modern plague. The good news . . . the only good news . . . is that the deadly pathogens, the viruses, seem to be exclusive to the populations of bats that have been found in the vicinity of the fatalities. We've found no abnormal, mutated, or new viruses in the bodies of other animal forms.

"But that's where the good news ends. Because each of the deadly outbreaks seems to have been caused by a different virus that, for reasons we don't fully understand, has undergone mutation. And, unfortunately, because the mutations come from different virus strains, finding a way of fighting them will be incredibly difficult. It's likely that prevention is the only cure.

"Let me explain the science. One common structure of a virus is the icosahedral or quasi-spherical virus. It's a solid object built up of twenty identical faces. The most elementary type of icosahedral virion is one where each of the triangular faces is made up of three identical capsid protein subunits, so that makes sixty subunits per capsid. Now some of these capsids have mutated and their external protein sheaths have developed new surface features that enable them to invade different cellular structures inside the human body. Think of it as a lock and key system, where the viral capsids have produced new keys that enable them to unlock the external membranes of particular cells, thereby gaining access so they can release their genetic material and instructions into a host's cell. The injected genetic material then goes about recruiting the host's enzymes that make more of the virus particles that then break free of the cell and infect new cells. But the rapidity of attack is unprecedented. My view is that the mutant RNA . . ."

She stopped talking when she heard the president clearing his throat. Looking around the table, she realized that she'd lost most of the non-scientific audience in the science.

"Sorry. Let me put it in nontechnical terms. The lyssavirus, which in its usual form causes numbness, muscular weakness, and sometimes a coma, which ultimately leads to death, has suddenly changed its capsid structure, the protein coat that covers all the RNA. What that means is that this change has made it much more aggressive as an invader of key cells in the human body, such as the blood, the liver, the brain, and others.

"It has mutated into a very aggressive form that causes brain swelling, internal bleeding, organ failure, and death within hours. Same story with a similar lyssavirus, the Lagos bat virus that up till now hadn't killed anybody but in some bat colonies has mutated with a slightly differentiated but new protein coat and has become, in effect, an incredibly aggressive offspring virus and is now causing deaths through uncontrollable hemorrhagic fever in Nigeria. Like I said, this is especially where bat populations are unable to find fruit due to the destruction of forests for their wood, and arable land has been turned into biofuel production; this and aerial spraying of insecticides has caused a massive reduction in the flying insect population which is also part of the bats' diet.

"The Melaka virus from Malaysia, which only used to cause respiratory problems and was probably linked to the avian flu virus, is now causing deaths where bat populations are under pressure from their jungle habitats being converted into fields of palm oil plants. When they come into contact with humans, their excretions are deadly. And in Britain, the virus that caused that terrible outbreak at the school in North London was a mutant variant of the SARS virus; again, it was structurally and morphologically slightly different from the types of viruses found in British bats, but that difference in capsid structure was enough to enable the virus to eat its way into a whole new set of cells in the human body.

"And the bats from Ramapo Mountain State Forest that killed those poor children in upstate New Jersey were suffering from a deadly variant of the Marburg virus. I won't go on, but as a last example, the vampire bats on the banks of the Orinoco River in South America have a form of rabies that we haven't seen before, and it is devastatingly potent.

"It's as if, in these bat populations that are affected, all the usual suspects, all the normal standard nasty viruses for which bats carry antibodies that don't affect them, have suddenly turned deadly. And it seems to have happened at the same time and throughout the world. We're getting reports almost every week of another unusual outbreak. But the key issue here, Mr. President, is that the viruses that are causing these human population deaths are in almost every case different. There's no common pathogen. It's not like the flu pandemic in the First World War, or the AIDS epidemic where HIV could be isolated. These are all different strains.

"I'll hand around a report that I've prepared that goes much deeper into the science, along with the electron microscopy that identifies each of the viruses . . . we've pictured the normal virus against the mutant variant and identified the structural differences that are causing the problems, but you'll see that each of the viruses we've identified is different. It's as if the normal bat viruses have been given an injection of testosterone," she said.

Her assistant, Professor Daniel Todd, stood and handed around a thick folder of their findings to each of the people at the table. They opened it and flicked through the pictures.

The president said, "We'll read these later with great interest, Debra, but meantime, what's your conclusion about how to deal with these outbreaks? And what can we do to prevent them happening again?"

She swallowed. Here came the crunch, which she'd discussed at length with the president before the meeting, and now would come as a bombshell to his advisors.

"Sir, I don't think we'll find a cure for ten, fifteen, maybe thirty years. Not even with every scientific lab in the world devoting itself to this problem. We can't solve the problem by finding a cure. The situation is too urgent. And the antiviral drugs we've created so far to fight diseases like the flu are going to be useless against these viruses. It's going to take years and years of pharmacological research to find a drug that might, just might, be useful against one or two of these new strains of virus.

"So the only solution is both prevention and direct action against the carrier, the bats. We can't inoculate the US population against an enemy that constantly mutates, even if inoculation against viruses worked."

"It works against smallpox," said Damien Close, the president's scientific advisor. "Jenner used cowpox to inoculate. Smallpox killed five hundred million people in the twentieth century, but today it's been totally eradicated."

"True," said Debra, "but Jenner worked in the nineteenth century and we didn't eradicate smallpox until 1980. We just don't have that long, Doctor Close."

"What have you determined to be the reason that these viruses are mutating and, to use your language, seem to be on testosterone?" he asked.

"We're only in the earliest stages of working on a hypothesis, but it's pretty clear from the mammalian biologists we've contracted around the world, people who specialize in bat populations, that due to very recent and very dramatic alterations in the environment where certain bat populations live, their bodies are responding to a sudden increase in stress by the exponential augmentation of their viral loads. Not every bat population . . . most are normal; but where there's a conjunction between the human world and the animal world, where there are great stresses on local bat populations due to the circumstances I've mentioned, or others yet to be defined, these traumatized bat colonies are reacting by the viral load in their blood going through the roof.

"Where you once had only an occasional outbreak of Ebola or SARS in isolated populations that found themselves in close proximity to humans, now you're having established populations suddenly endangering people in towns and villages in parts of the world where bats have lived in close relationships to people for millennia."

"But what's causing it? What's suddenly happened?" asked the vice president.

"Sir, we can only guess. But if there are two things that seem to have happened globally and at the same time, it's the alteration to the world's climate temperature regulation mechanism caused by effects yet to be fully understood. There's debate, of course, as to whether or not global warming is caused by the increase of greenhouse gases in the atmosphere. That's not an issue I can deal with, but what's apparent is that weather patterns are changing. Record high and low temperatures, unprecedented snowfalls and droughts, glaciers melting, and cyclones and tornadoes at record levels from elevated sea surface temperatures. I'm not a climatologist and I have no knowledge of whether it's anthropogenic or natural, but the climate is certainly changing worldwide and bats are hypersensitive to ambient and seasonal temperatures.

"Then there's the change in ten thousand years of agriculture brought about by modification of fruit and other crops that have altered the use of natural land for farming, and more recently altered farming land by converting it to the production of biofuels for the automotive industry. In brief, in certain populations of bat colonies, the atmospheric temperature is changing too rapidly for them to adjust, their food supplies are shrinking, and their habitat is getting more constrained. It's a perfect storm for some bat populations, and they've reacted to the stresses by what's happening in their bloodstreams."

"You keep saying 'some' bat populations, Debra," said the president. "So it's not all bats throughout the world."

"No sir, not as far as we can tell. I've had analyses done of the bloods of hundreds of stable bat colonies, and most don't seem to have experienced an alteration in the virus content or count in their bodies. But where there's friction between certain colonies under stress and a local human population, or where severe weather patterns have messed around with the food supply, that's where we have trouble. That's why these outbreaks are still isolated. But they're no longer confined to jungles or forests. Now they're wherever human populations reside. That's why we've seen it happen in the center of London, New Jersey, and other places. And with more and more bat populations seeking to live in human habitats like parks or botanical gardens in major cities where there's a ready food source, well . . . " She left the rest of her sentence unspoken.

Again, the vice president, a former World Bank economist until he became governor of Montana and then ran for president, only to be offered the vice presidency as running mate to President Thomas, asked, "But why bats? What is so special about bats that make them so damnably dangerous, as opposed to birds or fleas or rats or mice?"

Debra turned to Daniel, who stepped forward to the end of the table and replied, "I'm Daniel Todd. I specialize in bats at Harvard University. What you have to understand is the special niche that bats fill in the scheme of things. Firstly, their antiquity; they derive from an ancient ancestor that is hundreds of millions of years old, which has enabled them to adapt to and survive in conditions that would have killed later arrivals. Bat species are about fifty million years old, and the only mammals that have adapted to flight. Some mammals today glide, but bats are the only ones to actually have proper flight ability. Long, long ago, they diverged from other mammals by congregating in caves and the tops of forests, so they've had eons to coevolve with viruses that became symbiotic. Because they're not avian, this has given them the ability to isolate themselves in out of the way roosts, trees, belfries, and other places. And in this isolation, they've been able to harbor and adapt to viruses and make themselves immune to them."

"But how did the viruses get into the bats in the first place?" asked the vice president.

"Sir, you've got billions of viruses in your body. And bacteria. All living things, plant and animal, bacteria and fungi, have viruses in them. Few cause problems, but sometimes, they mutate, or a foreign and dangerous virus, like the common cold or flu is introduced, and it's a week in bed with whiskey and orange," said Daniel.

The VP smiled and looked at the president for permission to continue questioning. A nod enabled him to ask, "But why suddenly? Okay, you've said that global warming and changes in food distribution patterns, but it's all a bit sudden, isn't it, for these things to be happening at the same time, all over the world?"

Daniel nodded, everybody strained forward to listen, so he said simply, "I agree. It's a bit sudden. There have been species jumps throughout history, although we didn't know about it. For instance, the virus level in bats is usually quite low so direct transmission to humans would have been fantastically rare, except for the instances of rabies and bats biting people and infecting them directly. But the transmission of, say, the Hendra virus from bats to horses would have been a bit more common because they'd have deposited the virus through mucus or feces or urine onto horse food. The horse would have concentrated the virus at much higher levels, and then infection in humans who tended the horse would have been pretty certain.

"On the other hand, the SARS virus transmits from bats to a carrier, mutates, and when it crosses the species into humans, it changes again through its genetic structure and becomes very dangerous, often fatal," he said.

"Which means that hosts have to be either amplifiers to concentrate the virus or adapters to change it from relatively benign to dangerous," said Damien Close, the president's scientific advisor.

Daniel nodded. "That's right, Doctor Close."

"And would you acknowledge that even though bat viruses have probably been jumping species for a long time and even into humans, the spread from human to human is extremely rare?" said Damien Close.

"Yep. I'll acknowledge that. But that's not the problem we're dealing with here, sir. It's that once these new virulent viruses are in the amplifying or adapting host, the danger isn't so much them spreading from human to human; they're so dangerous that just infection, ingestion, or touch can kill. That's the problem. But we've seen in London and here that when people are infected, they'll become the source of new infections, because after the school kids went to that petting zoo and fell ill, the parents became infected and quickly died when they were attending to their sick children."

The table remained silent as it absorbed the implications of what Daniel and Debra had said. Everybody knew in general terms what had been the undercurrent of discussions for weeks, but now that the facts were on the table, the cold reality was shocking. Global warming and the annihilation of traditional farming structures to meet the demands of the biofuel industry, or the demands of the World Bank for indigenous people to plant cash crops to repay debt instead of their traditional food crops, were issues that had to be faced as an international emergency.

Debra knew that she had to center everybody's thinking back on the report she was delivering. "The issue has arisen because of the very special nature of bats in our biosphere. Bats are unique, as Professor Todd has said, not just because they're the only mammal that flies but because they're so genetically close to humans, they enjoy a special environmental and ecological niche. Because they carry so many viruses to which they've grown immune over the eons, the moment we start to pressure and stress them with the degradation of their forests and the diminution of their food supplies, we increase exponentially the risk of disease spill from their noses or mouths or urine or feces as they fly over farmlands or populated areas and infect the foodstuffs eaten by the human population.

"As we'll never find one or more vaccines in time, the only way is either to move human populations from traditional flight paths, which would be ridiculous if we're talking about the bats in botanical parks in our major cities or to find the endangering populations, and eradicate them."

"That," said the president, "is obviously the best course. Except that it'll pit us right up against the environmentalists. We can't stop global warming immediately nor change farming habits overnight, and even if we could it might not diminish the viral load in bats' blood until many generations have been and gone, so I'm afraid that the only course we've got is to find dangerous bat colonies and eradicate them, worldwide."

A voice from the edge of the room caused everybody to turn as Professor Daniel Todd, Debra's colleague, stood and spoke. "Mr. President, may I? Sir, ladies, and gentlemen, as you know, I'm a bat specialist. I've been foretelling what's now happening for quite a long time. Debra was the first person to take me seriously. My speciality being bats means that I've come to some conclusions that I need to bring to your attention. While a handful of bats throughout the world have turned deadly, and while those colonies that are dangerous have to be exterminated, we must understand the place of bats in the scheme of things. Sure, they're scary to most people, and lots of folk know they're carrying rabies, but what's not generally known is that bats are one of the most important natural ways of keeping down the numbers of moths and mosquitoes and flies. Over agricultural land, they prevent billions of insects from damaging fruit and wheat and dozens of other crops. On the wing, a large colony of bats can eat tons and tons of nasty insects every night, meaning that a lot more people would become very sick if it weren't for the bats. And they're a significant method by which plants and fruit trees are pollinated.

"What I'm saying, sir, is that you can't eradicate one species without it having severe repercussions on other species. And we haven't even looked at the effect of dramatically reducing the bat population. What we're planning on doing could have severe unintended consequences. We have to model all the contingencies before we start the wholesale slaughter. Thank you, sir," he said and sat down.

"Your point is well made, Professor Todd, but this won't be wholesale slaughter; we're going after specific colonies that carry the dangerous viruses, not the benign colonies who've lived in coexistence for millennia." The president turned to the secretary of agriculture. "Zac, can you put together a task force on how to deal with the unintended consequences of significant reductions in specific bat populations? I'm sure Debra will allow you to co-opt Professor Todd from her team for that purpose.

"Meanwhile, Debra and I will start to put together a working model of how we're going to deal with dangerous bat populations. I'll contact each of you in due course, asking for your expert input."

"Will you announce this working model or keep it secret?" asked the secretary of agriculture.

"I'm going to do this very publicly. We do this openly, transparently, and blatantly. With no apologies. We regret what we have to do, and we'll do it as humanely as possible to cause the least suffering, but we have to save human lives. If we try to do this thing without telling people, it'll leak out within minutes and make the environmental movement seem like the good guys. But we will allow no vigilantism. There'll be no cowboys out there killing bats. I'll invoke severe penalties for anybody or any group unofficially acting against bat colonies. No, this is the president's conflict, a humane, contained, and painless confrontation with an animal species that is endangering the human race. Normally we eradicate bacterial, insect, or rodent pests to protect ourselves. This is, perhaps, the first time in recent memory that we've been forced to exterminate mammals. We'll answer the animal liberationists point by point, item by item. And if you think that the American people will side with them and the bats when there's flying death right above their heads, you're misjudging the mood of the American people," said the president.

The director of the FBI asked, "How will you announce it, Mr. President? Television broadcast? Media conference? Over the Internet?"

"The first thing I'm going to do is to call on the secretary-general of the United Nations and give him Debra's report. Then I'm going to telephone the heads of government of all our major allies. At the same time, our ambassador to the United Nations will brief every other ambassador to every other regional bloc, so by the time I make the announcement at a media conference in the White House, the African, Asian, Middle East, Oceanic, South American, and European groups will all know what we're planning to do with our bats. Once that's done, we'll offer our scientific teams worldwide to every nation, friend or foe, who wants their bat population analyzed to see if they're carrying deadly viral loads. And we'll offer to assist with humane eradication."

"And how will you deal with the animal rights and liberation lobby?" the FBI chief asked.

"I'll make it very clear in my media statements that if it's a choice between diseased bats and us, the bats are going to lose every time, and I'll make it equally clear that healthy bat populations are essential in the ecosystem and are to be left alone. I'll also make the point that it's us, we human beings, who've caused this problem for the bats, and it's us that'll have to clear up our own mess.

"Sure," said the president, "the liberationists will yelp and holler and curse; they'll blame humanity and demand that we go back to the lifestyle of pre-industrialized humanity . . . but nobody will be listening because they'll sound like anarchists and fundamentalists, and they'll be up against world governments ensuring the safety of their people. No matter what they say, it'll be too little and too late."

"Sir, it's not what they say that worries me . . . it's what they'll do when they hear your plans."

"That, Director, is your problem," said the president.

13

At the request of the president of the United States of America, Debra remained seated when all others had risen from the crisis meeting and left the Roosevelt Room. They sat at opposite ends of the huge table, and it took some moments for her to stop arranging her papers and to realize that he was just sitting and looking at her. He was smiling.

"Well, that was quite a performance, Debra. You had them eating out of your hand."

"Except for me breaking into techno-babble at the beginning. I totally forgot that they weren't scientists but a lay audience. I'm so sorry, Mr. President."

He smiled. "They may be a lay audience, except for Damien Close, but they're very well-read and clued up. And don't underestimate Damien. He's pretty bright, y'know. He did win the Nobel Prize for chemistry."

"Sir, in no way was I seeking to denigrate Professor Close, nor any of your cabinet . . ."

Nat Thomas burst out laughing. "Lighten up, Debra. I'm making fun of you. Look, this was a pretty heavy meeting. It's laid out the whole of the problem for all of us to see, and we now know what we're dealing with. While your scientific colleagues are working on the cause and cure, you and I have to do some serious work on a strategy of how we're going to implement this search-and-destroy method. And it might surprise you, but I'm going to bring in the army chief of staff, General Coles because I'm going to give him the job of working on the fine details of our broad strategy. His people play war games all the time in the Pentagon so they'll have a way of approaching this and deploying materiel and forces that you and I just wouldn't understand. That okay with you?"

"Sure."

"Okay, then unless you have a pressing reason to get back to your offices, I'm going to do something for you that I've been promising myself I'd do for weeks now."

She put the papers down, looked along the length of the table, and said, "Sir?"

She felt her heart race. In the past weeks she'd been working eighteen hour days, traveling everywhere, negotiating, cajoling, demanding, and explaining; she'd not allowed herself a single moment of "me" time. Sometimes, she was so busy running from meeting to meeting that she didn't even have time to put on proper makeup. Now that the pressure of this presentation was over, now that she and the president had set the train in motion, she realized that this was one of the first times since she'd been appointed that she'd had a chance to breathe.

Nathaniel Thomas smiled. He had a devastating smile. With the enormity of the meeting behind her, she again remembered that she wasn't just in the presence of the president of the United States but was sitting alone in a room with a devastatingly gorgeous man. Tall, tanned, muscular, elegantly graying, and green eyes that made a woman's heart pace, he could have been a Hollywood matinee idol as easily as he was a Nobel laureate and America's most popular president since the early days of Bill Clinton and Barack Obama. And she also remembered how she'd been incapable of intelligent speech when they'd first met and how she'd felt his magnetic power drawing her in as he stood next to her in a palace in Rome. Was this how Monica Lewinsky felt when Bill Clinton stood near her?

Debra hadn't been romantically involved with a man, any man, in years. She'd accepted that she'd never be married to anybody or anything but her work and knew that she had become one of those women her mother disparaged as "professional spinsters," but the importance of her work and her reputation in the scientific community was all the relationship she needed. She realized again that she was holding her breath, like an estrogen-saturated teenager.

"I know it seems a lifetime ago, Debra, but I promised you a tour of the White House. I've had to put it off a couple of times, but now that we're going to be working together in here on this strategic plan, I was wondering whether today was an appropriate time for me to show you around?"

"Oh!"

"Is that a yes or a no?"

"But don't you have lots of things to do?" Then she bit the inside of her lip for asking such a stupid question.

"There are lots of good people around here that are quite capable of doing the things that need to be done. I'm not an interventionist president, Debra. I don't believe in micromanagement. If you put your faith and trust in good people, they ought to be allowed to get on with the job. My predecessors, like Bill Clinton and Jimmy Carter, were micromanagers. I've treated my presidency as if running a very large and complex company. I can't do everything myself, so I've gathered around me the very best people I can find, and I've limited my activities to decision-making, hand-shaking, back-rubbing, and ass-kicking."

"Yet you're working on the details of this strategic plan with me?"

He smiled again and shook his head. "No, Debra. You're working on the plan, along with General Coles. I'm just giving assent or demanding more."

"Oh!" Again, she bit her lip and wished she'd stop saying, "oh."

"I have ten meetings scheduled for today, starting in two hours' time. I'll be working through till after seven this evening when I have to dress in black tie and host a banquet here for the prime minister of Greece and assure him of our continued support in his continuing financial struggles. So my day is pretty fraught. But I have a couple of hours free this morning to show you around . . . although from the number of times you've visited the White House in the past weeks, I'd say you know the pathway from the portico to the Oval Office pretty well. But there's a lot more to see, and if we start now, I can give you an informative and personally guided tour. Interested?"

FBI REGIONAL HEADQUARTERS
MADISON, WISCONSIN

Inspector Marcus Stone prepared himself for what surely would be one of the most important briefings of his career. The large conference room was full of local agents and a contingent flown in from J. Edgar Hoover Building in DC to help out with the investigation into every microcosm of the life that Stuart Chalmers had led from birth until five minutes ago. He had been given the job of field team leader by Deputy Operations Director Zane Trobe after he and his team had won a bare-knuckle fight between two divisions of the agency, the Counterintelligence Division and Trobe's Counterterrorism Division. Intelligence had petitioned directly to the FBI Director Dennis Molner, but the director was of the opinion that it wasn't so much Intelligence as Anti-Terrorism at play, and so the responsibility had ultimately devolved onto the local Bureau chief, and Marcus Stone knew he was ready. But before he entered the room, he had to work out his first couple of sentences for the briefing to gain both attention and respect.

He took a deep breath and walked toward the closed door behind which forty of the most experienced agents of the Bureau were waiting, but before he could open it, his assistant ran up to him and said, "Boss. Before you go in there . . ."

"What?"

"Stuart Chalmers is downstairs. In an interview room off the reception lobby. He's asking to see you."

"Here? Chalmers is in the building?"

His assistant nodded. Stone thought quickly and told his assistant to explain to those in the conference room that the briefing would be delayed for half an hour but not to explain why. He paced downstairs, but before he walked into the interview room, he went into the adjacent monitoring room to check that the monitors were waiting ready to activate all the complex video and recording equipment. It gave him a few moments to look at the slight, hunched academic sitting there, lost in thought, as though he'd come in to report a bag snatch. Stone straightened his jacket and waistcoat and prepared to walk in on the suspect, but just before he left the antechamber, Chalmers turned to the one-way mirror, gave a ghost of a smile, and seemed almost to wave his fingers in greeting. It was as if he knew Stone was looking at him. It unbalanced the FBI agent. He'd interviewed hundreds of suspects in his career and knew most of the tricks of their trade, but this guy seemed different—as though he wanted to give the appearance of being a suspect, but in reality he was letting Stone know that he was very much in control.

"Good morning. I'm Agent Stone."

"And I'm sure you know who I am, Agent Stone. But you're probably wondering why I've come here."

Stone nodded. He was going to say as little as possible to draw more information from Chalmers.

But Chalmers just looked at him, obviously knowing the silent interrogation technique, and waited. And waited.

Eventually, Stone had to break the impasse and said, "Why are you here?"

"I would guess that either today or tomorrow your local agents, joined by a contingent of people from Washington, would raid my property. My problem, Mr. Stone, is that my land is planted with some very sensitive and precious root and plant stock from endangered species, and if your people trample over my land, they'll destroy what takes years to cultivate. So I'm here to answer any questions you might have in the hope that you'll respect my property. Or is that too much to ask?"

Stone found it hard to respond; he was so stunned by the opening gambit of Chalmers's approach. The forthcoming raid on Chalmers's property was a closely guarded secret. Was there a leak in his office? Had somebody warned Chalmers of what the FBI was planning? Or did it come from DC?

"And just how do you know that we're going to be knocking on your door in the near future?"

"Oh, come now. The president of the United States mentioned me by name as a suspect in the terrorist murder of a cabinet secretary. Once an allegation of my involvement was out in the open, it must have necessitated swift action to coordinate the investigation of me and my affairs.

"I assume that it would take a maximum of two days to get all the law enforcement organs into a coordinated operation. Contacts then had to be made between Homeland Security, CIA, Marshal's Department, FBI, and local police here in Madison. Then there'd be meetings, planning, consulting, and implementation . . . what . . . say another two days. Flying the people out from DC and making sure that all the ground logistics like accommodation, money transfers, sufficient transportation, and such were in order would, I assume, take another day. That brings us to today. So it's either today or tomorrow. Just as a matter of interest, which is it?"

"I'm not here to discuss operational procedure with you, Professor Chalmers," he said. In reality, Stone wanted to reach across the table and punch out the little academic's arrogant lights, but the cameras were rolling, and it would be a career-ending moment of gratification.

"But assuming you're right, why do you think that an appeal from you to protect your plants would prevent us from raking over every minute of your life and every inch of your property in order to determine whether you've been a murderer?"

"Because," he said leaning across the table and fixing Stone with an uncompromising stare, "I've been tipping you guys off for decades about who's really behind the assaults on America in the name of animal liberation. And you've missed every single opening I've given you. Every one! Each time I learned that there was going to be an attack, every time a laboratory or a factory farm or a vivisectionist was going to be murdered, I phoned the FBI in Washington or the city where the atrocity was going to be conducted, left an anonymous message, told you who I thought was behind it, and hoped to heavens that you'd have the sense to prevent needless loss of life in the future. But you've never been able to put two and two together."

"Explain."

"Oh really! C'mon, Mr. Stone. Surely, your computer programmers can put together a simple algorithm so that you can link assaults against similar organizations associated with animal welfare in locations throughout the nation with anonymous tip-offs, even over decades? I would have thought it was fairly simple."

Stone merely stared at him, waiting for him to continue.

"I've contacted your regional and head offices anonymously seventeen times and told you the connection between the particular organization which was going to perpetrate it and the crimes they were going to commit, many of which have been sheeted home to me. I'm as much their victim as poor Secretary DeAnne Harper. I also phoned the Washington Bureau and told them that CHAT was planning the murder of a cabinet secretary, but unfortunately, I didn't know which one. I phoned hours before the actual bombing and told your office that CHAT was the organization that was going to be doing the killing. I knew about it because I'd heard rumors whispered into my ear that the head of that ridiculous organization, Tom Pollard, was planning something seriously big, a high-profile murder, but I had no idea who would be the victim. I phoned and warned you, yet your people took no action.

"Y'know, Mr. Stone, connecting CHAT to a series of crimes isn't rocket science. Every time there was an assault against some group that treats animals improperly, one of the senior members of this particular organization was either in the town or had just left. I would have thought you could have put cause together with effect. You do, after all, have some awesome computing power in J. Edgar Hoover's Building, don't you?"

Stone looked at him, trying to hide his contempt for the man's smugness. But as though he didn't notice, or he just didn't care, Chalmers continued unabashedly.

"Look, in 1995, there was a carefully planned assault on a farm in California that was producing battery chickens from cruel and intensive hatchery methods. The cruelty to which the chickens were exposed was hideous, but whoever did the bombing obviously knew that if he released them, because of the way they'd been bred as egg-producing machines, genetic freaks that had lost the power to fend for themselves because they'd been bred for their meat, they'd not last five minutes in the farmyard . . . why, the poor things could barely even walk. So to put them out of their misery, he blew up the facility with five thousand chickens in it. Euthanasia. But he also killed four Mexican workers who were doing the night shift in the battery farm at the time. I phoned up your HQ in Washington and told them who it was, but nothing happened.

"Then in 1996, a conference of cosmetic chemists in Seattle, people who experiment on live animals for the benefit of ladies who want to wear perfumes, was attacked. Funny, really, except that two scientists died. The killer poisoned the food that was being served for their lunches. Apparently, it was only meant to make them feel sick, but the two who died were suffering from amoebic dysentery, which they'd caught in Thailand at an earlier conference two weeks prior and hadn't fully recovered. They were so weakened by the illness that their hearts gave out. The hotel was blamed for serving stuff that hospitalized one hundred people with food poisoning, but I know who did it. I phoned your Washington bureau and told them it was CHAT, but again, nothing happened.

"Now we come to 1997. Again, I tracked one of their senior staff to Memphis, Tennessee, where the university has been granted a vivisection license to conduct experiments on capuchin monkeys. Tiny, beautiful little balls of fur. And they were going to be strapped to dissection tables and have probes and electrodes poking and prodding them, their inner organs exposed and monitored in order to find a cure for some disease or other. Unforgivable, when you come to consider that there were other perfectly good ways to research human ailments without taking an animal's life. And what happened? As the chief scientist and two of his colleagues, all academics from the university, were getting into his car in the parking lot, the ignition triggered a huge bomb, and they were blown to bits. Again, Mr. Stone, I contacted DC in advance and told them what I knew, but . . .

"In 1998, a bomb in a genetics lab in Maine that had cloned rabbits, dogs, and sheep. Three scientists were left maimed and they are still in wheelchairs.

"In 1999, a Hollywood movie studio that had made a film glorifying men who go out hunting. Nobody killed, but a studio lot burned to the ground."

He shrugged. "I could go on and on. Through every year up until the present day and the assassination of Secretary Harper and her family. I've been monitoring CHAT and other liberationist movements for close to twenty years now and tipping you off every time they do some dastardly act. Oh, don't misunderstand me. I applaud what they're trying to do, but I fiercely, vehemently, and utterly object to the obscene ways they're going about it. To take human lives . . . it's abhorrent."

"If you knew all this, why didn't you make your information known? Why give anonymous tips?" asked Agent Stone.

"These people are fanatics. They kill without compunction. Just the leak of my name, inadvertently, and I'd have been their next target. No, Mr. Stone, I gave you all the information you'd need to stop these maniacs. But you and your colleagues chose to ignore it."

"How do I know you're telling the truth, Chalmers? How do I know this isn't rewriting history, reengineering the past to prove your innocence in the present?"

"Easy," he said, with a smirk on his face he could barely contain. This was the *coup de grace*, the moment he'd been planning and looking forward to for nearly half of his life. It had taken eighteen years of careful planning to reach this moment. There were occasions over the years when he'd been arrested by the cops, when he'd thought to pull out all stops during an interrogation to save himself by throwing the spotlight on those assholes from CHAT. But now, now that he'd been identified by name in front of a vast television audience by the president of the United States himself . . . now was the time to prove his innocence and humiliate Nathaniel Thomas and maybe even bring down his presidency.

He'd spent all those years monitoring the movements of CHAT senior personnel and then using their visit to some town or other to give the green light to any one of a dozen assaults he or one of his cells would unleash against animal murderers. And the tip-offs he'd given either hours or days before the incident had been sufficiently obscure to almost guarantee that the Feds wouldn't be able to follow them through. But it was all there on the record, and now it would prove his innocence.

He took out a book from his inside pocket. A handwritten leather-bound book containing details of each assault that he was blaming on CHAT and the name of each person in the Bureau to whom he'd spoken, as well as the time and other details of the call.

"Check this out," he said handing over the book. "I've kept a record of the assaults I can certainly sheet home to CHAT and the other murderous lunatics. . . and the tip-offs I gave you in advance. It's all here, Mr. Stone. The incident, the time, and place I contacted, and the person to whom I gave the information. And, of course, the CHAT staff member who was in the location at the time. There have been more, many more, but I just don't have their details. The information I gave you came directly to me from the late and lamented Ms. Christine Knowles, Deputy Secretary of Health and Human Services, who recently committed suicide because she couldn't bear to live in a world where her dear friend, DeAnne Harper, and her beautiful family had been murdered. She pretended to support CHAT to get inside information on them, but she was actually acting on my behalf so I could report their activities.

"All you have to do is to examine your records and you'll find that hours before each assault, you got an anonymous telephone call telling you that CHAT was behind the murder and mayhem. Okay, so they were spread out over eighteen or more years, but it shouldn't be beyond your computer programmer's ability to join assaults conducted against people who mistreat animals, with a tip-off around the same time."

Stone nodded. If Chalmers was telling even a fraction of the truth, it was a monumental screwup on the part of the Bureau. But he'd need time to get the information together.

"But if you knew these people from CHAT were visiting a state or a city to commit a crime, why weren't you more explicit? Why be so covert? You could have saved lives."

"I've already told you. I had to protect myself. And not only that . . . the CHAT people travel extensively, and Miss Knowles often didn't find out the specific information about which executive was in which city and who would do the evil deed. So we relied on your organization's professionalism . . . big mistake! Many of their personnel go all over the country raising funds and giving speeches. I didn't always know which one would commit the crime so I couldn't be too specific with the information."

"But Jesus Christ, all you had to do was to come in with this notebook years ago, and we'd have arrested the lot of them. Yet you've led us to believe that it was you and WEL that were the terrorists . . ."

"I've led you to believe nothing, Mr. Stone. I've led you to the truth, but you treated me like Tiresias, the blind prophet of Thebes. Instead of transforming me into a woman for seven years, for the past seven years and more, you've ruined my life by transforming me into a terrorist. I've been arrested and set free, harassed, tormented without remorse, but you've never once offered me an apology. And all the while, like the blind Tiresias, like Cassandra, I was trying to tell you the truth, but I was never believed."

Stone didn't follow what he was saying but asked, "Then Professor Chalmers, why didn't Ms. Knowles go to the police?"

"She was terrified that she'd be next on their hit list."

"We could have protected her."

"Like you protected Secretary Harper and her family?"

Ignoring the cutting remark, Stone flipped through the book. Even without the benefit of a forensic examination, he could tell by the fading of the ink in the reports starting eighteen years earlier that it had been written over a period of many years, and the likelihood was that Chalmers was telling the truth.

"Would you mind waiting in this building while I contact my HQ in Washington and begin investigations as to the veracity of what you're saying?"

Chalmers smiled. "It would be my pleasure, Mr. Stone. And when you've verified what I've told you, and now that I've closed down WEL, I'd be happy to assist the Bureau in apprehending these murderers at CHAT. They do the good and honorable name of animal and plant welfare no good at all."

Stone stood, still restraining the anger he felt at the hubris and arrogance of the man. Profoundly disturbed by the evidence he'd been given, he picked up the battered leather notebook and walked to the door, but before he even touched the handle, Chalmers said, "Oh, and maybe you could work out a way that the president of the United States could offer me a public apology."

THE WHITE HOUSE

As he escorted her from stateroom to stateroom on the first floor of the White House, all sounds of commerce and industry, of national and international commotion that ruled the lower floors seemed to lessen and become muted. As though absorbed into the thick carpets and luxurious furnishings of the upper floors, as she ascended the White House, it transformed from a center of activity to an ancient temple of a deity, of potency.

And another thing that Debra noticed was that whenever the president led her to each door, he'd put his arm around her shoulder as she exited. It surprised her, and she wondered, as they became more and more remote from the hordes of people who worked one floor below in the functional offices of the White House, whether their isolation in the vastness of the exquisite upper staterooms gave him more freedom to be less president and more man. And if he was now a man showing her around the president's home, alone and unobserved, was he was going to go further than just putting a friendly arm around her shoulders? Was he going to hold her hand, back her into a corner, and try to kiss her . . . take her into one of the state bedrooms, close and lock the door, and seduce her? Was this her President Clinton moment with Monica, the means of seduction used by President Kennedy to overwhelm Marilyn Monroe, the isolation used by President Eisenhower when Mamie was downstairs and he was alone with his driver Kay Summersby?

As they walked from room to room, her heart was thumping. Was this a calculation on his part to get her to lower the barriers that professionalism had erected? Would the uniformed guards who were stationed on walkways and the tops of flights of stairs suddenly disappear as the president rounded a corner and an unoccupied bedroom suddenly put her in the position of yielding to a man she was finding increasingly irresistible? Did she care that he was married and had a young family? Did she worry that his wife may be in the family quarters, doing what First Ladies did while their president husbands were getting more than advice from one of the young and vulnerable assistants?

Or was her mind playing ridiculous tricks on her? She was being escorted around his house by a man who had been offering her a tourist's eye view of the White House and who had been nothing but supportive, charming, and civil from the time they'd left the downstairs conference. Yes, he'd become more and more friendly and at ease with her as they walked through the first floor of the White House; he'd touched her far more than previously. But it had been the touch of a friend, the gentle touch of a mentor, the innocent arm around the shoulder of people who were suddenly relaxing in each other's company.

Leaving the magnificent East Room with its teardrop chandeliers and Steinway piano, they walked slowly along the eighty-foot long Cross Hall with its plush red- and gold-edged carpet toward the state dining room where he'd promised her a place at the next appropriate state banquet.

"This corridor isn't just a corridor. That's the genius of the architects. We use it for receiving lines after there's been an official arrival ceremony on the South Lawn. Often guests line up on either side, and I accompany a visiting national head of state as we walk down the red carpet. My wife and his wife, or her husband, walk behind us, as though we're walking down the aisle of some cathedral on the red carpet at a wedding," President Thomas said. "It looks all very formal, British pomp and circumstance, but you'd be amazed at how much private humor there is between world leaders, so long as the television cameras aren't eavesdropping. Once, I was escorting the president of France into a banquet, and I whispered into his ear, 'Maurice, will you marry me?' Without a second's consideration, he said, 'Yes, with pleasure, but you'll have to be the wife . . . I am French, you understand.'"

Nathaniel Thomas smiled, and Debra burst out laughing. "You'd be amazed at the language we use when the advisors have left the room, and we're alone. And I won't mention whom, but the wife of one of the European leaders is pretty fresh with her language as well. My wife was shocked, at first, but now she's a lot more used to it."

Debra realized with surprise that it was the first time that he'd mentioned his wife since the start of the impromptu sightseeing tour he was taking her on. The tour had begun warmly enough, with him showing her through the ground floor of the West Wing and introducing her to many of the people that she knew by name or she regularly saw on television. Then they'd gone upstairs where the frenetic atmosphere of the working house transformed into the staterooms of the White House and where ceremony replaced the commerce of political life. From the magnificent East Room, they were about to go into the state dining room when the president's press secretary came running up the stairs and said hurriedly, "Sir, can I have a word with you?"

The president stepped four paces away, and the press secretary whispered into his ear. Nathaniel turned to Debra, his face creased in sudden worry and said, "Sorry, but we're going to have to cut this short."

"That's okay, sir, I'll see myself back to my office."

"No, this concerns you." Suddenly the relaxed and avuncular president vanished and the hard-working, no-nonsense President Nathaniel Thomas appeared, striding meaningfully down the hall toward the stairs. They returned in silence to the Oval Office. Waiting for them were three of his senior aides, the secretary of agriculture, and Daniel Todd.

When she entered, she walked over to Daniel and asked hurriedly, "What's going on?"

"I have no idea. A car suddenly pulled up and whisked me back to the White House. I was told that the president's chief of staff had sent for me, but they haven't told me a thing."

The president walked to his desk, and everybody gathered in the seats that formed a semicircle. Without any preamble, he said, "Ross?"

The secretary of agriculture began, "Five hours ago, the governor of Texas was called out of a budget breakfast meeting and given some news about bats in her state. She immediately flew to Garden Ridge, near to San Antonio, where . . ."

Debra felt Daniel's body, seated beside her, suddenly go limp. "Oh shit," he said under his breath, but everybody in the room heard him. He was in no mood to apologize. From his reaction, Debra knew what was coming.

"She found a scene of utter carnage and devastation. The governor is on video link on your television right now, Mr. President."

An aide reached over and pressed a remote control. The blank video monitor suddenly came to life, and the governor of Texas was visible, standing in a field. The helicopter was in the background, and the camera, obviously a steady-cam, was transmitting a clear and immediate picture.

"Mr. President?"

"Good morning, Governor. I'm here with the secretary of agriculture and a number of other experts. Can you tell us what's happened, please?"

Governor Consuela Lopez cleared her throat and spoke into the hand-held microphone. There was too much crosswind in the open field for her to be heard over the distant camera's mike. "I'm in Garden Ridge, which is a couple of miles northeast of San Antonio. The field I'm in is owned by the Bat Conservation International organization. Bracken Cave is a home to millions and millions of Mexican free-tailed bats. They fly up here from their winter in Mexico. It's a thousand miles. They nest and roost in this cave. There are over twenty million bats, Mr. President. They come here to have their babies. Ten million babies. They swarm out at night to feed. It's one of the greatest sights in the world. One of the most important mass animal movements anywhere on the planet. And it happens every night.

"And during the early morning, after the bats had returned from their night's feed and were exhausted and were sleeping, some bastards have netted the mouth of the cave and they've thrown in dozens of petrol bombs that have exploded and set fire to the bats, and when they tried to escape they were caught in the netting, and they're dead, Mr. President. They're all dead. Millions and millions of them. Those bastards have killed them. They weren't diseased. We tested them. They used to fly out for hundreds of miles and they would catch two hundred tons of mosquitoes and moths and insects every night. They were harmless; they used to do only good and the farmers, tourists, and people loved them. And these bastards have netted and killed them. Burned the poor little creatures to death. Oh God . . . you should see the carnage . . ."

She tried to fight back tears and had to put the microphone down for a moment. Before he could say anything to console her, Governor Lopez continued, "You should see piles of bodies of the little things. The floor is littered knee-deep with millions upon millions of them . . . and their babies. They died in agony."

"Consuela," said the president, "have the police got any eye-witness statements?"

"They're working on it, sir, but you'd better put some laws into place, or these bastard vigilantes will kill every living thing. I know they're scared of this plague, Mr. President, but this is mass murder of perfectly healthy and important animals. It can't go unpunished."

The president continued to talk to her about the slaughter and if there was any hope for any bats that might still be alive. But the situation was beyond recovery, and everybody knew it.

"I assume that you're going to make a press statement when the news gets out," he said. She nodded. "Okay, how would you feel, Governor, if one of my people emailed you some talking points so that you can be part of the national picture of what we're trying to do up here? I'll make a statement immediately after you've informed the media and the citizens of Texas. Oh Consuela, I'm so terribly sorry. But I promise you that this murder of innocent animals by Americans will cease. We won't have these cowboy vigilantes taking the law into their own hands."

When the transmission had finished, the president gave instruction to his press secretary about the material to send to the governor of the state of Texas. Then he turned to Daniel Todd. "How significant is this Bracken Cave, Professor Todd?"

Before he spoke, Daniel glanced at Debra, who gave him a barely noticeable nod. "Sir, it would be hard to overstate the importance of Bracken Cave's bat population in terms of the global problems that these creatures are facing. For the past number of years, especially on the East Coast, we've been tagging bats with transmitters and are doing infrared flight analysis and testing their blood to try to solve a devastating problem that is already causing their numbers to crash, and that's without these vigilantes.

"There's a species popularly called the little brown bat that is dying off in the millions from a fungus called White-nose Syndrome. This white fungus grows on the faces of the bats during hibernation and irritates them. It upsets their natural rhythms so that instead of being dormant in their warm cave where their bodies close down in the freezing cold and lack of food, this fungus causes them to wake up, become active in the intense cold, and go out in a useless search for food that isn't there during the winter season. In some cases, sir, we're losing 100 percent of bats in caves and mines in upstate New York . . . but now it's spreading and is heading west and south.

"The point is, Mr. President, that this massive die-off from fungal disease is going to devastate US forests and productive agricultural farmland. Look, I know most people are scared of bats, but you have to think about them differently. They're one of our most important pesticides, as well as incredibly important in the cycle of nature, like pollination. One of these little brown bats can eat a thousand insects every night. So you lose a million bats to White-nose fungus, and there's going to be close to a billion nasty insects, nearly seven hundred additional tons of moths and beetles and mosquitoes each summer that will do terrible damage to forests and woodland. And that's just one species.

"Bats are voracious feeders on moths and beetles that attack crops like cotton, corn, and other things that farmers grow. So we'll have to use more pesticides that are already damaging our ecology. Dear God, they've survived for fifty million years, and the lot of them could be wiped out in the next decade.

"You asked how significant is the murder of these bats in Bracken Cave. I'll tell you, Mr. President. Multiply what I've just told you by twenty; and then twenty again and then again and you'll have trillions of additional mosquitoes, beetles, and other insects in the air over the southern states of America with all the devastation that'll cause. And there'll be far less pollination of our fruit trees.

"Mr. President, sir, it's a real problem. And all for nothing. These bats weren't infected. They were a successful, thriving community. I just hope that the American people realize how devastating this has been, and you can convince other vigilantes to lay off. It's the law of unintended consequences, sir. We wipe out one species that is threatening us, and suddenly, without realizing it, we're prey to other things we didn't even think about."

14

Although there were two FBI agents in front of him, two behind him, and one each at his left and right sides, Professor Stuart Chalmers wasn't handcuffed as he strode into FBI headquarters in Washington. Inspector Marcus Stone walked ahead of the group and ushered them into a large conference room. On the table were the ubiquitous conference phones and microphones; an electronic whiteboard was at one end of the room and a large glass mirror was at the other end. Stone seated Chalmers directly opposite the mirror and noted that as he sat down, he smiled and gave a little wave to his reflection, knowing that behind the two-way mirror there was a phalanx of experts recording, analyzing, and synthesizing every word, movement, and flicker he made.

One of the dozen or so people in the monitoring room who was watching Chalmers's every breath was Harry Clarfield, a covert operative often used for black ops and wet work, but never officially employed by White House Chief of Security Ted Marmoullian. Harry had been woken by an urgent phone call that morning and ordered by Marmoullian to go to the FBI's headquarters to listen in on the interview being conducted with Chalmers.

By arrangement, Clarfield's name appeared on no lists, no rolls, no pieces of paper. He only answered the telephone to three people—two were family, and one was the White House's head of security. Other than that, he was non-existent. The only way for anybody wanting to employ his services to contact him was via a messaging service in the Cayman Islands that relayed the request to a secretarial service in Ireland that passed it on to the message bank of a client they believed lived in Auckland, New Zealand, and who they only knew as "Mr. White." When he listened to his message bank, Clarfield bought a once-only mobile phone, contacted the person who'd made the inquiry, dumped the phone into the furnace of his Seattle apartment block, and took an immediate flight to where he was wanted. Ted Marmoullian wanted him in this FBI Washington office, right now.

Clarfield was a skeptic by birth as well as by training, and the thought that this animal rights anarchist had managed to pull the wool over the eyes of these FBI goons and was now presenting himself as their most valuable asset was more proof of how dangerous he was. Sure, the Feds were skeptical of his *volte face* and apparent willingness to assist them in bringing the killers to book, but they kept trying to convince Marmoullian of the fact that the evidence of the book he'd been compiling was accurate scientific proof. They'd chemically analyzed it and shown that the original entries were, indeed, nearly twenty years old and that the later entries, although vague, had been verified by monitored calls to FBI offices before the murder incidents. So, even though he was still a prime suspect, the evidence was pointing to the truth of what he'd told them in Madison . . . that he'd made anonymous calls to local FBI offices in order to warn them before each murderous incident and that the Bureau had failed to connect the dots.

But Harry wasn't buying it. Scientific evidence could be forged; it could be manipulated. And he'd always relied on his gut instincts, which right now told him that this guy wasn't just a mass murderer and anarchist, but a terrorist who had designs on killing the president of the United States. The difference between Harry and the FBI was that they sought evidence to bring a miscreant to trial, whereas if somebody threatened the occupant of the Oval Office, Harry would blow them away without a moment's hesitation and ask questions later.

It was such an obvious ploy to distract the investigation from Professor Chalmers and his Whole Earth League and pour a bucket load of shit on the heads of the other moronic dropkick group, CHAT—Citizens for Humane Animal Treatment—that Harry wondered why they were even wasting time with this interview. But on the principle that no stone must be left unturned, he'd go along with Inspector Stone and listen in.

The FBI man began the discussion. "For the record of this interview, my name is Inspector Marcus Stone. In the interview room with me is Professor Stuart Chalmers, who has offered his assistance with the apprehension of the criminals who murdered Secretary of Health DeAnne Harper and others. Professor Chalmers, since you gave us your notebook, we've checked the coincidence of your entries with anonymous phone calls made to FBI offices in Cleveland, Ohio; Boise, Indiana; Phoenix, Arizona; Charlotte, North Carolina; Tulsa, Oklahoma; and many other cities. As far as we can tell, these telephone calls were made, but our computer system didn't pick up a pattern in the warnings, and so we didn't view Citizens for Humane Animal Treatment as a likely culprit in the many different crimes over the past twenty or so years. Would you mind explaining why, if you knew that CHAT was responsible for these many crimes, you didn't come in and provide us with proof so that these crimes could have been prevented?"

Stuart Chalmers nodded sagely, as though thinking of the answer, even though he'd anticipated it and his answer was rehearsed.

As he explained why, citing their common objectives to save the flora and fauna of the planet, though their methods were entirely different, Harry Clarfield listened with increasing frustration. To him, as a trained and experienced interviewer, the answers given by this philosopher were right off a song sheet. Obvious questions, obvious answers.

No, Harry realized, the only way to get this bastard to confess was to trip him up . . . to lead him along a path so he felt totally comfortable and became arrogant—even if it took a couple of hours—and then hit him in the balls with a question that undermined his confidence . . . even if it were a lie. Like *but we have your fingerprints on a gun*, or *but Stuart, we have an eye-witness who has positively identified you as being there.* Say it with a completely straight face—even if it were a barefaced lie—and even the toughest and most hardened criminal would begin to doubt himself.

And then . . . nothing. Silence. Just sit there, and despite the protestations, banter, and denials, just sit there and look back at him, your face totally expressionless. Allow yourself just the merest raised eyebrow, just the slightest suggestion of a smile, and in your silence, the creep would begin to unpick himself, strand by strand. Sure, it would be difficult in a court of law for the lawyers to explain it away, but as he was unknown and unknowable, and never appeared in public, let alone in court, he didn't even have to say *Oops, sorry, I made a mistake*, but in the meantime, the perp had already confessed and was begging for a deal.

Yet this FBI *nudze* was using logic, conversation, pleading for Chalmers's better nature. Oh, please.

After an hour, the interview came to an end, with nothing of any value resulting from the session other than a renewal of the offer by Chalmers to assist the Bureau in apprehending the monsters from CHAT who had perpetrated this dastardly crime.

Before Chalmers was allowed to leave the interview room, Clarfield asked the Bureau chief, "Do you think I could have a crack at breaking him . . . just a dozen or so questions on behalf of the president of the United States?"

The chief looked and felt uncomfortable, but he knew that Clarfield was here at the request of the Oval Office's head of security, Ted Marmoullian, and that meant it was as good as a demand from President Thomas. He agreed reluctantly.

Stuart Chalmers was surprised when Harry Clarfield suddenly burst into the interview room unannounced. So was Marcus Stone. But in his earpiece, Marcus Stone was asked to leave the room immediately, and Clarfield told Chalmers to resume his seat.

"I'm afraid I don't know you. You're not wearing any ID. Would you mind introducing yourself?" said Chalmers.

But Clarfield just looked at him, then down at the file he'd thrown on the desk. Lifting the file up so that Chalmers couldn't see the contents, Clarfield opened it and read the first couple of pages. He remained in studied silence.

"I notice you haven't turned on the tape recorder. I assume that this is an unofficial interview."

Again, Clarfield ignored Chalmers and continued reading from the file, only glancing up in surprise as he read something to look at Chalmers and check that what he'd been reading was real.

"Oh, the strong silent type. I'm supposed to be intimidated, right? Okay, I'm scared. Is this when I'm supposed to make some kind of confession?"

The philosopher sneered in contempt and continued, "When are you going to open a bag and take out a hypodermic needle full of truth drug? Oh c'mon, this is getting silly. I'm here because I volunteered to help the Bureau bring murderers to justice. Or hasn't your boss told you that?"

Clarfield continued his silence, still reading. Chalmers also relapsed into silence, looking at Harry, wondering when the impasse would be broken.

Then, still reading for another full minute and not looking up at Chalmers, he said softly, "Your colleague, the guy who runs WEL with you, Jim Towney. He's a professor, isn't he?"

"Yes."

"He just told me he was one of America's leading agricultural scientists, possibly one of the best in the world. But I checked with people and they tell me he's a small-time player. A failed academic. So is he shitting me and using WEL to boost his standing, or is he nuts?"

"You have Jim Towney here?"

"Is he just exaggerating to impress me, or what?"

But Chalmers remained silent and just stared back at Clarfield, who resumed reading the notes in the file. And they remained silent for minutes, Clarfield occasionally looking up when he turned a page but looking down again as if his interest was waning.

Eventually, Harry closed the file and put it back on the table. He folded his hands behind his neck and rocked back on his chair. "You're quite something. Listening to Towney just now, he's got you figured as Noah and Moses and Jesus and Mohammed, all rolled into one." Harry shook his head, as though in disappointment. "Of course, that's the problem with having a lower order intellect as your number two. I guess it must make succession a problem for you. Not for him, though. He thinks he's ready to step into your shoes right now."

Stuart Chalmers looked back at him, his face inscrutable—a deadpan and unfathomable mask. But Harry had met people like him many times before, who thought they were a lot smarter than they actually were. Clever, this guy surely was . . . but not as smart as he thought. And to Clarfield's advantage, Chalmers didn't have street smarts.

Then Harry shook his head slowly from side to side. "But one thing you did that Towney couldn't understand was offing those little babies. Secretary Harper, he could understand—even her husband. She's visible, high profile, attention getting, and he's her handbag. And by blaming it on CHAT, it was worth killing her. But their kids? Townie was crying when I showed him the burned and mangled bodies of her babies. He pushed the photos away, but I insisted that he look at them, and then I showed him Secretary Harper's body in the morgue . . . a blackened skeleton, bits of hair, an eye still in its socket. Horrible. He told me he'd seen them in his nightmares ever since the explosion. Not her, not the secretary. But her children. Can't get those children's faces out of his mind. Big mistake."

Harry sniffed and mumbled, almost inaudibly, "second-rate intelligence," and then he just remained silent, rocking slightly back and forward in his chair. And Stuart Chalmers also looked back. His face didn't crack an inch. Not an emotion registered, not an eyelid flickered, not a line creased his forehead.

The two men stared at each other—minute after minute. And it was then that Harry Clarfield knew he'd won, and allowed himself a smile. Chalmers also smiled, thinking that by showing no emotion at all, he'd won by not being the first to crack.

"Tell me Stuart, have you ever studied psychology?"

Chalmers shook his head. "Nope, philosophy, history, literature, and some other subjects but never psychology."

"Thought not."

"Why?" asked Chalmers.

"The subject of my doctorate in psychology was criminal psychopathy. And you've just blown it, my friend."

Chalmers continued to smile and said, "Oh do go on. I can't wait."

"It was the kids that proved it. If I'd mentioned murdered kids to almost anybody, there'd be a flicker of horror or a sign of remorse. Almost any normal person. But not you, buddy. Not from you. You were totally untouched by it. You're a psychopath. You have no feelings for humanity. You have a Grade A personality disorder; you're unable to form any human attachment; you have zero empathy toward others, but masked by an ability to appear outwardly normal and even warm and friendly and jovial. But you'd just as soon kill an old lady to take her seat on a bus as you'd have a drink of water. So you ordered the killing of Secretary Harper and her family as though you were just doing a laundry list."

Chalmers smiled. "I think you're forgetting just one tiny little fact here, fella . . . I'm the president of WEL, the Whole Earth League. Before I was forced to close it down, we were dedicated to the salvation of every living creature and organism . . . plants and animals . . . and that, you moron, includes humans. I could no more kill Secretary Harper and her family than I could tread on an ant. What kind of a bozo are you, for crying out loud. Psychopath!" And he burst out laughing.

But Harry Clarfield just continued to look at him and smile.

"Oh," Chalmers continued, "and where's your evidence? What evidence have you got to bring into a court of law and prove my so-called guilt? Not a scrap. When my lawyers get hold of you, they'll . . ."

"Court of law?" whispered Clarfield. "What court of law?"

"What do you mean?"

"You said I'll need evidence for a court of law. Why?"

"Because our justice system depends . . ."

Harry Clarfield burst out laughing. "You just don't get it, do you? You're a fucking professor and you're too dumb to get it."

Now Stuart was worried, and it showed in his face. "Get what?"

"You're a terrorist. You're outside the reach of American justice. The president of the United States declared you to be a terrorist under Executive Order 13224 which President George W. Bush signed into law in September 2001. That means, my friend, you're in my jurisdiction right now and not the FBI's. They were just a bus service, a means of transporting you to Washington.

"Which means that as soon as I can arrange your journey, a little thing called extraordinary rendition, we're shipping you outta here in the dead of night, taking you to Andrews Air Force Base where you'll be put on board a plane and transported to . . . oh, I don't know . . . let me think. Afghanistan, Syria, Egypt, Sudan, Algeria, or Turkey maybe. One of those happy little Muslim countries where they still use extreme methods to extract confessions. You probably know it better as torture. And then, my friend, when we've got all the information that you can give us, we'll bring back what's left of you to a nice Arab country, tell them that you've committed a crime against Allah that carries a lifetime in prison, and pay them a couple of thousand bucks. That's all it costs for them to keep you in bread and water until you die of starvation, or you're fucked to death with baseball bats by a gang of Muslim fundamentalist thugs. That's what we do to terrorists."

Harry Clarfield picked up his folder, nodded, and walked toward the door. He didn't even look back at Stuart Chalmers, who was white-faced with shock, incapable of speech.

Outside the interview room, Inspector Marcus Stone, his face contorted in fury, confronted Harry Clarfield. "I don't give a good goddamn if you are White House, how dare you treat my prisoner in that manner? Do you realize . . ."

"Listen to me, and listen to me very carefully unless you want the president of the United States to order that you spend the rest of your career sitting at a desk in Chuathbaluk, Alaska. You get somebody Chalmers has never spoken to before in this building to take him to a cell in complete silence, and you leave that man alone tonight. And tomorrow. Totally and completely fucking alone. Just give him food and drink.

"You don't talk to him, offer him comfort. Do nothing. Understand me? Alone in a cell, he'll be panicking. Come Tuesday morning, he'll do a deal. He'll offer up Jim Towney and everybody else in WEL, as well as his mother and sister and beg you to let him kill a herd of buffalo by hand in order to avoid what he's now thinking is going to happen to him.

"But you refuse to do any deal. You concede nothing. You just tell him that a full confession will enable you to get him back from animals like me and into your jurisdiction for prosecution of criminal offenses conducted in the United States. Then you'll have your case and a confession, and you'll put him away forever."

Marcus Stone was ready to explode. "Are you stupid? Do you know what your little charade in there has done? There's no way we can get him into court now. Once he's armed with a lawyer, he'll . . ." Stone was lost for words. "Not after you just did that to him."

Harry Clarfield looked at Stone in shock. "Do what to him? I haven't been here. No interview took place. There's no recording. I'm not on anybody's radar. I have no name and no title. And don't think of involving Ted Marmoullian in this, because he's been holding a meeting in his office in the White House, attended by a dozen people, all of whom will confirm his presence; he has no idea I'm here and will sign a statement to that effect. When Chalmers's lawyer asks about me, you've never seen or heard of me and Chalmers is making the whole thing up. If he wants to proceed with a case against me, tell him to prove it. It's poetic justice, Inspector Stone; it's what he's been doing to the United States for the past twenty years."

Smiling, Clarfield walked past Marcus Stone and left the building, a building where he hadn't been for the past three hours, and where there was no record of his entry or exit.

OFFICE OF THE ARMY CHIEF OF STAFF
THE PENTAGON
ARLINGTON, VIRGINIA

Four Star General Douglas Coles sat at the end of a massive oak table, flanked on either side by majors, who were flanked by lieutenants, behind whom sat advisors and aides, aside of whom stood men and women in uniform ready at a moment's notice to fill water glasses, coffee mugs, and plates of biscuits. He looked carefully at Debra Hart and Daniel Todd before turning to the man who sat beside him. With the slightest nod of his head, the major flicked a button on his desktop control panel, and suddenly a huge map of the United States appeared on a screen.

"Since our briefing by the commander in chief," General Coles said, "we've drawn up this contingency map overlaid with information about bat congregation areas from the Department of Agriculture."

Another flick of another switch, and the continent of North America was suddenly filled with a mass of red dots, red lines to indicate flight paths and urban locations beneath the pathways; blue dots for hospitals; and black dots, which Debra was disturbed to read in the legend, for mortuaries. There were also larger circles around outer urban areas that she understood to be displacement camps.

General Coles continued, "Preliminary estimates of numbers and resources will be with us from our logistics teams within the hour. We'll also have good estimates of the quantity of people in urban areas beneath the flight path that may have to be evacuated until the infected colony can be eliminated. Meantime, the commander in chief has ordered me to liaise with you about which bats are most likely to be infected and what measures we have to take for eradication. Chemical, radiological, biological agents, personnel biohazard precautions . . . that sort of thing."

Debra knew she had to head Daniel off at the pass because on the way from her apartment, in preparation for this meeting, he'd expressed serious misgivings about the army being involved in the first place. Earlier that morning, he'd begged her to remember that no matter what the president or this general might be thinking, "this isn't a war, this is a necessary cull of a small number of infected animals in a confined space. You send in the army with their drones and weapons of mass destruction, and we're not going to have any bats left. Deb, this is a truly terrible idea; we need scientists to do this, not soldiers. "

She'd reassured him, but he'd still entered the Pentagon as a skeptic, a frightened academic too terrified of the certain destruction of his beloved creatures to allow reason to distract him.

Concentrating on keeping control of the meeting despite the formidable array of army firepower on the opposite side of the table, Debra said softly, "General, we'd love to tell you what bat roosts are infected so you could eliminate them, but so far there has only been one colony that we've positively found to be carrying viruses deadly to humanity and that was eliminated by your Chemical and Biological Warfare Division in the Pompton Lakes district of the Ramapo Mountain State Forest in upstate New Jersey. The reason for their infection was because their roost was for nursing mothers, and it was disturbed by a massive building construction in the immediate vicinity. Also, their food source had recently disappeared.

"As you know, sir, the other bat colonies were destroyed by terrified vigilantes. And it's these that we have to stop, because we can't have all healthy bats destroyed because of a completely unwarranted fear."

Daniel glanced at her and nodded.

"That's not a matter for the army, Doctor Hart; that's a local police issue," he said softly.

"And that's why," said Debra, "I'm going to present a proposition to the president that he declare all bats in the United States a protected species, save only for those bats in colonies found to be infected with a deadly virus capable of killing human beings. And I'm not talking about the ten thousand dollars or so fine for killing a member of an endangered species like a swan or a wolf. I'm talking about ten years in prison for the unlawful killing of a colony of bats, or at least a significant number of the mammals, as a deliberate act; naturally, the army would be exempt from such a charge."

Daniel turned and stared at Debra. In one simple, elegant maneuver, she'd come up with a scheme that would likely put an end to most vigilantism, allay the fears of the public by demonstrating that only a miniscule number of bat colonies might become infectious compared with the millions of healthy creatures in the nation, allow the army to do its job properly, and leave him and his precious bats with a lifetime of continued existence. He knew he shouldn't say anything, so he remained silent, as though he was in on the scheme. Truth to tell, Debra had only just thought of it when the map had appeared on the screen, and she looked in horror at the visualization of just how enormous was the cull being considered.

The lower ranks at their end of the table shuffled in their places, waiting for their general to speak. When he did so, he surprised the room by saying, "That's a good idea, Debra. Makes excellent sense. That way we don't have to harm the harmless. I like it. No collateral damage. Yes, I'll support you in your recommendation. Why don't we put it up jointly as a paper to the president? Your name and mine. He wouldn't dare say no to brains and brawn."

"Or beauty," Daniel whispered under his breath.

* * *

When the meeting was over, with plans to regroup again at the Pentagon the following day when facts and figures had been assessed for analysis, Debra and Daniel walked out of the immense military complex into one of the many parking lots where they'd left their security vehicle an hour and a half earlier. Sitting in the foyer was Agent Brett Anderson, her personal security man, who smiled as they handed back their badges and he escorted them to the vehicle.

She and Brett had been together now every day for a number of weeks, and they had become more than friendly. It had begun two days after he was assigned to her protection, and although he was a perfect gentleman, the occasional hand in the small of her back to guide her into a room, or moving ahead quickly to open a door, or shaking hands just a little too long as they said good night, made her realize that there was a personal, as well as a professional, element to their time together. She saw him looking at her, glancing more often than was needed, smiling as she talked to others. And he was a warm, sensitive companion, knowing, knowledgeable, wise, and cautious. Always the professional, always concerned with her protection, he was becoming more mother hen than Secret Service agent.

As the days wore on, he became the relief she needed after the intensity of her days, the *de facto* husband to whom she returned after a tough day at the office. Not, of course, that he ever strayed into her personal territory or even hinted that he'd like to become more private, but her womanly antennae were humming to the tune of an interest she presumed . . . hoped . . . was growing.

As they drove from meeting to meeting or sat in rooms alone waiting for others to arrive, she'd allowed herself to indulge in banter with him, some of it coquettish, some girlish . . . it was lovely to bring out into the open the person she'd hidden from herself all these years, and Brett seemed to enjoy her femininity. She'd even pecked him on the cheek last night as he bid her good-bye and handed her over to the night security shift. He looked at her, smiled, held her hand much longer than necessary, and kissed her back—politely and like a true gentleman—on her cheek. He could have remained in her apartment, taking the moment further, but said good night and disappeared, leaving her heart thumping and her face flushed.

Whether he sensed that a romance was budding between his boss and her security guard or whether he genuinely wanted to go somewhere, as they left the building, Daniel said, "You're going to the White House. I need to be at a meeting at Health. I'll just take a taxi."

"Daniel," said Debra, "we'll drop you off, it's on our way."

"Don't worry, I need to be alone to think," and he walked off toward the taxi rank.

"Where now, ma'am?" said Brett, his manner deliberately obsequious. He was the very opposite of a chauffeur but accommodated her every need. He stayed with her, morning and afternoon, and delivered her from her apartment to wherever she had to be and then back to her apartment at night. A separate detachment of security people were stationed outside her building overnight, and two people sat shotgun on her door until morning. At first, she'd objected to the people outside her front door and had taken them food and drink, but it soon became obvious that they were doing their job, and she was interfering.

But she missed Brett when he said good night to her and handed her over to the evening shift. During the day, she really enjoyed his presence, the closeness of a hunky man in the car driving her around, his masculinity, his intelligence and knowledge, and especially his sense of humor.

They got into the bulletproof car, and she asked him to drive her to the White House where she had a ton of paperwork to do. As they drove out of Arlington toward central DC, Brett cleared his throat and said, "I have some news to tell you, Debra. We're stepping down the security level. It seems that the head of WEL, Stuart Chalmers, has made a full confession of arranging to kill Secretary Harper and has confessed to numerous other crimes. He's confessing so much that it seems they can't shut him up. And we've tested many of his statements that appear to be true, so we're inclined to believe him." He cleared his throat and said softly, "He's being arraigned this morning, and they're assembling a grand jury, so it looks as though the danger has passed."

She turned to him in surprise. "But I thought that this Chalmers guy was a hard nut to crack. What happened?"

"Well, somehow, the FBI managed to crack him and he's confessing to decades of crimes. I have no idea how they broke him, but it seems as if everything he's saying checks out, so . . ."

"So the alarm is over?"

Brett nodded silently.

Debra remained quiet in the car. Then she said, "I'm glad that DeAnne Harper's parents will get the satisfaction of seeing her killer put away, even though they've lost their daughter and son-in-law and grandchildren. There are few worse things for relatives than to see their loved ones' murder go unpunished. But . . ."

"But?"

She didn't know if she could say it. So she remained quiet.

"I've really enjoyed working with you, Debra," he said softly, negotiating his way through the traffic. "It's been one of my most pleasant assignments."

"I've really enjoyed . . . I mean, it's been a real pleasure, Brett. I'm just sorry that we won't be seeing each other anymore. I mean, not seeing each other in a . . . not that I . . . I don't mean . . ."

He smiled at her. Such a brilliant woman, yet so easily tongue-tied when it came to trying to say something personal.

"We don't have to stop seeing each other, as friends, y'know Debra. I mean, you're in town for a while; I'm married to the job and have no family . . . if you want, we could go to a movie, go out somewhere for dinner. Now that you're not likely to get shot, I can take you somewhere public. If you'd like."

"I'd love that. I really would."

They continued to drive deeper and deeper into the heart of central DC, but as the administrative and government buildings grew more and more concentrated, Debra said, "Look, I've been working sixteen-hour days, every day for the past God knows how many days. I deserve some 'me' time. Take me somewhere lovely so I can relax. Let's do what tourists do. Let's go to Georgetown and go on a river cruise. Or let's go to Dumbarton House . . . I've always wanted to see the inside. Or we can go back to Virginia and go see Great Falls Park and walk along the banks of the Potomac . . . oh God, I sound like some giddy student tourist from South Dakota seeing Washington for the first time. You must think me an idiot."

"Not at all. I think it's sweet. You've been here all this time, and you've probably never seen more of the city than the insides of buildings. Even spending all day beside the president of the United States can make a woman yearn for the great outdoors. Or we could go to a mall and just browse, or I'll take you for the best burger and fries you've ever had in your life. Ever heard of Ray's Hell Burger on Wilson Boulevard in Arlington? Just about the best burgers, sweet potato fries, and onion rings you'll ever eat."

She smiled and said gently, "I couldn't think of anything lovelier. Let's do it."

Four hours later, full from the gourmet fast food, she felt close enough to ask him, "Wanna come back to my place for a cup of coffee?"

"Don't you have to work this afternoon?"

"I phoned the president's PA while you were in the john and told her that I wouldn't be in because I needed some 'me' time. I didn't lie and fib because I don't have to. But her reaction surprised me. Instead of being condescending and censorious, she burst out laughing. She just laughed. I asked her why, and she said that she and the president had been having little daily side bets of a chocolate biscuit about which day I'd break and take some personal time off. The president has been telling me to take time off for weeks now, but I just didn't think I could in this emergency. Both she and the president have been worried about the stresses I've been under, and they were hoping that you and I would become . . . well, she said 'friendly.'"

Debra stole a glance at Brett, saw him grinning, and continued, "And then she laughed and told me that she was really pleased that the president had won and that she'd ask his butler to put a chocolate biscuit on the president's coffee tray. You don't think the president thinks . . . you and me? He couldn't . . . right?"

Brett shrugged. "There've been lots of comments from my colleagues about how lucky I am to have you to guard. People say I have the best assignment because you're such a beautiful woman. My boss, Ted Marmoullian, and the president are very close . . . who knows what they talk about?"

She sat back in her seat, stunned. Not at the thought that her private life was being discussed in the Oval Office, but nobody, especially not a man, had called her beautiful in years. Only her mother had said that her beauty was wasted in test tubes and viruses—that she should get out more, meet more people.

Without warning, her cell phone buzzed telling her that she'd just received a text message. She looked at it and burst out laughing. She read out the words on the screen to Brett, who continued driving toward her apartment.

"As President of the United States, I order you and Agent Anderson to chill out this afternoon. It is normally a federal offense to interfere with a Secret Service officer, but I have just signed a Presidential waiver. Enjoy . . . you deserve some 'me' time."

15

The first time was, for her at least, less than satisfying. When he touched her, kissed her, fondled her, and massaged her in places she'd forgotten existed, her body, like a kraken, woke from a deep slumber, and began to respond to his urgings.

But unlike when she was a graduate student, the last time she'd enjoyed a profound and satisfying relationship, she climaxed far too quickly, surprising Brett and forcing her to apologize.

He laughed and told her that he was delighted. They shared a cup of coffee and within an hour were again in bed, kissing and fondling and touching until this time, both he and she, came in long, satisfying, and unfathomable measure.

They lay in each other's arms in bed and watched through the window as the day turned slowly into dusk. When night fell, she made him some supper, and they ate it in bed together.

And it was then that Brett Anderson said something that, innocuous as it was, light and airy and trivial and phatic as it was meant to be, changed the course of American history. Just a simple phrase, just a thoughtless wish. But enough to make Debra's scientific mind begin to reel and vault and cogitate and examine. And think.

"Y'know," he said munching on a piece of cheese as he sipped a Cabernet Sauvignon, "I'm going to be assigned somewhere else tomorrow or the day after, now that you're no longer . . . well, you know."

She nodded.

"Wouldn't it be wonderful if we could make this moment last forever? If we could just carve out a bit of America all for ourselves and live there in peace and harmony, just you and me. Nobody else. Just us, alone in our own little universe. No outside world to interfere with us, nobody to tell us what to do, no danger, no maniacs trying to interfere with us. Just us."

He smiled and continued to drink his wine. And Debra laid her head on his chest and played with the hairs as her body rose and fell with his breathing. But then, slowly at first but with increasing intensity, her body became rigid. Attuned to a sudden onset of danger and alert to the slightest alteration in attitude, Brett reacted to the unexpected stiffening of her body. He noted that her fingers had slowly stopped playing with his hair and become still, as though she was aware of danger, of something lurking in the room. But he glanced quickly and saw nothing out of the ordinary.

"What's wrong?" he whispered.

"Nothing."

"Debra, what's wrong?"

"Just something you said . . ."

"What?"

"Nothing. Let me think."

"Have I upset you?"

She laughed. "No, silly. But you said something and I need to think it through."

"What did I say?"

"Brett, shut up, this is important. Let me think."

And, to Agent Anderson's increasing irritation, Debra continued to lay there stiff as a board, thinking. She was still thinking deeply as she got out of bed and into the shower without saying a word to her lover; she thought as she got dressed, as she sat at her desk making notes while he showered and dressed. She was thinking when she called Daniel Todd and told him to meet her urgently at the White House; she was still thinking as she and Brett pulled into the underground parking garage and silently walked through security, Daniel knowing not to interrupt her when she was in one of these moods, something he called her "deeply cogitative states."

She was still thinking along the corridors that were now so familiar to her and into one of the basement conference rooms. And as Brett Anderson, still theoretically on duty to guard her, watched her and Daniel Todd plotting and planning and scheming and laying out her ideas, he realized that she'd stopped thinking in theory and was in action mode as she assembled plans for presentation. It was then that he understood why she'd reacted so strangely to the words he'd spoken in bed after they'd made love. And it was then that she sent a text message to the president's PA asking for a super-urgent meeting as soon as was humanly possible. A text came back almost immediately saying that the president could see her in two days' time, but her subsequent text said, "No, sorry, absolute priority; must see POTUS immediately. I'll take responsibility. Must be NOW."

* * *

The following morning, she and Daniel met with the president of the United States over breakfast. He squeezed them into his feverish schedule because he knew that Debra never would have asked for urgent access unless it was extraordinarily important.

She was bursting to tell the president what she'd conceived, but he forced her to eat a meal before they discussed business. During the bacon, eggs, and hash browns, he ribbed her about her absence from her office the previous day, hoping that the work she'd been doing with Agent Anderson privately had been productive and satisfactory. He stopped making fun of her when she flushed red.

"Okay, you two, what's so urgent that you have to take me away from my wife and children for breakfast?"

"We think we've come up with a way to minimize the danger of the diseases caused by bats and to reverse the problems by natural means," she told him.

Daniel firmly intervened and said, "We? No, it was Debra who thought up the idea and it's so brilliant and simple that I wish I could take credit. But I can't."

The president remained silent, waiting.

"Sir," said Debra, "in many parts of the United States, vast areas of land have been set aside in order to bring buffalo and wolves and bears back into nature as part of the natural cycle. Your departments in charge of agriculture, fisheries, and forestry set aside land to protect species at risk of extinction, and as you know, the Department of the Interior US Fish and Wildlife Service has an extensive Endangered Species Program that sets aside and protects habitats for animals and plants threatened with human activity. Well, we're proposing that parts of the United States be set aside for the bats to enable them to recuperate.

"There are massive marine parks throughout the world where fish, crustacean, corals, and other organisms can live without being assaulted. Why shouldn't we do the same thing for bats? I propose that we find huge areas of habitation where there are very few people, and we plant fruit trees for some species and encourage the growth of plants and flowers that will give rise to a multitude of insects for other bat species and, if necessary, build vast artificial cave structures with facilities for bats to colonize, and we make these areas into reserves where no human, industrial, or commercial activities are allowed. No building, agriculture, farming, factories, habitation. Nothing. Zip. Not even overflights of light aircraft. We leave the bats totally undisturbed for years without their interaction with human beings—so that in these areas, we live in harmony with bats and nature, and they will return to their natural state within a generation or two . . . or three. I don't know how long precisely, but I doubt it'll be a long time. We still need to do the research, but once this generation of bats dies out and we de-stress the next generation and the next, get the hell out of their lives, and allow them the grace of the natural lifestyle they've been living for the past fifty million years, they'll quickly return to the types of mammals they always used to be. And this land is set aside in perpetuity because where there's interaction between bats and humans and the bats become stressed, we can relocate the colony into safe areas and give them the environment they seek.

"Mr. President, I'm suggesting that we find stressed bat populations as well as colonies that are in decline, test them for their viral loads, and if they're marginal, we relocate these particular bat populations to specific wilderness areas free of the modern pollutants and noises and clutter of humanity, and in a couple of years, a few generations of peace and tranquillity, the bats will have returned to their normal state. And that this is our recommendation to other nations where there's a bat problem."

She'd blurted out the entire plan in moments and didn't hand over the written proposition to the president to read because his mind, trained in science, would be able to envisage the entire concept, and he'd pick through the problems without needing to get bogged down in the detail, something he could pass on to his people to check out later in the day.

President Nathaniel Jefferson Thomas continued to chew on his toast before answering. Daniel and Debra looked at him, waiting for a reaction. Any reaction. All he did was nod, chew some more, spread another piece of toast with butter, and chew again.

After he'd sipped his coffee, he said softly, "You're suggesting recuperation rather than elimination. But how do you know it'll work? How do you know that the new virus loads aren't passed on to future generations in the bat's genetic material? Where's your evidence that it'll be an effective way of lowering the viral load?"

Daniel was about to explain, but the president continued, "And how can we keep human beings out of such vast areas? Do we need to completely clear the environment so that it's only bats and other wildlife? Can't there be some human activity, supervised activity, so that the land we're returning to its natural state can still be productive—not factories or building sites or commerce, I agree, but surely, if we're sensitive to the needs of the bats, we human beings can still coexist with them? I agree we can't cause them stresses or change their feeding habits, but surely in nature there's room for two species to live and grow side by side. Respecting each other! And we're not dealing with bison and bears and wolves, you know. We're dealing with a flying mammal and we can't control the areas over which they're flying."

"Yes we can, sir. That's the brilliant thing about what Debra is suggesting," said Daniel urgently. "We're going to set up some sort of ultrasonic devices from the entrance to the caves or the trees where the bats are roosting, to the feeding areas. It'll be very wide . . . say two or three miles or so . . . along the flight path, so that if the bats stray into the umbra of the devices, it'll interfere with their radar and they'll regroup and fly along the straight and narrow. They'll quickly learn to adapt. Naturally, the area will have to be patrolled by the National Guard or whatever is the local state militia body to ensure that the devices aren't interfered with by vandals, but it'll ensure that the bats sleep, eat, mate, and roost in peace and harmony. My conservative opinion is that the overwhelmed viral loads will disappear in a generation, two at the most. After that, we'll have to see what we can do."

President Thomas nodded. "Okay, but how are we going to determine which bats are deadly to humanity? And when we've determined that, how are we going to gather millions and millions of them and relocate them simply and efficiently without increasing their stress levels so that they present a greater danger than they would if they were in their natural habitat?

"And then there's the problem of the deadly viruses the bats carry. At least for a generation or two, droplets of the bats' urine or nasal drips will be falling onto the ground. Sure, sunlight and fluorescent light and dry conditions can render a virus effectively dead, but in some cases, as I'm sure you both know, a virus stays inert until it enters a host. If a feral pig or deer or horse eats it, then the animal becomes potentially deadly to humanity, so we're going to have to solve that issue, as well. What do we do? Close off the land to all humanity as being too dangerous? And how do we keep the ground animals enclosed so that they don't wander into farmland that is adjacent to the protected area? There are many issues which we need to carefully consider, guys, before we launch into this scheme . . . and we still haven't solved the problem of global warming."

Daniel was about to answer, when the president continued, "And I'm going to face all hell in congress, because what you're proposing is vastly more expensive than the alternative of killing a diseased bat colony, which is a quicker and more certain method of ensuring that the problem goes away. I can just hear some congressional representative or senator saying that he's not going to give over vast swathes of his state's land for the benefit of diseased bats that don't vote."

"But think about the benefits you'll gain from animal lovers, Mr. President," Debra insisted. "You'll undermine the eco-nuts, join hand in hand with starlets from Hollywood who'll call you the god of animal lovers and every man and woman who owns a dog, cat, or bird will vote for you at the next election."

The president looked at her in surprise. She shrugged in apology and continued, "I know this isn't about votes, but with your popularity, now is the best time in your presidency to do something bold and brave and imaginative and fantastic. Look, sir, a short while ago, when all hell was breaking loose from the eco-nuts because it seemed that we'd have to kill diseased colonies, you stormed into the White House pressroom and turned the tables brilliantly on the animal protection groups and made them look like insane fanatics who were determined to put wildlife above the interests of human beings. That swung public sentiment behind you really strongly.

"But if you support this concept of ours, you'll make anybody who still insists on killing bat colonies seem like a mass murderer. You'll be seen as the first US president who is thinking of nature as a holistic environment for every creature to live cooperatively. It's the leadership that we in the scientific community have been looking for. Turning humanity back from progress at any price, to progress in harmony with our responsibilities to the world, to the earth, to nature. It'll bring religions, environmentalists, community groups, eco-conscious people, and other groups who are concerned about our pollution of the planet, of our use of precious resources, on board with us. This could be the turning point for humanity, Mr. President, because we're already at the tipping point. The earth is in trouble from the effects of humanity. Something is needed to make us stop and think. Somebody is needed to show the way. This could be just what we're looking for. It'll be a new way of our living in this world, a new way of living with nature . . . a new beginning . . ."

Both Daniel and the president looked at her in surprise. They'd never heard her sound more evangelical.

The president turned to Daniel and whispered, "Slip outside a moment, will you, Daniel, and tell my staff to build a giant cross. With this scheme of yours, I'm going to be crucified by congress, but according to Debra, I'll rise up to heaven after three days and sit on the right hand of the Almighty."

Debra smiled and she was going to apologize for her manner when the president said softly, "I'm going to go with half of your scheme, Debra. And I know that as a pragmatist, you'll understand my reasoning. You've devised a clever and imaginative idea and once you've proven the science, it's one that I'll implement but not in its entirety. I just can't take the risk.

"Look, we've seen beautiful little American and British children and kids from other parts of the world die from some of the most evil and virulent viruses we've ever experienced. Whole communities have been wiped out more efficiently than by some terrorist device of mass murder. Similar viruses could erupt at any time in any bat population, for all the reasons we've been researching these past weeks.

"As president of the United States, sworn to protect the people, I cannot and will not allow creatures that carry these deadly bugs to endanger the population. So my order will be to find and eradicate any bat colony in the United States that is found to harbor a virus deadly to human beings.

"However," he said, looking at Daniel and Debra, whose faces had fallen in disappointment, "I will instruct those departments responsible for our agriculture, fisheries, and forests to identify whatever wilderness areas are suitable for your scheme. Then, when a colony of bats is found to be in distress, and where the viral load is still below the threshold limit, we'll relocate them.

"To do so, I'll need to use the USA Patriot Act, Title V, or whatever, to compulsorily purchase the land if it's not owned already by the federal government. So, that's my decision. Much of what you've suggested will be carried out, but so will the protection of the American people. That's as far as I'm willing to go."

Daniel was about to argue, but the president interrupted him, "Daniel, I think I know what you're going to say . . . that it was we human beings who caused the problem the bats are now suffering, so it's ethically unfair, if not unconscionable, for us to destroy these creatures. I agree.

But someone or something has to lose in this unholy equation, and it's not going to be human beings. I'm sorry, but that's my decision."

Debra and Daniel remained silent for a few moments, thinking through what President Thomas had said. After a couple of seconds, Debra nodded and said, "That's a realistic compromise. We'd spent the night working out the risks of transporting a diseased colony, and we could have done it, but I hear what you're saying, Mr. President, and it makes eminently good sense. Even if the risks were absolutely minimal, the fear in the public's mind would be palpable. But if we say that we're destroying the killers, but putting those in danger into a sort of bat hospital until they're better, then it'll be a much easier job to sell."

The president nodded. "Good. I'm glad we're in agreement. It'll make it an easier sell to congress and the American people. How do you propose we progress from here?"

"Well," said Debra, "you should advise the secretary-general of the United Nations of the US decision. My group will work on the science, and General Coles and his Pentagon group will work on the logistics. You'll have to get the secretary of agriculture to work on land acquisition. I'll present the secretary-general with our paper, which presumably he'll then present to the General Assembly so that ambassadors can transmit it to their governments. Let's just hope that the rest of the world agrees with the way we're going about things."

"And there's our first major problem," said the president. "I'm confident that as a nation, we can set aside land to get our bats back to normal. I'm sure Britain and France and other European nations can do the same. China, Russia, India, and other such countries too, in all likelihood, and I don't envisage major problems in the rest of Asia, South America, or Australasia. But the real problems we're going to face are in Africa and the Middle East. They're still enormously tribal, and any attempt to compulsorily acquire land by a central government will be resisted in the most vehement and virulent manner, probably leading to insurrections, wars, or God only knows what else. Knowing the mentality of the people in these areas, especially the Middle East, they'd rather let people die than lose an inch of traditional tribal land to the government.

"But those aren't our problems, right now," he said, pushing back on his chair and standing. "I'm only concerned with the safety and security of the American people, and this is as good a concept as I've yet heard. Well done, both of you."

The breakfast was over, and they'd achieved most of what they'd been hoping for. As he walked them to the door, he said, "Okay, Debra, you get to work, and I'll start to bed down the administrative side. Naturally, I'll need a full analysis of your concept before I go too far, but on the assumption that it'll work and other scientists give it the green light, we could be in business within six months."

STARBUCKS CAFÉ
CORNER OF THIRTY-FIFTH AND FIFTH, MANHATTAN

Tom Pollard, president of CHAT, slowly stirred his coffee as he pondered the phone call half an hour ago. His chairperson, Donna McCabe, wanted to meet with him but out of the office. He'd agreed to meet her in what he called his boardroom, a nearby Starbucks where he could indulge himself in a grande white chocolate mocha, half of which he'd already drunk waiting for Donna.

He was looking forward to the meeting. His relationship with Donna had been cool when she'd taken over the chair from her predecessor six months earlier, but as the dollars had rolled in and CHAT had become one of the most media savvy and talked about animal rights organizations in the land, he became the golden-haired boy of the CHAT board of directors. Donna still treated him coolly, but he put that down to her being a New York attorney and a former state prosecutor.

Sure, things had taken a nosedive recently with the murder of the old guy in Florida and especially when CHAT, through some business card of a former employee, was linked by the FBI to the murder of the secretary of health and her family . . . linkages that he'd managed to evade by proving his and CHAT's innocence, and he would certainly have been axed by Donna had he not used his persuasive powers with the older board members and worked the numbers. Since then, he'd done some magnificent footwork over the bats issue, got Hollywood and the popular television media behind him, and raised awareness of CHAT so that it was the preeminent force that the government, universities, and others now had to reckon. Sure, Donna still was wary of him—cautious and cool to him in meetings—but he had most of the board on his side, and as the new chair, she was not on sufficiently solid ground to move against him. But now that the organization's coffers were overflowing, and as soon as she had a chance to read the plans he'd drawn up over the past few days, he was absolutely certain that he'd go from zero to hero in her estimation. It would be the turning point in appreciation of him.

Fortunately, since that moron, that idiot philosopher, that psychopath Professor Stuart Chalmers, had been arrested and incarcerated, singing like a songbird and probably in a straightjacket, all of his troubles were behind him.

Pollard looked down at the adjacent seat where the manila folder he'd placed there promised another year of spectacular success. It contained a four-page document, a plan for the next twelve months of CHAT activities; some were financial appeals, some were stunts that he wanted to carry out to keep himself and the organization on the front pages, and some were awareness raising activities in congress that he wanted to pursue through the appointment of a Washington political lobby group. He'd covered his tracks sufficiently and cleanly so that neither she nor anybody on the board would realize that he was a consultant to the lobby group, taking 25 percent off the top of their very handsome fee from CHAT.

He looked up when he heard the door open and saw Donna McCabe walk in. She smiled, waved at him, and ordered a short black from the service desk. She carried it over to his table.

"How are you, Tom?" she asked, putting her briefcase down on the chair next to her.

"Good thanks, Debra. How are things in the big wide world of Manhattan law firms?"

She smiled and didn't answer. "Tom, I'll come straight to the point. There's no need for you to return to your office this afternoon. Your desk is being cleared by a security team, your staff is being briefed by my assistant, the passwords on your computer are being changed as we speak, and your swipe cards will no longer work to get you into the building, the elevator, or the parking lot. Your personal effects are being bagged for return to your home, and you've been removed as the registered driver of your company car. In short, Tom, I'm firing you."

He looked at her in astonishment, his jaw dropping. But before he could say anything, she continued, "There are a number of reasons, but the most pressing is the fact that late last night, I was contacted by Ted Marmoullian, White House chief of security. Because of the terrorism and other security issues involving the arrest of this rogue professor, Stuart Chalmers, and knowing that I was a senior partner in a large law firm, Mr. Marmoullian did me the honor of giving me some confidential information relating to you and CHAT.

"Because of my position with my law firm, they believed me when I've assured them of my confidentiality, and they've let me know the outcome from a number of interviews they've conducted with Professor Chalmers since his arraignment. Why me and not you? Simply because some of the pertinent matters raised in these interviews relate to your activities within CHAT. Chalmers has implicated you in a series of very serious crimes. The Bureau has warrants to search your office, your computers, and your home, at the same time as they're interviewing you," she looked at her watch, "which should be in about ten minutes or so. I told them I was meeting you in here.

"The reason they haven't interviewed you yet, Tom, is because I've asked them to let me fire you first. However, as soon as I leave this coffee shop, they'll be taking you to Bureau headquarters because Chalmers has connected you with the crimes and has said that in a number of the more serious ones, you were a willing collaborator. He's saying that you provided him with the information he needed concerning laboratories that were experimenting with live animals and that you told him stuff that enabled him to commit his crimes."

Pollard shook his head vigorously and was about to deny everything when Donna held up her hand and said curtly, "Whether it's true or not,

Tom, isn't the point. I hope you can establish your innocence. What's crucial to CHAT is that the FBI is going to connect you to major crimes and even the murder of a secretary of state, and when the media gets wind of it, it'll have a drastic effect on the organization. That's just one of the reasons why I'm dumping you. I've been in touch by conference call with the entire board, and it was a unanimous decision. You'll be paid up for the month and, naturally, we'll pay your accrued leave and all your rights. And you should consider yourself extremely lucky that we're paying you these amounts. I'm sure you know what I'm referring to. Let's just say that my analysis of the financial irregularities and kickbacks from CHAT's suppliers to you is both illegal, criminal, and immoral. The fact is that we're making a clean break, and a press announcement of your separation is being emailed to all media as we're speaking."

Still in shock, Tom said numbly, "But if you fire me, it'll look like I'm guilty. Can't you see how disastrous it'll be for me? I never talked to Chalmers, never communicated, never . . . but if you . . . you can't . . . don't you understand . . . I'll be crucified . . ."

"That's not my problem, and nor is it CHAT's. As chair, I have to protect the organization and ensure its governance. If the CEO is interviewed by the FBI and horrific allegations are made, especially when they're to do with terrorism and the assassination of the secretary of health and her entire family, then whether it's true or not, we have to protect ourselves. We have to put distance between us. Sorry, but that's the way it is," she said, finishing her coffee.

"I'll need a lawyer. How am I going to afford a lawyer if you fire me? It's your responsibility to protect me . . ."

She breathed deeply. She had promised herself on the way into Starbucks that if he cried poor or threatened or even begged, she'd hit him with both barrels. She'd thought to buffer him from what was coming next because of his dismissal and the impending destruction of his reputation when the Bureau interviewed him, but now he was asking for a lawyer, she saw no reason to spare him.

"Tom, when I took over as board chair six months ago, I instituted a confidential audit of the organization. It's brought to light a number of really disturbing issues. Count yourself lucky that the board has agreed with me that we shouldn't pursue them, but just set you adrift. So why don't you use the thousands of dollars you've claimed on false expenses that our auditors have spent the past few months tracking? Or why don't you use the fortune we've paid to that San Francisco advertising firm, of which you're a silent partner, for ads that strangely never appeared? Or what about the three employees that are being paid a monthly salary, whose names and addresses are on our books but who oddly haven't ever appeared at work, whose paychecks go into an account where you're the only signatory and are registered as living in your parents' house in Oswego County and your sister's apartment in the Bronx?"

As the blood drained from his face, Donna continued, "By our reckoning, that's over two hundred thousand you've stolen from CHAT in the last year alone. We'd normally take action against you for its return, prior to sending papers to the police to prosecute you for theft. However, let's just say that we'll write it off to experience and you can put the money you've misappropriated to good use in defending yourself. And one last thing, Tom. Please don't contact me or any of your former staff again. They've been instructed not to accept your phone calls on pain of dismissal. Oh, and don't bother asking for a reference, because nobody who speaks to me will ever want to employ you. So like I say, good luck because you're certainly going to need it."

Donna stood, turned, and walked out. For reasons he would never know, he picked up the folder on the chair beside him and was going to run after her so he could give it to her . . . but then the depth and dimensions of the catastrophe suddenly dawned on him, and he sat down in his chair with a bump.

He looked at Donna's receding back as she pushed her way through the door and out into the crowded streets of Manhattan, his head spinning with the news of his radically altered situation. He saw her nod to two men standing on the street, and as she strode down the street toward a cab rank, he saw that they were walking toward the Starbuck's front door.

Tom Pollard watched the FBI agents enter the café and move toward his table. He felt as though he was suddenly teetering on the edge of a precipice. But his thoughts were interrupted by the server, who asked breezily, "Can I get you another white chocolate mocha? Don't they just make your day . . ."

16

Eighteen Months Later

It was a late start to the morning. They'd turned off their alarm clocks and allowed themselves to sleep in because last night's movie hadn't finished until 11:00 p.m.; instead of going straight home, they'd wandered the streets, deciding on impulse to pop into an all-night restaurant and indulged themselves in pancakes and hot chocolates, coming back to their apartment as the clock struck 1:00 a.m.

It was past 9:00 a.m., and Secret Service Senior Agent Brett Anderson was reading the Internet edition of that morning's *Washington Post* on his iPad. He glanced over the table to where his fiancée Debra Hart was reading her overnight emails. He didn't have to be in his office until midday, and he knew that Debra's first appointment, an interview with *Vanity Fair*, was scheduled for early afternoon.

Debra glanced across the table and asked, "So, what's happening?"

Without looking up, he answered, "His ratings are on the rebound, thank heavens. Latest poll from the *New York Times* says that he's now ten points above the Democrats, with six months to go before November. If he continues like this, he'll be a shoo-in."

Debra smiled. "Y'know, I honestly don't know whether I'm pleased or disappointed."

Now Brett looked up at her. "Why?"

"Well, I'm a lifelong Democrat so I should be voting for Wainer. But I'm still going to vote for Nathaniel Thomas. If only he wasn't a Republican."

Brett smiled. "You're still in love with him."

"'Course," said Debra, "so's every other woman in America. C'mon, he's brilliant and sexy and gorgeous and everything."

"But he can't dance."

Debra laughed. She and Brett had attended a White House ball three weeks earlier, and the president had asked her to dance, much to the excitement of the gossip columnists. But when he'd trodden on her toes three times and seen her wince in pain, he led her off the dance floor and every subsequent time they met, he still continued to apologize for his clumsiness. His wife had even sent her a gift certificate for a pedicure with a funny card one of his children had hand drawn showing the president as a huge bear and Debra as a little fairy called Twinkletoes.

Brett sipped his coffee and said, "Y'know, I honestly thought he'd dived too far down in the polls to recover for a second term, after all that compulsory land purchase and the difficulties in relocating the bats. But the public is very forgiving, and now that things are settling down . . ."

"This last email from Ohio University says that the latest test results on the relocated Oregon bats show the viral load has dropped significantly. It's very encouraging."

"Are you going to put out a press release?" he asked.

She shook her head. "Nope, the president is still insisting that we let the thing remain quiet and low profile until we're out of the danger zone with all the relocated colonies. But it does look very encouraging."

"Is that fair? Surely you deserve . . ."

"Nothing," she insisted. "This was the plan proposed to congress and the United Nations by the president of United States of America. He was generous enough in acknowledging me and my team, but . . ."

"And if it had failed," said Brett, "it would have been your plan and your neck on the chopping block."

She shook her head vigorously. "Bush, Clinton, Jimmy Carter, maybe, but not Nat Thomas," she insisted. "He'd never have used me as a scapegoat if the results hadn't been good. He's not like that. He'd have stepped up to the microphones, said something like, 'well, we tried and it didn't work,' and then he'd have worn the criticism. You know he would."

Brett smiled. "You are a bit in love with him!"

"The only reason I'm marrying you is because he's not available," she quipped.

They continued with their breakfast, pouring more coffee and munching on toast before Debra said, "Well, enough of this frivolity. I should go to my office and check on things. We're expecting results from tests of relocated at-risk colonies in New Mexico and Wyoming today, so hopefully that'll add more definition to our research on what's happening to the bats."

Brett nodded. "Must be frustrating, all this waiting and watching for the bats to calm down and to determine whether or not the viruses have diminished in their bodies," he said softly.

"Not as frustrating as having to answer all the questions from the townspeople and farmers near to their flight paths. Still, half the job is PR, the other half is administration. That's why I'll be so glad to get back to some real science."

He looked at her as she retreated into the bathroom to shower and dress for her office and her interview. The past year and a half had been the most glorious and satisfying in his life, a whirlwind of a professional assignment that turned into a friendship that became a love affair, the translocation of his and her place into theirs, and then an unspoken decision of them both to spend the rest of their lives together. Meetings with her family, with his family, and with his and her colleagues, and they were married in all but name. Even the White House, though not told officially, began to include him on invitations to her to attend dinners and receptions.

And he knew that she'd fallen deeply in love with him. They'd decided to get married a year ago, but the cloud on their horizon was where they'd live when her work came to an end with the UN's Emergency Task Force.

Most of the scientists whom she'd co-opted into the program before the policy of mass relocation of the bats had returned to their universities and laboratories, and the office that once boasted a staff of over seventy, overseeing the investigation of the disease outbreaks and dashing like fireman to remote parts of the globe when there was the sudden discovery of an infestation, were no longer a part of the team. All that were left were Debra, Daniel Todd, and ten or so men and women who were monitoring the worldwide programs Debra had put in place.

Soon, maybe this year, maybe next, when things had returned to normal with the relocated bats, or the infected colonies had been wiped out, they would have to make a huge decision. If Debra returned to the Atlanta Center for Disease Control, probably to take over the entire organization from her elderly boss, then they'd move to Georgia. The problem was that Brett was a senior officer in the Secret Service, and there was little if anything for him to do down there. Sure, he could probably transfer to the FBI, but he wasn't particularly interested in that work.

Maybe it was time for him to quit and find a post in a large organization as head of security, earning a fortune, driving a late-model company car, traveling first class, and working nine to five. He shuddered when he thought of it. How would he cope with the boredom?

* * *

Late in the afternoon, after the reporter from *Vanity Fair* had left her office, she and Daniel Todd left their office and drove the short distance to the underground parking garage of the White House, using their passes to take the elevator to the conference room on a lower floor of the building. It was convenient for them to be in the building so that there was communication between them and the administration so that they could keep the president and the secretary-general informed of developments.

They spent the next hour analyzing the blood results from the samples taken from the bats in New Mexico, Wyoming, and Ohio as well as monitoring the results that were flowing in from France, Italy, the United Kingdom, Australia, and other parts of the world. There were still hideous and murderous outbreaks in central Africa, South America, and parts of Asia, but now that bats had been defined as the source of the infections, there was no need for a flying squad of scientists. Instead, they sent in United Nations specialists from the World Health Organization who were trained in locating the bats' roost and in elimination using poison gas.

So the question that Debra and Daniel were deciding was whether they had sufficient information and substance to be able to candidly inform the president and the secretary-general that the bat offspring tested had far lower viral loads than their parents. Not only that, but the viral loads in the blood of translocated bats, not just bats born in the new stress-free landscape, had dropped significantly.

"If I was asked, Debra, I'd be happy to present these results to a conference of Chiroptera specialists as conclusive proof that moving the bats and de-stressing them, has worked. And that means that I'm prepared to present them to the president and tell him the same," said Daniel.

She nodded. "I guess you're right. We could wait another three months and put more weight behind our conclusions, but there's no way these figures could rebound on us, is there? Surely."

Both she and Daniel were startled by her cell phone ringing. She always carried two phones, one for calls that were personal or from media or her staff; the other she used exclusively for calls from the president and the office of the secretary-general of the United Nations. In the early days of the outbreaks, that phone had gone off a dozen times a day; recently, certainly for the past twelve months, it rarely rang.

"Hello," she said.

"Debra, are you in the building?" asked the president's PA.

She told her she was. "And is Daniel with you?"

"He is," said Debra.

"The president would like to see you both. Could you come up?"

It was surprising but not out of the ordinary. They left their room, walked to the end of the corridor, and took the elevator up a flight to the ground floor. They walked through three security stations, showing their IDs at each point and going through two separate metal detectors.

In the West Wing's inner sanctum, the hustle and bustle of the rest of the White House, where all the important work of the presidency was done, disappeared, absorbed by the thick carpets and the solid walls.

The president's PA smiled as they approached and said, "Go right in."

Daniel and Debra entered the Oval Office and greeted the president, who was sitting at his desk, involved in an animated phone conversation with some congressional representative. He motioned for them to sit on the couch, and when he'd finished, he came over and sat opposite. In his hand was a memo.

Debra was keen to tell him of the latest test results, but she'd been summoned, and so she waited for him to speak. His face was grave. There was no sign of his usual bonhomie nor the peck on the cheek whenever she walked into his office for a meeting.

"Daniel," asked the president, "what's the coldest temperature in which a bat colony can survive?"

"Well, sir, when they hibernate, their body temperature can drop to as low as . . ."

"No, not during hibernation. I'm talking about bats flying across land, looking for food."

Daniel shrugged, realizing that the president didn't want a scientific discourse but his conclusions verified, so he said, "well, not very cold. Why do you want to know, Mr. President?"

"Can they survive an Antarctic winter?"

"Not possibly," he said. "You're looking at temperatures thirty or forty degrees below freezing."

The president nodded. Debra asked, "What's this all about, sir?"

He handed over the memo he was holding. She and Daniel read it. It was clipped and to the point. She realized that the blood had drained from her face. Daniel was speechless and he was shaking his head.

"It's not bats. It can't be bats. Not there," was all he could say.

The president nodded. "Fourteen days ago, all communications with Shackleton Base in Antarctica was lost. At first, the scientists in the research establishment in Hobart, Tasmania, thought there'd been a huge storm and had knocked out the communications. But the satellite pictures showed just normal winter weather. After two days of silence, a mission was put together and flown down there. They relayed what they'd discovered. The entire base of fifteen men and women scientists had died. Their bodies were hideously bloated, as though they'd been lying on the floor of a tropical rainforest. They communicated with Hobart and another team of scientists and medical personnel was flown out but this time with biohazard gear. What they found was ghastly. Not only did they find the fifteen scientists, but all the members of the first rescue team were dead as well.

"The scientists quarantined the entire area and took samples of every-thing . . . body tissues, air, food, everything. It was tested under maxi-mum secrecy and security in the University of Melbourne's laboratories, and they came to the conclusion that the thing that killed everybody was the same virus that killed those people on the Indonesian island of Kasiruta. I remember, Debra, that you called it Ebola on steroids."

The president sat back on his couch. He looked drawn and exhausted.

"Sir, it's just not possible," said Daniel.

"It can't have happened. There's been some mistake," said Debra.

But Nat Thomas shook his head. "The tests have been repeated a dozen times. There's no mistake. The thing that killed all those fine people in Antarctica is the same virus that killed the fifteen hundred villages in Minangkabau and the evil cousin of the viruses that have killed the other people during these past couple of years."

Daniel was still shaking his head. "But no bat could live in those con-ditions. It's too cold . . ."

"I know. Which leads me to the conclusion that bats aren't the only agent that is spreading this damnable disease."

"But if not bats, Mr. President, then what?" asked Debra.

Nat Thomas looked at her blankly and shrugged his shoulders. "I guess that's something you're going to have to work out," he said softly.

Debra sighed and slumped back into the couch. Suddenly, she felt the weight of the entire world on her slender shoulders.